OUT OF
JERUSALEM

—◆— VOLUME FOUR —◆—

LAND OF INHERITANCE

OTHER BOOKS AND AUDIO BOOKS
BY H.B. MOORE:

Of Goodly Parents

A Light in the Wilderness

Towards the Promised Land

OUT OF JERUSALEM

✦ VOLUME FOUR ✦

LAND OF INHERITANCE

a novel

H.B. Moore

Covenant Communications, Inc.

Cover Image: Jorge Cocco Santangelo © 2007. For more information please visit www.jorgecocco.com

Cover design copyrighted 2007 by Covenant Communications, Inc.

Published by Covenant Communications, Inc.
American Fork, Utah

Printed in Canada
First Printing: September 2007

11 10 09 08 07   10 9 8 7 6 5 4 3 2 1

ISBN 978-1-59711-397-6

Dedicated to Les & Jeanie Moore
—for their tremendous support.

ACKNOWLEDGEMENTS

First and foremost, I'd like to thank my dear husband, Chris, and our children, for their faithful support and encouragement. In writing this volume, I have sought counsel from my father, S. Kent Brown. I'm grateful for his expert direction and ready advice. He and my mother, Gayle, were the first readers of the first draft. Their feedback was integral in taking the manuscript to the next step.

I am also grateful to the scholars of the Book of Mormon, including many contributors to FARMS; and more specifically to this volume—John L. Sorenson. A sincere thanks goes to Gordon Ryan for his insights, Dave LeFevre for his attention to detail, and to my critique group, who have been there from the beginning: Annette, Michele, Lynda, Stephanni, Jeff, LuAnn and James (and their spouses who put up with our weekly meetings).

Appreciation goes to my supportive editor Angela Eschler, and also to Kathy Jenkins, Emily Halverson, and the Covenant staff. Special thanks to Shauna Humphries, former managing editor, who gave me that first chance. This series is a result of her confidence.

I'm grateful for others who have helped me on my writing path, namely my father-in-law, Les Moore; Karen Christoffersen; Phill Babbitt; the LDStorymaker family; all the faithful readers who have followed the series; the excellent managers and employees at the various bookstores; and of course, my Wednesday Ladies' Lunch Group. See you next week!

ᴥ PREFACE ᴥ

This fourth and final volume, *Land of Inheritance*, concludes the *Out of Jerusalem* series based on Ishmael's and Lehi's family journey from Jerusalem to the promised land. This installment follows the scriptural text found in 1 Nephi 18:24 through Jacob 1:4.

My overall intention in writing this series was to illuminate the life and ministry of the prophet Nephi. Words cannot express the deep appreciation that I have felt for the Book of Mormon prophets, specifically Lehi, Nephi, and Jacob, as I've studied their lives.

Volume one, *Of Goodly Parents*, began with Lehi and his family's exodus out of Jerusalem. Eventually, Ishmael's family and Laban's servant, Zoram, joined them and five marriage unions resulted. Volume two, *A Light in the Wilderness*, covered the event of Ishmael's premature death at Nahom and the families' subsequent journey through the Arabian wilderness. After spending many arduous years living in the desert, the family enters the land of Bountiful. There, in volume three, *Towards the Promised Land*, Nephi is commanded to build a ship. The Lord then guides them across the vast Pacific to a new land—the "promised land."

Where was this promised land? Anthropologist John L. Sorenson supposes that Lehi's party arrived by ship on the Pacific coast of Guatemala or El Salvador. Shortly after their arrival, perhaps a year or two, Lehi dies. This leads to a chasm between brothers Laman and Nephi. The Lord commands Nephi to take his family and all those who will follow and flee into the wilderness (2 Ne. 5:5). Nephi's group then settles an area they refer to as the Land of Nephi, which is widely believed to be modern-day Guatemala City. Substantial inhabitation of the site dates between 600 and 500 B.C. (*Images of Ancient America: Visualizing the Book of Mormon*, 194).

Another question arises. Were other people living in Mesoamerica upon Lehi's arrival? History shows us that several major cultures lived throughout southern Mexico in 578 B.C.—Lehi's approximate time of arrival. The Olmecs predated the well-known cultures of the Aztecs, the Zapotecs, and the Maya. John L. Sorenson outlines the indigenous population that preceded Lehi to include the Tlatilco, San Lorenzo, La Venta, and Chiapa de Corzo (*Images*, 15).

Of interest, the Mayan Preclassic period includes the people of Kaminaljuyú—a culture that dates back 9,000 years. The center of Kaminaljuyú land was uncovered a short distance from Guatemala City. It has become one of the most well-known archaeological sites in Mesoamerica. I have included this tribe in the encounters that Nephi may have had with other people. Whether Nephi's family met indigenous tribes soon after their arrival at the promised land, or in later years, is likely but remains unknown.

As in the previous three volumes of this series, I have prepared a section of chapter notes, and many references include additional details. Along with the historical significance, they add to the era of Nephi's life.

After Nephi took his followers and left the land of their first inheritance, God revealed that Nephi's brethren were cut off from the presence of the Lord. Laman and his people had lost the Holy Ghost. Catherine Thomas clarifies that "the Lamanites cursed *themselves* when they chose to reject the Spirit of the Lord" (*Studies in Scripture, Volume Seven*, 111). As a result, the Lord set a mark of dark skin upon them. Thomas points out that "the sore cursing was not the dark skin, but the loss of the Holy Ghost, of which the skin coloring was but a mark" (*ibid.*).

How did this happen? Clues in the scriptural text include "the Lord God did cause a skin of blackness to come upon them," (2 Ne. 5:21) and "the Lord spake it, and it was done" (2 Ne. 5:23). Later in the Book of Mormon we learn that the mark of dark skin ends, as noted in 3 Nephi 2:15: "And their curse was taken from them, and their skin became white like unto the Nephites."

My question became: Did this happen suddenly? Or was it a gradual change caused by sun exposure or intermarriage with other Mesoamerican cultures? Taking the scriptural text and combining the literal interpretations of "the Lord spake it, and it was done," then later reading of the mark being removed by the Lord, "and their curse was taken from them," I've developed a plot that contains a sudden change of skin tone. This may be a liberty for some, but since this is a fictional account, it became a significant plot element when the mark was not placed on all those living under Laman's jurisdiction.

The most difficult part of writing this final volume was how to approach the death of Lehi. Second Nephi covers the period from about 588 B.C. to around 545 B.C. Within this period, twelve years passed from the time Lehi left Jerusalem to the time of his death. Scholarly estimation places Lehi at the approximate age of forty-two upon leaving Jerusalem; thus he would have been about fifty-four at the time of his passing. If the family spent eight years in the Arabian wilderness, two years building the ship, and nearly one year crossing the ocean, Lehi would have only lived a year or two in the promised land before death claimed him.

Another challenge that presented itself was the separation of Nephi and Laman. Granting this was for Nephi's protection and would fuel the building of a righteous nation, I had to consider the division between the sisters-in-law, Sariah and Ishmael's widow, and the cousins who were best friends. Who followed Nephi, and who was left behind? One vein of possibility is entertained within the story.

It is my wish that the reader will enjoy my account, but will also take the time to ponder and study the sacred words found in the scriptures themselves.

Second Nephi contains wonderful explanations of the Atonement, and it is filled with powerful testimony from men who were literal witnesses of Christ. Nephi wrote the things of his soul upon the plates for *our own* "learning and profit" (2 Ne. 4:15). It's my hope that we will trust in the Lord as Nephi did, and as we raise our voices in supplication, the Lord will become our "rock of righteousness" (2 Ne. 4:35).

FAMILY CHART

Two years after they reach the promised land

Lehi & Sariah—Lineage of Manasseh
Laman [m. Anah]
    Shem
    Canaan
    Ruth
    Mary
Lemuel [m. Puah]
    Javan
    Delilah
    Helek
    Abital
Samuel [m. Tamar]
    Govad
    Sam
Nephi [m. Isaabel]
    Aaron
    Sarah
Elisheba [m. Raamah]
Dinah [m. Tiras]
Jacob
Joseph

Ishmael (deceased) & Bashemath—Lineage of Ephraim
Raamah [m. Leah, deceased]
    Tiras [m. Dinah]
        Seba
Raamah [remarries Elisheba]
    Dedan
    Noah

Heth [m. Zillah]
   Jochebed
   Madai
   Tubal
Rebeka [m. Zoram]
Anah [m. Laman]
Puah [m. Lemuel]
Tamar [m. Sam]
Isaabel [m. Nephi]

Zoram & Rebeka—Lineage Unknown (likely the tribe of Judah)
Eve
Deborah
Rachel

⟊⟊ PROLOGUE ⟊⟊

When your fear cometh as desolation, and your destruction
cometh as a whirlwind . . . call upon me . . .
(PROVERBS 1:27–28)

The sweetness of their arrival to the promised land was still tender and young in Nephi's mind. Though his family had enjoyed its rich abundance for several weeks now, each morning when Nephi woke, gratitude hit him anew. And today had been no different.

After hours of clearing timber for the new field, Nephi had been pleased to sit down to a meal of beans, maize, chili, and wild avocado wrapped in leaves—new tastes to the family, but ones he enjoyed immensely. Long after the rest of his extended family had retired, Nephi read from the brass plates by the dim glow of an oil lamp. When the air turned cool with gathering dew, he blew out the small flame.

In the speckled moonlight, he made his way to the sleeping quarters he shared with his wife, Isabel, where she slept. He'd married Isaabel when she was a young woman of fifteen, but their experiences and hardships had matured them both beyond their years. He let his gaze dwell on her for a few moments, feeling his heart expand with love. In the next section of their tent slept their four-year-old son, Aaron, and two-year-old daughter, Sarah. In the morning, the work would begin again, and he would go his separate way as he cultivated the fields while Isaabel worked in the nearby garden in tandem with the children.

He missed her.

Nephi leaned over his wife and brushed away a stray lock that had fallen across her cheek. For a few precious moments, he listened to her gentle breathing, then lay down next to her. He pulled a light rug over himself, letting his body relax and his eyes grow heavy as sleep began its descent.

Just as he started to dream, his nose began to itch and his eyes watered. Soon his mouth tasted acrid, his throat burning. Sitting up, he rubbed his eyes, then covered his mouth to quiet his cough. Heart hammering, he rose and pushed his way out of the tent. As he stood in the quiet darkness of his secluded homesite, his fear was confirmed.

Fire.

Beyond the grove of trees where his family's tent stood, the unmistakable glow of orange pierced the black sky. Light from the flames unmasked the thick smoke billowing toward the settlement.

Even from his position, Nephi knew what burned. Only one possession could send flames thrusting so high.

The ship.

Nephi ran. He ran without alerting Isaabel or his children. All instincts propelled him toward the vessel he'd spent two long years constructing. The vessel that had—more than once—nearly brought him to blows with his two older brothers, Laman and Lemuel. This was the ship the Lord had instructed him to build—to carry his entire family from Bountiful to the promised land.

Pushing through the foliage like a spooked gazelle, Nephi arrived on the sandy stretch of earth that marked the edge of the great sea. The passive lapping of waves contrasted sharply with the burning visage upon the lackluster waters. The moonlight cast an eerie glow on the sides of the planked ship, but the pale illumination stopped just below the deck.

Hungry flames consumed the mast pole, and the sail hung in charred ruin. Other spots of fire sprang along the deck, as if one point of intrusion weren't enough. For a moment he couldn't move but simply stared at the terrible sight.

Finally he forced his body to respond, and he ran from tent to tent. "The ship is on fire!" he shouted. The families emerged, some pulling on robes, all running toward the shore, then stopping to stare at the burning mass upon the waters.

When Nephi found Sam, he said, "Tell the women to gather jugs." He turned from Sam and spotted Zoram in the assembling crowd. "Gather the men." Then he raised his voice and shouted above the din. "Father!"

Lehi pushed through the crowd and lifted his arm. "Over here, son."

Nephi ran to his father. "The women will pass us the water while we position ourselves on the ladder. Sam and I will go up on deck."

"Son, it may already be too late."

He stared at his father's wizened face, but Nephi couldn't give up . . . yet. "We have to try."

Zoram reached his side. "Raamah and Heth are on their way to the ladder, but Laman and Lemuel are nowhere to be found."

"Tell their wives to find them!" Nephi ordered, feeling a rawness in his throat.

Zoram nodded and hurried away.

"Let's go," Nephi said, gripping his father's arm. Together they ran to the shoreline and plunged into the mellow surf where they met Sam and the other men.

"Where's Laman?" Nephi called to Raamah as soon as he saw him.

Raamah lifted both hands indicating he had no idea.

Within minutes, the women and children had formed a line from the shore to the ship. The men perched on the ladder, passing jugs of water upward to the next person. Sam and Nephi stood on deck, tossing the water onto the growing blaze.

The flames reached above their heads in some spots, and Nephi took a couple of seconds to wrap his turban across his mouth. The smoke wafted through the cloth, permeating his mouth and stinging his eyes. He fought the coughs racking his chest as he poured jugful after jugful of seawater onto the blazing inferno.

"Watch out," Sam yelled.

Nephi turned and saw his brother pointing upward. Following the direction, Nephi looked up. The fire had reached the top of the mast. A horrible cracking split the air.

"It's going to topple!"

Nephi scrambled backward, releasing the jug he'd been carrying. Above the sound of shattering pottery, he could hear screaming coming from someplace, but where? He couldn't tell above the angry roar of the fire. He fell to his knees, gasping for breath. The pole swayed—toward him.

"Nephi!"

"Sam?" The smoke cut off Nephi's cry. He choked on the thickness and felt a burning deep in his chest. He wondered if it were possible to drown in a cloud of smoke.

The mast crashed against the deck, close enough to Nephi that he shielded his eyes to ward off the flying embers. A hand tugged at his arm, and he turned to see the blackened face of Sam.

"We're jumping off."

Nephi nodded numbly and let himself be half dragged to the edge of the deck. Before he could determine whether or not he really wanted to jump, his brother's strong arms pushed him off the edge. And suddenly, Nephi was falling, straight down.

He hit the water square on his stomach, which pushed the breath from his body for a moment. The abrupt coldness sharpened his senses, and he started to kick his way to the surface. When he broke through the top, he heard his wife screaming his name.

"Isaabel?" he gasped, sputtering against a mouthful of seawater.

Cold arms wrapped around his torso, pulling him toward shore. Nephi blinked against the sting of salt and looked at his rescuer. Zoram had reached him first. "Wait . . . what about the ship?"

"Your life is more important," Zoram said.

"Did Laman and Lemuel show up?"

"Not yet," Zoram said through gritted teeth.

Nephi's stomach twisted as he thought about the implication this presented—his two older brothers conveniently missing as the ship burned. He extended his legs in the water and touched the bottom. "I think I can stand."

"All right," Zoram said, gripping Nephi's arm to help him maintain balance.

The two men waded the last several paces to shore, where Isaabel watched. She ran to Nephi and flung her arms about his neck. "Nephi! You could have been killed." She buried her face against his chest.

"I was trying . . . to save the ship," he said, gasping. His chest seized as he coughed.

Isaabel shook her head, tears forming. "You could have died."

"I know," he whispered. He turned to see the ship, more than half of it now consumed in fire. The iridescent yellow and orange lit the night sky and reflected in the water below. It was as if his heart had left his chest and burned with the flames. He groaned and clutched his wife close. They rocked slowly for a moment, the cool surf lapping against their feet.

He finally relaxed his hold and looked at Isaabel with bleary eyes. "Any word from Laman or Lemuel?"

"No," she whispered, reaching to touch his face. "Do you think they're responsible?"

He simply nodded.

"I'm so sorry," Isaabel said. "It's unbelievable that they could do something like this."

He pulled away from her and took several steps into the sea. Isaabel grabbed his arm and followed. "I feel so helpless just standing here," Nephi said through clenched teeth. "Why? Why would they do this to me?"

His wife's warm hand slipped into his. After a moment of silence she said, "We all worked on this ship—two years of building and another sailing." She reached up and stroked the wet curls clinging to his neck. "They have to know that burning it hurts *all* of us."

He turned to face her, seeing the reflection of the fire in her gaze. Gently he cupped her face with his hands. "Every part of that ship was instructed by the Lord. This ship represented His promise to *us*, His blessings upon the entire family."

Isaabel wrapped her arms around his waist and laid her head against his sodden chest. "No matter what your brothers did, or will do, they can never change our relationship with the Lord." She lifted her gaze to meet his. "But the ship's purpose has been served." She hesitated, her expression hardening. "Your brothers will see that they have only damaged their relationships with everyone in the family."

Holding his wife quietly in his arms, Nephi let his head rest on hers. A tear surfaced as he watched his ship disintegrate into the night.

✦ CHAPTER 1 ✦

If ye be willing and obedient, ye shall eat the good of the land.

(Isaiah 1:19)

Two years later

The lapping waves rose and fell with each breath of the jade-colored sea, but Nephi wasn't watching the surf. In line with his gaze were his wife, Isabel, and their daughter, Sarah. The young girl hoisted a clay jar of seawater onto her hip—the salt to be extracted for curing meat. Isaabel patted her daughter's shoulder and nodded encouragement as they started back home together. Their home was simple, made of reeds—but most importantly, it was a home dedicated to the Lord and preserved with peace and love.

His family hadn't noticed him, so Nephi spent a few moments watching mother and child walk along the sand and turn toward home. With swift strokes, he finished paddling to the shore, anchoring his fishing boat with the weight of a rock. He had two baskets that brimmed with silvery fish, some still wriggling against their plight. Nephi had returned earlier than usual, due to the abundance of fish he'd caught. He marveled that each day his family seemed more blessed than the day before.

The cooking fires were in full force, stationed throughout the community that had grown in the last two years.

Two years. It seemed impossible that so much time had already passed since arriving at the promised land, but as sure as the sun rose each morning, time continued to move.

"Nephi!"

He turned his head and saw his younger brother Jacob sprinting toward him. Now that he was almost a man at the age of twelve, Jacob's voice had deepened, and he'd outgrown his lanky thinness.

"We have a new nephew," Jacob said as he reached Nephi. He gripped one of the baskets of fish, ignoring the seawater soaking the hem of his garment.

Nephi grinned. "Wonderful! Is Dinah in good health?"

"Yes," Jacob said. "Mother is waiting for these fish to prepare the celebratory meal. She sent me to scout for you."

Chuckling, Nephi grabbed the other basket and started along the shore, Jacob at his side. They had become spoiled in two years. Fresh fish for each meal—after so many months of limited food and water on the ship, preceded by dates and bitter water in the wilderness. Dinah and Tiras had finally married last year. Her stubbornness mixed with his made them the perfect pair. And now they had a child. He couldn't imagine his other sister, Elisheba, being a grandmother yet, but since she'd married Raamah, Tiras had become like her own son.

"Raamah and Laman returned just over an hour ago," Jacob said, pulling Nephi from his thoughts. "They found a stone quarry."

Nephi nodded, thinking of the temple that he and his father had begun to design. They had not told the family the entire reason for looking for a stone quarry. "Are there local people who claim the area?"

"No," Jacob said. "The closest population is a half-day walk."

"How far is the quarry from here?"

"Two days travel."

It would take them many months just to transport the hewn stone such a distance. But the quarries that were nearer to the settlement were already claimed by the people of Kaminaljuyú. The first time Nephi met the indigenous tribe, he was astounded by their architecture. Their temple was built over a great mound of earth, atop a hill. The people had covered the mound with stone sheathing. Steps led to the highest part of the graduated temple, with flat roofs holding sacrificial altars.

"They continue to jest that you want your *own* temple," Jacob said quietly. "It might seem their spiteful remarks are aimed at you, but they are truly hurting Father."

A prickle of irritation rose up Nephi's neck. *Not tonight,* he told himself. He didn't want to spend the evening warding off his brothers' taunting. Tonight would be dedicated to rejoicing in his sister's good health and her new babe. But when Lehi was affected, it was impossible to ignore.

Jacob wasn't ready to drop the conversation. "Father's health has not been good since Laman and Lemuel burned the ship." His voice took on a sharp edge. "I wish I could erase the pain I see in Father's eyes. It's unbearable."

"I know," Nephi said. A lump tightened his throat. His younger brother had not enjoyed an easy life. Since birth, Jacob had witnessed ridicule, torture, and intimidation. Nephi glanced at Jacob, realizing that despite the recurring tension among the brothers, Nephi couldn't help but be sincerely grateful. Both of his younger brothers, Jacob and Joseph, had discerned for themselves the correct path to follow. And Joseph had even begun to stand up to his young nephews when they sided with Laman's arguments. At times, Nephi had to calm him down when arguments erupted among the children. Jacob however, took a different approach—a quiet and contemplative one. It was as if nothing surprised him, and he took every setback in stride.

They neared the main shelter built for family gatherings, and Sariah rushed to meet them. "A new child has come to join us," she said with a grin lighting her face. "Little Seba is so handsome, and I've never seen Dinah more pleased."

Nephi marveled at his mother's exuberance. She had been at Dinah's side throughout the night and likely the entire day until the child was born. And here she was, looking clean and fresh, her joy uncontainable. Nephi placed his basket of fish on the ground and embraced his mother.

"Father and Joseph are preparing for the thanksgiving sacrifice." Sariah squeezed her sons tightly, then drew back. "Now, you and Jacob clean out the fish in the river. I want to have them cooking before the sun sets."

Nephi nodded. "Yes, Mother." He caught Jacob's smile above his mother's head. No one dared to argue with her; it proved to be an absolute waste of time.

Jacob hoisted his basket and started walking toward the river just south of the main settlement. Nephi followed, increasing his pace to match his younger brother's. Suddenly Jacob slowed.

"What is it?" Nephi asked.

Jacob lifted his shoulders in a half-shrug. "Maybe we should go downriver a ways."

Nephi looked in the direction of the bank and saw three girls washing clothing—Heth's daughter, Jochebed, a budding fifteen-year-old; Eve, Zoram's eleven-year-old daughter; and Govad, Sam's daughter, also eleven.

Jochebed spotted them. She raised her arm and waved. "Jacob, Nephi, did you hear about the baby?"

"Yes," Nephi called back with a smile then glanced at Jacob. He was surprised to see his brother's face redden considerably. "What's wrong?"

Jacob shuffled forward, his head lowered. "I just think we should have gone downstream."

Nephi nudged his brother. "I see a great opportunity to get some help cleaning the fish. And the sooner Mother has her fish, the happier she'll be."

* * *

Eve froze mid-motion when she heard Jochebed screech Jacob's name. Her back was turned toward the approaching men, but she waded farther into the river hoping that she wouldn't have to carry on any conversation with them. Although her father, Zoram, was known for his talkative nature, she was just the opposite. In fact, she despised the fact that the other girls seemed to converse so easily with the boys their age—Shem, Javan, and Jacob included.

She held the tunic under the clear water for another moment, realizing how she was unlike her cousins. Her mother required that Eve spend most of her hours caring for her grandmother. And she spent any spare time helping her younger sisters. As the oldest daughter of the oldest daughter, Eve had been taught at a young age that part of her duty in life was to care for her aging grandmother. This left very little time to play with the other children, and as her womanhood approached, she realized that she no longer had much in common with them anyway.

She had also noticed the way that Jacob seemed very nervous around Jochebed. They would make a match someday; at least that's what everyone said. Eve wasn't surprised. Jochebed was beautiful, very lively, and loved to laugh—everything that any man would desire in a wife.

"If we carry the clothing back for you, will you help us clean these fish?" Nephi's voice cut through Eve's thoughts.

She turned and was about to answer when Jochebed and Govad chimed *yes* in unison.

"Just make sure you clean them downstream from *our* wash," Jochebed said with a laugh. Her eyes were as bright as gemstones.

Surprisingly, Eve had never cleaned fish before, since she'd always been involved with caring for her family. She tried not to wrinkle her nose in distaste as she returned to her work. The tunic she held was more than clean, but she spent another moment wringing it out before returning to shore. Jacob and Nephi were hard at work, using their daggers to make neat cuts along the fish bellies.

Jochebed leaned over Jacob's shoulder, her excited voice exclaiming at the procedure. A string of scarlet spilled out from the fish Jacob held. He just laughed when Jochebed let out a little scream. Then Eve saw redness creep along his neck.

She turned away and grabbed the next handful of clothing. Moving into the shallow part of the river, she focused on the cool water cascading across her ankles and calves.

Govad passed by her, arms full of wet clothing. She winked and said, "It looks like Jochebed beat you to it."

Eve felt the back of her throat suddenly go dry. "What do you mean?"

"Just look at them," Govad said, tilting her head. Her brown eyes twinkled with laughter. "Like an old married couple already."

Eve spun in the water and saw that Jacob and Jochebed appeared to be arguing about something. The flowing river made it difficult to hear what they said. Eve turned to face Govad and shrugged. "Good for them."

She began to move to a deeper part of the river when Govad called to her again. Eve looked over her shoulder, but couldn't hear her cousin's words.

With a sigh, Eve plunged the clothing into the river, soaking the tunic thoroughly. Then she walked back to the bank and slapped the clothes against a large rock. When Govad finished with the square of soap, Eve took it in her hand and scrubbed every section of the clothing, inside and out.

"Sorry," Govad's voice whispered in Eve's ear.

"Sorry for what?" Eve asked, scrubbing harder, her hands turning a harsh red.

"I didn't mean to upset you over Jochebed and Jacob."

Eve straightened and met Govad's gaze. Her cousin was her only true friend, but Govad had one serious flaw. She couldn't keep quiet. And now Eve was regretting she'd told her friend about Jacob. "What I told you about Jacob was a secret. Besides, it was over a year ago, and I don't feel the same way anymore."

A smile tugged at Govad's lips, but her eyes were filled with remorse. "I understand. I won't mention it again."

"I hope you will scratch it from your memory and never even *think* about it again."

"I promise." Govad extended her hand, and Eve reached out to grasp it. Over the years, the two girls had formed this sign of truce. Only it seemed that Eve had been extending her forgiveness to Govad too many times in the past months.

Eve swallowed against the pain in her chest as Jochebed's laughter rang loud and clear, followed by Nephi and Jacob chuckling along. Typically Jacob was the quietest among the older cousins, but Jochebed could drag a smile or a laugh from him, seemingly at her will.

Placing the soap on a rock, Eve entered the river once again to rinse off the newly scrubbed clothing. She wished she could soak herself in the water and forget about her envious heart. Or at least ignore it.

As she trudged back to shore, Nephi waved her over. Eve had always been a little intimidated by him and his profound Sabbath sermons. She often asked her father to explain further. What would begin as a simplified version of Nephi's words often turned into tales of traveling in the wilderness. These fascinated Eve, and she loved to listen to her father's deep voice recall the early trials and great miracles on the trail between Jerusalem and Bountiful. Eve's earliest memories consisted of living in Mudhail as a slave, then traveling through the desert until they reached Bountiful. She had been eight years old then.

But her father's descriptions of Jerusalem and his growing-up years, followed by the time spent at Laban's court, intrigued her, as did his reminiscences of her grandfather, Ishmael. Eve's widowed grandmother, Bashemath, spent most of her time inside Raamah and Elisheba's home and was hard of hearing. But Eve still tried to pull as many stories as possible from her only living grandparent.

Eve reached Nephi's side and watched his capable hands demonstrate how to clean the silvery fish. "Here." Nephi handed her his dagger. "You try the next one."

Crouching near the stilled water of the bank, Eve held the dagger in one hand and the limp fish in the other. Carefully she pricked the shiny flesh, and a small drop of blood oozed out. She hesitated, looking for Nephi's encouragement. Several paces away, he helped Govad. Eve's eyes locked with Jacob's, and he moved away from Jochebed's side and crouched beside her.

"You'll have to cut more than that to get the fish clean," Jacob teased.

"I know," Eve said. Still she hesitated, feeling ridiculous as tears brimmed her eyes. "You're foolish," she whispered to herself.

She hadn't realized she'd spoken aloud until Jacob mumbled, "Sorry," and stood. He moved away before Eve could explain. *I was talking about me, not you*, she thought miserably. *I can't even clean a small fish.*

Frustration burning at the back of her eyes, Eve took a deep breath and sliced open the fish like Nephi had shown her. She submerged it in the water and quickly scraped it clean. Then she grabbed another. She worked as fast as she could until she had cleaned a sufficient pile. Determined, she ignored all conversation and only answered once when Nephi asked her a question about her grandmother's health. She avoided Jacob's gaze until all the fish were prepared. *Of course, he's not looking in my direction anyway*, she thought.

She was the last to leave the riverbank and the last to arrive at the family feast. More and more she felt entirely disconnected from everyone. They all seemed to be in a celebratory mood, but Eve just wanted to be alone. Out of habit, she rushed to her grandmother's side and helped Bashemath settle onto a fur-covered pillow.

"Thank you, dear," Bashemath said, placing her trembling hand over Eve's young, browned one. "You'll make a wonderful wife someday."

As her grandmother continued extolling Eve's virtues, she couldn't help but let her mind drift. *If only*, she thought. *If only every word that came out of my mouth weren't so wrong.*

* * *

The dimness in the small birthing hut was cut by a single light from a clay oil lamp. The place was set apart from the main settlement to offer the mother privacy. Rugs hung against the walls, protecting the room from any cross breeze that might penetrate the slatted reed walls, giving the hut a secluded feeling. Sariah moved quietly around her youngest daughter, Dinah, as the babe—a boy—slept nearby. Tiras was proud, and it did her good to see his worries gone. She'd never seen anyone pace so much, even after the baby had arrived.

"Is it really over, Mother?" Dinah's voice sounded weak, childlike.

Sariah smiled tenderly and knelt by her daughter's side. "You did exemplary work. I'm so glad you tried the willow bark. I think it really helped with the pain."

The weariness showed plain on Dinah's face. "I have nothing to compare it with."

"Of course not," Sariah said, placing a wet cloth against Dinah's perspiring forehead. "But I feel confident that chewing the bark *did* make a difference, and we'll use it next time, too."

Dinah closed her eyes as Sariah continued wetting the cloth in a bowl of petal-scented water and dabbing her daughter's forehead.

"What did Tiras say?" Dinah asked.

"It is difficult to know because all I heard was his hollering."

Dinah smiled, her eyes glowing with pleasure. "He will be a good father."

"And he loves you dearly." Sariah returned the cloth to its bowl then pressed her fingers against Dinah's abdomen. "This will hurt, but it's important to release any extra blood."

Nodding, Dinah closed her eyes against the pain. She drew her breath in sharply as her mother's hands continued their work. When Sariah finished, she again dabbed Dinah's forehead.

The babe let out a small cry.

"Oh, Mother," Dinah said, a tear shining against her cheek. "I can't believe that sound belongs to my child."

Sariah retrieved the babe and helped place his rooting mouth to his mother's breast. "You'll be sore for the first few days, but by the day of your purification, you won't remember what it was like *not* to be a mother."

Dinah winced as the baby began to feed. "I'll trust your advice." But doubt had filled her eyes. "I thought childbirth was ordeal enough for a woman."

"It is enough. But it may surprise you that physical pain is the least of the trials a mother will face—" Sariah cut herself off, embarrassed to have spoken so boldly, and to her youngest daughter at that.

But Dinah seemed to understand. "Because things of the body are temporary, but things of the soul are eternal."

"Yes," Sariah said, leaning over her daughter and kissing her forehead. "It touches my heart to watch you become a new mother, full of hope and love. You have a lifetime of joy ahead of you." Even as Sariah spoke, she felt the heaviness of her many burdens. But she had just watched her daughter deliver a healthy baby, and she knew Dinah was now recovering well. That was a blessing indeed. Other concerns could wait.

Since arriving at the promised land, family life had been relatively tranquil. In truth, everyone had been so busy building their homes and farming that there hadn't been much room left for tensions between brothers. After they had recovered from the devastating fire that destroyed the ship, relationships had been peaceful. Her husband, Lehi, had given a strong lecture to Laman and Lemuel, all but accusing them of burning the ship.

Neither ever admitted to such an act, but Sariah still suspected them in her heart. They'd been afraid that Nephi would command them all to take a second voyage to another faraway land. She had watched her older sons closely over the past months and was happy to see that they at least tried harder than in the wilderness or in Bountiful. They spent more time with their children and spoke less sharply to their wives, Anah and Puah. Each had four children now, and Anah had just announced another child was on the way.

Sariah wished that Anah would wait the typical three years between each birth. But she had stopped nursing each child too early, so she always seemed to carry another too soon. It was as if she were competing with the other wives. But seeing Dinah's radiance now, Sariah could well understand Anah's desire for children. Sariah just hoped it was based on correct principles and not competition.

A soft call came from outside, and Sariah rose to see who it was. She smiled at the sight of her older daughter, Elisheba. "Come in."

Elisheba stepped into the room and immediately moved to Dinah's side, marveling at the new babe.

"You are a grandmother now," Sariah said with a smile.

"I suppose I am," Elisheba said. "A grandmother and an aunt."

Sariah smiled at the tender exchange between the sisters as Dinah relayed the details of the birth. Elisheba had married Raamah and became the stepmother to his son, Tiras. Then, last year, Tiras and Dinah had married, making Elisheba a grandmother by marriage.

After several moments, Elisheba rose from Dinah's side. "The others are waiting for you, Mother. I'll stay here with Dinah while you help with the celebration feast."

"Are Nephi and Jacob back with the cleaned fish?"

Elisheba smiled. "Of course. They are the ones who sent me to tell you."

"Good boys," Sariah said. "They know how to please their mother." She took a lingering look at the new mother and child, then slipped out of the room.

╼═╋═❖ CHAPTER 2 ❖═╋═╾

For every purpose of the Lord shall be performed.
(JEREMIAH 51:29)

"We've been looking for you," Shem said, slapping his hand on Jacob's back.

Jacob stopped just outside the gathering room where the family already ate supper. It was nearly dark, and the tempting odors of food wafted through the entryway. With sharp realization, he knew his hunger pangs would be stayed a little longer. He turned to see his two grinning nephews—Shem and Javan—identical images of their fathers, Laman and Lemuel. In the warm, moist climate, his nephews wore little clothing. Gone were the long tunics and robes of Bountiful—replaced by short pieces of cloth wrapped around their middles. Instead of turbans, they wore headdresses made of leather and colorful feathers, similar to those worn by the local tribes.

"Why do you need me?" Jacob asked.

"Found a new cave," Shem continued. He waved his hand in the direction of the eastern mountain range, then he lowered his voice. "A whole litter of baby foxes are in it, almost old enough to leave their mother."

"You want to keep them for pets?" Jacob asked.

Javan let out a bellow of laughter. "No, Shem wants a coat of fox hair."

Jacob nodded, not surprised. That sounded more like his nephews. "What about the deer you killed last week?"

"The fur is too rough," Shem said, a mischievous twinkle in his eye. "I want something to impress the girls."

Javan licked his lips. "You should see the little foxes and their soft gray fur—"

"I think a coat of a grown animal that was difficult to catch would impress the girls more," Jacob interrupted. "A baby fox is just like a helpless lamb."

"Ahh," Shem said, throwing his hands up. "You're too serious for your own good. If you don't take care, you're going to get stuck with one of Zoram's younger daughters."

Javan guffawed. "And she'll suddenly change and talk so much in your home that you won't get a wink of sleep."

Folding his arms, Jacob glared at his two nephews. "Since I'm only twelve, I don't see a reason to choose a bride quite yet."

Smirking, Shem let his hand rest on Jacob's shoulder. "No reason not to, either." His face brightened. "Yesterday we came across several girls from the Kaminaljuyú tribe near the rising hills. They came to the upper falls to swim."

Javan let out a laugh, then stifled it, whispering, "We were just going to watch them, when Shem knocked a rock loose." He elbowed Shem, who had a grin pasted on his face.

"It couldn't have been prevented." Shem's eyes filled with delight. "We were impressed by their friendliness . . . and beauty." He winked at Jacob. "At least we don't have to worry about competition from you, since you won't go against Hebrew convention and take a bride outside our lineage."

Javan offered a quick nod. "Maybe next time you should come with us."

Recoiling at the thought of spying on foreign girls, Jacob shook his head. "No thank you."

"Come on, cousin." Shem pulled Javan toward him. "Supper is being served. Let's leave Jacob to his brooding and brass plates."

Jacob entered the gathering room and watched the two take their places at the meal, then let his gaze move across the crowded enclosure. He heard the tinkling of Jochebed's unmistakable laughter coming from the food storage room. Then his eyes settled on Bashemath. Without having to look, Jacob knew that Eve, as faithful as ever, would be at the woman's side.

He'd heard Shem and Javan discuss Eve's quiet nature before, and it always bothered him. Why, he didn't know, but there seemed a goodness in her that was purer than the springs that bubbled from the highest mountain. It didn't seem right to tease her for being so shy. For a moment, Jacob was glad that Shem and Javan had diverted their interest toward the tribal girls.

But Eve thinks I'm foolish. Jacob tilted his head as he remembered the incident at the river. He was sure she referred to the way he encouraged Jochebed's lightheartedness. Her cheerful demeanor was contagious, and all who spent time with her came away laughing.

As if to emphasize his thought, another trickle of Jochebed's unmistakable laughter came from the adjacent storage room. It was then he realized that Eve was watching him. He glanced away quickly, embarrassed that she had caught his stare.

Girls . . . Women. Maybe Shem was right. Jacob might be better off sticking with the brass plates. *The writings of Isaiah are straightforward compared to females,* he thought. In fact, tonight he was to meet his father and discuss some of its passages. He looked forward to it more than he had expected.

* * *

In the gathering room that stood in the center of the settlement, Nephi tapped a small chisel against the ore plates he'd fashioned. The hour was late, but this was the only time he could find to write. By the light of two oil lamps, the delicate words formed beneath the chisel, and he thought back to when he'd received the instructions from the Lord.

Make a record of the ministry and the prophecies. The more plain and precious parts of them thou shalt write upon these plates.

Plain and precious. According to whom? Some men esteemed spiritual events to be of great worth, while others belittled the things of God. He wanted to assure future generations that he would only write what he had been commanded to record.

Nevertheless, I do not write anything upon plates save it be that I think it be sacred. Nephi painstakingly etched the words then reread them. An explanation was due.

And now, if I do err, even did they err of old, not that I would excuse myself because of other men, but because of the weakness which is in me . . . Nephi flexed his fingers then resumed his position.

. . . according to the flesh, I would excuse myself.

He leaned back and surveyed his words. Then he bent over the ore plates once again and blew away the tiny metal shavings. He continued explaining his thoughts, hoping that those who would read his record would understand the intentions of his heart.

Warmth spread through his being as he felt direct inspiration flow from the heavens. His testimony burned steady in his bosom, and the chisel seemed to guide itself. Gone were the weariness and aching hands. The next words he wanted to sing, to shout, to share with every living being.

And behold he cometh, according to the words of the angel, in six hundred years from the time my father left Jerusalem.

He knew it. He felt it. He had seen it, and he cherished the knowledge, though he would not witness the event from this earthly estate. No, but he had seen it in a vision at the Valley of Lemuel eleven years ago. *Wherefore they scourge him, and he suffereth it; and they smite him, and he suffereth it. Yea, they spit upon him, and he suffereth it, because of his loving kindness and his long-suffering towards the children of men.*

Nephi closed his eyes, thinking about the events he'd seen leading up to Christ's death. A shiver of dread passed through him as he thought about the torture the Son of God would experience—torture and pain Nephi had yet to see equaled. Even in his darkest moments, his despair was nothing like what Christ would experience. Nephi had only two brothers who fought against him on every angle of doctrine, every instillment of virtue. Christ would have an entire people against Him, and that was just during His mortality.

Nephi had seen the wars and battles that would rage over the divinity of the Lord. Those who believed versus those who didn't. Sheltered in his home, surrounded by a peaceful landscape, it was difficult to picture the hatred that would eventually consume the hearts of unborn civilizations.

A host of prophets had already predicted Christ's death: Zenock, Neum, Isaiah, and Zenos to name a few. They had foretold the crucifixion of the God of Israel. Nephi continued to write, pressing the words in permanent form into the ore plates. *Yea, and all the earth shall see the salvation of the Lord, saith the prophet; every nation, kindred, tongue and people shall be blessed.*

Nephi relaxed his hold on the chisel and bowed his head, thinking about the one thing he wished he could instill in his family. *O, remember the Lord. Remember your Redeemer.* Exhaustion set in, slowing his reflexes, hindering his movements. He released the chisel and relaxed on his side against a pillow, thinking of the next phrases he wanted to write . . . *perhaps with these records I might persuade my people to remember the Lord their Redeemer.*

As the lamps flickered into the night, Nephi bent once again over the plates. *For behold, I have workings in the spirit, which doth weary me even that all my joints are weak* . . . The sound of footsteps came from outside the structure, and he put down the chisel. Stretching, he walked to the entrance and saw his father walking toward him, the moonlight glinting off the man's silvery beard.

Lehi's head was wrapped in a dark turban, and the whiteness of his robe contrasted sharply with his sun-browned skin.

"I thought I'd find you here." Lehi's gentle voice parted the stillness.

Nephi smiled. "Welcome." He noticed with surprise that the horizon had begun to lighten. He had written the entire night. As his father neared, Nephi noted the deep crevices in Lehi's expression. Age had caught up with his parents. Lehi reached out a hand in greeting, and Nephi saw the hands of an old man—gnarled, spotted, and wizened.

He grasped his father's hand, then embraced him.

"Jacob will be along in a few moments," Lehi said. "He had to fetch some day-old bread because he said his mind couldn't work if his stomach was empty."

Nephi grinned. It was a sure sign that Jacob was growing into a man—the ever-increasing appetite. "We can wait patiently. The other boys his age are still sleeping, dreaming of the next hunt." He arched his back and stretched with a yawn. "I don't think I could bribe my Aaron to rise so early."

A hand grasped his arm, and Nephi looked at his father with surprise. Tears clouded Lehi's vision. "Don't you see, son? Jacob will succeed you as prophet in your aged years."

Nephi felt the words creep into his heart, swelling with clarity and knowledge. He placed his hand over his father's, feeling the trembling beneath. Questions about his own son, Aaron, collided in his mind, but he took a steady breath and listened for the Spirit's whisper. "Has the Lord made this known?"

"The Lord has shown me in a vision that Jacob will be a prophet, and someday, so will his son . . ."

The sure witness came, and warmth passed through his body. Nephi's questions about Aaron were quelled, and all he felt was a deep sense of humility for his brother. "Does Jacob know?"

Lehi shook his head. "I think we should wait awhile. Let him enjoy his unencumbered youth. The Lord will make it known to him when the time is right."

Nephi smiled tenderly as he thought about his younger brother. Jacob was the picture of righteous accountability. He seemed to carry the weight of their family on his shoulders already. Footsteps sounded outside the structure and an instant later, Jacob's eager face shone in the doorway.

For an impulsive moment, Nephi wanted to burst out the news, take his brother into his confidence, and tell him about what to expect and how to pray for guidance. But instead he remained silent, suppressing the joy he felt, knowing that opposition would accompany each of Jacob's accomplishments.

"On the Sabbath tomorrow, you will discuss the scattering of Israel." Lehi looked pointedly at Nephi. "I want you to read Isaiah's words directly from the plates of brass." He turned to Jacob. "Our brethren must learn to understand the sacred prophesies within their context, not cut up and made sweet."

Nephi watched as Jacob removed the brass plates from their dugout hole beneath the floor, all the while asking his father questions. Nephi's skin tingled with affection as he realized his father was training a prophet. Feeling protective, Nephi's heart both soared and trembled at the thought of Jacob leading their people someday. From an early age, even as young as seven, he had shown uncommon wisdom. Interpreting the language of the scriptures had come easily. The Spirit had dwelt with this young man for many years, conditioning and honing his spirit.

Lehi read the words of Isaiah. "'Thus saith the Lord God: Behold, I will lift up mine hand to the Gentiles, and set up my standard to the people; and they shall bring thy sons in their arms, and thy daughters shall be carried upon their shoulders.'" He lifted his head and looked at Nephi. "Tomorrow we will focus on this statement." His gaze slid to Jacob. "Do you know why?"

"A temple," Jacob breathed. "We need to build a temple to prepare for the fulness of the gospel of the Redeemer."

Lehi's mouth fell open. "Yes. But how did you know?"

"The 'standard' mentioned by Isaiah is the everlasting covenant and the fulness of the gospel that will be brought by the Holy Messiah Himself." Jacob spread his hands as if the reasoning should be clear to anyone. "By having a temple we can fulfill the old law until the new law is established."

Nephi rocked back on his heels, amazed by his brother's insight. Neither Nephi nor his father had mentioned their temple plans to anyone. They were still scouting for sites and giving the rest of the family time to complete their homesteads. Nephi could only imagine Laman and Lemuel's reaction to devoting months of labor to building a temple.

"Just as King David said in his psalm, 'Lift up, ye everlasting doors; and the King of glory shall come in.' David told us that we shall receive blessings and become righteous through temple ordinances. We will become holy as the temple is holy," Lehi said quietly.

Nephi nodded, feeling the presence of the Spirit permeate the room. "Worshipping in the temple is like participating in scripture. Instead of reading the words of the Lord, we become active participants in those words and become sanctified."

"Like an exalted highway," Jacob said.

"The strait and the narrow path can be found within the temple walls, an exalted highway, a mountain unto the Lord," Nephi finished, smiling at Jacob for using Isaiah's words.

"A strait path is not only narrow, but it may also be circular," Jacob added.

Lehi furrowed his brows and looked at Jacob. "How so, son?"

"A circular path that begins and ends with the Lord. All holy thoughts and actions circle to one thing: the Redeemer. The holiness of the Lord's house will bring us *back* to eternal life with the Lord Himself . . . right where we began." Jacob looked at Nephi.

"Into His arms, encircled with love," Nephi said. "Just as the Tree of Life is God's love. And He will send His Son so that we can *return*, or circle back to Him."

"Yes!" Lehi slapped his leg and grinned. He reached out and clapped Jacob on the shoulder. "And that is why we need to build a temple!"

* * *

As the sun dipped against the horizon, Sabbath began. Jacob stood in the center of the room he shared with his younger brother, Joseph. On his mat made with woven palms, his newly cleaned robe was spread out neatly. A thrill ran through him as he thought about the announcement that would be made to the family tonight—they were building a temple.

In the next room, he could hear his parents' muffled conversation. Jacob smiled as he thought about how his mother fussed over Lehi. Although her step was slower than it used to be, her mind and countenance continued to be bright.

"Jacob." It was his mother's voice.

"I'm coming." Jacob slipped on his robe, then adjusted his prayer shawl. He smoothed his hair with the water in the basin that sat in the corner of his room. Finally, he put a round, woven cap on top of his head.

He met Joseph and his parents at the entrance to their home, and noticed how his father clung to his mother's arm for support. Yet Lehi's expression was filled with eagerness and anticipation.

Most of the family had gathered by the time Jacob arrived.

Lehi raised both hands and waited for silence. Then he began his Sabbath sermon in the customary manner. "Welcome, everyone, on this blessed day which we have set apart for the worship of the Lord." After a few moments of speaking, he said, "And now, Nephi will read from the words of Isaiah."

When Nephi rose, Jacob noticed that Shem and Javan, who sat together, whispered then laughed.

"'Hearken and hear this, O house of Jacob, who are called by the name of Israel . . .'" Nephi began.

Shem met Jacob's gaze and grinned. He made the shape of a house with his fingers then pointed to Jacob. *House of Jacob,* he mouthed.

As Nephi continued reading, Jacob looked away from his nephews, not wanting to draw attention away from his brother. He didn't want to let their teasing have any impact on his mood tonight. He glanced in the opposite direction and was surprised to see Eve looking at him. She quickly moved her gaze back to Nephi.

She must have been looking at someone sitting behind me, Jacob decided. But even as he thought it, he knew no one sat behind him.

"'Nevertheless, for my name's sake will I defer mine anger, and for my praise will I refrain from thee, that I cut thee not off—'"

For behold, I have refined thee, but not with silver; I have chosen thee in the furnace of affliction, Jacob thought about Isaiah's words as Nephi read them. His gaze strayed to Eve. She wore a look of rapture on her face as Nephi read.

Does she understand the meaning of Isaiah's allegories? Jacob wondered. *If not, she at least seems to recognize the spirit behind the words.*

Nephi continued reading for some time. When he finished, Lehi stood and thanked Nephi, then turned to the family.

"We have been blessed with abundance in this promised land. For the past two years, we have sown and reaped a bountiful harvest from the seeds we brought from Jerusalem. We have found beasts of every kind—the cow and the ox, the horse and the wild goat, and many animals which have been for our use. We have also been blessed to find ore, gold, silver, and copper." Lehi spread his hands wide, his voice trembling. "All that we have around us has been given to us by the Lord."

Jacob's heart warmed at his father's powerful words. A complete hush had fallen over the family, and everyone seemed to know that their patriarch was about to say something important.

"And now we must meet the Lord's request. Just as the Lord promises not to forget the house of Israel, we must show the Lord that we will not forget Him." Lehi hesitated, his watery eyes passing over each person. "We will build a temple and dedicate it to His name."

A collective gasp sounded as Lehi continued. "With this temple, we will be able to fulfill the first law until the Son of God establishes the second law."

Involuntarily, Jacob's gaze landed once more on Eve. Her excitement looked like it was barely contained beneath the fair skin that framed her shining eyes. A smile crept to his own lips. *My family will have our own temple.* It would be an incredible achievement.

After Lehi closed with a prayer, the men separated from the women and walked to Lehi's home. Jacob usually joined the men, and tonight Shem and Javan came along, too.

"I bet you've known about this temple idea for a long time, Jacob," Shem said, catching up to Jacob, Javan in tow.

"No." Jacob shook his head. "Today was the first time."

"I thought you were in cahoots with the old man," Javan said.

Jacob threw Javan a harsh glance.

"So can we start guessing who the high priest is going to be?" Shem asked, his eyes dancing with mischief.

"Uh, let me go first," Javan said. "Nephi?"

Shem laughed. "I'll bet Nephi can't wait until that temple is finished. He'll probably sleep on the construction site."

Jacob let out a sigh, feeling annoyance creep along his neck. "You sound like your fathers." Even as he said it, he regretted his words. Shem and Javan were repeating what they'd heard at home, but truly they didn't possess the disposition of their fathers. At least he hoped they didn't.

But before he could apologize, they were pulled into Lehi's home by Zoram and instructed to sit and be quiet.

A heated discussion was already underway.

"You contradict yourself, Nephi." Laman's voice carried clear and strong across the small room. "How can you say there are *two* ways to interpret Isaiah's words—the spiritual way and the way of the flesh? It sounds as if you are interpreting the words at your own convenience."

The murmuring of voices rose until Nephi spoke. "They were manifested unto the prophet by the voice of the Spirit. As you know, it is through the Spirit that all things are made known unto the prophets."

Laman narrowed his eyes and folded his arms. Jacob felt his chest grow tight, and silently he prayed that an argument wouldn't erupt.

"This spirit of prophesy will come through the prophets and settle upon the children of men . . . according to the flesh," Nephi said, trying to make Isaiah's words more clear.

Jacob nodded to himself, having heard his father and Nephi discuss this very thing many times. He could almost answer the question himself.

"The things I have read to you are both spiritual and temporal. The house of Israel will be scattered upon all the face of the earth and among all nations," Nephi continued.

"So, you're saying that Jerusalem is already destroyed?" Laman asked.

"No. I am saying that regardless of the timing of Jerusalem's physical destruction, knowledge has already been lost by those in the city. This relates to the spiritual. And the physical separation is yet to come. A mighty nation will rise up among the Gentiles, and it will be the Gentiles who will nurse the scattered tribes back to the Lord's covenants."

Laman scoffed. "You are just trying to frighten us." He rose, his large form towering over those who sat. "You can frighten the women and children all you want. But I'll not be intimidated by a destruction that none of us can see."

Nephi's demeanor remained calm. He continued speaking, but now he wasn't merely answering questions, he was prophesying. Jacob looked at his father and saw his agreement.

"Our seed *will* be scattered," Nephi countered, his voice gaining volume and his eyes filling with passion. "And after our seed is scattered the Lord God will proceed to do a marvelous work among the Gentiles. This work will be of great worth to our seed, and we will be essentially carried in their arms and upon their shoulders."

Through temple ordinances, Jacob thought. His breath stopped short as he realized the implication of Nephi's words. A flood of warmth burst through Jacob's veins as he realized the Spirit was now whispering to *him.*

Laman simply turned and strode out of the room.

CHAPTER 3

Thus saith the Lord, shalt thou build me an house for me to dwell in?

(2 SAMUEL 7:5)

It didn't take long to clean up the Sabbath meal. With the help of many of the women, the work was light. Isaabel saw Bashemath and Sariah lingering over the challah bread. Their voices were animated, their gestures excited. Isaabel smiled to herself. The women continued to confer about the building of the temple long after the men had retired to Lehi's home for discussion.

Except for Laman's scoffing, everything is going well in the family, Isaabel thought. The sermon from Nephi was well received, and there had been no argument against building plans. Even Laman and Lemuel had remained quiet. She hoped that was a sign of their willingness to help. Building the temple would be a marvelous event if everyone participated. And once the family was able to perform temple ordinances again, their blessings would be multiplied.

Isaabel let out a breath as she swept the accumulated dust from the gathering room's corners. The evening sea breeze was soft and soothing.

She watched as Rebeka's daughter Eve hovered over Bashemath, ready to help with any small thing. Isaabel sighed. She thought it was wonderful that Eve was so attentive, but worried a little that the poor girl never did anything other than care for others. She couldn't remember the last time she saw Eve weaving or making pottery with the other girls. Isaabel thought about the embroidery that she enjoyed doing during her children's nap times or slow parts of the day. It was something she took pride in, ownership in. And she always felt a sense of accomplishment when she finished working on the hem of a shawl or robe.

She wondered if she might teach Eve the unique stitching skills that she had honed over the years. It would be several years before she could hope to train her own daughter in such a craft.

Isaabel finished sweeping and crossed over to Eve. As she approached, Eve quickly moved from Bashemath's side, as if she didn't want to be in Isaabel's way.

"I've come with a proposition for you, Eve," Isaabel said.

The girl looked genuinely surprised. She brought a hand to her chest. "Me?"

Isaabel smiled. "Yes. I thought about teaching some of the girls how to embroider. We could meet each afternoon at my home."

Eve glanced around her, as if searching for those "other" girls, then her forehead furrowed. "I usually bathe and massage Grandmother's feet in the afternoon."

"After you are finished, you could come over for a little while."

Eve nodded, her expression doubtful. "I don't think my mother—"

"I'll speak to your mother," Isaabel said, placing a hand on the girl's arm.

Suddenly Jacob's voice broke through the conversations. "It's Father! Come quick!"

Sariah stood, clutching Bashemath for support—who didn't provide much steadiness. Isaabel rushed to Sariah's side and latched onto her arm. "I'll take you."

Through the gathered darkness, the two women half ran, half stumbled along the path that led to Lehi's home. Isaabel focused her gaze on Jacob's back as he led the way. Behind, the rest of the women followed. No one spoke, but a myriad of thoughts tumbled around Isaabel's mind. Pushing through those gathered in the courtyard, she helped Sariah across the threshold. By now, her mother-in-law shook violently.

They entered the front room that was hot and humid. Men and boys stood against the walls, shoulder-to-shoulder. Some shuffled around, making room for Sariah and Isaabel to enter. Isaabel looked at the scene before them and immediately her heart dropped. Lehi lay on the floor, his eyes closed.

Nephi and Sam were bent over him, Nephi's hands rested on Lehi's head, his lips moving in reverent cadence as he offered a quiet blessing. Sariah gently knelt by her husband as Nephi continued his words. Isaabel found a place in the crowd, disbelief settling over her. Just as Nephi finished the blessing and opened his eyes, Joseph burst into the room.

"Father!" he cried and was captured by his mother's arms.

Sariah reached a trembling hand toward Lehi and stroked his cheek. "He is warm and breathes." Her voice began to gather confidence. "Something caused him to faint." She ran her hand along his neck, then allowed it to rest on his chest. After a moment, she leaned over Lehi, placing her ear against his chest.

"It beats steady," she said, her voice wavering. Then she lifted her head, her eyes searching for Isaabel.

As the two women made eye contact, Isaabel moved to Lehi's side and sank to the floor. She took Sariah's hand and wrapped an arm about Joseph.

"His heart is not as strong as it should be." Sariah brought a hand to her mouth and stifled a cry.

With her other arm, Isaabel drew Sariah close. "Please Lord," she whispered. "Allow him to stay with us."

Nephi began clearing the room until only he, his wife and mother, and his brothers remained.

"We need to get him to bed," Sam said, stepping forward.

Without further conversation, Laman, Lemuel, Sam, and Nephi lifted their father and transported him to the bed in the next room. As Isaabel watched the four men carry their father out, she felt as if her heart would break. The image of Nephi and his brothers coming together in their mutual love for their father imprinted itself onto her soul. She could almost forget Laman's recent outbursts. Almost.

And suddenly the emotions she'd felt at her father's passing came rushing back, so much that she almost staggered where she stood. Instead, she gripped Sariah and Joseph tightly against her. That was when she noticed Jacob kneeling in the middle of the room—his head bent in prayer.

* * *

Morning couldn't come too soon as Nephi kept watchful vigil over his father's quiet form, with Isaabel sitting quietly nearby. The steady rise and fall of Lehi's chest was the only comfort Nephi received. He had given him a blessing, and the entire family prayed continually for the patriarch. Sariah and Bashemath had spent most of the night in consultation, discussing medicinal remedies that might help. Finally they settled on jengibre, and Sariah and Isaabel had applied a warm plaster made from the ground root against Lehi's chest.

Just as the first hint of light began to dispel the gloom, Lehi took a deep breath.

"Son."

Nephi opened his eyes, suddenly alert. He scrambled to his father's side. "Father. How are you?"

Lehi's eyes flickered for a moment, then closed to slits, the deep brown irises hidden beneath his wrinkled lids. "Son." He tried to rise, but collapsed back onto the bed.

"Stay where you are, Father. You've had a fall."

"I am not well," Lehi said, his voice raspy. He took a jagged breath. "I've known it for some time."

Dread grasped at Nephi's heart as he stared at his father.

"Build the temple," he said.

"Of course," Nephi whispered. He reached out to touch his father's forehead and found it hot.

Isaabel moved to Nephi's side. "Should I call your mother?"

Nephi nodded, his throat too thick to speak. He held his father's hand until his mother arrived.

"He's awake?" she asked quietly when she entered the room.

Nephi stood and moved back, allowing his mother to be near her husband. "Yes, for a moment."

Her tone was practical as she leaned over Lehi. "Dear husband, it's time you wake and eat something."

Repressing a smile, Nephi moved to the door, where Isaabel now hovered. "Bring some broth and we'll see if we can get him to eat."

Isaabel nodded in acknowledgement and disappeared from the room.

Nephi turned to see his mother stroking Lehi's hand, gently humming a Sabbath song the family had sung just the evening before.

Lehi's eyes fluttered open and for a moment Nephi saw an exchange of love between the two as they looked at each other. Sariah—her countenance radiant with purity; Lehi—content and peaceful.

"That's better," Sariah said. "Now we can feed you properly."

A gentle smile creased Lehi's face, and he lifted his hand slightly. "Make sure Nephi builds that temple."

"Oh, stop ordering him around. When you get out of this bed, you can do it yourself."

Lehi's smile turned sad, and he moved his head slightly.

Sariah tightened her grip. "Don't you dare consider leaving me now. We have too much work to do."

Nephi backed against the wall, his heart pierced at the passion in his mother's voice. He felt as if he was witnessing something very personal that was meant for just the two of them.

"Besides," Sariah continued, adjusting the coverlet about Lehi, "we aren't quite settled in our home. There is plenty left to be done before either of us can even consider our earthly work to be finished."

Lehi's gaze followed his wife as she rose and bustled about the room.

"And," she said, turning to cast him a stern look, "there are a few passages in the books of Moses that need better explaining. I heard Jacob and Nephi discussing them the other day." She paused, her voice growing tremulous. "And they most certainly need your help with the matter."

"Sariah," Lehi's soft voice cut through her chatter, "come here."

Nephi watched his mother's shoulders droop as she moved to Lehi's side again.

"Tonight, I want to speak with our children."

Sariah nodded, swiping at the tears falling against her cheeks. "Of course."

* * *

Jacob greeted his father, pleased to see him propped against a mound of pillows, throwing out directions to anyone who entered. Most of the family had assembled outside the home and were waiting for Lehi's instructions. Tightness formed in Jacob's throat as he approached his father's side.

"Son," Lehi said, stretching out his hand. The color had returned somewhat to his face, but his voice sounded raspy and sore. "Are all my children gathered?"

"They are waiting outside with their families."

Lehi nodded and swallowed thickly.

"Father, you are recovering by the hour." Jacob gazed into his father's eyes, not liking the passive acceptance he saw in them.

But Lehi shook his head slowly. "I am old, Jacob, and my days are numbered upon this earth. Yet I have much to say before I depart— whether that time is tomorrow or next month."

Jacob sensed a peaceful stillness in the room, as if the reed walls themselves were respectfully waiting in tranquility. His face felt hot; his eyes stung.

Lehi lifted a trembling hand and reached under the neckline of his tunic. He lifted a gold object that hung from a leather necklace. "Here." Lehi's raspy voice filled the terse silence. "Nephi made this from the first gold discovered in this promised land. He told me it couldn't begin to replace all that we lost to Laban."

Reaching out his hand, Jacob took the rough-hewn ring from his father. What it lacked in decoration, it made up for in weight.

"It's the only thing I can give you now," Lehi said, his voice cracking. "Someday, son, someday you'll take on the mantle which the Lord has prepared for you. You'll continue the writings on the plates. But until then, I want you to remember all that I have taught you . . . all that I have hoped for you . . . and all that I have blessed you with."

Jacob's fingers folded over the heavy ring, his eyes watering. "I am honored to have something I can always remember you by," he whispered. He leaned over and kissed his father's cheek.

With a satisfied nod, Lehi said, "Call your brothers." He took a deep breath and offered a tremulous smile. "Do not be afraid."

Backing out of the room, with the ring and its leather strap clutched in his hand, Jacob wanted to find a place where he could be by himself and try to digest the feelings pulsing through him. Had his father's time really come? His father was a prophet—a servant of God, who had seen angels, received visions, and heard the voice of the Lord. Wouldn't Lehi know when his time had come? *He does,* Jacob realized, but it was his family who couldn't part with their father—the patriarch who had brought them to this blessed land. Jacob didn't know if *he* could part with him.

He turned and moved through the doorway, nearly running into Nephi, who stood by the entrance. Nephi reached out and took Jacob into an embrace. Jacob kept his emotions clenched inside, willing them to stay buried for the time being.

The sons of Lehi filed into the small room, and Laman moved close to his father, taking his hand. "We are all here, Father, ready to listen to your words." His dark eyes flashed at his brothers, as if challenging them to argue with his place as eldest son.

"Take me outside, that I might speak to the entire family," Lehi said.

Laman nodded curtly and instructed Lemuel, Sam, and Nephi to help carry their father.

Jacob and Joseph hurried out of the room, making way for their father to be brought outside and placed on a pillow covered with rugs. The women organized their children in small groups, sitting on the ground. Zoram and Raamah lit several torches, sending an orange cast over the solemn audience.

Jacob found a place next to his mother and waited with anticipation. Sariah reached over and knowingly clasped his moist hand. When Lehi was settled comfortably with a rug placed over him, he began, "Last night, the men were discussing the method of building a temple when I suffered a setback. I have lived many years, all of them greatly blessed by the Lord. I owe Him my all, and I have dedicated my life and family to Him."

Sariah squeezed Jacob's hand, a tear trickling along her cheekbone. He felt his chest harden and his body tingle.

"Some members of the family rebelled as we crossed the high sea, and we nearly perished in the great storm. But we were spared by the mercy of God." Lehi's focus landed on Laman.

Next to Laman, Lemuel elbowed his brother. Laman shook his head then turned from his father's gaze, catching Jacob watching him. He glowered, then turned his mouth into a half-smile.

Jacob looked away quickly. His brother didn't even seem the least bit repentant.

"This same merciful God warned us to flee from Jerusalem to preserve our lives, and has given us the land of promise where we now live." Lehi moved his gaze to Nephi, who sat near the front of the group. "I have seen a vision."

Frustration over Laman fled Jacob's mind as the hair on his arms rose. His pulse throbbed as warmth spread through his body.

"Jerusalem has been destroyed. If we had remained there, we would have also perished."

The knowledge seared itself into Jacob's heart. His father's testimony became his own as Lehi's voice carried across the hushed gathering, imprinting his words onto each heart and mind. "I prophesy, according to the Spirit which has testified to me, that no people will come to this land except those who are led by the hand of the Lord. It will be a land of liberty . . . and the righteous will be blessed forever in it." His face shone with perspiration. "This land will be kept from the knowledge of other nations so that it will not be overrun with no place left for an inheritance."

As Lehi prophesied about the nations eventually dwindling into unbelief, and the subsequent scattering, Jacob felt his heart swell. It was awe-inspiring to hear the things that Nephi had told him restated by his father.

"Just as during our period of captivity in Mudhail when we had to rise above slavery, you must shake off the awful chains by which you are bound, so that you are not carried into the eternal gulf of misery and woe." Lehi leaned forward, his voice growing stronger. "Hear the words of a trembling parent, whose limbs you must soon lie down in the cold and silent grave, from where no traveler can return." He paused and wiped the tears streaming down his cheeks. "A few more days and I will go the way of all the earth."

Jacob felt as if someone had just twisted his heart from his chest. A choked sob came from his mother, and he drew her tightly against him.

"But the Lord has redeemed my soul from hell, and I have seen His glory." Lehi's voice lowered to a whisper, but it still rang clear. "I am encircled about eternally in the arms of His love." He dropped his head, his breath coming in exhausted gasps.

No eyes were dry among the family members. From his rebellious sons to even the youngest child present—all seemed to understand that this was the patriarch's final testimony. Jacob held his mother as she openly wept, his own eyes blurred with emotion. The words of his father were powerful, sure, and filled with the spirit of God.

"Laman, Lemuel, Sam, and my sons who are the sons of Ishmael, listen to the voice of your brother Nephi so that you will not perish."

Jacob stared at his father, his vision clearing. Then he moved his gaze to Nephi, as Jacob realized his father had just turned over the leadership of the family to Nephi. The silence among the family was tangible. *But it feels right,* Jacob thought—*to the very core of my soul.* He knew Nephi was chosen of God.

Nephi's head was bowed, and his shoulders shook—from fatigue or emotion, or even the witness of the Spirit, Jacob didn't know. He was drawn to look at Laman again, whose eyes were saddened but whose hands were clenched into fists. But Laman said nothing, staring ahead with a dull gaze.

Gripping the edges of the rug, Lehi focused on the men. "If you will listen to Nephi, I will leave you my first blessing. If you do not listen to him, I will take away that blessing, and it will rest upon him." His eyes traveled over the group and stopped on the tall, lanky figure of Zoram. "Zoram, you were the servant of Laban. Nevertheless, you have been brought out of Jerusalem and have become a true friend to Nephi. Because you have been faithful, your seed will be blessed with his seed. Your seed will prosper in this land as long as they are faithful, and if you keep the commandments of the Lord, your posterity will be secure."

"Thank you," Zoram said, his expression mirroring gratitude.

Jacob smiled and felt his heart fill with joy for Zoram, even though the parting words of his father were difficult to hear. Zoram had always been faithful, and to be counted among the seed of the next prophet was a blessing indeed.

"And now, Jacob, I speak to you."

Jacob snapped his head around and found his father's gaze penetrating through him. He swallowed quickly and stood, feeling the light from the torches cast their full glow upon his head and shoulders.

"You are my first born in the days of my tribulation in the wilderness. You have suffered afflictions and great sorrow because of the rudeness of your brothers."

Jacob stared at his father, his eyes brimming with heat. He had never heard his father acknowledge these events this way. Yes, they had been the cause of great affliction—a lot of it before his birth. But the friction and endless threats from Laman and Lemuel stood clear in his mind.

"You *know* the greatness of God, and He will consecrate your affliction for your gain," Lehi continued.

Nodding, Jacob realized he did know the greatness of God. Not only in a spiritual way, but because he had studied the words of God nearly his entire life. *My afflictions will be for my gain. They will make me stronger.* Laman and Lemuel could threaten all they wanted. Their sons, Shem and Javan, could try their worst on him. But he would not falter. He would only become stronger.

Lehi continued speaking directly to Jacob about how all people could be saved through the Atonement of the Redeemer. Then he said, "There needs to be opposition in all things. If not, my first born in the wilderness, righteousness could not be brought to pass, neither wickedness, holiness nor misery, neither good nor bad."

Jacob reeled at the significance of it all. Now he truly understood how Nephi held onto his faith all these years—why he never wavered. While Lehi spoke, the doctrine became clear, solidifying the sacred words of the scriptures.

As his father's voice continued into the night air, Jacob felt as if he were practically lifted up and only he and his father were present. Lehi's words benefited the entire family, but they thundered into Jacob's heart so fiercely that he wondered if he could contain all of the knowledge. He forgot about his older, rebellious brothers, forgot about the charge to Nephi to be the next leader, and forgot about his weeping mother. He now existed on another plane, another place on earth that only the Spirit could take him.

He was witnessing firsthand the unspeakable depth of God's love.

CHAPTER 4

Set your hearts unto all the words which I testify among you this day.

(DEUTERONOMY 32:46)

Eve stood in the shadows as Lehi addressed his sons, prophesying and sharing his testimony. Her heart ached and burned with fire at the same time. She had also watched her father, Zoram, practically transfigured when Lehi had addressed him. To have his seed be considered the same as one of the sons—like Nephi—was astounding indeed.

Nephi was so full of humility. Every word that came from his lips was filled with kindness and compassion. But he'd also struggled many times with his older brothers. Stories circulated throughout the family from time to time, but most of what Eve had heard came from her grandmother. Bashemath had a tender spot in her heart for Nephi and loved him like her own son. Eve's favorite story was when Nephi and Isaabel were yet unmarried, and she begged Laman and Lemuel to spare Nephi's life.

It was such a tender moment to think about. Eve couldn't imagine being thrust into that situation—to plead for the life of a man before his own brothers. It was unthinkable. And it had happened so long ago she could hardly imagine that Laman and Lemuel had been so awful.

But she remembered what occurred on the ship. Even though she hadn't been allowed to go up on deck at the time, she remembered the anguish Isaabel, Lehi, and Sariah went through during that trial. She had never known pure fear could be so palpable.

With the hushed audience, Eve listened as Lehi spoke to Jacob. It was difficult for Eve to look at Jacob's profile because each time she did, she felt a tremor in her heart. She was sure someone might notice the flushed appearance of her skin, so she kept her eyes diverted.

When the patriarch turned to Joseph, Eve raised her head. Lehi began his address to Joseph as his "last born" in the wilderness. "You were born in the wilderness of mine afflictions. Yea, in the days of my greatest sorrow did your mother bear you."

Eve brushed at her moistened eyes as her gaze moved to her grandmother. Bashemath sat a few paces away, wrapped in a soft animal-skin. Her head bobbed a little, and anyone who didn't know her intimately would have thought the elderly woman was asleep. Not so. Bashemath would remember and discuss every word that fell from Lehi's lips.

From her grandmother's memory, Eve learned of Shisur—the place where Joseph had been born—and the difficulty Sariah and Lehi had faced due to Laman, Lemuel, Raamah, and Heth's disappearance for several months. Soon after Joseph was born, the family was waylaid by a group of desert marauders. The leader was none other than Laman.

Yes, it was a time of great sorrow when Sariah bore Joseph—a time when she thought two of her sons were lost forever. Eve looked down at her twisting hands, listening to Lehi tell of Joseph's namesake and how he was a descendant of Joseph who was carried captive into Egypt. Young Joseph would be blessed because of the covenants made by his forefathers.

"Your seed will not be destroyed, for they will listen to the words of the book."

The words of the book. Which book? She could reasonably guess that it would contain the Lord's commandments. She'd heard that Nephi wrote on plates of ore nearly every day. And the brass plates contained the words of Isaiah and the books of Moses. Was there more? Was God also speaking to other prophets in far-off lands?

The light breeze from the ocean had chilled with the late hour. Eve pulled her cloak tightly about her. On an ordinary night, the families would be tucked inside their homes. But this was no typical meeting. Lehi called up the children of Laman. Shem, Canaan, Ruth, and even Laman's infant Mary, carried by Anah, gathered around their grandfather. Lehi admonished them to keep the commandments.

Then Lehi called up the sons and daughters of Lemuel. Javan, Delilah, Helek, and Abital moved to stand in front of their grandfather. The patriarch began, "I leave you the same blessing which I left to the sons and daughters of Laman . . ."

Lehi continued speaking to his entire household—Sam and Tamar, Raamah and Elisheba, Heth and Zillah, and their families, too; then Tiras and Dinah. Finally he called up Zoram's children. Eve located her two sisters, Deborah and Rachel, and led them to Lehi's side. She looked into his wise eyes, feeling warmth and kindness radiate from him. "Blessed art thou and thy seed, for you will inherit the land like the seed of Nephi. If you will remain faithful like Nephi, you will be blessed all of your days."

The words were simple, but they stitched themselves into Eve's heart. She would hold the Lord true to that promise, she decided. She would do her best to remain faithful. The path before her headed in only one direction.

* * *

Nephi sat outside his parents' bedchamber, waiting for the dark shadows of the night to lift. Any little sound or movement sent his pulse racing. In the silent moments following, he thought about the prophecies his father had delivered over the years—from his preaching in the streets of Jerusalem to his most recent sermons.

Before addressing each son, Lehi had told them about the fall of mankind. An angel had fallen from heaven, becoming the devil, and subsequently sought to do evil. He had tempted Eve in the Garden to partake of the forbidden fruit. Nephi thought about the times that he had been tempted, and the consequences of his choices.

Adam and Eve were driven out of the Garden of Eden to till the earth and bear children. Lehi taught that because of the Fall, the days of the children of men were prolonged so that they might repent while in the flesh.

"*All* men must repent." Lehi's words were clear.

Even I, Nephi thought. *I have much to repent of.*

"Adam fell that men might be; and men are, that they might have joy." Lehi's words echoed in Nephi's head. Men and women could repent. Through repentance they could find joy again. Lehi had also spoken about the Savior's Atonement. "We are free to choose liberty and eternal life, through the great Mediator, or to choose captivity and death."

Nephi thought hard about his father's words. The freedom to choose was a part of finding joy, of receiving happiness. If the adversary's plan was followed, there was no joy in keeping the commandments. But because choosing the right was a choice, true satisfaction could be obtained. *I am happy because I chose to be happy. But I am also miserable when I make poor choices.*

The clarification inside Nephi's heart continued. The anger that reared toward his brothers again and again conflicted with staying close to the Lord and tangibly feeling His Spirit.

A soft murmuring came from inside his parents' room. Nephi held his breath and listened for any sign of distress. The curtain was pushed aside and his mother's lined face appeared through the slit. Her eyes were swollen and her wrinkles seemed to have deepened. But her lips held a gentle smile as she spoke, "He is asking for you."

Nephi rose to his feet, feeling unsteady. He made his way into the room and was surprised to see his father standing. Lehi took a couple of steps forward and spread his arms. Nephi walked into his father's embrace and stood for several moments, the emotion of the past several hours surging to the surface.

Then Lehi pulled away and looked tenderly at Nephi. "In the morning I would like to resume our studies with Jacob." He paused, the early light brightening his features.

"But for now, you need to return to your family and get some rest. I have the best care I could ever ask for."

A grin spread across Nephi's face as he nodded. "Of course."

"And now," Lehi said, "I will take a short walk with my wife."

Sariah moved to Lehi and took his arm, supporting him. Nephi watched the pair slowly walk out of the low room. He marveled at his father's resilience. A huge yawn worked its way to the surface, making his eyes water.

Nephi's demeanor softened with hope as he watched his parents move about the courtyard, albeit slowly. It was time for him to go home.

CHAPTER 5

I have beheld his glory, and I am encircled about
eternally in the arms of his love.

(2 Nephi 1:15)

Isaabel heard footfalls outside her home. She had been awake, trying to find a comfortable position. Only four months with child, she was experiencing the discomforts earlier than usual. She rose to her elbows, careful not to disturb her sleeping husband. Dawn was at least an hour away, and Nephi had slept so little lately that she wanted to protect him. Then came another sound of shuffling.

She grabbed her outer tunic and pulled it across her shoulders, then walked through the moonlit-bathed rooms until she reached the outer courtyard. A soft breeze stirred her uncovered hair.

Someone stood at the gate, and as she drew closer, she recognized it was Jacob. "You're early," she whispered. Then she caught his full expression in the moonlight. His eyes looked swollen and his cheeks wet.

Isabel reached for her young brother-in-law. "What happened?" She took his arms and drew him into her embrace.

"It's Father."

Isabel pulled away and stared at Jacob. His shoulders were shaking. "Is he—?"

"Not yet. He's asked for Nephi."

She released Jacob and turned without another word. Hurrying back inside, she hesitated for the briefest moment over Nephi's still form. The instant she touched him, their lives would change. Slowly she extended her hand and squeezed his shoulder. His eyes fluttered open. If he had been pleasantly dreaming, it was all for naught.

"Nephi, it's your father. He's grown worse."

"Umm," Nephi said, his voice thick. He rolled over and rose to a sitting position. Letting out a long sigh, he met his wife's gaze. Then he reached out for her.

Isaabel leaned forward and buried her face against the crook of his neck. He was so warm and strong . . .

After a long moment, she straightened. "Go to him."

But Nephi wouldn't release her, his gaze pleading. "Come with me."

She brushed the budding tears from her eyes and nodded. "Of course." She watched him silently dress, then followed him outside, her hand clasped in his—secure and safe—ready to face the next stage of life together.

Jacob turned when he heard them approach. Nephi strode to him, and, releasing Isaabel's hand, enveloped his little brother in his arms.

Tears stung Isaabel's eyes as she remembered the words of Lehi when he had told the family that he was encircled about eternally in the arms of God's love. The brothers parted, and with one arm draped over Jacob, and the other across Isaabel's shoulders, Nephi propelled them toward his father's home.

They walked without speaking, but their hearts communed. The predawn air held a slight chill, though threads of warmth from the previous day still remained. Lehi and Sariah's home glowed softly as if several fish oil lamps burned within. The night was still present and dawn had yet to surface, but Isaabel was surprised that the other family members hadn't arrived yet.

Sariah stepped into the entryway, and Isaabel hurried to her mother-in-law and held her for a moment. When Sariah stepped back she fell into Nephi's embrace. She simply whispered, "He is waiting for you."

Nephi entered the home and walked the short steps to Lehi's bedchamber. Isaabel, Sariah, and Jacob waited just inside the entry.

Isaabel watched Nephi crouch next to his father and take his hand. Lehi turned his head and focused on his son, his eyes blinking several times.

"I'm here, Father," Nephi said quietly.

Lehi's lips parted, and he spoke in a guttural voice, "You shall lead this family, son. Build the temple and raise your seed unto the Lord. And . . . you will have to excuse me from this morning's scripture study."

"Of course," Nephi said, his voice trembling. He leaned forward and kissed his father's cheek, then he took a deep breath. "Farewell, Father."

Isaabel felt her throat catch as her mother-in-law clasped her hand. Amazingly, Isaabel felt a surge of peace flow between them. The peace became more substantial until it seemed to fill the whole room. Nephi rose from his father's side and walked toward them. He bent to kiss his mother, then led Isaabel and Jacob out of the home.

* * *

Sariah felt as if part of her heart left when her children stepped out of the bedchamber. On one hand she wanted to go with them, to take comfort in their presence. On the other, Lehi needed her. He was barely coherent, but at least he had acknowledged Nephi's presence. As she approached her husband, his breathing deepened and slowed.

The light from the two clay lamps in the room softened the signs of age on Lehi's face. His complexion glowed with warmth. It was difficult for her to accept how close to the end he really was. She knelt next to him and brushed her hand across his forehead. His eyes opened, and he attempted to speak.

"Dear husband," she whispered, stroking the sides of his face. "Please stay with me."

Lehi made a sudden movement, and Sariah pulled away, startled. His hand had shot up from the coverlet and grasped her arm. She saw determination in his eyes, similar to when he was about to prophesy.

"I know," Sariah said. "I know." Trembling seized her heart, and it was difficult to breathe. "I love you, too."

His hand remained, and he let out a deep sigh. Eventually his eyes closed, his breathing growing quieter.

Sariah leaned over him and rested her head just below his shoulder, above the soft spot of his heart. The thumping rhythm comforted her. She stayed there for a long time, weariness eventually relaxing her body. Her eyes closed, and when she opened them, she was surprised to see the sun's rays streaming through the narrow window slits. She straightened from her cramped position and noticed the lamps burning low. How long had she slept? *It must be late morning at least.*

It was then that she looked at Lehi's tranquil face. His body was motionless. She reached out her hand, feeling the breath leave her own chest as she touched his cool, already stiff skin. His heart had stopped. Instinct propelled her to lay her head on his chest, just to make sure.

Nothing.

Tears gathered as she raised her head and touched her husband's unmoving hand that still encircled her arm. She gently removed his fingers and laid his hand on his chest. For a moment she stared at her husband of thirty-nine years. They had aged together—gray hair, wrinkles, stubbornness, and all. She knew every line, every shadow, and every angle of his features. She had seen him worried, sorrowful, angry, loving, concerned, and tender . . . and now he looked peaceful at last. His worries had been washed away, cleansed in death. His burdens finally lifted, he was now literally encircled in the arms of his Redeemer.

"Oh, Lehi." Hot tears splashed against her cheeks as she murmured his name and kissed his cheeks. "Farewell, dear husband, farewell."

She stood, feeling the weakness in her knees. She took several shaky breaths before opening the door. When she exited the chamber, she found the room filled with people. Everyone turned to look at her when she entered. Sam reached her first, and she laid her head against his chest as the sobs finally came.

* * *

Wailing pierced the air, jolting Eve from a restless sleep. In the instant between sleep and wakefulness, she knew Lehi had died.

"Oh, no," she cried, bringing her hands to her mouth. Tears stung her eyelids as she listened to the mournful cries.

On the mats next to hers, her two younger sisters awoke. Four-year-old Rachel woke first. Eve rose from her mat, her feet slapping against the hardened earth floor as she made her way to her sisters. Eight-year-old Deborah's eyes were as wide as a full moon.

"What's happening?" Deborah asked.

"Lehi died," Eve said, trying to remain calm for their sakes.

"Why?" little Rachel asked.

Eve swallowed deeply, and settled onto the mat. "It was his time to leave."

Deborah nodded, her expression contemplative.

"Who's crying?" Rachel asked.

"Your aunts. They are very sad because they miss him." Eve stopped to catch her breath. She could feel intense emotions surfacing.

"Are you sad?" Rachel asked, looking up at Eve.

Eve nodded, feeling a tear spill onto her cheek.

"Eve!"

She jumped when she heard her mother call her name from the next room. Eve kissed the top of Rachel's head. "I'll be back." She left her sisters on their mats and hurried to answer her mother.

Rebeka stood in the doorway of their home, her hair disheveled. Her narrow face and dark eyes revealed sorrow. The mantle she usually wore over her head hung loosely about her shoulders. "Lehi has passed on. The other women are too distraught to prepare his body for burial." Her pointed gaze seemed to assess Eve. "We must do it."

Surprise pulsed through Eve. "Me?" She heard the tremble in her own voice.

Her mother's expression softened. "The body needs to be ready for burial by this afternoon. This will be a great service to Sariah and her daughters."

Rebeka crossed the room and started to examine her jars filled with dried herbs. "Bring a basket."

Eve complied and watched her mother.

After choosing a half-dozen sweet-smelling herbs and placing them in the basket, Rebeka looked satisfied. "Now," she said, turning to look at Eve. "We need a jug of fresh water. Can you fetch it and meet me at Lehi's home?"

Eve nodded, grateful to delay going to the place of mourning if even for just a few moments. After changing her clothing, washing her face, and plaiting her hair, Eve collected a water jug from the corner of the cooking room. While her mother spoke in quiet tones to her sisters, Eve scurried out of the house and along the well-worn path that led to the river.

The wailing faded as she neared the river, and she took solace in filling the jug with water. The peaceful, rippling sound of the water helped reduce her anxiety over helping to prepare Lehi's body.

It was an honor to be sure, to take care of a man who was so dear to the entire family. He had never shown anything but kindness toward Eve. Her father revered Lehi, and her mother unconditionally obeyed him.

She hoisted the full jug onto her head and traipsed back to the settlement. The gurgling of the river faded, replaced by the high-pitched sound of grief. Her heart thudded as she grew closer, but she was not prepared for the actual sight before her.

Eve stopped in her tracks and stared. The women of the family were gathered in a circle, standing together with their arms linked across each other's waists. Their wailing seemed to have an order to it, louder shrieks rising periodically. Their heads were uncovered, and Laman's wife, Anah, threw ash across the backs of the other women.

There was an inner circle of three women—Sariah and her two daughters—clinging together and swaying back and forth. Several of the women tore at their clothing, creating long rips in their tunics. Eve remembered the many hours spent on hot afternoons weaving the very cloth the women now tore.

But she sensed the rending eased their inner pain. It wrenched her heart to witness such violent mourning. Suddenly, Eve wanted to return to the river where she could think, reflect on all she saw, and remember Lehi in his times of good health.

She looked toward Lehi's home, hoping to see her mother. Eve didn't want to enter the silent house alone. Beyond the outer courtyard where the women grieved, she saw several men gathered together—a couple were in quiet conversation, but most stared ahead, unseeing, unhearing. She saw Nephi standing next to Jacob, his arm around his brother. Young Joseph clung to Sam's leg, his fearful eyes focused on the stricken women.

A hand touched her shoulder, and Eve turned to see her mother.

"Come," Rebeka said, her eyes sad yet determined.

Eve followed her inside the house, the jug of water still balanced on her head. The atmosphere of the home was different. The air seemed reverent somehow, as if it were preserving the memories of a prophet. Her mother led the way to Lehi's bedchamber, and they entered without speaking. Eve hesitated at the door, not sure of what to expect upon seeing Lehi's body. It was strange to see him in repose, not moving or speaking. As she gazed at his unmoving limbs, she could remember his crackling tone. In the silent room his voice seemed to resound in her ears.

She bit back her anxiety and stepped forward to join her mother at Lehi's side.

"Place the jug on the floor, and I'll prepare the herbal mixture." Rebeka crushed several herbs and mixed them into the water. She produced two squares of cloth and dipped them into the scented liquid. She handed one to Eve. "Begin to wash his feet and legs."

Eve nodded, taking the damp cloth. Still she hesitated for a moment as she watched her mother gently wash Lehi's face and neck.

Eve tried to follow suit, but her pounding heart caused her hands to tremble. She lifted the coverlet to reveal Lehi's cracked and weathered feet. Immediately tears flooded her eyes. As she moved the cloth over his stiff toes, she felt overwhelmed with the sensation that the Spirit of the Lord was nearby, watching over the two women as they cared for His beloved prophet.

She brought the cloth to his thin ankles, rubbing and cleansing. His body would soon be buried inside a tomb, but for now, it received final regard. The wailing from outside had diminished, or perhaps Eve had just stopped paying attention to it. All she knew was that participating in the cleansing was sacred. She heard her mother sniffle and knew she felt the same as they continued working in tandem, preparing a cherished man's body for its final event on earth.

* * *

The afternoon sun shone fierce upon the funeral procession. Sariah walked first in line behind her sons, who carried her husband's shrouded body upon a bier. Yellow-backed orioles fluttered along with the moving crowd, their cheerful song lost on the sorrowful procession.

Sariah stared straight ahead as she walked, focusing on the back of Zoram's head. Her legs felt weak and her breathing labored. Even with Isaabel's steady arm on one side and Elisheba's on the other, the support didn't seem to be enough.

"Not much longer, Mother," Elisheba whispered in her ear. The wailing from the women had stopped for the moment, but the sound of the dulcimers played by a few of the children continued to accompany the families' march.

Sariah gave a small nod, knowing that it was not much farther to the burial site that Lehi had designated for the family. She remembered that over a year ago, Lehi had showed her the natural cave and told her about his plans for a family burial chamber. Sariah had not returned since. Until now.

The clearing was just as she remembered it. The men lowered their father's body, still upon the bier, next to the cave opening. Sariah's heart melted when Joseph rushed to help the men adjust the bier.

One by one, the children came forward and placed flowers on top of their grandfather's enshrouded body. Then the family sat on the ground in front of the tomb, surrounding Lehi. Sariah walked to the side of her husband and stood for several minutes, gazing at the shrouded form. Then one by one, the men approached Sariah and kissed her cheek. She murmured a thank you to each one. Nephi was the last to embrace her.

"Please speak to the family, Nephi," Sariah whispered. She knew the Lord had commanded that her son be the next leader of the family, and she thought it would be fitting for him to say some final words about Lehi.

Nephi straightened and met his mother's gaze. "Very well."

The emotion worked on his face as he turned to face everyone. He waited for a few moments, then said, "Our father, the patriarch of this family, has now reached the Tree of Life. As in Father's vision, he has partaken of the fruit and waits for us to join him." Nephi gazed out over the family. "Just as Father explained, the Lord will continue to bless us if we are righteous. We, too, can obtain eternal life and partake of the fruit with him." He lowered his head for several moments.

Sariah felt her heart thumping. Her oldest sons listened with quiet respect, but she wondered if she should have asked Laman to speak, too. As soon as Nephi finished, she would invite Laman to say something.

Nephi continued to speak about the Tree of Life vision, focusing on the strait and narrow path that they all needed to follow. Letting her gaze drift, Sariah looked again at her husband's shrouded form. The flowers the children had gathered seemed to radiate in the sunlight streaming through the trees.

When Nephi finished, the group began to embrace each other and weep.

Sariah turned, looking for Laman, but didn't see him though his wife and children were all together. She scanned the other faces quickly. He must have left, she realized. A lump hardened in her throat as she hoped he would return soon and find solace in the shared grieving.

The women seemed reluctant to leave and let the men work on the burial tasks. Sariah watched Jacob kneel by Lehi's body one last time. She fought back another round of tears as several in the family came to embrace her. When the women and children finally began to leave, Sariah closed her eyes, letting the whispering wind soothe her being. Lehi had lived a full and righteous life, just as she had tried to do. She'd seen weary age in his face and witnessed his weakening body.

She, too, had grown old. Her heart knew many trials and tribulations, but also great joy and love. Her step was slower, her speech more methodical, her actions delayed. But inside, she felt twenty years younger than her age. Even as she stood next to her husband's body, she felt an overabundance of blessings. To have witnessed so many miracles in their journey from Jerusalem, to have heard the literal words of God resound from her husband's and Nephi's lips, and to have heard the whisperings of the Lord Himself—were treasures that would never leave her heart.

Her sons and sons-in-law lifted the bier again and entered the cave opening. Sariah waited for a moment, imagining her sons lovingly arranging his body on the shelf inside the tomb. Then she pulled her mantle around her shoulders and turned away. Tears blurred her steps, and not too far down the path, she felt an arm encircle her shoulders. Without looking up, she knew Elisheba had waited for her. Together the two women walked slowly away from their husband and father. They would carry out his final wishes and do everything they could to partake of the fruit.

CHAPTER 6

*Keep thy father's commandment, and forsake not the law
of thy mother.*

(Proverb 6:20)

Nephi read over the words he had just etched onto the ore plates.
*And upon these I write the things of my soul, and many of the scriptures
which are engraven upon the plates of brass. For my soul delighteth in
the scriptures, and my heart pondereth them, and writeth them for the
learning and the profit of my children.*

Several days had passed since his father's death, but today was the
first chance he had had to reflect on all the events leading up to his
father's final hour. Lehi's words of counsel and his patriarchal blessings to all of his children were engraved in Nephi's memory. As Nephi
wrote in the quiet afternoon, he relished the chance to be alone for a
short time. Isaabel had taken the children to gather wild berries that
grew near the river. Although the majority of work had slowed as the
family grieved, food preparation could not be delayed.

He worked in a small courtyard behind his house, grateful for the
shade that several trees provided in the sultry heat. Just beyond his
home, the jungle rose in full height, climbing against the brilliant
blue sky. Nephi could spend hours watching the exotic animals and
birds that ventured to the edge of the tree line. But today, he didn't
have hours. His heart brimmed with emotion, and he felt compelled
to write his thoughts.

Behold, my soul delighteth in the things of the Lord; and my heart pondereth continually upon the things which I have seen and heard.

"There you are."

Nephi looked up, startled to see Laman watching him from the side of the house. His brother moved into full view; following behind were Lemuel, Raamah, and Heth.

None of them smiled or greeted him. They did not look like they had come for a pleasant social visit. At the sight of the four men, Nephi felt as if his heart had plunged into a deep well, leaving the rest of his body behind.

Nephi laid his chisel down and slowly stood from the animal-hide cushion. He moved in front of the low table that held the ore plates and folded his arms across his chest. "Is something wrong?"

A sneer lifted Laman's upper lip. "What are you doing?"

"Recording our history." Dread pressed against Nephi's chest. He'd seen the same disgusted expression on Laman's face many times, and there had never been a good outcome.

"How nice," Laman said. He glanced at the men next to him. "And I'm sure the Lord *commanded* him to sit here in the shade while we labor clearing timber . . . for what?"

"For the temple," Lemuel answered.

Laman shot him a harsh look. "I wasn't speaking to you." His gaze shifted to Nephi again. "We're building *your* temple, while you do nothing."

Nephi felt his anger bristle. He thought that their father's death might have pacified Laman from his usual outbursts. It seemed that today he was just seeking out trouble of any kind. "This is the first day I've written since Father's death."

His oldest brother's eyes clouded with contempt. No sorrow. No regret. "He's not here to protect you anymore."

Nephi raised a brow, trying to understand what Laman meant. He'd always been able to protect himself—with the help of the Lord, of course. "Protect me from *what*?"

A scoff rose from Lemuel, but Nephi ignored him.

Smiling, Laman tilted his head to one side. "As the new patriarch of the family, I think *you* should build your own temple. After all, I didn't hear the Lord tell *me* to build it."

The men chuckled, and Nephi looked hard at Raamah. His brother-in-law was usually the most reasonable out of the group, and Nephi knew he had loved Lehi like his own father. "You heard Father's words. They did not come from me, but as a commandment from the Lord." He felt his audience slipping away from belief. "*And I did not choose* to be the leader of the family. The Lord made His own choice."

Raamah said nothing. He hovered in the back of the group, shifting from one foot to the other.

"Choice? Who said anything about a choice?" Laman interrupted. "I think you have *plotted* to become the leader. You've spent all these years since Jerusalem with our impressionable father, slowly convincing him that he should turn the leadership over to you."

"No," Nephi said. "You know that's not true."

"Using the Lord's name might convince the women, but not us," Heth said. He took a couple of steps in front of the group.

Nephi looked at his brother-in-law in surprise. "I'm not trying to convince anyone. It's just as the Lord has said, nothing more."

"Your modesty is laughable," Laman said, placing a hand on Heth's shoulder as if to support him. "You act as if you have been imposed upon. Leading this family is what you've aspired to since leaving Jerusalem. First you used God's name to take us away from our inheritance, and then you used His name to marry Isaabel."

Shaking his head, Nephi couldn't believe Laman still harbored ill feelings about the betrothals. It was unbelievable. His brother listened to no one's opinion but his own.

"Establishing your own kingdom where you can manipulate the laws of birthright and first born to your benefit are all that you have ever dreamt about." Laman passed Heth and entered the courtyard. "I don't think you ever really had a vision from God. Those 'visions' have been nothing but aspirations to serve your own greed."

Raising his hand to stop the accusing words, Nephi said, "I have only followed Father's counsel which came directly from the Lord."

His shoulders felt heavy. Laman had never changed his complaints—
they were all the same. And no matter what Nephi said, his brother
persisted in his false accusations.

Laman hooted, then his eyes narrowed. "Well, you can't hide
behind Father anymore."

"I'm not hiding." Nephi crossed his arms, trying to rein in his
anger. "You are disrespecting Father's blessings—his very memory."

"Forget Father!" Laman shouted. He took another step forward,
until he was a breath away from Nephi. He spoke in a low growl.
"Tonight we will have a family meeting, and the true order of the
family will be laid out. There will be no doubt in anyone's mind as to
who leads this family. You, your wife, and your children, will be taken
off your pedestal, and if you value your standing in the community,
you will acknowledge your allegiance to me."

"Laman," Nephi said in a harsh whisper. "You might have been
deaf to Father's dying words." He let his gaze fall on the other men.
"But I know that each of you heard his last pleadings. I know this,
and the Lord knows this. And by acting this foolishly, you will break
Father's heart . . . again." He stood his ground, unflinching, trying to
suppress the indignation that consumed him. "Heed Father's counsel—
if not for the sake of love, for the sake of your souls."

His brother merely threw back his head and laughed. "I'm
looking forward to hearing more from you tonight." Then his
expression grew serious. "But I'm afraid there are very few you'll be
able to convince."

* * *

Isaabel had pressed herself against the wall as Laman spoke her
name. She pulled Aaron and Sarah close and hushed them. Nephi's
pleading voice rose above Laman's.

"Come," she whispered to the children. "We must go inside."

"But I want to see my uncles—" Aaron started.

"Later," Isaabel said, giving him a stern look. Aaron bowed his
head and followed his mother and sister into the house.

The cool interior was a welcome respite, but it did little for Isaabel's pounding heart. It had been less than a week since Lehi's death, and already it had begun.

Little Sarah tugged at her mother's hand. "Why are they angry with Father?"

Isaabel crouched to meet her daughter's eyes, realizing that the five-year-old understood more than most children. "They are very sad that Grandfather died, and sometimes when we grieve we feel angry."

The young girl nodded, her eyes solemn as if everything had just become clear.

"Wait here," Isaabel told her children. "I'll be back soon."

She slipped out of the house and walked around the opposite way. She did not want to chance meeting the angry men, so she moved through the bushes, staying concealed should they round the corner. Just as she came within hearing distance she heard Laman laughing. His next words were muffled.

Heart pounding, she waited for what was to come, but all went quiet. After several moments, she realized that they must have left. Isaabel stepped out of the brush and rounded the house, seeing Nephi bent over the plates of ore. He was not writing anything, just staring at them.

He looked up to see her, his eyes rimmed in red. "Did you hear?"

"I heard enough," Isaabel said quietly. She entered the courtyard and crossed to her husband.

Nephi let out a frustrated breath, then slammed his fist on the table. "I thought they'd at least wait a month or two before starting."

Isaabel touched his shoulder. "It fills me with sorrow to think of their defiance, not only all the grief they caused your father in his life, but the disrespect they show him in death."

He turned to her, his face shadowed with anger and confusion. "I just don't know what to do, Isa." He hung his head. "They want to hold a family discussion tonight."

Dismay touched Isaabel's heart. "Oh, no," she whispered. She grasped Nephi's arm and leaned close. Eventually, he wrapped his

arms around her, his breathing heavy. She bit her lip, not wanting to
cry when the children would surely notice. "Your poor mother."

* * *

Jacob checked on his mother for a second time, but she still slept.
Her afternoon rest period seemed to increase in length each day. He
backed quietly out of the room and moved to the front of the house.
Just then his sister Elisheba entered.

She greeted him with a frown. "Mother's still sleeping?"

Jacob nodded, eyeing the basket of bread and pot of steaming
food she carried. Joseph came scurrying into the room, no doubt
smelling the aroma.

Elisheba patted the young boy's head. "You two start eating, I'll
go and check on Mother." She laid the food on the low table in the
corner, then paused. "Jacob, tonight there will be a family meeting."

By the tone in her voice, Jacob could tell she wasn't pleased with
it. "What about?"

Elisheba glanced in Joseph's direction, who, bending down, had
already started devouring the cooked meat. She met Jacob's gaze and
said carefully, "Laman is not settled with the idea of Nephi as
leader."

Not again, Jacob thought. Instinctively he knew that his oldest
brother was seeking a confrontation. And this time his father would
not be there to mediate. "Maybe it's best that Mother continues to
sleep."

A soft smile crossed Elisheba's face. "If it were possible, yes. But
her presence and influence may be greatly needed tonight." She took
a deep breath then continued. "Oh, how I long for peace."

Jacob gazed at her with renewed understanding. He knew her
husband, Raamah, often sided with Laman. He wondered whose side
his brother-in-law would be on tonight.

When Elisheba left, Jacob settled next to Joseph. "Have you
already thanked the Lord for this meal?" he asked his brother.

Joseph looked up, his mouth displaying bits of bean and meat.

"All right, I'll just do it for the both of us," Jacob said, bowing his head and hiding a smile.

Just as he and his brother finished eating, Sariah entered the room, followed by Elisheba. She looked surprisingly well rested, giving Jacob hope that the family council would turn out all right.

As it was, the hour grew late, and Jacob stood to allow room for his mother to recline at the table.

"I need to take food to Dinah and Tiras, then I'll meet you later," Elisheba said, her hand lingering on her mother's shoulder.

Sariah nodded and watched her daughter duck to leave the house. "She works too hard. Her husband is a good man, but I worry his stubbornness will overshadow his love for her someday."

Jacob was surprised to hear his mother speak so frankly. Whatever the reason, her unrestraint did not bode well for the family gathering.

She rose to her feet without touching a morsel. "Bring me my mantle," she told Jacob. "We have a meeting to attend."

He hurried to do her bidding, noticing the steely determination in her eyes. Since Elisheba hadn't left too long ago, Jacob assumed they would be early to the gathering. He was surprised to see most of the family already assembled in Laman's courtyard—at least the men and a few of the women. Joseph was the only young child in attendance.

Laman paced along the back side of the courtyard. Lemuel, Heth, and Raamah stood together talking. Zoram and Sam stayed near Nephi, none of them saying anything. The women stood in the opposite corner. Sariah immediately crossed to them and began asking questions. Jacob could see a look of clear distress on Isaabel's face.

With the arrival of Sariah, Laman turned and faced everyone. The gathering grew quiet almost immediately, and Laman smiled at his guests. "Welcome to my home," he boomed, spreading his arms wide. "We have some important family matters to discuss." He paused for a moment. "With the unfortunate passing of Father, a debate of leadership has arisen."

"There has been no debate," Sariah said.

Everyone turned to look at her in surprise.

"You are correct, Mother," Laman said.

Now it was Jacob's turn to be surprised.

Laman continued, "There is no debate. I am the first born, and I am the birthright son. The laws of nature and the laws of *God* dictate that I inherit the leadership of this community." His gaze swept toward Nephi. "Our younger brother thinks he can rule over us. But I say . . . *no*. He is the cause of our tribulations, both in the wilderness and upon the high sea."

Jacob felt his skin grow cold. These were all things he'd heard Laman say before, but with the absence of Father . . . the cloak of security had been lifted.

"Oh, Laman," Sariah's voice came again. All eyes focused on her. Isaabel and Elisheba flanked her sides. "You have driven grief straight into my soul."

Jacob watched in horror as she reached out, her knees buckling beneath her. Everyone gasped, and Isaabel and Elisheba supported Sariah on each side.

But Laman didn't flinch. "It is not I who spreads sorrow, Mother," he said to her sagging form. "It is Nephi." He turned to the rest of the family. "See what you have done. You have entertained foolishness and believed that Nephi's words come from God. I say they do not. Nephi has deceived each of you."

Jacob's heart pounded as Nephi strode to Laman. "You have nearly killed our mother. Your wrongdoings hastened Father's death, and you have not hesitated to try to murder me." He raised his voice. "You have done enough. I am the rightful leader of this family, called by the Lord Himself. And I say we are finished hearing you rant."

Laman's wife, Anah, pulled herself away from the women—her sister, Puah, close behind.

"You are wrong to speak to my husband that way." Anah's eyes flashed with fury, and her tone increased another notch. "You have caused us grief long enough."

Laman nodded, bringing his wife by his side. "We will not bow down to you any longer, Nephi. Nor your God."

The silence that followed was palpable. Jacob realized he was holding his breath. Finally Nephi spoke. "My God is your God. He is the same yesterday, today, and forever. Destruction of your entire posterity will be upon your head if you do not repent. How can you deny His hand? How can you say He did not bring us to this promised land?"

Nephi picked up a rock and hurled it into the night air. "Do you not see this stone? This sky? This earth? Are we not in a new land, as *promised* by the Lord? Your sons will inherit more than they ever could have in Jerusalem." His breath came in ragged gulps. "Jerusalem has been destroyed, and the Lord that you deny has saved your life, preserved your posterity, and given you abundance that eleven years ago we could have only dreamt of!"

The expression on Laman's face twisted into revulsion. "Your words are not worth listening to." He grabbed Anah's hand. "Leave my property."

Nephi shook his head slowly and turned. He walked through the gathering and out of the courtyard. Jacob watched Isaabel hurry after him, tears streaming down her face.

Jacob felt sick. He couldn't even look at Laman. Turning, he crossed to his mother and Elisheba, and together they helped Sariah to her feet. The other women backed away, watching him. He could hear their sniffles but he knew he couldn't meet their eyes either. He didn't trust any of them. Not anymore.

* * *

Eve blinked back the drenching tears as she huddled on her bed. She had fled the gathering as soon as Nephi and Isaabel left, barely arriving home in time to expel her sorrow. While she hadn't been in the group of women, she'd heard everything from her place in the courtyard. Laman's voice came to mind again, causing her to squirm and clutch her stomach. And his face—eyes devoid of humanity and mouth uttering wrongful accusations—could a person really hate so much and still breathe?

In her heart, she knew Nephi hadn't vied for the leadership of the family. The Lord had commanded it. Eve wondered why the Lord chose Nephi over Laman. Especially when He must have known the discord it would cause. Perhaps Laman would be a better person if Nephi hadn't upset the birthright.

Then she understood. Laman was a despicable man—despicable with or without power—and the Lord was protecting the rest of the family. Sam was just as righteous as Nephi, but she knew that Sam wouldn't have been able to stand up to Laman like Nephi did. Nephi's large stature definitely commanded attention and gave him the physical advantage over his older brothers.

Eve rolled over onto her back, detecting the soft tones of her parents' voices coming from the next room. They couldn't sleep either.

She rose quietly so as not to disturb her sleeping sisters and padded across the floor. Standing at the entrance to her parents' room, she whispered, "Father?"

Zoram sat up in bed. "Eve? Why are you still awake?"

"I can't stop thinking about what happened."

Her father must have heard the tremor in her voice because he came out of his bedchamber and ushered her into the cooking room. "Let's go outside." He fetched a cloak and wrapped it around her shoulders.

The pair stepped into the moonlit courtyard and settled onto a bench. Zoram put his arm around her. "We must put our complete trust in the Lord."

Eve nodded. "But what if something terrible happens?"

"Terrible things have already happened," her father said. "You are still young, but the conflict between Laman and Nephi has arisen many times over. Nephi has been preserved by the Lord again and again. Nothing that Laman or Lemuel can do is more powerful than God's protection."

Her stomach twisting, she said, "I never felt so awful as I did tonight while listening to Laman. I'm afraid of what might happen to Nephi . . . and his other brothers." Eve breathed in her father's spicy scent as his warmth encircled her shoulders. She leaned her head against his chest.

"Whatever might happen," Zoram said in a grave tone, "I will always protect you. And Nephi can defend himself. Besides, as long as we are righteous, we have the added protection of the Lord."

Together, they watched the myriad of tiny lights twinkle through the canopy of trees. Beneath the vast glittering, Eve felt small but peaceful in the same breath.

"Nephi has saved my life more than once," Zoram said quietly.

"I know he rescued you from Laban's household," Eve said, wondering why she hadn't heard the other stories.

"*Rescue* is a good word." He chuckled then sobered. "I would have never made it out of Jerusalem alive with my status as a slave."

Eve felt a shiver trail her arms. "You would have been killed just because you were a slave?"

"Slaves are protected under Israelite law, unless a crime is committed, especially a crime against one's own master," Zoram said. "If Nephi had left me in Jerusalem, I would have surely died for the death of Laban. Nephi also saved the entire family from starvation when he constructed a wooden bow." He looked down at his daughter, holding her innocent gaze. "Not only did he save me physically, but he also saved my soul."

He let out a long breath and blinked rapidly, then added, "Because of Nephi's goodness, we were led to this beautiful land, where one day, your sons and daughters will live in peace and harmony."

Eve wondered at the words. Things had certainly been peaceful since arriving at the promised land, until tonight.

Her father's arm tightened about her shoulders. "Someone's coming," he whispered. "Go inside now."

She rose to her feet and hurried inside the house. Heart pounding, she crouched near the window to hear. If anything was wrong, she certainly wanted to notify her mother.

"Zoram?"

Eve recognized Laman's voice instantly. Her heart pulsed with alarm. What did Laman want with *her* father?

"It's late," Zoram said.

Eve couldn't see the men, but she imagined that her father stood to face Laman and whoever else might be with him.

"Where are your loyalties?" Laman's voice came again.

"Are you asking me to choose?"

"The time has come to decide whom you will follow."

Eve strained to hear, catching every word. Her father's voice came next.

"How about following the Lord?"

Laman chuckled softly. "Indeed." Eve heard a horrible slapping sound, then, "Well, Zoram, you've always been a coward. I guess I couldn't expect much from a former slave who was so easily deceived by Nephi's disguise as Laban. But that's understandable, because you couldn't even provide a living for your widowed mother, and she had to sell herself—"

"Enough!" Zoram cut in.

Eve covered her mouth to stifle a gasp. What was Laman talking about? Her father had been forced into servitude after his mother died. And his mother had been a seamstress.

"I guess I'll have to make the choice for you," Laman said.

"How so?" Zoram asked. "My days of slavery are over, and I am free to choose my own path."

"Not if Nephi is no longer around to worship."

She heard the footsteps receding. *If Nephi is no longer around?* Was Laman planning on killing him? Her heart beat wildly as she realized that someone had to warn Nephi, somehow. By the time morning arrived, it might be too late. With increasing anxiety, she waited for her father to come into the house. He never did.

✦ CHAPTER 7 ✦

Blessed are all they that put their trust in him.
(PSALM 2:12)

Aaron and Sarah rushed to their father, throwing their arms about his legs. Nephi patted their backs, meeting Isabel's gaze over their children's heads. He was on the verge of losing all sense of reason, and he needed to be alone. Desperately.

Isaabel understood and pulled the children away. "Father has work to do. Let's get ready for sleep."

Sarah smiled at her father. "Why are you still sad?"

Feeling as if his heart might split at the brightness of his innocent daughter's face, Nephi crouched to be level with her gaze. "I shouldn't be sad because I have so many beautiful things to be grateful for." He looked at his son, then Isabel. He wished he could put up a barrier around his house and never leave, surrounded by only his wife and children.

Aaron put a stout hand on Nephi's shoulder. "Go and do your work, Father. I'll be the man until you return."

A sweet smile spilled from Isaabel, and Nephi joined her. But it was bittersweet. He never wanted to put his son in that position. "Children, let us pray, then off to sleep."

The two young heads nodded eagerly, and the four family members knelt together. At Nephi's request, Isaabel began, "O Lord, through Thy mercies we have been blessed. Please restore harmony among the family members. We are grateful for Thy loving hand, O Father, and Thou knowest all our needs. We will follow Thy will, O God. Amen."

Following his wife's prayer, Nephi met her gaze, and a look of understanding passed between them.

They all rose, and after kissing his children and wife, Nephi grabbed two oil lamps. He left the house and walked to the back courtyard. He pried up the loose stone in the corner and lifted out the ore plates. After lighting the lamps, he bowed his head for several moments, gaining composure and trying to consolidate his thoughts.

The entire family had grown so much in faith, and they had experienced great hardships together. Yet through it all, they stayed together—with Lehi as the anchor. But now that steady beacon was gone, and Nephi felt destitute as never before. The way that his brothers angered him at times—he wondered if he had the strength to endure their obstinacy.

He lifted the thin chisel and began to write. *O wretched man that I am! Yea, my heart sorroweth because of my flesh; my soul grieveth because of my iniquities.* The words flowed faster than he could etch them, and for a moment it was as if he were the only being in existence. As he wrote, he felt his words extend toward heaven.

My God hath been my support, he hath led me through mine afflictions in the wilderness; and he hath preserved me upon the waters of the great deep.

"God has loved me. He has confounded my enemies—my brothers—until they quaked before me," Nephi whispered into the night air. "He has heard my cries by day and has given me knowledge by vision at night."

And angels came down and ministered unto me. And upon the wings of his Spirit hath my body been carried away upon exceedingly high mountains.

Nephi had seen great and marvelous scenes, scenes which he was told not to write. He relaxed his hold on the chisel and hung his head, staring at the engraved words that seemed to leap in the lamplight. He knew the Lord was merciful. "So then why does my heart weep and my soul linger in the valley of sorrow?" His voice was just above a whisper, but his soul wanted to shout.

He wrote as his heart twisted, his hands aching with the motion, but on he continued. *Why should I yield to sin, because of my flesh? Yea, why should I give way to temptations, that the evil one have place in my heart to destroy my peace and afflict my soul? Why am I angry because of mine enemy?*

Why? He had seen the hand of the Lord. Nephi was a living witness and had knowledge beyond the earth and beyond this life. An argument with his brothers shouldn't have the power to thrust him into bitterness. The death of his father didn't mean that the Lord had changed His mind. Everything was still the same as it had been since the beginning of time. The Lord loved all of His children, and He was merciful. Nephi's life was in the Lord's hands, not Laman's or Lemuel's. Wallowing in sorrow was not part of the Lord's mission for him.

Awake, my soul! No longer droop in sin. Rejoice, O my heart, and give place no more for the enemy of my soul.

Nephi rubbed his swollen eyes, pushing back the fatigue, the pain of betrayal, and the worry he'd seen on his wife's face. He had been given everything by the Lord, and it was for the Lord to give or take, not Laman.

Gripping the thin engraving tool, Nephi's determination renewed. *Rejoice, O my heart, and cry unto the Lord, and say: O Lord, I will praise thee forever; yea, my soul will rejoice in thee, my God, and the rock of my salvation.*

Tears splattered onto the plates, but still Nephi wrote. His heart and mind were one now, repentance seeping through his fingers onto the ore below. *O Lord, wilt thou redeem my soul? Wilt thou deliver me out of the hands of mine enemies?*

He knew he only had to ask. The Lord had delivered him so many times, why would tonight be any different? Nephi's heart had been broken by his brothers, again, and his spirit was contrite. Responsibility had settled upon his shoulders, and he would walk the path of righteousness. The Lord knew the answers. All Nephi had to do was listen.

O Lord, wilt thou encircle me around in the robe of thy righteousness!

He continued writing, listening as he did so. *O Lord, I have trusted in thee, and I will trust in thee forever. I will not put my trust in the arm of flesh . . .*

Tears again clouded his vision, but he somehow completed the final words of the psalm. *Yea, I know that God will give liberally to him that asketh. Yea, my God will give me, if I ask not amiss; therefore I will lift up my voice unto thee; yea, I will cry unto thee, my God, the rock of my righteousness. Behold, my voice shall forever ascend up unto thee, my rock and mine everlasting God. Amen.*

At last, Nephi released the chisel and pushed away from the table. He sank to the earth, and in the light of the flickering lamps as the jungle hovered around, he continued to pray.

* * *

Eve stumbled along the path in the patchy darkness. The heavy limbs of the trees provided excellent shade in the daytime hours, but now they blocked the moon from lighting the already obscure path. Her toe hit a rock in the middle of the trail, and Eve nearly went sprawling to the ground. Instinctively she reached out in front of her and caught a branch. Her breathing rapid, she decided to slow her pursuit. Her father never came back into the house after speaking with Laman, and when she dared to venture outside again, Zoram was nowhere to be found.

Eve decided that she had already wasted too much time as it was and slipped outside without alerting her mother. She hoped her father had gone to find Nephi and tell him of Laman's threat. If not, it was up to her.

The night was warm, but the quiet darkness chilled her, whether it was because she was alone or because she feared Laman could be lurking somewhere . . . If he was angry enough to kill Nephi, what would Laman do if he found out Eve's intentions to intercept the plot?

A branch tugged at her sleeve, and she let out a gasp. Quickly covering her mouth, Eve halted for a moment, trying to calm her pounding heart. A waft of pungent smoke reached her nose, and she stood still, trying to recognize the scent. It was similar to incense, but more woody.

Eve trudged on, moving away from the smell, the fear of her news arriving too late propelling her forward. It was not much farther to Nephi and Isaabel's home. Surely she'd see their courtyard any moment. Then she could warn them and question them about the smell of incense at the same time.

Suddenly, a hand grabbed her arm and pulled her into the trees. She started to scream, but another hand clamped over her mouth.

Just kill me quickly, Laman. Afraid of a fate worse than death, she tried to size up her attacker. Maybe she could wriggle away or let a scream escape loud enough that someone in Nephi's household would hear.

"It's not safe out there," the voice said in her ear, the grip relaxing.

Eve tore herself away and turned, seeing Jacob. "It's you."

"Eve?" Stepping out of the shadows so that she could see his concerned expression, Jacob said, "I'm sorry for grabbing you. I thought you were Isabel, and I didn't want you to be seen alone."

"By whom?" As Eve asked the question, she already knew the answer. She took a deep breath. "Laman and Lemuel came to persuade my father to join their cause."

Jacob nodded. "So you know already." His brow wrinkled with worry, and he lowered his voice to barely a whisper. "Zoram came to tell me, and I said I would speak with Nephi. I was on my way when I saw you. I worried that Laman had beat me to Nephi's house and you were Isaabel rushing into his trap."

"Where is my father now?" Eve asked, casting a furtive glance at the nearby homes.

"He went to find Sam, then he'll meet me here."

"So Nephi doesn't know yet?"

Jacob shook his head. "Come with me. When your father arrives, he can take you safely home."

Eve looked toward the direction she had come. The branches hung heavy over the trail, twisted and dark. She shivered slightly and pulled her cloak tighter across her torso. "All right."

Stepping onto the path, Jacob brought a finger to his lips, then motioned for her to follow. Eve joined him and together they moved quietly toward Nephi's home. She heard nothing, but twice Jacob stopped her to listen. Nephi's home was dark inside, and the sliver of light from the new moon cast a silvery, bare illumination on the courtyard and garden.

Jacob's hand touched her shoulder, at first startling Eve, then she understood. He guided her through the edge of the encroaching jungle so that they arrived at the back of the house. The wind picked up, carrying with it the pungent scent again.

"Do you smell that?" she asked Jacob.

His mouth formed a tight line, then he whispered, "I think some of your cousins have adopted a few unsavory practices."

Cousins? That meant it was someone around her age. But before she could mentally calculate who, Jacob interrupted her thoughts.

"My brother often writes and sleeps out here," he whispered. His hand remained on her arm.

Eve's eyes adjusted more sharply to the dimness, and she noticed the faint stir of lamplight. Then she saw him. Nephi knelt next to a table, his head bowed. "Oh . . . he's praying." She felt an awkwardness rise in her chest. "Perhaps we should wait."

"Laman wouldn't wait," Jacob said. He drew her along until they reached the clearing. At their approach, Nephi raised his head and looked around.

"It's me, Jacob, and I've brought Zoram's daughter."

Nephi rose from his place and squinted through the dark. "What's wrong?"

Jacob pressed Eve forward. "Tell him what you heard."

Taking a deep breath, Eve relayed the words between Zoram and Laman. She was surprised to see Nephi's expression remain placid. He merely folded his arms and nodded here and there.

"Thank you for letting me know," Nephi said when Eve finished. "I know now that Laman's anger has ripened." He turned from them and moved to the table. Lifting the ore plates and chisel, he then placed them in the underground vault.

Eve watched in fascination. She had seen the brass plates on many Sabbath occasions, yet these were different. Nephi had been writing on them. Curiosity burned in her heart, but she held her tongue.

"Let's go wait for your father," Nephi said, directing them alongside the house.

Eve wondered at those who slept within—Isaabel and her two children. She felt fiercely protective of them, knowing that they would suffer the most if Nephi's life were taken.

Just as they rounded the home, Eve saw two men standing at the front. In an instant her heart froze until she realized it was her father and Sam.

When Zoram recognized Eve, he rushed forward. "Eve."

Nephi explained how she came to warn him, but Zoram's face showed disapproval.

"You shouldn't have come alone," Zoram said.

Eve hung her head, regretting the danger she had put herself in.

The men moved away, and they spent several moments whispering together. Eve waited with Jacob until the three men returned.

"Zoram and Sam will keep guard tonight." Nephi looked at Jacob. "Take the girl home to her mother, then make all haste to your own home."

Jacob started to protest, but Nephi hushed him. "Nothing will happen tonight. Laman will not execute his plans in secret. He wants the rest of the family to know his plot so that he can establish fear and control."

"Wake your mother and tell her where I am," Zoram instructed Eve.

She followed Jacob out of the courtyard. Neither said a word as they walked to Eve's home. But she wondered if Jacob was afraid of his oldest brother, who possessed a murderous heart. Each small sound startled her, until Jacob took her arm, bringing a measure of comfort. Any other time, she would have been embarrassed, but tonight her inhibitions somehow seemed irrelevant.

As they reached her home, Eve was grateful to see the familiar outline, peaceful and tranquil. Jacob let his hand drop, and Eve instantly missed the warm pressure. "Thank you," she whispered, meeting his gaze.

He looked past her, the formality between them returning.

She watched him turn and walk away, then he paused.

"Did you leave something cooking?" Jacob asked.

Eve turned toward her home. "No." But by then she had smelled it, too. *Smoke.* She turned toward Jacob. "Maybe one of the homes nearby?"

Jacob shook his head slowly, then scanned the dark horizon.

Joining his search, Eve looked at the tree line at the edge of the settlement. She knew it would be difficult to see smoke on such a black night. But finally she saw it. The white wisps curled ever so gently, sparse at first, but within moments they grew into a cloud of gray.

"The temple site," Jacob whispered with dismay.

Just yesterday, Eve had marveled at the immense clearing prepared for building the temple. Stacked around all sides were great timbers that had taken many weeks to cut and prepare. The men had just started laying the foundation a couple of days before Lehi's death, according to his adamant request to build it.

She covered her mouth, staring in disbelief.

Jacob was the first to break her trance. "You'd better go speak with your mother. I'm sure that soon everyone will know, and you don't want her to worry."

Eve dipped her head, her heart pounding at the atrocity. She now knew where Laman went after speaking to her father.

"I need to inform the men," Jacob said. But instead of hurrying away, he walked slowly, head down, as if he knew it was already too late to save anything.

* * *

The morning has come too quickly, Isaabel thought as she turned over on her mat. She reached out her hand to find Nephi's place cold and empty. *He never came back inside.* Sitting, she pushed away the panic that rose in her mind. He had simply fallen asleep in the court-yard. It wasn't the first night that he'd done so. And there were times when he rose and left for the fields or the temple site before she and the children awoke.

Isaabel relaxed onto her blanket and basked in the warmth of her covers for just a little while longer. The children would be up soon, and then her day would not be her own. She remembered with a grimace the harsh words of Laman from the night before. She hoped that a good night's rest and the brightness of the new dawn would soften everyone's heart and change Laman's perspective.

With a sigh she pulled herself off her mat and dressed. Mentally she went through responsibilities—first she would prepare the morning meal of guava and mashed beans picked from the garden on the side of the house, fetch fresh water before the day grew hot, and harvest the chilies. *And,* she thought, *I'll seek out Eve and a couple of the girls and begin embroidery lessons.* She worried about the haunted look she saw in her niece's eyes—too young to look so sad and lonely. But if Isaabel could bring some confidence to Eve's countenance, it would be worth her time.

A pang of hunger stabbed at her belly, and Isaabel smiled at the sensa-tion. The child within her womb was already demanding sustenance.

"All right, I'll hurry." Isaabel patted her growing abdomen, then entered the cooking room, smiling again. It was wonderful to have such a nice, permanent home. Although the bare floors and walls weren't much to look at, they were *hers.* The pottery was hers, the cooking pit was hers, and the colored baskets were hers. She took great joy in moving about her duties each day, knowing that in the process she built a family and continued the traditions of mothers before her.

Isaabel broke off a piece of dried bread and ate it, staving the hunger pangs as she worked. First, she stoked the fire in the cooking pit and added more dried tinder. Once she had a subdued blaze she placed a ceramic pot filled with water onto the cooking stone. Then she mixed day-old water with ground maize. She knew once the children smelled the boiled cakes of maize, they would wake of their own accord.

She scooped the mixture onto a leaf and wrapped the leaf around the ground maize. Then she dropped the cake into the hot water. The maize took only a few moments to cook. She was just about to open the first warm cake when she heard someone calling her name from the courtyard. Not calling—but shouting.

Isaabel removed the rest of the cakes from the heat and rushed outside. To her surprise, Eve stood there, hair uncovered and unkempt, eyes wild.

"What is it?" Isaabel asked, fear immediately registering in her heart.

"They burned the temple site." Eve's breath came in jagged gasps.

The girl trembled, and leaves and dirt clung to her outer garment. "Who burned the temple and why?" But Isaabel's initial concern turned to dread. She knew who was responsible.

Eve's shoulders slackened, and despair filled her face. "The men have been there for hours and now . . ." She bit back a sob. "Laman and Nephi are arguing. Laman openly threatens his life. I couldn't listen any longer. I didn't know where else to go."

Rushing to Eve, Isaabel took the girl into her arms and held her trembling body. "I will go, then. Thank you for coming."

Eve sniffled and drew away. "I'll stay with the children."

"Thank you." Isaabel hesitated. "I was just preparing their meal."

Nodding, Eve wiped her eyes. "I'll finish it."

Isaabel touched Eve's shoulder, wishing that she could explain to the girl that this conflict had happened many times before, and that the Lord had always preserved them. Even so, Isaabel dreaded what she was about to see.

She left Eve and walked around the house to find the path Nephi liked to take to the temple clearing. She moved through the jungle brush as quickly as she could. Each step brought her closer to the tragedy of the burned site, but she hoped that each step also meant the conflict was closer to being resolved.

Her early morning sentiments had been way off, she realized. The new day had not softened Laman's heart. With Lehi's death, Laman had only grown worse in his defiance.

"O Lord," she whispered as she hurried, "preserve my husband from Laman's anger. Protect him with Thy hand. Protect Eve and my children while I am away." Before she realized it, tears were coursing down her face, but she pressed forward, feeling branches tear at her clothing as she made all haste.

The burnt smell surprised her as the trail dipped and angled north. The changing wind carried the smoke, hitting her full in the face. Isaabel coughed, feeling her eyes sting. She wondered if the timbers still burned or if the smoke continued to rise from the smolder. The next moment told her.

She arrived at the edge of the clearing to see the foundation of the temple completely charred. On the east end, the stack of ruined timbers still glowed orange, although it didn't look like the wood could become any blacker. The tent that provided relief for the working men hung in ruin. Its goat-hair panels reeked of burnt animal.

Isaabel saw instantly that she was the only woman on the premises. The men gathered on the west side of the clearing, but Isaabel was too far to hear what they said. She saw her brothers, Raamah and Heth, standing next to Laman and Lemuel—across from them stood Sam, Zoram, Nephi, and Jacob. Isaabel's heart lurched at the sight of Jacob standing there, hearing all that went on. *He's a man now,* she told herself, but it still hurt to see him exposed to the vileness of Laman and Lemuel.

And my brothers, Isaabel thought. *How dare they treat Nephi so?* She remembered with sadness that it was Heth who had helped save Nephi's life when Laman and Lemuel bound him in the desert and left him to be devoured by wild beasts. And it was Raamah who pledged to Lehi that he would keep the Lord's commandments.

But all that changed with Lehi's death, Isaabel realized. She watched with alarm as Laman yelled incessantly, his face dark with hatred.

True hatred.

Isaabel felt a new nausea, one that wouldn't be reversed with a morsel of bread or a piece of fruit. The nausea was the realization that

Laman had gone too far to ever change his heart. And that maybe nothing, not even God Himself, could stop the man's murderous intentions.

"O my Lord," Isaabel whispered. "Is there any hope?" She sank to her knees and felt as if she would melt into the earth with this descending burden of sorrow, disgust, and anger. She let her head hang as tears dripped onto the dusty ground. A hand touched her shoulder, but she didn't have the strength to look up.

"Isa." It was Sam's voice. "Return home to your children."

Isaabel lifted her head to see her brother-in-law, one who had never wavered in his loyalty or faithfulness. But today his kind and jovial face was etched with deep suffering.

"Please," he said, drawing her to her feet. "Nephi has asked me to send you away. He cannot risk Laman using you to his advantage." He lowered his voice to a whisper. "Your husband wants you to return home where you will be safe."

His meaning sank into Isaabel's anguished thoughts. "He thinks Laman will harm me?"

Sam closed his eyes and nodded. "Please go. Now."

Taking another look at the men, Isaabel turned away and stumbled toward the settlement. With each step, her anger grew. Who was Laman to dictate how her family lived? How the rest of the family lived? The Lord had made it clear whom He wanted to lead the family, and it was for a good reason. Laman had been vile, and his occasional repentance was offered only in fear. The Lord didn't want a man like that responsible for His people and carrying their salvation in his hands.

And he had burned the temple site.

What other witness did she or anyone else need that Laman would never govern in righteousness? She thought of her sisters, Anah and Puah, who were married to Laman and Lemuel. They'd never had strong feelings about the Lord from the beginning, and living in the shadows of their overbearing husbands had not been helpful. She and her sisters had come from the same mother, the same father—yet one man could thwart all the human decency they had been taught.

She veered off the trail and walked to the north end of the settlement. Zoram's household was the closest to the temple site, but just beyond that lived Laman's family. Since the air was permeated with smoke, Isaabel was sure Anah knew what had happened.

When Isaabel reached her sister's home, she was surprised to find that Anah still slept. Shem, Anah's oldest, regarded Isaabel with suspicion as he stood in the entryway of his home.

"Is your mother ill?" Isaabel asked her nephew.

Shem shook his head. "She sleeps late since she became with child."

Isaabel furrowed her brow. "Even on this morning when the air is heavy with smoke?"

A flash of interest crossed Shem's face. "Have you seen the fire?" A sly grin erupted. "Father says we don't need a temple to house altars. The ones we've used for years are good enough."

Isaabel felt her face burn at her nephew's words. But she did not blame him. How could she? He had been taught as a child to despise the things of God. For an instant she wished she could draw him to her bosom and tell him the true nature of life, how beautiful and peaceful it could be. She wished she could show him what it was like to live in a household filled with love and righteousness.

But Shem had already sped around her, on some other errand of his own. Heart pounding, Isaabel entered Anah's home, surprised to see the cooking fire long grown cold. She wondered what the children had eaten for their morning meal. The house was silent, signaling that the children must be in the garden or playing with cousins.

She spied Anah's sleeping form and hesitated to wake her. But the arguments she had just witnessed pushed her forward.

"Anah," Isaabel said softly, waiting for her sister to stir.

Finally, Anah lifted her head and peered over the covers. With a groan she fell back again and brought her arm up to shield her eyes. With annoyance in her voice, she asked, "What do you want?"

Isaabel stiffened. "To talk about our husbands."

With that, Anah lowered her arm and looked at Isaabel as if she couldn't believe her sister had said such a thing. Then a slow grin broke across her face. "They are like children, no? They fight and make up, fight and make up." She let out a huge yawn, then rose from her mat.

Standing nearly a head taller than Isaabel, Anah looked at her sister with bleary eyes. "Not much we can do. Discussing it is a waste of time. I'd rather be eating."

Isaabel followed Anah out of the room, feeling deflated. But her sister wasn't really angry, so that gave Isaabel hope.

"Laman burned the temple site," Isaabel said quietly as Anah dipped a cup into a jar of water.

Lifting the cup to her lips, Anah drank for a moment. She didn't seem bothered in the least by the event. Then she shrugged. "Less work for my husband, I say."

Isaabel clenched her fists. "The Lord commanded it, Anah. Less work should not be the deciding factor in whether or not we do His bidding."

Anah met Isaabel's gaze. "Not all of us joy in laboring till we nearly drop dead." She scooped another cup of water and drank eagerly. When she finished she wiped her mouth. "Just think, you and Nephi can start all over, by yourselves. That will really buy your place in heaven."

"Heaven doesn't have a purchase price," Isaabel said, not liking the turn of the conversation. But she was in no mood to back down now.

"Have you seen heaven, Isa? Not even your husband can claim that. For all you know, death is the end. There is no judgment, no Atonement, no forgiveness, no repentance." Anah's voice trembled with emotion. "I'm tired of the fighting, too. I'm also tired of feeling second best every time I'm around you or your husband."

Isaabel shrank away. "The Lord loves us all the same . . . *I* love you."

But Anah shook her head. "You don't understand. No matter what you say or do, I will always support my husband. And if that means going against you, or your husband, so be it. Laman is *my* master. Not Nephi or his God."

With a sinking heart, Isaabel understood. Her sister was bound by her marriage vows. Laman didn't know how lucky he was to have a wife who would follow him through bitterness, no matter how degrading or painful it might be to her or her children.

The atmosphere in the room had changed from resentment to sad reconciliation. There was nothing more she could say.

CHAPTER 8

*Yea, I have loved thee with an everlasting love: therefore
with loving kindness have I drawn thee.*

(JEREMIAH 31:3)

Amidst the smoldering smoke and his brothers' fierce expressions, Nephi thought of his wife and children. Sam had sent Isaabel away when she'd come to the clearing. One part of Nephi wanted to run to her and bury his face in her neck—seeking peaceful solace. But the other part of him wanted to rage against his stubborn brothers, setting them in their places for the last time.

"Let us slay him now." Laman spat on the ground. "I will rejoice in the day of his death, and today, I am in the mood for rejoicing."

Lemuel's eyes lit with fire as he nodded in agreement.

But Nephi wasn't swayed. He stood his ground and didn't back away from his advancing brothers. Granted, he had Sam and Zoram at his side, as well as Jacob—but at that moment the Spirit whispered to him that his life would be preserved. He would not die here, not now, and not by the hands of his brothers.

"We are tired of being afflicted by your high and mighty speech," Heth joined in. He looked at Laman and grinned. "He will no longer be our ruler, Laman, for that role belongs to you."

Laman merely grunted and withdrew his dagger. "He is mine to kill. You men may hold him down, but my knife will do the honor."

He paused, sneering at Sam and Zoram. "But first, I want him to bow to me. Worship me as he does his god. Call me his savior."

Lemuel and Heth laughed out loud, and even Raamah cracked a smile.

"No." Nephi shook his head. He was suddenly more than tired. After a night without sleep and now a verbal battle with Laman, he wished for the day to be over, for peace to be restored. But reality reared up as Sam and Zoram withdrew their daggers. Nephi knew these men would offer their lives to preserve his. But that didn't seem right. In his heart he pled with the Lord. *Stop these men and cause them to listen to reason.*

Jacob stepped to Sam's side, his face confused and hurt. Nephi caught his gaze and wished he could undo the last two days. Every bit of it. He'd change his anger against Laman. He'd repent of his strong words and beg Jacob and Joseph for forgiveness.

Nephi was ashamed of his failure to teach his oldest brothers the ways of God. He looked at the ground, staring until the dirt and leaves blended to one color.

"He's bowing," Lemuel said with a chortle.

"A little lower," Heth joined in. "You're almost there."

But Nephi raised his head, feeling swelling behind his eyes. The disdain was clear on Laman's face, and Lemuel's held no trace of mercy. Heth showed signs of unbreakable hatred, and Raamah—his expression was as dark as ever.

"Nephi," a voice cried. Without turning, he knew his mother's voice. Despair sailed through him as he thought about his mother's grief. It was about to be multiplied.

"Joseph," Sam whispered.

Nephi turned and saw his five-year-old brother leading his aged mother toward them. He looked at Laman, whose face hardened.

Sariah walked right into the middle of their group and faced Laman. She stared at him for a moment, then let her gaze slide to Lemuel.

"Is it true?" she finally said. "Is it true you burned our Lord's temple?"

Laman held her gaze, unflinching, admitting nothing.

She looked at Heth, then Raamah. "Leave. Go home to your wives." She bid Zoram to do the same. Nephi was about to protest, but then he saw the wisdom in his mother's actions.

When only the sons of her womb were left, she spoke. "My hair is gray, my body is weak, and I have no wisdom left to offer." Her steely gaze settled on Laman. "You have desecrated a holy site that had yet to be dedicated to the Lord. You spit on your father's memory, and although he is not here in body, his spirit is with us."

She brought a hand to her cheek and wiped at the dampness. "He suffers still. The whole family suffers because of the actions of my sons."

Nephi felt a slow burn spread through his body. There was no softening in Laman's or Lemuel's features, but they had relaxed their grips on their daggers.

"A mother's love cannot shore up so much hate." Sariah's voice wavered. "You have been warned by the Lord Himself. You have been taught in your youth and still you deny all that is good and righteous." She sniffled, but remained steady. "My work is done. I have prayed for your souls night and day, and all that has come of it is more grief."

Laman took a shuffling step backward and mumbled something. Nephi watched him closely, hoping that his mother's words would have some effect.

"Each of you I bore from my own flesh and blood." She looked at all of her sons, then let her sharpened gaze rest on Laman and Lemuel. "But now it is no more. I cannot take honor in claiming sons such as you. Your days are numbered, and although only a few days have passed since your father's death, you have already lost his blessing."

The hairs on Nephi's neck rose. He had never seen his mother so calm and decisive, her words cutting to the very bone. She had nearly disowned Laman and Lemuel.

Slowly she turned, grasping Joseph's arm, and walked away. Nephi looked at his mother's stooped body, feeling his throat swell. His long-suffering mother had finally reached her threshold of tolerance.

"We'll see how many days the old woman has herself," Laman said.

The bitterness in Laman's voice seared into Nephi's heart, and he closed his eyes. Sam grabbed his arm, as if he knew Nephi needed to feel constrained. But when Nephi opened his eyes, Laman and Lemuel had turned away. He watched with surprise as they headed back to the settlement.

I have been delivered once again, Nephi thought. *But at great cost to my mother.* He looked at Sam, who shook his head. Jacob just stared at the smoldering ruins, his face as ashen as the smoke.

After several moments, Jacob joined Nephi, and together they walked home.

* * *

Nephi fell into an exhausted sleep, blocking out everything that had happened in the past few hours. Upon arriving home, he'd found Isaabel very quiet, her eyes bordered in red. She'd told him that she went to visit Anah, but that there was no tenderness between the two of them.

That brought another weight onto his shoulders. As the sun hit midday, blessed sleep claimed him, strengthening him for what was to come.

In the late afternoon, Nephi woke and found himself alone in the house. For several moments, he lay still on his mat, dwelling on the words of his mother. He knew he'd been protected once again by the hand of the Lord. Preserved for another day. His anger was replaced by sadness for the disarray of his family. How could he make reparations?

Depart from your brothers and flee into the wilderness.

Nephi felt his heart pound as the whispering of the Spirit came again.

Go into the wilderness and take all those who will go with you.

Leave his father's settlement? His brothers had threatened his life many times, so why was he to flee this time? Nephi moved to a sitting position, then knelt on the floor. He had been commanded to rule over his brethren in righteousness. How could he accomplish this if he left the settlement?

The whisperings continued, more urgent now.

Your brothers seek your life. Flee with your family into the wilderness. There is much work yet to be done.

Nephi buried his face in his hands, emotion creeping over him. Everything they had built over the past two years would have to be left behind. Who would go with him? Sam? Jacob? Mother and Joseph? Zoram? His sister, Dinah, and her new child? But what about her husband Tiras, son of Raamah?

What about his sister, Elisheba? As Raamah's wife, what would her choice be?

Nephi wiped the moisture from his face, his heart already grieving over the potential loss of his sisters. Then he thought of his wife leaving her sisters, Anah and Puah, and Heth's wife, Zillah. No matter how cruel and iniquitous Laman and Lemuel were, he knew that Isaabel truly loved their wives and children.

He rose to his feet, his chest expanding with purpose and resolution. The Lord had commanded that he take his family and flee. From past experience, he knew the wounds of separating siblings and cousins could begin to heal—but now, those wounds would be reopened.

Leaving the bedchamber, Nephi passed through the tidy cooking room. Isaabel took great pride in keeping house, and another pang shot through him as he thought about all that she would have to leave behind. He found her in the garden, working alongside Aaron and Sarah.

He stopped for a moment, taking in her appearance—the way her scarf covered her head and knotted at the nape of her neck. Tendrils of dark hair had escaped, framing her copper face. Her thick lashes were lowered as she dug up manioc roots, her swollen belly already making the work difficult.

When she looked at him, her eyes widened in understanding. He knew that she saw his changed countenance. Without a word, she left the children to their tasks and followed him inside the house.

Nephi stopped at the center of the cooking room and turned to face his wife.

"What is it?" Isaabel whispered.

Gently he placed his hands on her shoulders and took a deep breath. "The Lord's voice came to me."

Isaabel's eyes grew incandescent as she listened.

He lowered his head for a moment, preparing for his wife's reaction. Then he looked at her and touched her cheek. "Isa, we must leave this place. The Lord commands that we take our children, and all that we can carry, into the wilderness."

"All of us?"

"We will travel with those who will come." He hesitated, seeing the moisture gather at the corner of her eyes. "But the Lord has made it clear that this is the only way to be safe from Laman's murderous intentions."

Isaabel began to nod even as tears trickled along her cheeks. "We will be free . . . finally free."

"The price is high, I know," Nephi said softly. "All that we have worked for in the past two years will be left behind. But we will start anew and raise our children without the contentions that beset our journey across the desert."

"Yes." Isaabel nodded as the path her tears took widened. She turned from him and folded her arms, staring at the colorful pottery that lined the cooking room. She waved her hand, pointing to the walls that they had built by their own hands, the fire pit that she had fashioned with just the right sized rocks, the woven palm mats on the floor. Finally she covered her mouth with a hand, stifling a cry. Turning, she buried her head against Nephi's chest.

Then she pulled away abruptly and looked up at him. "What about your mother?"

"She will come with us." Nephi brushed his fingers against her tear-stained cheeks, wishing they could stay and live peaceably among the entire family. Even after all the pain, anger, hurt, and iniquity, he feared that without his presence, Laman and Lemuel's families would only grow more willful—their souls sliding beyond the reach of divine mercy.

Isaabel bit her lip and took Nephi's hand. "Will she leave her first-born sons?"

Then he told her about what had happened at the temple site, how Sariah denounced her nurturing role over her eldest sons.

Fresh tears fell as Isaabel said, "The price of freedom has always been great, so why should it be any different now?"

Nephi wrapped his arms about her enlarged torso and held her close. They cried together, for sorrow, for disappointment, and for hope.

Several moments passed as they clung to each other.

Isaabel pulled away first, drying her wet face with her mantle. She gave a final, loud sniffle, and asked, "What will we tell the children?"

He cupped her face with his hands. "Tell them we are going on a journey—a journey to find a new place to build a temple."

"All right, dear husband."

Nephi smiled and kissed his wife. "When the moon begins to set tonight, we will leave." He straightened, rubbing the short beard on his face. "I will go and speak with the other men and tell Mother to gather her necessary things."

Another thought entered his mind, one that saddened him. "If Laman, Lemuel, Heth, or Raamah find out, they may stop us."

Isaabel nodded, her face distraught as the full weight of what was happening seemed to settle on her shoulders.

Nephi felt the lump harden in his throat. "I'm sorry that you won't be able to say good-bye to your sisters."

"Perhaps in time we will see them again, when things can be reconciled," she said.

He couldn't respond. It was likely they would never again see the family members who remained. But he knew his wife needed that hope. "The Lord will direct us," was all he could manage.

Isaabel's face paled. "I must speak with my mother. She would never understand if I left without saying good-bye . . . and Elisheba." She looked at Nephi, her eyes imploring. "Raamah will surely find out if Elisheba knows."

"It's her decision whether or not to tell her husband," he said. "We'll just have to trust that if she tells him, Raamah won't cause a disturbance. And your mother will be in good hands with your sisters."

Isaabel remained quiet for a moment. "I will go to the children, and we'll begin preparations."

Nephi watched her leave, then he looked around the room. Their first real home—one they had hoped would be permanent—where they'd live out their days.

He moved into the courtyard, breathing in the fragrant air tinged with the smell of the sea. How far inland they would travel, Nephi didn't know. Whether or not they'd be within sight of the great sea was yet to be determined. Resolutely he set out on the trail, walking to Sam's home first.

Eventually, he met with Zoram, his mother, and finally arrived at Dinah and Tiras's small home. Dinah was still in confinement, so he hesitated outside the door. But he knew his sister well, and guessed she would defy tradition and travel with them regardless.

"Hello, Nephi."

He heard his name called. He turned to see Tiras in the nearby field. Nephi raised his hand in greeting.

As Tiras walked toward him, Nephi marveled at how much the young man had changed since leaving Bountiful. In the past couple of years, Tiras had grown taller than his father, Raamah, and had developed a full beard.

Tiras's eyes were filled with both concern and curiosity as he neared Nephi. Obviously, he'd heard about the dispute between Nephi and Laman.

Nephi spoke first. "I need you to discuss something with your wife."

"What's happened?" Tiras asked.

"Tonight I will take my family and leave the settlement, for good. We will journey until we find a new land in which we can build homes and raise up a temple to the Lord." He noted the incredulous expression on Tiras's face. "The Lord has commanded it. Otherwise I don't know if I would have the courage to part with my family in this way."

"It's so unexpected, yet . . ." Tiras looked away, his eyes clouding over as he thought about Nephi's plans.

Nephi reached out and clasped his brother-in-law's shoulder. "I would like you and Dinah to accompany us. Mother, Sam, Zoram, and their families are also preparing to leave."

Lost in thought, Tiras finally met Nephi's gaze. "What about my father?"

Nephi felt his shoulders sag. "Your father doesn't know of our plans yet. But you are the man of your household, and you have made marriage covenants to follow God." He tilted his head. "The decision is yours alone to make."

"My grandmother would never leave her sons."

Nodding, Nephi let out a sigh. "I am aware of that, yet I'm certain she'll be well taken care of if she decides to stay."

Tiras brought a hand to his brow and rubbed his temple. "It will be impossible to keep this a secret."

"You may be right," Nephi said. "But I hope that we'll be advanced in our preparations before any confrontation develops."

* * *

Isaabel hovered outside her mother's home as dusk enveloped the settlement. She could hear the murmur of voices coming from inside, so she waited, watching the twilight hour advance. Nearly everything was prepared for the journey, but she still had one more farewell. Finally, she knew she could wait no longer and still make haste for the journey. Tentatively, she entered the home and found Eve sitting at her grandmother's feet. The girl immediately rose and made motion to leave.

Isaabel gave Eve a halfhearted smile as the girl passed by, wondering if she knew anything about the journey yet. Normally she would have asked Eve to stay as she visited with Bashemath, but not this time. She was grateful Eve had left them alone.

"Mother," Isaabel said, settling in the place that Eve had just abandoned.

Bashemath turned her worn gaze onto her youngest daughter. "Where did Eve go?"

"She'll return in a few moments. I know how you depend on her."

"She is a very good girl and takes care of all my needs," Bashemath said, somewhat absentmindedly.

Isaabel patted her mother's hand. "Yes, I know. Eve is truly a gem." Then her voice turned serious. "Mother, you need to listen to me."

Bashemath arched a spidery brow. "What do you think I'm doing?"

Ignoring her caustic remark, Isaabel dove into explanation. "Laman and Lemuel have threatened to kill Nephi again. Every day grows worse and is more fearful than the next."

"Will those men never learn?" Bashemath lifted her sunken eyes and stared at the ceiling.

Isaabel squeezed her mother's hand. "Nephi is moving us away from here. The Lord spoke to him and told him that it was time to leave." She stopped, waiting for her mother's response.

"Perhaps a separation would settle the hard feelings." Bashemath brought her hand to her stomach. "I am not feeling well myself and will be glad when peace returns."

"That's exactly why we need to leave, Mother. To restore peace." Isaabel clung to her mother's hand, wondering if she really understood.

Bashemath brought her gaze to meet her daughter's. "Will Sariah travel with you?"

Isaabel nodded and saw the instant pain in her mother's face. The two matriarchs were closer than sisters. They had delivered grandchildren together, prepared meals out of next to nothing, comforted each other in widowhood, and been friends in all things.

"How long will you be gone?" Bashemath asked quietly.

"Oh, Mother," Isaabel cried. "I don't know if we'll ever return." She wrapped her arms around her mother's neck as her tears fell.

Bashemath patted Isaabel's back, the most affection she'd shown in a long time. "Go with your husband, child."

Isaabel drew back and saw the glint of determination in her mother's eyes—the same determination that had given her the strength to follow Lehi's family across the barren desert when her own husband was buried in the strange land of Nahom. Isaabel bit her lip, hesitating to deliver the rest of her news. She took a shaky breath. "Tamar and Rebeka are coming with their husbands, too."

Bashemath visibly stiffened, and Isaabel tried not to take offense that her mother would miss one daughter more than the other.

"But that means Eve . . . ?"

"Yes," Isaabel whispered. "Eve, too."

Bashemath's eyes closed and her lips pursed shut. Isaabel knew that she was being dismissed. It wasn't the tearful good-bye she may have hoped for, but at least she knew her mother wished her well.

"Anah, Puah, and Zillah will be here to care for you."

"Phhh. They have been tainted by their husbands and only care for their own interests." An eye opened. "What about Elisheba? Don't tell me Raamah and Elisheba are going with you."

It was as if a dagger had entered Isaabel's heart as she spoke. "Over the past days, Raamah has supported Laman. I think he'll stay."

Bashemath nodded, her expression softening. "Elisheba will care for me then. Any woman would be a fool to leave her husband."

The old resentments stirred in Isaabel's heart. *Not now,* she told herself. *This may be the last time I see my mother.* "Your sons have always been good to you. And their wives will take over where Rebeka and Eve leave off."

Bashemath didn't meet her gaze. "Send Eve in." Her tone was sharp, but Isaabel sensed emotion beneath the words.

She silently left her mother, who sat and stared ahead, and exited to the courtyard. There she found Eve and took her hands. "Your grandmother is asking for you." She looked deeply into Eve's eyes and saw that the girl had since learned of the journey. "I told her you were coming with us."

Eve's eyes brimmed with unshed tears, but let out a relieved sigh. "I was afraid to tell her. I don't want to cause her any pain."

"Of course not," Isaabel soothed. "It's nearly dark now, so we must hurry. Do you want me to wait for you?"

"No," Eve said. "I must do it alone."

Footsteps sounded behind them, and Isaabel turned to see Nephi. His expression looked pained. "What is it?" Isaabel asked, hurrying to his side.

"I've come to bid farewell to Bashemath." He moved past her and entered the small house.

Isaabel and Eve hovered at the entryway. Isaabel marveled at how easily Nephi seemed to bend over and kiss his mother-in-law, murmuring endearing words. Bashemath hugged him back and even shed a tear at his departure. Then he walked outside, Isaabel following in order to leave Eve alone with her grandmother.

"What's happened, Nephi?"

"Everyone knows now. At least the women. Fortunately, Laman and Lemuel are nowhere to be found."

"Hunting?"

Nephi shrugged. "I don't think so. They'll probably return later tonight. But I'm not worried about Raamah and Heth stopping us."

"Then hopefully we'll be able to say a proper good-bye before your brothers return."

Nephi nodded curtly, but Isaabel could tell that something else bothered him. She walked with him back to their home, when suddenly Nephi stopped and turned toward her, distress clear on his face. "What is it?" she asked.

"I met Elisheba on the trail. She was in tears."

"She knows?" Isaabel asked.

"Mother told her a short time ago. She doesn't want to lose Elisheba," Nephi said.

Isaabel felt her chest tighten. Elisheba had a difficult choice to make. "Is there any hope of Raamah softening his heart?"

Nephi shook his head. "Not now, at least. I don't know if he'll change his mind after a time." He brought a hand to his face and rubbed his forehead. He frowned, lost in thought. Finally he said, "I'm going to speak with him."

"No," Isaabel said, her instinct driving her. "You don't want to risk his wrath."

Nephi lifted a shoulder and studied his wife. "It's a risk I must take . . . for my sister."

Isaabel understood, but a seed of fear had sprouted within her breast. "Let me come with you."

He reached for her arm. "It would be too dangerous."

"If only to say good-bye to Elisheba," Isaabel said, her voice trembling at the thought.

Nephi nodded briefly and took her hand. Together they turned on the trail that led to Raamah's home.

One part of Isaabel hoped Raamah wouldn't be there, that they could convince Elisheba alone to leave with them. But in her heart, she knew her sister-in-law had a strong bond with her husband, even when he was at his worst.

As their home came into view, Raamah's frame filled the entryway. It was almost as if he'd been waiting for them. Nephi stopped inside the courtyard and waited. As Raamah walked to meet him, Isaabel moved toward the far end of the courtyard. Just as she suspected, Elisheba was sitting in the cooking room, within plain view of the entrance.

"I know why you've come," Raamah's deep voice boomed.

Isaabel slipped into the darkened enclosure and walked to Elisheba's side. The two women embraced, and Elisheba shuddered. Isaabel felt her own tears form at the obvious distress of her good friend.

"He will not allow it. He says that I have made a covenant to him," Elisheba whispered. She drew back and looked at Isaabel. "And I know he is right." She lowered her wet eyelashes and in barely audible words said, "He even told me that if I considered leaving, I would have to leave my sons behind."

Isaabel stroked her sister-in-law's hand.

"I could never live without my Dedan or little Noah," Elisheba said through trembling breaths.

"And they could not live without their mother," Isaabel said. She leaned forward and kissed Elisheba's moist forehead. "Do you understand why we must leave?"

Elisheba nodded. "I have felt it since my father's death. I know it is the only solution." She grasped Isaabel's hand. "Oh, how I wish my stubborn husband would be a man unto himself. Why does he have to follow Laman? I can't stand the way he treats my husband, but Raamah doesn't see it."

"In time, dear sister." Isaabel looked at her with tenderness. "I'll never stop praying for your family."

"Neither will I," Elisheba said, then the choking sobs started.

Isaabel gathered her into her arms and held fast. "Nephi is speaking with Raamah right now. Perhaps he'll be able to soften your husband's heart."

But the next instant proved her wrong. Nephi appeared in the doorway, his face reddened. He crossed to his sister and kissed each cheek.

"Continue to stay faithful in the Lord, sister, and raise your children in righteousness. For that you will always be blessed."

Elisheba nodded, tears streaming down her cheeks.

Nephi took Isaabel's hand and led her from the room to the outer courtyard. There Raamah stood, his arms crossed and face like stone.

⊰⊱ CHAPTER 9 ⊰⊱

*If ye will obey my voice indeed, and keep my covenant,
then ye shall be a peculiar treasure unto me above all
people: for all the earth is mine.*

(EXODUS 19:5)

The moon sat low, casting its thin silvery light across the moving party. The mood was somber, and sniffles could be heard among several of the women. Sariah walked slowly as they climbed the incline above the river. They had loaded their belongings onto their backs, only bringing what they could carry. A few domesticated deer traveled with them, and the animals carried some of the heavier items.

A piece of her heart had been left behind in Lehi's settlement—with her daughter, Elisheba; her daughters-in-law, Anah and Puah; her dear friend, Bashemath; but most of all, her grandchildren. Oh, how she would miss them.

She wanted to cry at the heavens and pound on God's door. For a moment, she wondered if death held a better option than seeing her family go their separate ways. She was old, and she could feel age in her very bones. Her skin had lost the fulness of youth and the elegance of womanhood. She felt as if she were a washed-up fig on the sandy shores, withered and alone. She missed her husband.

Her farewell with Bashemath had been quiet and hurried. Sariah didn't have much hope of seeing her friend again. Bashemath's health had declined over the past few months, and Sariah feared what this journey would do to her own body.

Ahead of her, she could see Eve's youthful form, and thoughts of Bashemath renewed. Eve would be sorely missed by the woman, and Sariah wouldn't be surprised if Bashemath's health deteriorated rapidly after losing Eve's gentle care.

Sariah hadn't been given the chance to say good-bye to Laman or Lemuel. With an inward sigh, she thought about the choices they'd made since leaving Jerusalem. The pattern began years before, and now the consequences had set in, for better or worse.

"Mother," a voice sounded close to her.

Sariah looked over and saw Isaabel. "We are close to Lehi's burial ground. Would you like to stop for a while?"

"Yes," Sariah whispered, forcing the words beyond the emotion constricting her throat. She walked with Isaabel as they made their way to the clearing. Several of the family members had gathered and knelt upon the earthen floor in front of the cave.

Sariah joined them, bowing her head. Would she ever come to this quiet grove again? She had never traveled without her husband, and in doing so now, she felt utter loneliness. Being surrounded by her dear children and grandchildren somehow didn't make up for the absence of her beloved. After offering a silent prayer for protection and guidance, she bid farewell to Lehi one last time.

* * *

Elisheba paced into the night, wearing a path along the carefully baked tiles of the cooking room. Raamah had left after supper and never returned. She suspected that he went in search of Laman and Lemuel—to inform them of Nephi's departure. She could well imagine the rejoicing that Laman would show. His thorn had finally fallen off the family branch.

Only a few hours had passed since Nephi and the others had left, but already Elisheba felt as if it had been a lifetime. She knew when the sun rose on the settlement in the morning, its rays would find empty homes, untended gardens, and somber trails.

"O Lord," she whispered. "Remain with me in this time of hardship. Do not abandon me in my need."

She wanted a glimpse—if even for an instant—of the future. Where was Nephi's group going? Where would they settle? How far from here? Would the separation change her husband's heart? Would Raamah see Laman for what he really was?

Be patient.

Elisheba halted in her tracks, wondering if the words came from her own mind or from someone greater. Regardless, she clung to the message and savored it. "Be patient," she whispered out loud and continued her path. Nephi's last words came to memory. *Raise your children in righteousness.* She slowed her step and changed direction. Moving silently she walked into the back room and spied upon her sleeping babies. Six-year-old Dedan and three-year-old Noah slept side by side. Their lives had not been simple, but they were happy here.

She bent over them, listening to their sweet childlike breathing. For a moment, she was tempted to stroke the soft, black hair framing their faces, but she knew her touch might wake them.

Distinctive footsteps came from the courtyard. She stiffened, trying to decide if she should hasten to bed and keep still, or confront her husband.

She opted for the first. Whatever had happened tonight, the morning would soften any potential argument. Quickly, she moved to her bedchamber and settled onto the mat, pulling the covers to her shoulders. She turned and faced the wall then listened to the motions of her husband entering the house.

A tear slid down her cheek as she thought about the emptiness of the settlement. Just knowing how many family members had left, including her mother and sister, created emptiness inside. She felt alone, very alone.

As her husband lay down next to her, Elisheba squeezed her eyes shut, her mind turning in desperate prayer. Her last thought before succumbing to sleep was that she hoped Isaabel would keep her promise to pray.

* * *

When the morning light flooded through the airy clouds on the horizon, Eve turned her face to the new day. The followers of Nephi had traveled all night, urgency laced with fear in every step. And now Eve welcomed the new day, thinking about the significance it brought. They had a new life—free of Laman's disdain, free of Lemuel's cajoling, and free of the disapproving stares from the sons of Ishmael. Throughout the night, Eve had stayed close to Sariah, finding comfort in the grandmother of many.

Nephi's weary voice rang across the group, and the travelers staggered to a halt. "We will rest here for several hours. Do not erect the tents. Save your energy." He moved through the crowd and the small flock of sheep, reaching Eve just as she settled Sariah on a dry rug.

He smiled his gratitude and placed a hand on her arm. "Be sure to rest, Eve. You need it just as much as anyone."

"Of course," Eve whispered. She cleared her throat in an attempt to say more, but nothing would come. She had been surprised at the attention Nephi gave her. She watched him walk away and help Isaabel settle their tired children.

But Eve was far from sleepy. Her mind kept going over the past few days, again and again. She quietly stepped away from the bedrolls and walked along the edge of the trees. A narrow stream that was small enough to hop over cut through the undergrowth. She crossed to the other side and followed its meandering course for a few paces. Then she heard someone speaking. It was so faint at first that she wondered if it were the wind. She moved cautiously past the first row of trees, then the second.

Not too far away, Jacob knelt, his head bowed in prayer. Eve drew back into the drooping branches, laden with yellow fruit and dark leaves. The gigantic cashew tree offered the concealment she needed. She hadn't meant to come across Jacob as he prayed, yet the scene of him kneeling alone intrigued her. After a moment of watching, she felt guilty for seeing him unaware, but it was impossible to pull herself away.

When he rose and moved down the bank for a drink, she realized that he might be able to see her from his new position. She moved farther back into the trees, startling a group of chattering birds. As they took flight, her heart started to pound. It only increased when Jacob stopped what he was doing and looked around.

Eve held her breath and only let it out when Jacob left the area. As the waning light filtered through the dense escarpment, Eve knew she must return; it would be dark soon. But something held her interest. Something she had discovered just before noticing Jacob.

It was an intricately carved statue, an incense burner. It was used to keep evil spirits away.

"Sssss."

Eve whirled to see a young girl peering down from a high branch. The girl was perched in a tree, watching. She let go of the branch and leapt to the ground. Eve stared at her, not sure what to say. The girl smoothed back her long dark hair and grinned.

"Hello?" Eve said, smiling, although her heart pounded fiercely.

"He-lloo," the girl mimicked. Standing eye to eye, Eve realized this girl was probably her same age. She wore red feathers and a short cloak of brilliant green. The girl tilted her head and stared openly at Eve.

"What's your name?" Eve asked.

"Wat yoo nime."

Eve laughed, and the girl started to giggle. Rows of bracelets lined the girl's arms. At her throat, she wore several exquisite necklaces. Eve had seen Kaminaljuyú girls wear such jewelry, but she stared in fascination at the amount this girl wore.

Raising her hands, the girl pointed to her necklace and smiled. In one swift motion, the girl removed one of the necklaces and held it out to Eve.

"Oh, no," Eve said. "I can't take it." She waved the gift away.

The girl's face fell, but she stepped forward, her hand outstretched. "Oo no?" she repeated. The necklace was made of a long, thin piece of animal hide that had been threaded through the center of a polished jadeite, turquoise in color. *Good fortune.* Eve remembered hearing that jadeite jewelry was worn for good fortune. She also remembered hearing it was rude not to accept a gift from the tribal people.

The girl pressed the necklace into Eve's palm, chattering in a language that Eve couldn't understand.

"All right," Eve said, feeling her face heat with pleasure. "Thank you very much."

"Ve-ree mush."

Eve laughed, and the girl grinned. Then before Eve could say another word, the girl disappeared, leaving only the rustle of leaves behind. "Hello?" Eve called. "Where did you go?" She listened for further sounds, then looked down at the necklace in her hand. She glanced over at the pile of leaves that held the incense burner. Was the girl worshipping when Eve disturbed her privacy? She'd heard about foreign worship from her father when he'd told her about the demise of Jerusalem. Trees, stones, and animals were idolized. She crouched over the object, fascinated by the intricate metalwork and design.

The top of the incense burner was sculpted in the form of the temple that she'd heard about from Nephi when he visited the village on the other side of the far hills. Looking closer, Eve saw a miniature figure had been placed inside. An acrid smell reached her nostrils, and she realized that it hadn't been too long since the burner had been used.

Eve backed away from the burner and stood abruptly. What if the girl brought more of her people with her? Meeting the girl alone had been fine, but if there were more of them . . . She frowned, looking at the surrounding trees with new eyes. They didn't seem so benign anymore.

What if there were a hidden civilization deep within the jungle that the family didn't know about? What if they were hostile, unlike the friendly Kaminaljuyú tribe? A shiver crept across her back as she recalled the stories of cannibals she'd heard about—the ones who had captured Sam on the outskirts of Nahom.

Eve took another step backward, the necklace clutched in her hand. She looked around, wanting to remember this place, committing the details to memory. The log by the stream, the flowering yellow-green manioc on the other side of the bank . . .

Turning, she pushed through the foliage quickly, wrapping the leather of the necklace around her hand. She started to run. She would show the necklace to her father and he would know whom it came from. But meanwhile, she suddenly did not want to be alone in the forest any longer.

"Eve?"

She stopped, petrified to hear her name called. Trying to still her labored breathing, she clutched the stone to her chest and spun around.

"Eve." Jacob stepped into sight. He looked just as surprised to see her as she was to see him.

"What—?" they both began.

Eve lowered her gaze, feeling her already heated face grow warmer.

"I heard someone running through the brush," Jacob said. "Were you following the stream?"

Eve looked up, her eyes meeting his. "Yes, I—" She hesitated, knowing how foolish she probably looked. Her plaited hair had come undone and hung in a stringy mess. Her tunic was stained with perspiration, leaves and dirt covering most of it. Her palms sweated against the turquoise stone, which she was sure Jacob had noticed by now. "I didn't mean to come across you, I had just met a girl . . ." she held out the object, "who gave me this."

He took a step forward, interest softening his features. "Who was she?"

"I'm not sure. I think she was from the Kaminaljuyú tribe."

Surprise creased his brow. "It's beautiful." His gaze met hers briefly. "She just gave it to you?"

Eve nodded and at that moment their eyes locked—both of them coming to the same conclusion. "We are not alone here."

"Nor have we ever been," Jacob said. "Shem and Javan have encountered girls from the tribes throughout this entire valley." He shook his head as if to erase some memory, then his expression filled with wonder. He reached for the object and Eve handed it over. Viewing it from all angles, Jacob concentrated on the engraving. "I don't think these are letters of any sort. Perhaps a depiction of food—grain or vegetable?"

Eve lifted a shoulder. "That was my guess. I don't suppose there could be more like it in the area?"

Jacob lowered the object from his scrutiny and looked at her. "Where exactly did you see the girl?"

"Maybe a dozen paces from the bank where you were . . . kneeling."

He pressed his lips together. "You saw me praying then?" he asked quietly.

Eve felt the ease of conversation flee and her awkwardness return. "I'm sorry. I didn't expect to see you."

Raising his hand, Jacob shook his head. "It's all right." He handed the necklace back to her. "We should show this to the family. See if it's similar to those made by the Kaminaljuyú tribe." His gaze trailed toward the sky above. "Let's go, it's nearly dark."

They traipsed through the jungle undergrowth side by side, following the stream. Eve's heart thudded fiercely against her chest. From being discovered by Jacob or from carrying a necklace that she wasn't sure she should have accepted, she didn't know. But she did know that she could barely contain a smile—a smile because she might be an ordinary girl who could talk to a boy after all.

Once they reached camp, all seemed quiet. So Eve tucked the necklace away, planning on showing her parents in the morning. Jacob waved a silent good-bye and Eve went to make her place by Sariah. Several of the children were already asleep. A small shelter had been constructed to offer privacy for Dinah and her new baby. She noted the men had gathered for some sort of a meeting, Jacob included. Eve hoped her father would come and apprise her later, since she was curious to know how far they'd be traveling.

A shadow fell across her bedroll, and Eve looked up to see her mother.

"You are sleeping here then?" Rebeka asked, looking from Eve to Sariah.

Eve nodded, hoping that her mother would allow it.

Rebeka gave a half-smile and said, "Very well. We are next to those trees."

When her mother left, Eve burrowed against her rug, finding comfort in the warm folds. As her eyes finally closed, she realized she wouldn't have to watch Jochebed chase after Jacob any longer.

Her eyes opened. Jochebed—her friend. Although it was not a close friendship, Eve would still miss her. Feeling envious of the girl's easy laughter and bold statements seemed trite right now.

Eve watched the men disassemble and join their families. For an instant, her heart froze. What if Jacob came to sleep near his mother? She let out a low breath when she saw him follow Sam. Realization dawned on her as she thought about what caring for Sariah would mean. She would encounter Jacob more than usual. Maybe she would have to let Isaabel take over the primary care of Sariah. But in Isaabel's delicate condition, Eve knew that the responsibility might still fall to her until Dinah was fully recovered.

Eve squeezed her eyes against her thoughts, knowing that she wouldn't be able to share them with anyone, especially Govad—unless Eve wanted the entire company to know. Regardless, she was glad she at least had Govad to keep her company.

Turning to face Sariah's sleeping form, Eve felt the hard lump of the necklace against her side. She wondered about the girl who'd given it to her. Then she wondered if she should have accepted it.

* * *

On the sixth day of travel, Nephi and his family came to a wide valley. He and Jacob stopped and looked upon the expanse of vegetation below. It was less humid than the tropics near the sea, and the forests had thinned. Birds soared above the treetops, and the afternoon sun brightened the deep green of the surrounding forest.

"Look at that river," Jacob said.

The meandering blue cut through the escarpment. Nephi felt the pressure of Isaabel's hand as she grasped his arm.

"It's beautiful," she said.

Nephi could only nod. His wife had said that many times on their journey thus far. They had traveled mostly north, covering challenging terrain. But this view made the taxing journey worth it.

"It is beautiful," he agreed. Then he wrapped an arm about Isaabel's shoulders. As they gazed over the valley together, a slow, sweet prompting came to him. He squeezed his wife's shoulder. "This will be our home."

Isaabel let out a whoop of joy and wrapped her arms around his neck. "Wonderful! Mother will be so pleased."

He glanced at Jacob and saw a grin spread across his brother's face.

"I'll go tell the others," Jacob said and moved away, leaving Nephi and Isaabel to revel in the pristine beauty of the mountain valley.

"Oh, Nephi," Isaabel's voice came softly. "Now we can raise our children in the Lord's way, away from the anger and threat of your brothers."

Nephi's grip tightened around her shoulders as he thought of the first time he had spotted the shores of the promised land with his father. He remembered the elation and sweetness of finally arriving at the blessed coast after so many months upon the sea and so many years of travail. Looking upon this new valley did not bring the same ecstatic joy, but instead, a quiet knowledge of obedience and acceptance. Here he would raise his children. Here he would see Jacob fulfill his calling, and here he and Isaabel would grow old together.

With his free hand, he swiped at a tear. If his wife noticed, she didn't say anything. He heard the sounds of joyful exclamation behind him, and Nephi turned to watch the reaction of his beloved family as they learned of their destination. He saw the plain weariness in their bone-tired faces, the relief of a journey finally ended, and the shadows of painful memories of lost family members left behind.

His father's words came to mind. *Awake, my sons; put on the armor of righteousness. Shake off the chains with which ye are bound . . .* Nephi knew the words were meant for Laman and Lemuel, but they seemed fitting for today. Nephi had followed the Lord's command to flee into the wilderness—for a second time—and he had shaken the heavy chains of his brothers' malice which had bound him for so many years.

Isaabel moved away from him and ran toward her children, telling them the good news. At their smiles and shouts, Nephi grinned, freedom soaring through his breast. At last they were free to turn their lives over to the Lord.

Nephi began to move among the group, embracing his brother Sam and kissing his mother, Sariah. She placed a trembling hand on his arm and kept it there as she gazed into his eyes.

"I will be buried here," Sariah said, her eyes gleaming with emotion.

"Mother, you have many days left yet," Nephi said. He knew that the journey had been difficult for her, but a few days of rest would greatly improve her health.

Sariah pointed to the spot where she stood. "Here."

Nephi followed her direction and looked at the ground.

"When I have passed through this world, I want to be buried in this spot—overlooking this beautiful valley—overlooking all my righteous posterity." Tears clouded her eyes and stopped her speech.

Nephi gathered her in his arms. "I understand, Mother. You shall have your wish." He turned to face the rest of the family, waiting a moment for his voice to steady. He looked at the faces of those he loved so dearly, those who had chosen to faithfully follow the Lord—Jacob, Joseph, Sam, Zoram, Tiras, and their families. "We will descend into the valley and create an altar of thanksgiving. Then we'll set up camp and rest. In the morning we'll begin to organize the settlement."

Cries of happiness echoed around him.

* * *

The animal prints began to fade as the trail narrowed. Elisheba knew the rain from the previous day had washed away most of the evidence of Nephi's departure. Already eight days had passed. Eight long days. She didn't tell her two young sons that they followed the footprints of their uncle. She merely led them along the winding trail above the river. Dedan and Noah loved the adventure, and their questions came faster than a running jaguar.

"How come I can't play with Samuel anymore?" Dedan asked.

Elisheba felt her heart wrench as she thought about Sam's five-year-old son. He and Dedan had been inseparable since they could crawl.

"Does he like Sarah better than me?"

"No, son," Elisheba said, trying to keep back her emotion as his small hand tugged at hers. "Sarah went with her mother and father, and so did Samuel. They had to go and live someplace else for a little while."

Dedan nodded somberly, but his questions continued. "Why did Nephi take so many people? Because Laman was so mean?"

Elisheba wanted to laugh and cry at the same time. She smiled at Dedan. "Let the adults worry about Laman. I don't want you to be sad about Samuel anymore. We can pray for him every day, and I'll bet he is praying for you, too."

Dedan let out a sigh and looked at his younger brother, Noah. "I don't like playing with babies all of the time."

A smile skittered across Elisheba's face. "Three-year-olds can be lots of fun if you give them a chance."

"Maybe I can play with Helek," Dedan said, doubt in his eyes.

"That's an excellent idea," she said, straightening. In the past, Lemuel's six-year-old son, Helek, had pushed Dedan around. Maybe now with Samuel gone, they'd form a friendship. *Please don't stay away too long, Nephi,* Elisheba thought. But even as she thought it, she knew her wish was futile. The men showed no signs of softening. Just that morning when she prepared for their walk, Raamah had stalled her by saying, "Remember your duty to your husband and children, Elisheba."

She had nodded and replied, "Of course." But as soon as her husband left the house, she'd let the tears fall. That's why she was still here—because of duty. But most of all, because of love. Yes, she loved her husband, dearly. And her sons were her life—her world. But she wanted it all. Perhaps it was selfish of her. Perhaps she was just envious of her sister, Dinah, who left with her husband to follow Nephi.

Following each step along the trail that Nephi had taken, Elisheba felt her heart grow heavier. Not even the two small hands enclosed in hers brought her comfort. She felt lost and abandoned.

Then the rain began to fall. Each drop created another barrier between her family and her, since each drop further obliterated their footprints on the trail. Soon her tears joined the rain upon her face, and she guided her children several paces off the path to take shelter beneath a canopy of trees.

"We'll wait here until the rain eases," Elisheba said, hoping her children wouldn't notice her tears.

"Why did Grandfather Lehi die?" Dedan's young voice cut through Elisheba's thoughts.

She silently berated herself for feeling so much self-pity. "He lived a long and full life. It was time for him to return to the Lord's presence."

"Can he see us from heaven?"

Elisheba smiled at her son, feeling the tears fade beneath her lids. "I believe he's watching over us and cares about everything we do."

"Can Grandfather see us through the trees?"

Elisheba chuckled. "I don't know about that." She picked up Noah and balanced him on her hip, then pulled Dedan close to her as the air gave off a slight chill. *Raise your children in righteousness. For that you will be blessed.* Nephi's words returned again. She knew she needed blessings right now. She decided this was a good time to follow his advice.

"Grandfather taught us many things about heaven," she began.

Dedan looked up at her. "How far away is it?"

"He didn't tell us that. But the Lord is always near us, just waiting for us to follow." She wiped the moisture from her face. "In fact, I once heard the Lord's voice."

"In Bountiful?"

Elisheba smiled at the way he said *Bounti-fool*. "No." She touched his shoulder gently. "It was long before that, soon after Grandfather Ishmael died." She took a deep breath and recalled the events leading to Nahom and her father's eventual death.

"All of us were very sad when he died. We wanted him to come with us to the promised land, but he had to be buried in Nahom, a place where we lived among strangers."

Dedan's expression was serious as Elisheba continued.

"Some in the family were angry with Grandfather Lehi because he led us away from our homes in Jerusalem. But Lehi was only following the Lord's commandments. And we know that when we do what the Lord asks of us, we will be blessed." Elisheba sensed a tremor in her voice and took a deep breath. "So when some in the family were very angry, the Lord had to tell all of us to remember to choose the right."

"What did He sound like?" Dedan asked. "Was His voice louder than the thunder?"

"No," Elisheba said with a tender smile. "It was quiet like a whisper, but more powerful. It was the kind of voice that you not only could hear, but you could actually *feel* deep inside."

"In your heart?"

"Yes, and all through your body." She met her son's brown eyes. "I want you to always remember I heard the Lord's voice. I know He's real, and He will always bless us as long as we choose the right." She ruffled his curly hair. "Do you think you can do your best to choose the right even when those around you don't?"

Dedan's gaze didn't waver. "Yes."

Noah squirmed in Elisheba's arms, and she put him down. It had stopped raining, and the brilliant sun pushed its way through the leafy branches. It was time to head home.

The three of them stepped back on the trail and started their southwestern journey. Elisheba's heart felt lightened. She knew she had seized an opportunity to teach her children, instead of letting it slip away, to be lost forever. Dedan was quiet on the walk back to the settlement, and Elisheba silently prayed that what she had told him would make a difference, even at his young age.

The land appeared renewed after the rain. The moist ground was rich and dark, and the surrounding trees seemed stoic and graceful, bringing peace and assurance. As Elisheba walked toward her house, she raised her chin in hope as she thought about the home that she had lovingly created with her husband. A home she now had to keep as a heaven on earth—a refuge from the storms that would surely come.

With each returning step bringing her closer to the settlement, she was filled with love and conviction that as long as she taught her children well, they would be blessed in the eternities.

✦ CHAPTER 10 ✦

In his days shall the righteous flourish; and abundance of peace so long as the moon endureth.

(PSALM 72:7)

TWO YEARS LATER

The months and years had slowly passed as Elisheba tried to maintain the order of her former life. But each day it grew harder. She missed those who'd left with Nephi. Her mother and sister in particular. And Tiras, who'd been just like a son to her. Her young sons, Dedan and Noah, played with their cousins and brought home raucous tales, many of which Elisheba immediately discredited. She told her sons over and over that they needed to listen to the Lord's guidance, yet never tell the others about her teachings. But in her heart, she dreaded the day that Raamah found out that she continued to teach their children after the manner of God, as Lehi and Nephi had taught.

As the sun set on a particularly hot day, Elisheba went about her usual evening tasks of cleaning up supper. Finally, as the last bits of daylight fled, she called her boys in from the garden. They tumbled against each other as they entered the cooking room, their youthful faces filled with combined excitement and exhaustion.

"Mama," Dedan shouted, his brown eyes alive.

"Hmmm?" Elisheba asked, not too concerned about this new

excitement. Her sons often shouted with glee even when discovering nothing more than a colorful lizard.

"Tomorrow we will go on the hunt with Father," Dedan said, jumping in the air, then landing sideways in a crouch. "We'll find the wild beasts and slay them!"

Noah laughed, clapping his hands.

Elisheba turned and studied her son. She had never been apart from her children for any length of time, and she wasn't sure she was ready for it. "You are quite young to join the men, Dedan. A boy of eight years would only slow the journey."

"But Father said they are in no hurry, and they want to teach Helek and me all about it."

Nodding, Elisheba said, "I'm sure they do. I'll speak with your father when he comes in." Helek was Lemuel's son, and that added another worry—Dedan spending so much time in Lemuel's presence. She shooed her children to bed and lit an oil lamp against the lengthening shadows. She didn't know how long it would be before Raamah came inside. Often, he ate with his brothers and spent long hours visiting and drinking fermented agave juice. In the beginning, Elisheba had been upset at the time he spent away from her. But when he was around, his temper was so foul that Elisheba decided she was better off with his long absences and the peaceful quiet they brought.

Soon after the boys fell asleep, she heard Raamah's footfall. He was unusually early. He stooped to enter the doorway, his large frame filling the space for an instant.

Elisheba rose, holding a bit of embroidery in her hands. She tilted her head and looked at her husband. He didn't meet her eyes and tried to pass without a word until Elisheba reached out and touched his arm.

He grunted, and she suddenly felt reluctant to broach the topic. But it was too late. Raamah's eyes bore into hers. She already had his full attention. "You are taking Dedan hunting tomorrow?"

He nodded, a dark brow arched. "Did you need him for something else?"

"No," Elisheba began. "But he's only eight."

"Lemuel is taking Helek." He pushed past her, mumbling something about being tired.

Elisheba watched him go, then sat on a stool. But instead of resuming the embroidery, she felt her eyes sting. *Not now,* she chided herself. *The boy will be fine with his father. And it's no secret how an animal is killed.*

She should have asked if Laman was going, too. When Raamah was gone from home, she never felt comfortable being alone in the house. She had little contact with the other men and felt ostracized from the women. Although their children played together, she felt very little kinship with her sisters-in-law.

An hour passed, and Elisheba hoped Raamah had long been asleep. She crept into the bedchamber, careful not to disturb his slumber. She stared above her into the darkness, waiting for sleep to come. She tried to forget the pagan dancing that took place nearly every night, the unnecessary animal sacrifices, the idleness of both men and women, the children arguing freely with no supervision . . .

Elisheba opened her eyes in the pale light, realizing she must have dozed after all. The house was still quiet in the early morning, and Raamah's breathing was steady and deep next to her. She turned her head toward him.

Seeing his arm slung across his chest, she let out a gasp. His arm was nearly black. She wondered if he had cleaned out the ashes from the main fire the night before. Then her eyes traveled to his neck. It too was dark.

Elisheba brought a hand to her mouth, stifling a cry. Raamah's face, eyelids, ears . . . were all dark.

Had he been in a fight? Thrown into the dirt and ash? How could she not have noticed when he'd entered the house?

She reached out and touched his arm, rubbing it gently. No dirt or bit of ash came away on her hand. Her tanned skin looked pale in comparison.

Elisheba fell back on her pillow, questions boiling in her mind. *Perhaps he has an illness of some sort.* She stole another look at him, but saw that he slept peacefully as ever. Then she bolted upright. *My children.* She moved quietly out of the bedchamber, then entered the adjacent room and spied on them. Their heads were nearly touching as they slept curled up on their mats. Dedan's arm extended from his cover, and his round face held a dreamy look. His skin was still fair, and Noah's too. She sighed with relief and crept out of the room.

Elisheba moved toward her bedchamber again and hesitated at the entrance. Raamah's even breathing filled the small room, nothing but peaceful sleep upon his darkened brow. She decided that there must be a simple explanation for the change in color, and she turned away to begin preparations for the morning meal.

She went to the cooking room and lit dry tinder beneath the metal pot. Soon tiny flames gained courage and began to heat the morning air. Elisheba straightened and retrieved her mantle from a peg on the wall and tied it over her hair. The other women no longer covered their heads, and sometimes her sons would ask why she still did. She would promptly tell them it was because she wanted to show the Lord respect. But that didn't sit well with her sisters-in-law.

Elisheba left the house and walked through the courtyard to her cherished garden. She had spent hours each day laboring over the produce growing there—breadfruit, sweet potatoes, and jicama. She bent to dig up the sweet potatoes when she heard a cry coming through the trees from the direction of Laman's and Anah's home.

Immediately, Elisheba dropped the sweet potatoes and hurried along the trail toward the sound. Anah was carrying her sixth child, but was not expected to deliver for two more moons. Fear entered Elisheba's heart as she thought about the devastating consequences that an early birth might bring. The unborn babe would have little chance of survival.

Skirting the final clump of trees, Elisheba came to a full stop. Ahead of her, Anah stood in the outer courtyard of her home, tearing at her clothing.

Bees, Elisheba initially thought. Then, with horror, she saw the cause of Anah's anxiety. The woman was the same dark color as Raamah.

"Anah!" Elisheba rushed toward her and grabbed her arms. "Are you hurt?"

Anah stopped, her eyes wide as she looked at Elisheba. "No!" she screamed. "Look at me!" She scratched at her arms, then crouched to the ground and rubbed dirt on her hands, trying to cleanse the dark. Her clothing hung in shreds across her shoulders.

"How did this happen?" Elisheba adjusted Anah's tunic so that she was covered modestly. She felt her pulse increase its pace. "Raamah is the same color."

"Raamah?" Anah stopped her movements for a moment to stare at her. "I want to see him."

"Wait, have you checked your children, or Laman?"

"Laman didn't come home last night," Anah said, a hardened look coming into her eyes. "What about your children?"

"They remain untouched. Maybe it was something in the meal last night?" Elisheba suggested, hope in her tone.

Anah bit her lip, her eyes watering. "I must check my little ones . . ."

Just then, Anah's children stumbled through the doorway—obviously awakened by their mother's screeching. Elisheba covered her mouth in astonishment. They, too, were as dark as the earth.

Anah flew toward them, pulling at their clothing, inspecting their hair, their ears, and mouths. "Oh, my dears, what has become of us?" she moaned.

"What is this illness?" Elisheba finally managed to say as she watched Anah's frenzy. "Did you eat something poisonous?"

Shem bent over and picked up a rock. He ran the stone along his arm, trying to rub the color off. He sneered with anger and met Elisheba's gaze. "Why is *your* skin unchanged?" He looked at her with undeniable spite, as if it were her fault.

Self-consciously, Elisheba pulled her mantle tighter about her head and tried to speak calmly. "Were you all together last night? Something must have caused the change. I was home with my children."

Shem shifted his gaze and looked at his mother. "What about Father?" he shouted.

"I don't know, he didn't come home last night," Anah said, her voice flustered. "Go find him. He'll know what to do." She watched Shem hurry away, then turned to her other children.

Elisheba looked at Anah, feeling a wrenching in her heart for her sister-in-law's plight. "I am sure we can find some herbs to remedy the situation." She thought back to some concoctions she'd learned in slavery while living in Mudhail—something that would lighten the skin or remove dark stains, although she hoped that it wouldn't come down to that. "It may wear off in a day or so," she suggested hopefully.

A flash of doubt crossed Anah's face. "I must watch for Laman," she said, wringing her hands. She looked at her children and ordered them inside. "Stay there until your father returns. I don't want the sun making it more permanent."

Forgotten, Elisheba slipped away, back into the grove of trees, along the path to her home. Raamah might be awake by now, and hungry.

Once she reached home, she scooped up the abandoned sweet potatoes and entered the house. Everything was still quiet, but her heart felt heavy as she worked alone. Finally, she couldn't put it off any longer and went into her bedchamber to wake Raamah.

When he opened his eyes, he didn't look too pleased to be disturbed.

Elisheba began slowly, "Raamah, your skin is stained dark. Is it from something you did last night?"

Raamah rose up on an elbow and examined his forearms. "I did nothing last night except come home early and sleep." He moved to his feet, inspecting his torso and legs. "How did this happen?"

"Anah and her children have the same dark stain all over their bodies." She eyed him closely. "Did you eat something strange in her household?"

He met her gaze, confusion in his eyes. "No. I did not eat with Anah or Laman, or any of them."

Elisheba was about to ask him what he did eat, when he turned, doing a cursory check behind him. "I don't understand it." Then he lifted his eyes to look at her. "You are not changed. What about the boys?"

"They are unchanged. But they played close to home yesterday. Perhaps there was something in a drink or fruit that everyone else ate, but us."

Raamah rubbed his beard, his eyes narrowing in thought. "I ate nothing different than I have on any other day." He rubbed his forearm furtively. "I need some water."

Elisheba followed him to the cooking room and watched as he splashed the stored water onto his face. But there was no change. He looked at her. "Did you see anyone besides Anah and her brood?"

She shook her head, watching her husband pull on his outer garment. The finely woven robe had been dyed dark red—a color that seemed to bleed against his new complexion.

"Will you still take Dedan hunting?"

"Not today." His gaze lingered on her as if he was seeing her in a new light. Then he strode out of the room without another word, not even stopping to sample the morning meal as it lay simmering over the cooking fire.

Elisheba moved to the courtyard and folded her arms about her torso. What was the curious nature of the stain? When the boys awoke, she would take them for a walk to gather herbs that might help remove it.

* * *

The Land of Nephi sprawled from one end of the valley to the other. Nephi surveyed the progress on the temple site from a distance. It was just days away from completion, and there was a pulse of excitement in the air. His gaze landed on the exquisite structure on the hillside. Every rock—quarried, transported, and cut—had his approval. The stones had been carefully laid in the rectangular fashion of the temple at Jerusalem.

The pillars and door of the temple were not of gold as in Jerusalem, but gold had been found in the surrounding hillsides and was used on the altar.

"Over here, Nephi."

He turned to see Sam crouched next to the furnace in the smelting yard. It was situated just outside the line of houses below the temple site. Nephi walked over to inspect his brother's work.

Sam held up the glowing shard of steel, which was equal in size and quality to the sword of Laban.

Nephi bent and looked at the workmanship, then nodded. "It's a very close likeness." He straightened, the weight of worry insistent upon his brow. "We will put this sword replica in the Holy of Holies, and there it will represent our resolve to follow the Lord's commandments."

He watched Sam pound the blade for another moment, then he walked toward the temple to inspect the final touches. He passed the homes and courtyards that had been built the first few months after arriving at the new land. They were all situated to face the temple site, so that each family had an excellent view of the raised building. Their homes were made of lashed sticks and stalks with thatch roofs.

Beyond the nest of houses, fields of maize stretched across the wide valley, interrupted by orchards of young fruit trees. Soon he would ceremoniously carry the replica sword and replica Liahona to the temple and place them beneath the altar in a stone vault. The original artifacts were hidden on the other side of the valley, almost ready to be buried in a secret vault. He and Jacob had spent several weeks working on the project, digging a hole and lining the earthen walls with rock. No matter what contentions arose among his people or the people of Laman, the sacred items would be protected. Only he, Jacob, and Sam knew their true location.

As he stepped onto the stone tiles of the first level, he felt awed once again at all of the blessings from the Lord. They had lived the last two years in peace and raised their children in quiet communion. He and Isaabel now had three children—Aaron, Sarah, and young Lehi.

Everything was peaceful, but at the back of his mind, Nephi couldn't shake a foreboding. At first he attributed it to his mother's declining health, but he knew that that wasn't all.

He ascended the steps and entered the interior of the temple to find Zoram hanging the great tapestries handcrafted by the women.

Jacob and Joseph worked by his side as they fastened the edges of the material with iron nails and pounded them into the cracks of the stone. For a moment, the pounding stopped, and Zoram turned and waved, then he wiped perspiration from his face. The weather had been calm, offering no breeze to pass through the window openings.

"Nephi!" Isaabel's voice reverberated off the stone walls.

The men turned, and Nephi saw his wife's face pale with distress. "It's your mother."

He moved into action and hurried to meet his wife at the entrance of the temple.

"She's calling for you, Nephi," Isaabel said, placing her hand on his arm. "She says that her time has come."

They ran down the steps and hurried to her home, followed by the others. Nephi felt the pounding in his chest increase as he braced himself for what he was about to see. His mother had been a champion since arriving in the Land of Nephi. She never complained but took her ailments as they came.

He stooped beneath the entry of her small home and nearly ran into Tamar, who stood in the cooking room. When he entered his mother's bedchamber, Eve stood from her place at the side of the raised bed. She nodded at Nephi, then left the room.

Sariah's head seemed haloed in gray, her once ebony hair faded to the color of veined rock. She smiled gently at the sight of Nephi. It was not one of joy, but more of relief.

"Mother," Nephi said as he took her hand. He felt her bony fingers through her loose skin, but her hand was warm.

Isaabel settled on the opposite side of the bed and held Sariah's other hand.

Before Nephi could speak, Sariah said, "Son, you have created a beautiful place here for us to live." Her eyes clouded. "But it's time for me to bid farewell."

Isaabel brought a hand to her mouth as Nephi shook his head. "Not yet, Mother. We won't let you leave us. You must live to see the temple dedicated."

Sariah squeezed Nephi with her trembling hand. "I'm afraid that won't be possible. You see, I've already spoken with the Lord, and He agreed that I have waited long enough to be reunited with my beloved husband."

Tears came quickly, stinging Nephi's eyelids. But still he was not swayed. "Father will have to wait a few more hours yet. We will dedicate the temple now." He looked at Isaabel and saw her eyes brimmed with tears. "Isa, ask the others to make preparations quickly. We will dedicate the temple before sundown, with Mother's presence."

She nodded, then rose and quickly left the room.

Nephi gazed at his mother. "It has been many weeks since you've seen the progress on the temple. Father would have been proud."

A thin smile stretched across Sariah's lips. "It was his dying wish, and now it is mine."

Nephi bent over his mother and kissed her papery cheek. He smoothed the stray wisps of hair from her forehead and looked into her earth-colored eyes. He could see the depths of endurance that she'd exhibited over the years, mixed with the triumph of righteousness.

He slid his arms beneath her frail body, gently lifting her and carrying her from the room. Eve still waited in the cooking room. "Bring more rugs," Nephi said.

Sariah's head lolled against his chest as he walked. "We're almost there, Mother." His mother's weight in his arms reminded him of when she had carried him both physically, as a child, and spiritually as a man. She had always been there to listen to him and support him. She knew the struggles he had faced with his brothers and understood the challenge it was for him to assume leadership of the family.

Jacob and Zoram came to help him settle Sariah at the base of the temple stairs. Eve had spread a rug on the ground and placed cushions to go with it. Nephi walked to the raised platform that supported the altar built of unhewn stones. He took his place, standing behind the altar, and waited for the others to arrive. The rest of the family began to trickle onto the temple grounds, from the women and men to their children. Everyone respectfully greeted Sariah, then took his or her place.

Jacob released the sacrificial lamb from a small pen behind the raised platform. He gathered the unblemished animal and delivered it to Nephi, who placed it upon the altar.

"O Lord," Nephi began in prayer. "We dedicate this temple to Thy holy ordinances. We have been blessed to enjoy the freedom of this land and to live in righteousness without persecution."

He quickly slit the animal's throat and drained it into a bowl. Then he sprinkled the blood around the altar. "For Thy mercies, we praise Thee, O Lord."

With the conclusion of the sacrifice, Nephi met his wife's gaze. She sat next to Sariah, supporting her. Sariah's head had slumped against Isaabel's shoulder. He washed his hands in the bowl of water that Sam held ready. Then he hurried down the stairs and knelt at his mother's side. Taking her hand he saw that she was still breathing. But she would not open her eyes. Her voice came in a whisper. "Thank you, Nephi."

Sam stepped out of the gathering crowd, and together they carried her back home. Isaabel and Tamar hurried ahead and prepared the bed for her comfort. Once Sariah was settled, Sam and Nephi returned to the temple.

The family sat in various places, waiting for further instruction. When Nephi raised his arms for attention, everyone grew quiet. "Mother is resting quietly now. The move to the temple proved a strain for her."

Several heads nodded, then Zoram stepped forward. "Nephi, this may not be the opportune time to discuss this, considering your mother's ill health, but . . ." He looked to Rebeka, who nodded her encouragement. "We all would like you to be our official ruler—our king."

Nephi stared at Zoram in surprise, then let his gaze stray to the other family members. Everyone he looked at gave his or her consent. He felt humbled at the request, but deep inside it didn't feel right. Nephi cleared his throat. "I do not wish to be made a king, nor do I desire to rule over you as one."

Zoram lowered his head, his mouth slack. Noticing the disappointment on his face, Nephi continued, "But I will do everything for this community that is in my power. I will dedicate every day to you and to the Lord. We will continue to labor and to be industrious. We will become a strong people, devoting our lives to the Lord." He looked at Sam, Jacob, and Joseph. "No, I cannot be your king, but I pledge to serve you the remainder of my days."

Zoram dipped his head for a moment, then raised his moistened eyes to meet Nephi's gaze. "We are honored."

The other family members murmured their consent and soon the crowd broke up—each resuming his or her daily tasks.

Nephi walked slowly to his mother's house.

Isaabel greeted him at the door. "She sleeps comfortably, and her breathing is strong and steady."

"Very good," Nephi said, his thoughts eased with the report of his mother's comfort.

Isaabel touched his arm. "What is it?"

"The people have asked me to be their king," Nephi said, seeing the astonishment on Isaabel's face. "Yes, I was surprised, too. But I told them I could not be king over them."

Isaabel nodded. "They just want to honor you, and—"

"I know," Nephi said quietly. "But the request honors me enough." He looked away from her, toward the hills that housed the hidden vault.

"Something else troubles you, Nephi," Isaabel said.

"I don't know what is wrong. I just feel different." He let out a breath of air. "I will go walk for a while. Perhaps the Lord will give me the answer." Nephi looked at her with a slight smile. "I'll be home before dark."

He turned from his wife and left his mother's home. He made the trek through the thick evergreen trees along the incline. Less than an hour later, he sat just above the vault. Soon he and Jacob would move the sacred artifacts to their new resting place. His heart felt heavy from something barely tangible, just out of his mind's grasp. For two years they had lived in quiet peace. Was asking for more years of peace too much? Contrary to his hope, he somehow knew that the anger of his brothers hadn't dissipated with the long absence.

Nephi shifted to his knees and bowed his head, his hands clenched in familiar reverence. His heart pled before any words reached his lips. The Lord's answer came immediately as if He had just been waiting for Nephi's preparedness to hear the message—the awful truth.

They have not hearkened unto my words and have been cut off from my presence.

Nephi gripped his hands together tightly, trying to grasp the full meaning of the words. His brothers and their families had lost the spirit of the Lord.

I have caused a cursing to come upon them, yea, even a sore cursing because of their iniquity.

Nephi felt his body literally tremble as his breathing shortened. He immediately thought of Elisheba and her small children. Dedan would be about eight and Noah five years old by now. Had they been cursed, too? The lump in his throat grew.

They hardened their hearts against me like flint and I did cause a skin of darkness to come upon them.

So it had finally happened. The Lord had kept His promise and taken away Laman and Lemuel's blessings, and the blessings of all those who followed them. His brothers had received a curse—a curse that caused them to lose the Spirit. The skin of darkness was a mark of the curse.

I will cause that they shall be loathsome to thy people, unless they repent of their iniquities.

The first shred of hope bloomed in Nephi's chest. If Elisheba followed his counsel and taught her children in righteousness, they would surely avoid the Lord's wrath.

And cursed is the seed of him who mixes with their seed, for they will be cursed even as they are.

Nephi felt pressure on his shoulders as if someone were pushing him toward the ground. Then the Lord showed him that because the people of Laman became an idle people, full of mischief, they had been cursed.

They will be a scourge to your seed in order to cause them to remember me. And if they do not remember me and hearken unto my words, they will destroy them.

As the Lord's voice repeated itself in Nephi's mind, he recalled another part of a vision he'd seen years before in the wilderness—his seed and Laman's seed battling against each other. The awfulness of the prospect settled in his stomach, and he thought about the far-reaching consequences of Laman's hatred.

After spending several more minutes on his knees, Nephi finally rose, feeling weak and exhausted. But his conscience was clear; he now knew why the sense of foreboding had followed him for so many days. Changes had occurred in Laman's settlement, and if Nephi's people wanted to be safe, they would have to work harder. They would have to be prepared. Nephi realized that in the near future his people would begin to prepare for their defense in case Laman's people tried to attack.

CHAPTER 11

Blessed is the man whom thou choosest . . . that he may dwell in thy courts: we shall be satisfied with the goodness of thy house, even of thy holy temple.

(Psalm 65:4)

Looking for herbs to help the others back at the settlement, Elisheba strode along the familiar trail with her two sons. It was the same trail that Nephi and the others had taken over two years ago— to flee to a better life—a life consecrated to the Lord and to fulfilling their righteous purposes. She was grateful that the emptiness she had felt had dimmed over the past months. Nothing had necessarily improved, but she'd accepted her situation. Her sons were the most important thing to her, and she spent her days focusing on nurturing them.

As they walked, Elisheba kept a sharp eye out for new herbs that might help lighten skin, all the while carrying on a conversation with her boys.

"Hurry, Mother," Noah yelled, as he galloped on the path ahead of her.

Surprisingly, Elisheba felt tired already. And she knew it wasn't because of little sleep the night before. She'd often experienced sleepless nights—it was something she was accustomed to now. Smiling, she paused on the trail. "Why don't both of you race to the large tree up there, and I'll catch up with you in a moment?"

Dedan and Noah whooped as they sprinted for the same target.

Elisheba used the few moments to catch her breath and wipe the perspiration from her forehead. A sudden dizziness passed over her, and she felt a sharp nausea clench her stomach. Surprised, she rushed to the side of the trail and had barely knelt on the ground when she became sick.

When it was finished, she drew back, shaking. She looked at her skin and wondered if it would turn dark also. Maybe this was part of the disease, and this was how it started. But Raamah hadn't been sick.

Then the realization hit her. Something she or any other woman could have foretold. She was with child. With her other two boys, she hadn't become sick until the third moon. She placed a hand on her belly and noted the soft roundness she had been too busy to notice before. Judging from the sudden onset of nausea, she was sure she was at least in the third moon. She wasn't a normal woman like her sisters-in-law, who would immediately know by the second month.

Turning her head, she looked at her playful boys far up the path, shoving each other and arguing who had run the fastest. She loved them so much, but they had been born in a time when she'd had tremendous family support. Now, she spent most of her days isolated. And now, she would bear another child amidst animosity.

Elisheba rose from her knees and retied her fallen mantle. She took a sip of water from the sheepskin slung over her shoulder. When she reached her boys, she said, "Dedan, Noah, it's time to return."

They grumbled, but hurried along the path, talking about seeing their cousins. The lump in Elisheba's throat hardened as she thought about what her boys would say about the darker skin. She wondered if it had touched anyone else besides Anah's family. At least her basket was full of clipped herbs, and she could take them to Anah immediately and see if anything helped.

Suddenly her eyes filled with emotion as a clear image of Sariah came to her mind. Elisheba had tried to tuck away her mother's memory for many months. It was just too painful to remember what a sweet and gentle soul she had been. And how much she'd endured. *As I am enduring.* Elisheba almost stopped walking as the thought hit her. It was painful but oddly comforting to think she had something in common with her mother—not only the love for herbal remedies, but the challenge of living a dedicated life among those who mocked the Lord. How did her mother endure so many years? "Oh, Mother," Elisheba whispered as her children explored the trail in front of her. "You were a supreme example. I have nothing to complain about."

The nausea hit again, and she hurried into the brush, hoping not to alarm her boys. When she exited, they were excitedly studying an iguana perched on a tree branch and hadn't noticed her momentary absence. She gripped the basket of herbs to steady her trembling hands and urged her boys away from the reptile.

When Elisheba and her sons finally arrived home, she wished she'd tarried a little longer in the serenity of the trees. The entire clan had gathered at her home and waited for her in the courtyard. The sea of faces that met hers were dark—just like Raamah and Anah. Everyone but her and her two sons had stained skin.

Raamah walked forward to meet her. Dedan and Noah immediately latched onto their father, but when it became clear that he was not in good humor, the boys scuttled away. Elisheba met her husband's gaze, holding out the basket as if it would somehow make things right.

"Where have you been?" he hissed.

"I took the boys to gather some herbs . . . I hoped to concoct something to help with the skin color—" Her eyes flitted to the rest of the family members. Most of them stared at her as if she were the strange one.

"What's wrong? Why is everyone here?"

"They are waiting for you," Raamah said. His eyes had changed from the hardness of the past several months to a genuine fear.

Elisheba's pulse throbbed with anticipation. "For me? For the herbs?"

"No," Raamah said gruffly. "They want to see your light skin for themselves. They wonder why yours hasn't changed." He glanced at Dedan and Noah, who stood a ways off, examining their cousins' new features.

Through the gathered people, Laman pushed his way forward. Elisheba tried not to stare at the darkened skin of his same features. His face was grim and his eyes seemed to bore into her.

"You have conveniently returned," Laman said. His gaze trailed her body, from the top of her head to her toes. "I see you've not been touched with the malady."

Elisheba could feel Raamah tense beside her. She was glad when her husband stayed near and faced her older brother. "No," she nearly whispered. She lifted the basket of herbs. "I've collected these in hopes of making something that will take away the stain."

"Stain?" Laman chortled. His wife and children pressed forward and joined his side. "Did you hear that? She thinks it's a stain— something to be rubbed off with a little poultice or salve. Something she can *fix*." He looked at Raamah, hesitated slightly, then sneered. "I think your wife has been trying to *fix* us for too long."

"What do you mean?" Raamah said.

But even in her husband's question, Elisheba sensed suspicion. The two of them had hardly had a decent conversation in such a long time that she wondered how steadfast Raamah would be. She glanced in the direction of her children, fighting emotion with the realization that they heard every word spoken by their uncle.

Her oldest brother folded his darkened arms across his broad chest. They practically rested on his large belly. "I think you have cursed us, Elisheba." His face worked in fury. "You have preached to our children about Nephi's lies long enough, and now you have devised some plan straight from the devil you serve to bring a plague upon us."

Raamah stepped forward. "Wait a minute. Are you accusing my wife of sorcery?"

"Who else attends every birth and makes herbal remedies that seem to work only by her hand? Who else continues to talk about things beyond this world that concern none of us?" Laman looked from Raamah to Elisheba. "She separated herself from our tribe as soon as Nephi left. She mourned him and neglected her duties to family. She has placed herself above us."

Raamah's expression faltered and Elisheba wanted to run away, screaming. The now-familiar nausea welled up inside her. But that didn't stop her from responding. "I have only tried to serve the women in their time of need. No ill attempt was made. All the herbal practices I used I learned in Mudhail."

"Yes, Mudhail." Laman's eyes narrowed. "A place where we were slaves for five years—because of you!" He pointed at her. "I'm tired of suffering for your mistakes or your misdeeds—call them what you may."

Elisheba felt as if he'd slapped her. She couldn't believe he still blamed her for their period of slavery. She wanted to scream that it wasn't true, but her voice caught.

Laman turned to the rest of the family. "I say Elisheba brought this curse upon us, and she is not welcome among us anymore."

"Laman—" Elisheba began.

He turned to her, his eyes blazing.

She felt as if her throat and eyes were on fire. The nausea combined with the horror of her own brother's accusations collided into one burst of devastation. The next thing she knew the faces around her blurred, and the ground beneath her moved.

* * *

Night blended with day, and day with night, until Elisheba wasn't sure how much time had passed. All she knew was that she lived in a dream—or more accurately, a nightmare. One thing she was certain of was that she was covered in her own blanket, although the walls surrounding her were not familiar.

She heard rather than felt her husband's presence. The sound of arguing floated in and out of her mind, fierce and seemingly ceaseless. Voices cut into her torrid thoughts and vague memories of what happened after Laman's confrontation. At one point she'd even heard her children's high-pitched voices.

Elisheba tried to move her mouth, but her lips wouldn't budge, and her tongue felt swollen and heavy. She couldn't tell if she was hot or cold, or if she was hungry or tired. She just existed, but she knew Raamah had cared for her.

With great effort, she opened her eyelids, only to see mottled shapes and shadows—nothing distinguishable. Closing her eyes again, Elisheba worried who had prepared meals for her family, who had put her sons to sleep amid all this chaos.

The shouting began again. Desperately, she wished to cover her ears and block it out, but her arms wouldn't obey. Again, Elisheba opened her eyes, fighting to focus on something. A crashing sound echoed nearby, and she flinched. Suddenly the room jumped into focus, and she saw that she was not at home at all. The walls were made of awkwardly spaced timbers. Sunlight peeked through the slats, and the roof slanted overhead, heavy and oppressive. It was one of the hunting shelters Raamah often used. *But why have I been carried so far from the settlement,* she wondered.

Elisheba lifted her head, seeing a stool and a low table near her feet. There was no fire pit or rug in the small room, only a dirt floor and the mat she lay on. She rose to her elbows, finding that the small effort left her exhausted. *What is wrong with me?*

The shouting continued, and slowly Elisheba was able to concentrate enough to make out voices. One of them was definitely her husband, and the other could have been Laman or Lemuel.

Then she smelled smoke.

Propelled by fear, Elisheba stood unsteadily, gripping the sides of the timber walls for support. Her head throbbed, and every muscle in her body ached. Instinctively she looked at her arms to check the color. Nothing had changed. She limped to the entrance and leaned against the doorway for a moment. She was already out of breath. Pushing through the sheepskin hanging, she stepped into brilliant sunlight.

The brightness momentarily blinded her as she searched for the source of the shouting. The smell of smoke grew stronger, but she couldn't see or hear any fire. As her eyes adjusted to the glare, she saw two men standing at the edge of the clearing. They hadn't seen her.

Laman waved his hands frantically, and Raamah crossed his arms in defiance. Then Laman's gaze found her, and he pointed in her direction. Raamah turned to look at Elisheba, and she could tell from his expression he wasn't pleased. *Where are the children?* She wanted to shout, but nothing came. She gingerly took a step away from the lean-to and started to walk toward the men. Laman slunk away before she reached Raamah.

His expression filled with disapproval. "You need to stay inside," he said, turning her around and propelling her back to the hut. His voice softened. "Are you feeling better?"

Elisheba stopped, refusing to take another step. She faced Raamah, finding it hard to stare into his face without remembering Laman's harsh words. "Why did you bring me here? And where are Dedan and Noah?"

"They are with Puah," Raamah said, bitterness crossing his face. "The family decided to evict you from the settlement."

"Why?" Elisheba said. Her throat burned, and she felt as if her heart had been twisted right out of her chest. "I have done *nothing.*" She noticed the vacillation in her husband's expression.

"They continue to accuse you of sorcery and blame you for the darkened skin." Raamah let out a heavy sigh. "I've run out of explanations. Look at me, then look at you. What is the meaning of this? Everyone in the entire family has been touched but you and the boys."

"Why do they accept the boys and not me, then?" Elisheba shot back.

"They are children, innocent of wrongdoing," Raamah said softly. "The family sees them as *my* sons."

Elisheba brought her hand to her throat. "And do you agree with them? Am I no longer their mother?"

Raamah's eyes were hooded, his face twisted in confusion. "Regardless of what *I* think, if you return for the boys, your brothers will take your life."

Elisheba's knees crumpled, and she reached out for her husband— a man who seemed to have lost faith in her. Raamah helped her back to the hut and made her lie down on the mat again. "Do you smell the smoke?" he asked.

She nodded, watching his every movement as he paced the small space.

"They're burning down our home. They want to rid the settlement of all traces of your influence." Raamah paused and straightened to his full height, dominating the room.

Elisheba covered her mouth in horror. Her home? They were burning her home?

"Because of your insistence to follow the ways of Nephi and to teach our children the same, you have lost your children, and now you have lost your home," Raamah said.

Elisheba felt numb as he delivered the cold words. She tried to grapple with the reality of her home being burned by her own brothers. She was having another bad dream, wasn't she? "Can't you explain to them, Raamah? I never meant to harm anyone. I only followed my heart." For an instant, she thought she detected a brief understanding in her husband's face, but it passed quickly.

"I can do nothing but hide you, Elisheba. I can only preserve your life—as I promised your father long ago that I would." He shifted from one foot to another. "As far as what you've taught the children, I can't very well blame you for that. I should have put a stop to it before it became apparent to the others. Did you really think you could keep it a secret?"

Elisheba shook her head as tears spilled onto her cheeks. "You see, my husband, I've been given two choices. Do I follow the Lord and be saved for eternity? Or do I follow Laman and be saved only for a lifetime?"

Husband and wife stared at each other for a long moment.

Then Raamah finally spoke, his voice guttural. "That may have been your choice in the beginning, but now you only have one choice left. Laman has threatened to kill you if he sees your face again." He knelt beside her and took her hand. "I will honor my agreement and move you to a safe location. After that, you will be responsible for what happens next."

"I need my boys, Raamah." She reached out a hand to touch him. "All of them."

Pulling away from her touch, he said, "I cannot give you that, or we'll all be killed." He held her gaze. "You must choose. Give up your happiness and let the children live. Or take the boys and risk all our lives."

Smoke wafted around them, and Elisheba's eyes watered as her emotions surfaced. Brief images of her beautiful yet simple home passed through her mind—but that paled in comparison to the image of a life without her family.

"What about us?" Elisheba whispered.

Raamah stiffened. "There has been no *us* for a long time."

Elisheba hung her head, hating his words, but knowing they were true. Their hearts had gone different directions. He had turned indolent and preferred spending time with their brothers instead of with her. He did not defend the teachings of the Lord, but instead followed along with the other men. He had lost the tender influence of the Spirit. And she . . . she had turned inward and kept her deepest thoughts buried inside her soul.

She wondered where it had all gone so wrong. Surely they couldn't really believe she had the power to cause their skin to darken. That power was only in the hands of God.

Elisheba snapped her head up. She knew the answer. It wasn't her fault—not at all. "My brothers have cursed themselves for their own wickedness. They have separated themselves from God. *That* is the curse, not the skin. The darkened skin is only a mark of what they have done."

Raamah's face was steeped in anger. "You are impossible even to speak with. This moment may be the last I lay eyes upon you—my wife of many years—yet you insist on rebuking us. I have never done anything but protect you, yet you carry on Nephi's tradition of preaching."

"We can leave, Raamah. All of us," Elisheba rushed on, pleading. "I know that Nephi would welcome you and our children. He wouldn't have to rule over you if you are living righteously—he doesn't share the same contention with you as he does his brothers. And as the Spirit is restored in your life, the Lord will lift the mark."

"So this has been your plan all along?" he said, vehemence in his eyes.

"No," Elisheba said. "Like you said, I made a choice. I'd rather come under the judgment of the Lord and be found clean than conform to Laman's evil ways."

"By calling Laman evil, you call me evil."

Elisheba avoided his piercing gaze, hoping he wouldn't discern her thoughts. But it was too late. He had seen her meaning behind her eyes. She heard his footsteps take him from the hut and across the clearing. He was gone.

Pulling her knees to her chest, she bowed her head and wrapped her arms about her torso, squeezing as hard as she could. She wanted to chase him and scream at him to repent, to quit his foolish behaviors and become the husband he'd once been. Not only had her husband left her, her children were also gone, as was her home. In her pursuit of worshipping the Lord, she'd had everything that she loved stripped from her.

She was so alone. And for the first time in her life, she wondered if following the Lord was worth the heartache. Lowering her head onto her knees, she rocked back and forth as grief consumed her.

Hours passed as Elisheba waited outside the hut in the night air for Raamah to come to her. He had said he would take her to a safe place, but that was before they'd argued. Maybe he'd changed his mind. If he knew her condition, he wouldn't have abandoned her. But she didn't know if she could bring herself to tell him. *At least not yet*. What if Laman tried to take the baby from her, too?

The smoke hung thin in the air, just enough remaining to remind her of all she'd lost. The changing wind did nothing to dispel the acrid scent which permeated every part of her clothing and hair. Strangely enough, the musty smell helped to ease the nausea in her stomach.

Elisheba watched the leaves on the nearby trees shiver in the moonlight. She felt oddly protected by the night's darkness, as if it were a cloak of comfort. How could such a peaceful night be bordered by such hatred? She let out a low breath, trying to remain alert, listening for any sound of Raamah. In the farthest reaches of her mind, she pushed back the images of her two boys—their freshly scrubbed faces, their dimpled hands, their bright eyes and eager questions.

Were they sleeping in their cousins' room on a bed? On a mat? Were they cold or did Puah cover them with a rug? Did they eat all of their supper? Did they look around longingly for their mother? Elisheba bit her lip hard, trying to quell the trembling. What had Puah and the others told her sons about her absence? Would they turn them against her? Did they think she was alive or dead? And where was Raamah? Now that their home was gone, whose home would he share tonight?

A nearby branch shuddered, and Elisheba nearly gasped out loud. A sudden image of Laman's menacing face came to mind, causing her to flee into the opposite grove of trees. What if the person who came for her wasn't Raamah, but Laman?

A figure slowly entered the clearing and walked toward the hut. But the huddled form was much smaller than Raamah or Laman. Heart pounding, Elisheba waited to catch a glimpse of the face in the moonlight. The person entered the hut, then exited a moment later.

The colorful scarf about the person's shoulders was familiar.

"Anah?" Elisheba whispered.

Her sister-in-law turned and scanned the trees.

Elisheba stepped forward. "What are you doing here?"

Anah brought a finger to her lips and scurried toward her. "I thought you might still be here," she whispered, appraising her.

"Where else could I go?" Elisheba asked, feeling the tremble in her voice.

Anah shook her head. "I am fortunate to find you, regardless." She looked about her as if she expected someone to discover them at any moment. "I bring a final warning."

Anger seared through Elisheba's breast. She didn't want to hear any more threats. She turned from Anah.

"You must leave now. Laman discovered this place today when he saw you earlier, and now everyone knows where you are hiding." Anah touched her arm. "I can only say a few more things, then I have to leave. Raamah was beaten when Laman found out your husband intended to move you again."

Elisheba gasped and faced Anah. "I must go to him."

"No," Anah said sharply. "That's exactly what they want to happen."

A flash of guilt crossed Anah's eyes, and Elisheba wondered how much remorse her sister-in-law felt for Laman's actions.

"Your sons will be well cared for," Anah continued.

A stab of pain shot through Elisheba's heart as tears fell rapidly. "I cannot bear to leave them behind."

"For all our sakes, you must." Anah lowered her hand. "For your unborn child as well."

Elisheba stared at her. "How did you know?"

Anah patted her own protruding belly. "It's the way of women, I suppose." She gazed at Elisheba for a moment. "This is farewell, sister. You must not return. Take yourself and your child and find a new life."

But Elisheba shook her head. "I will wait nearby, and you can tell me when it's safe to return."

"No," Anah said. "If it's discovered that I have visited you, I will be beaten . . . or worse." She looked behind her, then said, "I have tarried too long." She moved away, her face hidden in the shadows of the night.

"Wait," Elisheba cried, but Anah's figure had melted against the silhouette of trees. After several moments, Elisheba entered the hut, and in the dark, she located the remaining bread brought by her husband. She wrapped it in a cloth and tucked it in her waistband. She picked up the empty sheepskin and slung it over her shoulder. She knew that if Raamah ever did return, he'd see the sheepskin missing and know she'd taken it. It would be her message to him that she'd done his bidding.

Hesitating at the entrance of the hut, she knew leaving was the right choice to preserve her family, even though it meant she might never see them again. But that did not make the loss any easier to bear.

Elisheba took a deep breath and crossed the clearing. Gazing at the moonlit sky, she determined the direction she had to take. She knew that this hunting lean-to was just a short walk from her father's burial site. Going there would bring her a little closer to the settlement, but it would also provide a place where she could think about what to do next.

Plunging forward, with only the moon and the stars as her guidance, she moved as quickly as her weakness would allow. Gratefully, the nausea had faded for now, but she felt the lack of energy from little food or water over the past couple of days. She listened attentively for the sound of a nearby stream where she could fill the sheepskin.

The smell of smoke had diminished with the night, but it seemed to hang thinly in the air, reminding her of her eviction. Still her chest constricted, and she struggled to even her breathing as sorrow engulfed her. She wondered what Raamah was doing. Was he thinking about her? Did he regret leaving after their argument? Were any of the other women caring for him? Would his anger against her be solidified even further? Maybe he would not return to the hut after all, unless a chance hunting trip took him there.

She continued to walk into the night, her heart heavy with grief, until she reached the clearing that held her father's grave. The stillness of the area was like a peaceful balm. Even the pungent smell in the air had faded, although she was actually closer to the settlement than she had been at the hut.

Elisheba hesitated before crossing to Lehi's resting place. Foliage had nearly covered the tomb's entrance. She sat near the cave's opening and whispered, "Oh, Father, you understand my angst. I have only followed your teachings and tried to raise my children unto the Lord."

A tear slipped down her cheek as the magnitude of the recent events weighed upon her shoulders. She did not want to leave her children. With or without Raamah, her place was as a mother. She hung her head in sorrow. Raamah had been beaten for hiding her—and yet that diversion may have been what had prevented Laman from coming and taking her in the middle of the night.

She raised her head and looked at the numerous stars in the sky. Her husband may very well have saved her life. Should she now steal into the settlement to snatch her boys, ignoring his warning that this decision might result in all of their deaths? She shivered as the wind came through the clearing, stirring the trees around her. She wondered, even if she found a safe way to retrieve her boys, if she would have the ability to provide her children with the food and clothing they needed.

She knew the answer already. Moving to her knees, Elisheba bowed her head and began to pray for strength for what she was about to do.

CHAPTER 12

I will not justify the wicked.
(Exodus 23:7)

The months passed quickly as the Land of Nephi continued to thrive. Everything seemed peaceful and ideal, but Jacob felt uneasy nonetheless. Since the temple dedication, he had noticed something different about Nephi. Worry, concern, fear? All seemed to be evident on his brother's face. Everyone worried about Sariah's health, but Jacob sensed that it wasn't Nephi's only concern. Was it because his brother regretted turning down the kingship? No, that couldn't be it.

Jacob straightened from his sitting position just inside the temple. Each morning he studied the brass plates until Nephi joined him. Suddenly a strain of conversation reached his ears, and he peered through the partially open doors. Eve passed by with her sisters, each of them carrying jugs of water. He glanced down at the plates quickly, but soon his gaze strayed again. It seemed that one day she was a quiet thin girl, and the next . . .

Jacob shook his head. Thinking about Eve's womanhood would do neither of them any good. It would only fuel the whispers that had already begun. And he hated being the center of attention in any way. He was happy to spend as much time as possible with Nephi in study and to do his share of the labor. Things like women and marriage intimidated him. Growing up, he'd heard several lusty arguments between married couples, and he couldn't imagine how to even begin consoling an upset woman.

But shaking his head didn't remove the image of Eve from his mind. Then he heard another set of footfalls. Jacob glanced up and saw Sam approach. He waved in greeting, and Sam smiled. "I passed Nephi a short time ago and he wants you to meet him at the vault."

Jacob rose and stretched.

"I'll store the plates for you," Sam said.

Jacob nodded and set off toward the vault. The sword of Laban and the Liahona were already at the location. The only thing left to carry to the hillside was the brass plates. Reluctant to hide away the plates, Jacob considered every delay in finishing the vault a hidden blessing.

He had nearly cleared thoughts of Eve from his mind as he left. Nearly. Perhaps it was the efficiency that Eve had inherited from her mother that caused him anguish. Both women were busy from dawn until dusk—and in recent weeks, Eve had been sent to Sariah's side more and more often as her illness progressed. Perhaps that was why she appeared in his thoughts more—he had seen her more than usual.

That was the explanation. Jacob began to whistle. Now that he understood, he would have no more qualms about Eve encroaching upon his thoughts, interrupting his study on a regular basis.

A half hour later, he neared the site of the vault. Just as he started the climb, he heard a sound coming through the trees. He hid himself . . . just in case. Even as he did so, he questioned what he should be hiding from. There was no real danger nearby, except for wild beasts. But his dagger had proved a hardy companion for those occasions.

The figure crashed through the underbrush, undoubtedly in a hurry.

"Nephi," Jacob said, stepping from his concealed spot.

His brother turned, surprise on his perspiring face.

"Is something wrong?" Jacob asked, noticing the twigs and leaves latched onto Nephi's clothing. But even as he asked, something in his brother's eyes seemed familiar. It was as if Nephi's skin literally glowed. It was somehow brighter, fairer.

Catching his breath for an instant, Nephi nodded. "The Lord has spoken."

Jacob was taken aback by his brother's throaty voice. It had changed for the moment, drawing up deeper tones. "What . . ." He tried to recover from his astonishment. "What did He say?"

Nephi took a step closer to Jacob and motioned for him to sit on a nearby rock. Then Nephi joined him, still struggling for a steady breath. He wiped the beaded perspiration from his forehead, then turned to look at Jacob.

"It was some months ago that the Lord revealed it to me. But now, I am allowed to share with you." His gaze was steady. "The Lord has fulfilled His word."

Jacob automatically nodded. The Lord always did. That fact had been proven time and time again—often to the desolation of those who didn't follow Him.

"They have been cut off from His presence." Nephi let his hand drop to Jacob's arm.

A shiver spread from Nephi's touch, making its way to Jacob's neck where his hairs stood on end. *They* referred to those family members who remained with Laman. Jacob couldn't imagine what life would be like being cut off from the Lord—not receiving blessings, and not enjoying comfort in times of tribulation. "So they did not repent of their ways—even after we left so they could rule themselves?"

The sadness in Nephi's eyes was plain, and Jacob felt the same grief penetrate his heart. "What about all our nieces and nephews? And . . . Elisheba?"

Nephi brought his palms to his eyes. "I . . . don't know." His voice was weighed with sorrow. "If only Raamah had let her come with us."

"But she couldn't leave her children," Jacob said softly.

Nephi raised his head, tears sparkling against his lashes. "You're right. If only Raamah had come." He placed his hand on Jacob's shoulder and squeezed. "I only hope that she kept her promise to rear her children unto the Lord."

Letting out a jagged breath, Jacob nodded. He couldn't imagine Elisheba doing anything but that, no matter how brutal her circumstances.

Nephi's hand slipped from Jacob's shoulder, and the dark brooding returned.

"What else did the Lord say?" Jacob asked. A long moment passed, and Jacob was about to repeat the question when Nephi began to speak in a low voice.

"The Lord has put a mark upon them."

Jacob stared at Nephi, his heart pounding. He almost couldn't believe what he heard, but in his heart the Spirit confirmed the truth of Nephi's words.

"The Lord caused a skin of darkness to come upon them, so that their seed will be loathsome to our people," Nephi said. "The people of Laman have caused this curse to come upon themselves through their idleness and iniquity."

It took a few moments for Jacob to grasp the impact of what Nephi had said. He shook his head as he thought about the consequences that the people of Laman had undergone—were still undergoing.

Nephi's voice fell to a near whisper. "The Lord said that Laman's seed will be a scourge to our seed, so that we will be continually stirred up in remembrance of Him."

"We have become like the people of Moses. So close to receiving all the blessings imaginable, yet because of our own foolishness, we are cursed," Jacob said.

"*They* are cursed. They have alienated themselves from the Spirit, and we will suffer because of it," Nephi clarified.

Jacob hung his head. He had known this was coming. Nephi's visions had revealed what would happen as their posterity grew. But somehow, Jacob had thought he would be an old man before he witnessed it firsthand.

"There is more."

Jacob lifted his head and gazed at his brother. "What?" How could there be more? Wasn't the curse enough?

"We must prepare for battle—build swords and weapons so that we may defend ourselves against our brothers."

Jacob felt as if the sword of Laban had been thrust into his chest. The battles would not take place when he was an old man, but sooner than he could have ever imagined. He saw the grave concern on his brother's face. So this was what had weighed upon Nephi for so long.

"I must return home now," Nephi said, rising to his feet. "The Lord's commandments are not to be delayed." With a nod and a long, sorrowful look, Nephi was gone.

Jacob stared after him for several moments, then stood, feeling the weight on his shoulders grow. At fifteen, he felt he had already seen and heard enough to last him a lifetime.

* * *

Isaabel sat next to Sariah's bed, feeling hope fade with each staggered breath her mother-in-law took. She wished for Nephi to return, and soon. Even though he could do no more for their dear mother, his presence was a comfort.

It pained Isaabel to see her mother-in-law's health fail. In some ways, Isaabel felt closer to Sariah than she did her own mother. Isaabel and Sariah had both endured similar heartaches and burdens being the wife of a prophet. Sariah was always someone Isaabel could turn to when no one else seemed to understand. Bashemath had remained with Raamah and Heth—her sons—to live out her old age. And although Bashemath had been a good and diligent mother, she had lacked the tenderness and seamless love that Sariah offered.

Sariah had been more than just a mother-in-law to Isaabel, more than a grandmother to her children—she had been a friend. A friend who truly understood the changing emotions and feelings that the wife of a prophet underwent. Together they had commiserated when times had been difficult and rebellions took place in the family. When Isaabel's sisters had spoken negatively of Nephi's role as a prophet, Sariah had understood, for she'd had her own children rebel against Lehi.

Sariah had even fully embraced Bashemath—an oftentimes hardheaded woman with a sharp tongue. But through Sariah's unfailing love, the two matriarchs had become the closest of friends, sharing in their hardships with their sons, bringing grandchildren into the world, and grieving over the loss of their husbands.

Looking at Sariah now, Isaabel wondered what was going through her mind during her last days on earth. Was she looking forward to joining her husband? To living in the glory of the Lord's presence? Or resting from the taxing burdens of earthly life?

Isaabel sighed, feeling emotion well within her. She could truly say that Sariah's example had nourished her testimony of the Lord and had strengthened her conviction of living righteously.

Aside from worry over Sariah, life couldn't be more peaceful than now, Isaabel reflected. It had been painful to separate from the rest of the family, but she knew it was commanded of the Lord. And she took comfort in that. She had watched her three children learn and grow, unencumbered by violence and torture to their father. She'd watched her nephews develop into fine men, and her nieces mature into kind women.

Sariah stirred and licked her dry lips. Isaabel immediately moistened them with a wet cloth. She was surprised to see her mother-in-law open her eyes and stare at her for a steady moment.

"Mother," Isaabel whispered. "Nephi will return soon. He wants to give you another blessing."

Sariah's lips moved, but no words sounded.

Isaabel placed her hand on Sariah's arm. "Just rest. We are taking care of everything. There's nothing you have to be worried about." She sensed, rather than heard, a presence in the doorway. She turned to see Eve standing there. "Come in," Isaabel said, motioning for the girl to sit on a stool.

Eve hesitated, then offered a quick smile. She settled onto the stool and focused on Sariah. "How is she doing?"

"She woke a moment ago, but now she is resting again," Isaabel said.

Eve nodded, her young face drawn into a serious expression.

"What is it?" Isaabel asked.

"I can't stop thinking of my grandmother," Eve whispered as she wrung her hands. "Sariah was always the stronger one."

"Yes, I often wonder how Bashemath fares. You took such excellent care of her." Isaabel was dismayed to see Eve's eyes well up in tears. "Oh, my sweet Eve, she will be taken care of by Anah and Puah."

"I know," Eve said, her shoulders sagging.

"Do you still miss it?"

Eve looked up, a startled expression in her eyes. "Lehi's settlement?"

"It wasn't easy for any of us to leave," Isaabel said.

With a shrug, Eve said, "It's mostly just my grandmother I miss. I worry about her."

Just then, Sariah's eyes flew open. Both women turned to look at her. Sariah brought her hand to her stomach and started gasping.

"Get the apazote seeds!" Isaabel said.

Eve stumbled to her feet and rushed out of the room.

"Oh, Mother," Isaabel said, stroking the woman's face. "Hold on. We'll ease your pain."

Eve dashed into the room. "There's none left."

Without delay, Isaabel followed Eve out of Sariah's bedchamber. She searched the jars of herbs. Nothing would substitute for apazote. She turned toward Eve, seeing her wide eyes filled with worry. "You must find some more. It grows at the head of the north stream." Isaabel handed Eve a basket. "Make all haste."

Eve nodded without a word and disappeared through the cooking room.

With a heavy heart, Isaabel returned to Sariah's side, praying that Eve would return in time and that Nephi would be close behind.

* * *

At thirteen, Eve had matured into young womanhood. Had she lived in Jerusalem, she might already be betrothed. And because of that she was grateful she lived in a country far away from the traditions of her ancestors. Though they still kept many of the Hebrew traditions, with a smaller family group, some had become relaxed. She wondered what match was in store for her future. Her father, Zoram, had come from the tribe of Judah, and her mother from the tribe of Ephraim. Sariah had told Eve often enough that the combination was pleasing to the Lord, but she still did not know what that would mean for her own future.

This thought of Sariah added a renewed urgency to Eve's errand, and she kept close to the trail that led to the far hills. The afternoon was young, but she didn't want to waste any time. As she hurried along, she thought about how she often felt separate from the rest of the family. Moving away from Laman and his people hadn't really made a difference in her interactions with others. Within Nephi's tribe, Eve still felt alone and out of place. She still missed Grandmother Bashemath dearly. On some days, it seemed Eve just existed day to day, moving through her tasks with little joy or interest.

Her mother was usually too busy to talk, and Eve's sisters only wanted to play childish games. The times that her mother did pay attention to Eve, she only called attention to her shyness. "You are pleasant to look upon, Eve," Rebeka said. "You must stop being so shy and interact with Jacob. He will think you don't like him."

Eve dreaded when her mother made comments about Jacob. Eve's old fears surfaced, and she felt self-conscious with every word she spoke to him. She prayed for Bashemath each day and wondered how her health fared. If Sariah's health was so poor now, Eve could only guess whether Bashemath still lived.

The terrain changed pitch, and Eve put more effort into her hiking. She had plenty of endurance, although she knew she was too thin, even though her body had changed with womanhood. But she wished she could remain in a little-girl body forever and not have to face the feelings that boiled inside her—feelings that left her too inept to even speak to someone as kind-hearted as Jacob.

But today she had something else to focus on. With Sariah's urgent condition, Isaabel implored Eve to find and collect the apazote plant. The new errand took her to a hillside that she'd never explored before.

She'd often seen Nephi and Jacob headed in this same direction, so her heart pounded as she thought about running into one of them. But soon her fears were allayed with the silence of the surrounding forest.

Eve pushed through sections of thick brush, following Isaabel's instructions. Eve had been told to find the stream that came from the mountains. As the hillside grew rockier, she was soon out of breath, but she didn't let it slow her down. About halfway up the hillside, Isaabel had instructed her, the apazote grew in abundance on the banks of the small river. Once she collected the small tropical herb, she'd wade through the stream and hurry back.

She found the reddish-stemmed plant growing plentiful, just as Isaabel had said. It didn't take long for Eve to cut the branches of oval leaves and green-spiked flowers with her small dagger. Soon her basket was full, and she'd remove the seeds once she returned. When she finished, she looked longingly at the river; its slow run made it seem almost like a pool instead of a moving entity.

Quickly she unlashed her sandals and slipped into the cool water. Her feet sank into the riverbed, the silt squeezing between her toes. It felt refreshing and soothing on her cracked feet. But she'd already spent one precious moment too long and it was time to return. She didn't want to make Sariah wait longer than necessary.

On her way out of the river, Eve bent over and splashed water on her face, then straightened, feeling rejuvenated. It was then she noticed something reflected in the water next to her. With a gasp of surprise she turned around, coming face to face with a man whose skin was nearly as dark as night.

He was not much taller than she, but his ample muscles gave him the appearance of a warrior with the strength of ten men. Even more surprising was the little clothing he wore. Just a girdle and a loin cloth.

Eve stifled a scream as the man took a step closer to her. Her heart thudded in her ears, making it difficult for her to decide what to do. Was he the only one from his tribe here, or were there more? Would she be carried off and made a slave or concubine?

"What do you want?" Eve finally managed to ask. Her voice came out high-pitched and breathless, and she knew that even if the man couldn't understand her words, he'd understand her fear.

He stiffened, and the expression on his face twisted. Then he grunted and took another step forward.

Eve moved backward, feeling the water rise to her knees. She knew the middle part of the river would be well over her waist, but she was not afraid to swim for the other side. Her pounding heart told her she couldn't outrun him, so what was the use? She wondered what manner of things she might suffer at this man's hands, and she regretted leaving her dagger on the bank with the basket of herb cuttings. She moved her feet along the riverbed, feeling for a rock to use in defense.

"Eve?"

She stared at the man, hardly believing he'd spoken her name. How could he know it?

"It's me. Shem."

Eve brought a hand to her throat. This dark man couldn't be Shem. The last time she'd seen him, he'd been a boy—although older than she. And his skin had been fair like hers.

But something in his eyes and the set of his jawline told her the truth.

"So this is where you live?" Shem waved his hand in the general direction of her settlement.

She nodded, her surprise too great to respond.

He laughed. "You look like a scared monkey standing there shaking. Come out of the water."

Eve hesitated then followed him, noticing the long, curved dagger hanging from his girdle. She glanced away, feeling awkward around his near nakedness. But she was drawn again to the color of his skin. Could this darkened man really be her cousin?

He perched on a nearby boulder and watched her, a mirthless smile splayed across his face.

Eve noticed how the white of his teeth contrasted with the dark of his lips.

"You didn't recognize me, did you?"

Eve shook her head, tearing her gaze away, suddenly feeling embarrassed that he'd caught her curious stare.

"It's the color of my skin," Shem said, almost to himself. "The woman Elisheba has cursed our settlement."

Eve's eyes widened as she looked upon Shem in amazement. "Elisheba? What happened to her?"

"You worry about the woman? Look at me! She did this, and you are concerned for her?"

Eve shrank at the rebuke. She didn't like the instant anger she saw in Shem's eyes. Looking at the ground to avoid his glare, she noticed the water from her tunic dripping steadily about her feet. Her mind raced at how to diffuse her cousin's temper, yet gain information at the same time. She struggled to make sense of what Shem was saying—that Elisheba had darkened their skin. How was that possible? And yet Eve could not shake the feeling that something had changed within her cousin that went much deeper than skin color.

Run. Eve shook the command out of her head and looked up at Shem. "How did this happen?"

"Elisheba is a sorceress."

Eve stared at him, startled. "Impossible." She bit her lip, thinking hard. "Everyone has the same skin as you?"

"Everyone does *now*. At first, Raamah's two boys remained pale like their mother, but now they are quite dark." He reached toward a bush and ripped off a dead branch. With a swift motion, he began to whittle the stick with his dagger. "I'm used to it now, and until I saw you wading in the river, I hadn't remembered how dark it seemed in the beginning."

Eve looked down at her twisting hands.

Shem scoffed, then tossed the stick several paces. "You should have seen the look in your eyes when you first saw me."

Clearing her throat, Eve said, "You startled me. I didn't hear you come into the river."

"No," Shem agreed. "I've learned to move quietly—especially when stalking my prey."

Eve looked away, feeling her trepidation increase. The way he kept staring at her made her want to cover her face and hide.

"I'd forgotten how pleasurable the fair skin is to look upon," Shem said, his voice dripping like honey.

Eve swallowed hard against the panic building in her throat. Why was he so far from home? And were there others with him? She needed to make some excuse to get away.

Shem climbed down from his perch and in two steps he stood before her. He reached out and touched her arm.

Instinctively, Eve flinched and moved away.

Shem responded with another laugh. "You have grown beautiful in your womanhood, Eve. Not that I'm very surprised. You always had a look about you that held promise."

Her neck absolutely burned at his words. "And you have grown bold in your words," she said.

"Not so, dear Eve," Shem said, grinning. "My words have always been bold." He circled her, and Eve felt like she was being hunted.

"You must come and meet Javan. He's camped not too far from here."

Eve's hand moved to her chest. *Javan is here, too?* "I have to hurry back. Sariah is suffering terribly, and the herbs I collected will relieve her pain." She made a move to pick up the basket.

"So the fair one still cares for the aged grandmothers?" Shem said, stopping in front of her, preventing her from reaching the basket. His gaze held hers. "Did I tell you how fair you are to look upon?"

Her throat tightened again until she was sure she'd fall to the ground unconscious. No man had ever looked at her like this, and no man had ever said these things to her. In fact, no man had even seemed to care enough to notice what she looked like.

"Don't worry. I won't marry you right away. You still need a few good months to reach your full bloom. The anticipation will be very pleasurable." He laughed. "And I must consider that some of the other men might want to fight me for your favor."

Eve paled. His words were outright raucous, and she could no longer bear to be in his presence. She'd rather drown in the nearby water than be Shem's wife.

He stretched his arms over his head. "Yes, Javan will surely be full of envy when he sees you."

She couldn't stomach his leering any longer. The basket of herbs forgotten, she turned to flee. But his strong hand landed on her arm, his grip firm.

"Come, little Eve," he said, his breath hot upon her face. "Let me show off my spoils to our cousin."

Eve pulled away and tried to scream, but Shem's other hand clamped over her mouth.

"You don't want to get hurt," he hissed in her ear. He twisted her other arm, forcing her to walk.

Each footstep echoed her fear, bringing her closer to an unknown fate.

CHAPTER 13

The Lord will be the hope of his people, and the strength of the children.

(JOEL 3:16)

The surrounding forest of trees looked vaguely familiar to Eve, but she couldn't be sure. As Shem kept his grip strong on her thin arm, she kept thinking about Sariah and the additional suffering she'd experience because Eve couldn't deliver the apazote seeds.

On several occasions, she tried to wrench from Shem's grasp, but each time he increased his pressure. How much farther he planned to lead her she was afraid to guess. But she wasn't looking forward to reuniting with Javan—or being at the mercy of her two estranged cousins. And as hard as she tried to appear unbothered, she could not get over Shem's darkened countenance—or the reason for his incredible transformation.

The terrain grew steeper, and Eve tried to catch her breath as Shem pulled her along at a swift pace. His dark hand contrasted with her sun-bronzed arm. She couldn't help but stare in fascination at his coloring.

"Why don't you come to the settlement and see everyone?" Eve had asked more than once.

His reply came in the form of laughter. Eve stumbled against a protruding branch. She cried out in pain, but Shem didn't slow. She saw a trickle of blood appear on her ankle. Her feet aching, she was still in disbelief that her cousin hadn't let her strap her sandals back on. She felt hot breaths of anger surge through her chest. What gave Shem the right to treat her this way? Her father would not be pleased.

"Almost there," Shem grunted, his breathing heavy.

Maybe he'll grow tired soon, and I can escape, Eve thought. But could she outrun him?

They arrived at a small clearing where the branches had been cleared from the ground, and a bed of leaves and soft undergrowth was arranged in a circle.

"Where is he?" Shem grumbled. He pulled Eve into the clearing, still holding onto her. "Javan!"

Eve drew her breath in, listening. In the silence, she only heard Shem's breathing next to her. And it was not a comforting feeling. Suddenly the sound of crashing came through the trees—toward them. Shem spun around, keeping Eve in his grip, withdrawing his dagger with the other hand.

Eve tensed, looking for a wild animal that was about to pounce on them. At the same time she calculated how she could use it as an opportunity to escape. The crashing grew louder, and Eve felt a scream tearing at her throat as the dark shape tumbled through the final line of brush.

"Javan!" Shem yelled.

Eve stared, hardly believing her eyes. A young man skidded to a stop, his eyes wide with fear. His skin was as dark as Shem's, but instead of being short and muscular, he was just the opposite—tall and lean.

"What's this?" Javan asked, stepping closer. He carried a large object wrapped in cloth. His fear temporarily stayed, he peered at Eve.

"Our lost cousin—Zoram's daughter," Shem announced.

Javan circled her now, his eyes taking in every feature. Surely he didn't miss the fact that Shem held her captive.

New hope sprang in Eve's breast. She wondered if she might find a sympathizer in Javan, for Shem had not loosened his grip in the least.

But Javan's lips broke into a sneer—wide and calculating. "We've met good fortune at last." He cocked his head to one side. "I was just running from one of your own, dear cousin." He looked back toward the trees he'd just pummeled through. "I believe his name is one you'll know well—Jacob."

"Jacob?" Eve said, relief consuming her. Jacob was nearby. Then she wondered why Jacob was chasing Javan.

"Look," Javan said, thrusting the wrapped object toward Eve. "I found what we came for—and after only a short time of looking for it."

Shem chuckled and lifted one end of the cloth to reveal the hilt of a sword.

Eve gasped. Instinctively she knew it was the sword of Laban. A family heirloom protected by Nephi and Jacob. In fact, she'd heard that they'd buried it far from the settlement.

"How did you find that?" Eve asked, feeling the loathing grow in her stomach as she stared into Javan's greedy eyes.

When he lifted a shoulder, Eve noticed a bleeding gash along his arm. "It wasn't easy . . . but I think I got him as good as he got me."

Had he fought Jacob? Eve felt her stomach churn. She wanted to escape these men more than ever. If they were inclined to injure or kill one of their own cousins, what would they do to her?

"If he was able to chase you, then you didn't get the better of him," Shem said, his grip tightening as if he were transferring his frustration to Eve.

She winced in pain, but held her gaze steady as she looked at Javan. "Let me go, and I will stop him from pursuing you. No sword is worth battling over."

Javan laughed, his eyes alive with excitement as his gaze combed over her. "Taking *you* just adds to the excitement."

"Jacob doesn't know we have Eve," Shem said, his voice doubtful. He then added sarcastically, "He probably values this *sacred* sword over a girl anyhow."

"It will be interesting to find out which he values more," Javan said, peering at Eve.

Her face heated up, and she was sure that Javan noticed her flushed complexion.

"I wonder how long it will be before Zoram notices his lovely daughter is missing?" Glancing at Shem, Javan said, "She'll make a more interesting traveling companion than you have been."

Eve felt her knees weaken as she realized they were talking about taking her with them. *Are they really going to take me to their settlement?* she wondered in disbelief. *Or is this all a game?*

"She's a great prize indeed," Shem said, pulling her close to his side. "*My* prize."

"Perhaps." Javan threw Shem a sharp glare. "But, the last fair woman who lived at our settlement was cast out because of her skin."

"Ah, but our aunt wasn't a prize of war," Shem said.

"War?" Eve interrupted, not liking the tone of their voices. "We are not at war with your people."

"*Our* people?" Javan said. "So you have cast us from your family heritage already?" His eyes darkened with anger. "We'll have to remedy that." He circled her again, touching her hair. "I wonder if our children would be dark or light-skinned."

Shem laughed. "Maybe both." Then his tone grew serious. "But she is not yours to touch, Javan. She is mine." He pointed at the wrapped sword. "You have your prize already."

"Hmmph." A scowl crossed Javan's face. Then he stiffened, listening. "We've used up too much time. I hear someone coming."

Eve tried to scream, but Shem was quick to clamp his hand over her mouth.

Before she could catch her breath, she was propelled between the two men and forced to run. They climbed higher until they neared the summit of a hill. They struggled through thick undergrowth and finally reached a faint trail. Continuing on the trail for some time, Eve watched with dread as the afternoon light faded. Darkness descended, enveloping the three as they rushed along an animal's path that was barely visible.

"Where are we going?" Eve cried out, hoping to be heard by

whoever was pursuing them. But she was swiftly silenced by Shem's strong hand to her mouth.

Javan turned, bearing the sword of Laban in his hand. "If you make one more sound, dear cousin . . ."

She saw desperation in his glance, but as they moved, seemingly hour after hour, she strained to hear any sound of a pursuer. Squeezing her eyes shut for a moment, she mouthed a prayer.

Suddenly she was jerked to a stop. Eve opened her eyes and saw that they had reached the edge of a narrow valley. The massive tropics sloped toward the sea.

It had been two years since she had seen the high seas—but even in the moonlight, the vision was awe-inspiring.

"Which way?" Javan whispered, looking from Shem to Eve.

Eve shuddered against the cool breeze that swept in from the sea.

"We can hide more easily in the forest." Shem's voice was scratchy and tired-sounding.

Eve felt exhausted. "Perhaps we should rest until morning." As loathsome as it seemed to sleep under their watchful eyes, she wanted to give whoever was looking for her the chance to catch up.

"No," Javan said, doubt crossing his face. "We can make better speed if we stay near the sea. Besides, it will be easier terrain."

Shem hesitated for a moment. "All right, but let's trade."

In an instant, Javan latched onto Eve, and Shem shouldered the heavy sword. The lonely call of a quetzal bird sounded, and Eve felt a shiver trail along her back as she imagined just how the forlorn bird felt. Knowing the male quetzal slept at night, she determined they must have disturbed its peace.

But Javan held his hand up for silence. "He's close."

"I don't hear anything," Shem said.

Javan looked down at Eve. "My uncle does a poor imitation of the quetzal."

Shem crouched to the ground and motioned for Javan to follow. The three cousins half crawled, half walked through a tangle of vines. Several paces in, Shem stopped them. Beneath the filtered moonlight, a shape appeared on the trail.

Jacob? Eve wondered. She couldn't be sure, but she hoped it was someone from her family. Maybe Nephi or Sam. The man moved quietly, then paused and looked around him. As the moonlight illuminated his features, Eve saw that it was Jacob. She tried to call to him, but Javan's hand clamped securely over her mouth. She struggled to wrestle out of his grasp, knowing this might be her only chance. Shem's powerful arm slid around her waist and both men held her out of sight, the sword of Laban pressing against her chest.

Jacob disappeared through the foliage that sloped toward the sea, and Eve wasn't sure he'd seen her. Javan kept his hand over her mouth for several more moments.

"If you try to scream again, Jacob will recover only your head," Shem hissed in her ear. "And I'll keep your body for myself."

Javan pulled Eve to her feet and roughly pushed her forward, away from the sea, away from Jacob, and into the unknown forest beyond.

* * *

The night had fallen fast—swallowing the trail that seemed so easy to follow in the daylight. But Jacob didn't slow his pace. His mind reeled at all that had happened in the past few hours. First, he'd learned of Nephi's revelation about how Laman and his people had been cursed. Then no sooner had he reached the site of the buried vault than a young man jumped out at him and wrestled him to the ground—a man with skin like ebony—just as Nephi had said.

When Jacob realized it was Javan, he hoped he'd be able to talk some sense into him. But the dark man he struggled with was not interested in conversation. His nephew was angry that Jacob had interfered with his plans. When Jacob tried to make amends, Javan lunged at him with his dagger. His hostile nephew had no intentions of resuming a friendship.

Javan had uncovered the sword of Laban, and when it was clear that he was about to use that very sword in defense, Jacob backed off. Then, in an instant, Javan was gone. This surprised Jacob. Where was he going? Did Javan really think he could escape that easily? Jacob knew the woods very well and doubted his nephew was familiar with any of the trails.

Jacob was forced to make a hasty decision—follow Javan and try to get the sword back, or return to the settlement and warn his people. Adrenaline mixed with youth sliced through him, and he chose the first. It wasn't difficult to follow Javan's route, and Jacob marked the trees with his dagger as he went, hoping that Nephi or Sam would be able to track him if the worst happened.

When he arrived at a clearing, he saw that it had been recently occupied. He skirted the edges, analyzing the lay of the leaves and undergrowth, trying to gauge how long Javan had spent in this place. How long had he been watching . . . and waiting? Was it Lemuel's cruel design to send his son to the Nephite village and bring back the sword? Then Jacob saw something in the center of the clearing that stopped him cold.

It was a piece of clothing, but not one that could have come from anything Javan wore. He had seen the piece somewhere, very recently. Walking toward it, the scrutiny confirmed his fears. The embroidery edging was unmistakable. It was a pattern that Isaabel had often used—and one that she'd taught Eve.

In Jacob's mind, he could almost hear his mother complimenting Eve on her new head covering. The one dyed a soft blue, edged with intricate embroidery. He had noticed it again at the temple dedication. And here it was. Its abandonment could only mean one thing.

Javan had Eve.

Panic shot through Jacob as he picked up the head covering and held it in his hands, scanning the circle of trees surrounding him. Which direction had he taken her? He squeezed the finely woven cloth as if it held an answer. Jacob walked along the border of the clearing, searching for the imperceptible breakage of branches, signs of trodden undergrowth . . .

It didn't take him long to spot the signs, and after hanging Eve's scarf on a high branch, he started the chase again. Marking the trunks as he passed, he hoped that if anyone tried to learn where he'd gone, they'd assume that Eve had befallen the same fate.

He moved with added urgency now. Not only was a sacred relic and family heirloom missing, but more importantly, so was the daughter of Zoram and Rebeka. And by witnessing Javan's wrath firsthand, Jacob knew the outcome would not be congenial. In addition, he worried about Eve's constitution. She was so quiet and timid that he knew she would not be able to fight back if necessary. If he was a poor match for Javan . . . how would Eve fare?

Jacob found himself praying silently as he scouted Javan and Eve's path. Typically he'd spend hours in prayer to understand the Lord's holy words, but now he sought immediate guidance. Strangely enough, the moon gave just enough light to keep Jacob going. Each time he felt discouraged, he'd see one more miniscule indicator of Javan's trek. He was careful not to make any sound, so he was surprised when he heard voices coming from the thick trees ahead. Then suddenly the voices stopped. Worried that they'd seen him, Jacob immediately veered from the trail and hiked down through the thick foliage. He found a secluded perch where he could watch the movements above. Everything stayed quiet for some time, and Jacob wondered if he'd mistaken the rustling leaves for human voices. Then he saw the pair. No. There were three of them. Javan, Eve, and . . .

Jacob stared in the darkness, trying to make out the third figure. The man was shorter, broader, and his skin the same color as Javan's.

"Shem," Jacob whispered under his breath. His heart sank. Eve stood no chance of escape now.

He continued to watch them pick their way along an outcropping of boulders on the hillside. He winced as Javan pushed Eve roughly. But she kept moving. Every so often, they would stop and listen—surely waiting for any signs of being followed.

So they know I am still pursuing them. He would have to catch them when they let down their guard—when they thought they had lost him.

As Jacob made his way back up the hillside to the group of boulders they'd just abandoned, he began to formulate a plan.

CHAPTER 14

Thou wentest forth for the salvation of thy people, even for salvation with thine anointed.

(HABAKKUK 3:13)

It's been too long, Nephi thought. He looked at the dark horizon, calculating how much time had passed since he'd seen Jacob. At least three hours. Although he wasn't worried about Jacob being in the forest after dark, a new problem had arisen. Eve was gone, too.

At first a few of the women had made comments of the budding romance between the two—and how Jacob and Eve must have taken matters into their own hands. But Nephi quelled their joviality with a stern glance. His recent revelation from the Lord made him more wary than usual.

Nephi looked back from where he stood with Sam and Zoram toward the outline of his mother's home. She was failing fast; he would be surprised if she lived until daybreak. But he didn't know if Jacob . . . or Eve . . . was in danger. What had befallen them? Eve was sent on an errand to help his mother—and Eve would not delay her return while someone she knew was suffering. The only consolation he felt was the hope that since they were both missing, perhaps they were together. Jacob was definitely capable of protecting Eve and leading her back home to safety.

Just then, Nephi recalled a detail that he'd forgotten about. When he had knelt and prayed that afternoon in the construction area of the vault, he'd noticed the disturbance of a pile of dirt. He'd just assumed that Jacob had been working there earlier. But when his prayers were finished and he began the trek back to the settlement, he'd run into Jacob *going* to the vault.

Nephi reached into the recesses of his mind and tried to piece the events together. Could a patch of disturbed earth mean more than it first appeared? And if so, what did it imply? His brothers knew that Nephi's people had possessed all of the valuable artifacts since their separation. And even though the promised land held plenty of precious metals for everyone, he was sure his brothers coveted the Liahona and the items from Jerusalem—if only because they were the last tangible connection to their homeland.

He turned to face Zoram and felt his heart drop at the man's distressed features. "I have something to tell you."

As he spoke, Nephi felt the whisperings of the Spirit that they should not delay looking for Jacob and Eve any longer. Even though the night was upon them and the moon only half-sized, thus allowing less than desirable light, no more time should be wasted.

Zoram's expression increased in consternation. "It's started already?" His words were a statement more than a question.

"What's started?" Sam asked, his round face reflecting the light from Zoram's torch.

"The prophesies that we have heard from both Lehi and Nephi." Zoram rubbed his beard, his eyes lined with dread. "Our posterity will battle their posterity." He met Nephi's gaze. "The Lord has commanded us to make weapons of war for one reason only; because there will be battle. And it appears that it has begun."

Zoram turned from the two men and pointed to the dark tangles of forest beyond the settlement. "Somewhere . . . out there . . . they have my little girl."

"The Lord willing, Jacob will find a way to protect her," Nephi said.

Sam nodded, his usual jovial expression serious. "How many should we send after them?"

Nephi looked at Zoram, knowing that he would not stay behind. "Zoram and I will go. We need some to remain behind to protect the settlement."

"Right," Sam said. "I'll gather everyone to the temple. It's the most secure location."

"And Sam?" Nephi said quietly. "Explain to Isaabel what has happened, and if I do not return in time for Mother . . ." His voice faltered and he couldn't continue.

Sam merely placed a hand on Nephi's shoulder and nodded. "Make haste, dear brother. Our prayers are with your journey."

Nodding against burning eyes, Nephi secured a sword at his waistline, then he and Zoram each grabbed a skin of water and a couple loaves of bread. Their journey was too urgent to delay any longer.

The two men melted into the night without sparing another moment.

They ran until Nephi thought his chest would burst open. But he continued to drive Zoram, who carried the torch, leading the way to the only location he could think of that held signs of intrusion. That the intruders might be his own kin only chilled his heart. *Brother against brother.* The visions he'd seen of the future had caused him many sleepless nights, and days filled with grief.

Like others in the Nephite settlement, he thought any battle between the families would take place decades in the future. And there was always a small part of him that hoped the family of Laman would not become so hardhearted, but somehow repent of their wrongdoings. But the revelation of the curse that had come upon Laman's people had squelched the seeds of optimism.

How could his brothers, who had witnessed so many miracles, turn their backs on the Lord? They owed their very lives to Him. Not only had He guided them out of Jerusalem—a city doomed to destruction—but He'd led the family across the hostile deserts of Arabia. Just crossing the high seas was miraculous by itself. And yet through it all, Nephi continued to teach his brethren. And only when the Lord commanded Nephi to flee did he leave them behind.

Nephi's thoughts refocused as they reached the clearing where mounds of dirt surrounded a vast pit. Zoram came up behind Nephi, then stopped and stared.

Zoram's breathing came in rapid bursts as he fought for normal breath. "So which pile was disturbed?" he asked when he finally regained his voice.

But Nephi wasn't searching the dug up earth. He moved from tree to tree, looking for any markings, broken branches, or kicked up undergrowth. Several paces into his search, he stopped, heart thumping loudly. Crouching, he touched the ground littered with leaves. One leaf had caught his attention in particular. He picked it up and lifted it toward the sky.

Zoram crossed to him and held the torch close. "What did you find?"

"Blood," Nephi said. "Perhaps Jacob's . . ."

"Perhaps Eve's," Zoram whispered.

Nephi didn't answer. He knew it could also be the blood of whoever disturbed the vault site. Then a new fear arose as he wondered if the dirt had been the only thing moved about.

He rose to his feet and bade Zoram to wait in the clearing.

Walking by memory in the dark, Nephi moved into the western trees and walked the short line that led to the hiding place of the sword of Laban. He'd just brought it to the site the day before in preparation for the completion of the vault.

He crouched next to the tree where he'd buried the sword. Unmistakable signs of digging showed at the base of the trunk.

The sword of Laban was gone.

He stared at the hiding place—the dug up earth, the scattered leaves . . . whoever had found it made no pretense of covering his tracks. Nephi turned away, anger pressing against his chest. He found Zoram still in the clearing, examining the front line of trees.

"The sword has been taken," Nephi said when he reached Zoram.

"Maybe Jacob used it to defend himself?"

"Possibly," Nephi said, although feeling doubtful. Jacob wouldn't have had time to dig up the sword. He would have used his dagger.

"I found more blood," Zoram announced quietly.

Nephi moved to his side and peered at the streak of crimson on the pale tree trunk. The mark was positioned high, and Nephi estimated the height of Jacob against it. "If it was Jacob, it was probably his shoulder." He glanced at Zoram. "It's too high for Eve."

Zoram let out a breath of air. "Let's go."

Before Nephi could ask where, Zoram pointed to another tree, farther in from the first. "I also found this dagger incision. I wouldn't be surprised if Jacob left it."

Nephi moved to the tree, and in the light of the torch he saw that a thin, sharp blade had pierced the young tree's skin. It was not from the sword of Laban, that much was clear. Holding the torch higher, Zoram moved through the forest slowly, discovering marking after marking.

"It was Jacob," Nephi marveled. "He left us a trail." He felt new hope filling his soul. "This means that Jacob is leading us, telling us something . . ."

"Yes," Zoram said, increasing his pace. His voice had softened, its dreary heaviness lifted.

They moved swiftly through the trees, following Jacob's markings. After awhile, they arrived at another clearing. Nephi walked to the center of the small space and rotated. "Can you see where the markings start again?"

Zoram scouted the perimeter, carefully examining every tree along the edge. Then he stopped. "Look," he said, pointing to a high branch. Dangling from it was a scarf. He reached and pulled it down. "It's Eve's."

Nephi stared at that soft cloth, knowing that it had been left to show them the way. But was it left by Eve herself as a cry for help, or had her captor left it—as a mockery?

"She was here," Zoram said, bringing the scarf to his face for a moment, closing his eyes. Then he tucked the scarf inside his tunic. He returned to his inspection of the tree trunks. After a moment, he said, "I found another mark."

Nephi joined him. "Well done."

Together they plunged ahead, following the marks and climbing the steep terrain until they reached the top of the hill. They paused, both out of breath. To the west was the fantastic landscape that descended to the ocean; to the east, a heavily forested area that stretched as far as they could see.

* * *

Like a beast of prey, Shem and Javan had tied Eve to the tree, her arms twisted painfully behind and her legs bound together at several points. Eve inhaled through her nostrils, desperate for a full gulp of air, but they had ripped a piece of cloth from her tunic and gagged her. She could not scream, could not even move her mouth.

As they slept, she watched them apprehensively for any signs of awakening or movement. But their snores only joined together to mock her capture. Eve twisted against the ropes as she thought about the irony of her plight. She'd gone to collect herbs to spare Sariah's pain, when in return she was the one placed in the path of destruction. At least they had not attempted to ravish her. Yet.

The exhaustion had been evident in their eyes when they strapped her to the tree trunk, but something evil propelled them regardless. That same malevolence had apparently deadened their consciences as they chose to mistreat her.

And now her hope of Jacob rescuing her had faded. Maybe he hadn't seen her and had taken the other path, and because of it, Shem and Javan had chosen this one. Surely they would lead her deep into the forest until they came to Laman's settlement.

Eve shuddered to think of what she would see when they arrived—assuming she'd live that long. Her time with Shem and Javan had taught her that two years of debauchery, of living without the Lord's presence, and of existing merely for their own sake had clearly taken its toll. She had dreamt of being reunited with her dear grandmother, but not as a broken and battered woman.

She'd asked Shem how Bashemath fared. He'd merely grunted and said, "Last I saw her, weeks ago, she could barely lift a hand to support herself."

"Then who is caring for her?" Eve had cried out.

She was immediately silenced with a slap.

Seething in the dark, Eve ignored the slow damp that crept into her skin. Daylight was still hours away, but the dew had begun its pilgrimage. It settled along her clothing, saturating every section of her tunic until her skin absorbed the cold. Her legs ached at first, then went numb. She closed her eyes, trying to block out the greedy faces of her cousins when an equally horrifying image entered her mind. That of Nephi tied to the mast of the ship. She had been only a child then, but she had caught a glimpse of the torture.

And she could never forget when his brothers had finally freed him and carried him below deck. His twisted limbs and swollen hands and feet were grotesque in appearance. *And I have only been in this position for a short time, with no wild pitch of a ship or lashing rain pounding on my head.* Eve felt hopelessness creep inside her heart, and she tried to push it away. *Think,* she commanded herself. *No.* She hung her head. *Pray.*

She poured out her soul, her heart, her angst and desperation. Her pleas stayed silent, but reached to the heavens above to the God who she knew always kept His promises. *But what if my captivity is part of what has been prophesied? What if it is the catalyst that will bring the sons of Lehi to battle one with another?*

Her father had explained in great detail the prophesies of Lehi and Nephi, and Eve had assumed she was well acquainted with the destiny of her people. But now she was not sure. Shem and Javan had taken matters into their own hands and seemingly instigated the warnings of the Lord to the people of Nephi.

The husky call of a tropical mockingbird brought Eve from her thoughts into full awareness of her desperate plight. The call came again, and she watched her sleeping cousins, fearful that they would awaken and resume the relentless journey back to their homes.

Then she heard a soft voice behind her. She couldn't turn her head, but she squeezed her eyes shut against her quickening pulse. She was hearing things, she was sure of it.

"Eve," the voice said again.

She felt a hand on her arm, and she nearly wrenched from her bindings with surprise.

"It's me . . . Jacob. Don't move."

Her eyes flooded with tears of relief, mixed with the increased hammering of her heart. She had to remain very still and quiet while Jacob released her. He tugged at the ropes, deftly untying them. He removed his turban, cut it in half with his dagger then bound her sore feet.

"Run fast," he hissed in her ear.

Eve leaned forward and stood, keeping as quiet as possible. She turned and concealed herself in the surrounding trees, but she couldn't run. She couldn't tear her eyes from what she sensed Jacob would do next.

Leave the sword, she wanted to shout.

The next moments were a blur as she watched Jacob close in on the wrapped sword that Shem kept tucked under his arm. Ever so slowly, Jacob moved Shem's arm and tried to manipulate the weapon from his grasp at the same time.

Just leave it! We can retrieve it later! Eve wished she could yell at Jacob. But he continued to work methodically, with patience. She thought her heart would stop as she watched the scene before her.

Then in an instant, it changed.

Javan leapt up and tackled Jacob. The two struggled for a matter of seconds before Shem added his weight to the skirmish. They tied Jacob's arms behind him, then his legs together.

Eve watched, sickened, as they pummeled Jacob's face over and over. She closed her eyes, muffled sobs ripping at her throat. When the beating stopped, she heard a shuffling sound, and—even though she dreaded doing it, opened her eyes. Jacob's face was covered with blood, his nose and cheekbones likely broken. In the dirt, like a child's abandoned toy, he laid motionless, legs twisted at an odd angle.

Then, without a thought for her own fate, she ran to Jacob's side.

* * *

Elisheba retched in the bushes again. Her arms and torso had grown thinner than ever, and she feared for her babe's life. If she couldn't keep any nourishment down, how could she expect to deliver a healthy child? The thought made her shudder. Although she'd born two children already, she had always done so with at least one other woman to assist her. Now there was no one.

The chattering of tree monkeys seemed to mock her despair. She rose from her knees—feeling better, though still weak—and walked to the makeshift shelter she had fashioned about a half-day's walk from the city of Laman. She couldn't bring herself to stray any farther, since this location afforded her the possible glimpse of her boys. But it had been months since she'd seen anyone except for Shem and Javan, who spent a lot of time in the forest. Fortunately, they had yet to come across her encampment.

Elisheba decided that she'd wait for a time to see if Laman's heart would soften. But if it became apparent that he would not change, she was prepared to take matters into her own hands. She wanted nothing more than to be with her sons. Even if it meant taking her sons to Nephi's settlement—without her husband.

She sparked a fire and watched the young flames lick the dry timber she'd assembled. Not far from the small fire pit was a fish wrapped in leaves. She'd speared it that morning in the river. She usually caught at least one fish a day, sometimes two—but it was still difficult to keep down the little food she did eat. So she had to wait until she felt strong enough to cook it without the smell making her queasy.

"Be patient. We'll eat soon," she whispered as she patted her growing abdomen. Elisheba often spoke to the child growing within her, partly due to the lack of conversation she had with anyone else, and also because she felt that she had to explain, out loud, how she had become so destitute. After the first week, she settled into a routine, using the survival skills she'd learned while enslaved at Mudhail. She still remembered Hadi, the woman she served, and the herbal remedies she'd been taught.

The fire crackled, and Elisheba took a deep breath. Quickly she unwrapped the slippery fish and placed it onto a thin stone which she then moved next to the flames. She had already chopped off the fish's head—the reason for her recent visit to the bushes. While she waited for the fish to cook, she walked to the river and scrubbed her dagger clean. Above all else, she was grateful for this one thing. The small dagger had saved her life in more ways than one, and it would eventually be the instrument to cut the child's cord.

On her way back, she stopped at a beehive that she tended. She listened to the merry buzzing that came from within and knew that in a few days there would be several slabs of honeycomb ready to extract. Continuing to her small campsite, she found the fish nearly cooked. Quickly she moved the stone away from the fire to let the heat dissipate. She took a long drink from the sheepskin she'd taken from the hunting shelter. As she did so, painful yet ever-present questions about Raamah swirled through her mind. Did he think ever about her? Wonder what had become of her? Whether she was safe, or even alive?

In the rising hills above Laman's settlement lived the Kaminaljuyú people whom she and others had crossed paths with from time to time over the past couple of years. And often, especially when she was suffering from a bout of severe nausea, she thought about walking to their village and finding some way to make a livelihood. But for some reason, she hesitated. No matter how tough her living conditions became, she did not want to live out her days with a profaning tribe—not only for her sake, but for her unborn child's as well. No, she would make it on her own as long as she could; and eventually, after the baby came, she would try and make it back to Nephi's settlement. With *all* her children.

She glanced at the makeshift bird pen she'd created out of reeds. She had captured two large quetzals to keep until some time after the baby was born, in hopes that their cawing would mask any sound her infant might make. If nothing else, she could use their feathers for trading.

The refreshing water made her feel better for a short while, and Elisheba used the opportunity to eat the cooked fish. She swallowed quickly, trying not to think too much about the slimy meat. The flesh was slightly bitter, but she reminded herself that she'd tasted worse.

She buried the scales and the silver skin she'd picked off, careful not to attract a wild animal to her secluded spot.

Before the afternoon faded to night, she walked again to the river and waded in until the water rose past her knees. Then she bent and splashed water on her face and neck. Above the rush of the water, she thought she heard a new sound. Quickly she backed out of the river and crept over to a group of trees. She listened, trying to decipher one sound from another over her pounding heart and the gurgling river.

She knew the sounds of the forest well—branches bending against the wind, the call of the birds, the slither of the snakes, the scurry of small critters, even the step of the larger beasts. But this was something different. The sound reverberated against the trees, sounding almost musical. *Could someone from Laman's camp be playing an instrument nearby?* she wondered.

Then the sound became clearer. Someone was crying, followed by a short burst of laughter.

Her body automatically stiffened as she tried to make out any words. The laughter died away, and the low murmur of voices reached her ears. Then another cry. The hairs on Elisheba's neck prickled as she realized the cry sounded like a woman.

Pulse racing, she knew she had to move from her concealed hiding place. She had to find out what was happening and see if she could help in some way. Perhaps it was one of the local women who lived in one of the high mountain villages. She shuddered to think of what could happen if one of the young girls became lost and ran into Laman or Lemuel—or even one of their sons. She closed her thoughts to even considering Raamah as a man who could harm a woman. And yet—

The unmistakable sound of footsteps passed just above her along the path on the ridge. She knew she had to move now, or she would never be able to catch whoever it was. Gripping her newly cleaned dagger, Elisheba forced herself to leave her place of security. She knew it was a risk at the very least, and perhaps she was also putting her life in danger.

Climbing stealthily, she found she needed both hands, so she gripped the dagger between her teeth and continued upward. She grabbed onto protruding roots and sturdy plants as she scrambled up the sharp incline. Although she was thin from her illness, her body was agile and responsive to the pulsing adrenaline. As she neared the top, she realized she was ahead of whoever it was on the path, which meant that they would pass right by her. She maneuvered behind a group of scrubby bushes and pulled her legs in tight against her torso. It would be difficult for them to spot her, even if they were looking right at her.

What Elisheba saw next nearly broke what was still intact of her heart.

She recognized Shem and Javan right away. Although she hadn't seen them up close for some time, it wasn't difficult to make out the two young men who looked almost exactly like their fathers. Shem walked in front, his stocky build moving in a sure-footed fashion. He laughed, and Elisheba recognized it as the sound she'd first heard. Javan brought up the rear, his tall frame easily distinguishable over that of Shem's.

But it was the sight of the two poor souls who walked between the two men that caused Elisheba to nearly bite her tongue in order to keep from crying out.

A young man and a woman had been tied together at the arms and legs so that they walked in awkward tandem. Their bands were wrenched tight, and blood was caked around their swollen wrists and ankles. The girl's mouth was gagged, and she struggled to breathe just through her nose. A gash on her forehead had appeared to stop bleeding, but the unmistakable stains of blood spotted her tunic.

However, now that the group was closer she could see that the man was far worse off than the battered woman. His features had been so deformed that he could open only one eye to a slit. She could see a festering wound along the length of his arm—the gash open and nearly black with disease. It was obvious by his ragged breathing that each step was painful.

Her gaze swept back to the woman and Elisheba noticed her fair skin, lighter than those of the surrounding tribes, and much lighter than Shem and Javan's. She realized that these captives were from Nephi's tribe.

Elisheba tensed, holding her breath as the pitiful group walked along the trail just above her. Then she felt a wave of horror pass over her. The woman was Eve—little Eve who would never hurt even the smallest animal. She was grown now, but even through the dirt and despair, Elisheba could see goodness radiating from the young woman. Then who was the man? She couldn't make out his features well enough beyond his injuries . . . but surely he was one of her nephews.

Where were Shem and Javan taking Eve and the other man? Her mind raced as she thought about what lay ahead for the two poor souls. If Shem and Javan had treated them this harshly already and now led the two as captives, Eve and her companion would probably be put to death or at least tortured by the rest of the clan.

Her body trembled at the injustice of it all—at her helplessness, and at the realization that her own two sons undoubtedly witnessed such wickedness every day. What would the fate of these two be, with skin as fair as hers? Her stomach curdled as she thought about what they may have already endured.

When their footsteps faded, Elisheba moved from her cramped position. Even at the risk of her own life, she couldn't just return to her shelter and do nothing. She believed they had passed nearby for a reason. Somehow, she was to be an instrument in their release. Her heart burning with determination, she scaled the last few paces to the trail and began to follow the group. She didn't know how she would stop Shem and Javan, but she knew she must try.

CHAPTER 15

Deal courageously, and the Lord shall be with the good.
(2 CHRONICLES 19:11)

I'm standing on the threshold of three ills, Isaabel thought. Her stomach twisted in worry as she scanned the line of trees to the east. On the other side of the valley the land rose and fell into a mass of tangled jungle. *Where are they?* Nephi, Zoram, Jacob, Eve. All had departed two days before, with no sign of any of them since.

Holding one-year-old Lehi on her hip, Isaabel listened to the sound of hammering. At the edge of the settlement, the men worked furiously, smelting steel and pounding swords into shape—enough that each person could wield two or three weapons if needed.

Behind her sat Sariah's home, and inside, she rested—too weak to rise from her bed and almost too weak to eat. Isaabel had been feeding Sariah one morsel of food at a time. But she had made no improvement during Nephi's absence. If anything, she'd grown worse.

Isaabel turned her back to the reverberating of metal upon metal and moved into the quiet home. Her sister Tamar glanced up from the stool where she kept vigil, and Isaabel nodded to her. The two didn't even need to exchange words. They already had said all they could and worried until both were spent. Tamar rose and left the room while Isaabel bent over Sariah and kissed her cheek.

After several moments of patting young Lehi on the back and sitting near her mother-in-law's bedside, Isaabel felt a new seed of worry growing. She had not seen her oldest sister, Rebeka, for the better part of the day. When Tamar came back in the room, Isaabel rose to her feet. "Have you seen Rebeka today?"

Tamar shook her head.

"I'm going to look for her," Isaabel said. She gathered up young Lehi and left Sariah under the watchful care of Tamar. Making her way through the settlement, Isaabel noticed that the children must have been playing indoors this afternoon. Perhaps they found all the activity of building and metal forging disconcerting. When she arrived at Rebeka's home, she called through the cornstalk outer wall and waited for the familiar voice to welcome her. No one answered, so Isaabel stepped into the cool interior.

Typically she'd find Rebeka grinding flour from maize, stitching, or weaving. Instead, she saw the hunched over form of her sister, her arms moving back and forth. "Rebeka," she called, but her sister didn't seem to hear her. Isaabel stepped closer. "Rebeka."

Finally, Rebeka stopped scrubbing, but she kept her head lowered and her body hunched over. Isaabel placed baby Lehi on the floor to scoot around, then knelt beside her oldest sister and put an arm around her shoulder. Rebeka had her eyes closed, but her cheeks were raw with tears.

"Any sign of them?" Rebeka whispered in a chaffed voice.

"Not yet," Isaabel said. The two women knelt together—silence between them—as the sound of pounding metal vibrated throughout the settlement.

"What has become of my Eve?" Rebeka asked. She turned and buried her head against Isaabel's shoulder. Both of their husbands were gone—both in danger—but Isaabel imagined it was Eve's safety that Rebeka feared for the most. The men were better equipped to face the elements of the jungle, but Eve had little experience being at the mercy of the unknown.

"Your husband is very good at tracking," Isaabel said.

Rebeka sniffled, then nodded.

"In the desert, he was able to see what others could not." Isaabel squeezed her sister's shoulder. "We must put our trust in that. And between the three men, who all care for her and would give their life for her—" Her own voice cracked. "Eve will be protected more than any of us, should we leave this moment and begin to search."

Rebeka pulled away. "I know. But if it weren't for my husband's strict instructions, I wouldn't be able to remain at home and just . . . wait."

"I know," Isaabel said. "We would all be searching for her." The clanking of metal drove through her senses. "But we must prepare, too."

Rebeka lifted her hands, reddened from work. "The scrubbing helps keep my fears at bay."

"I understand." Isaabel took her sister's hands and turned them over, holding them. "Let us pray for your daughter and the men, then we will heed the Lord's counsel."

Nodding, Rebeka shifted her position so she faced Isaabel. The two women bowed their heads. When Isaabel finished the prayer, she embraced Rebeka for a moment. She sensed her older sister's strength returning. Then she scooped up young Lehi, and Rebeka joined them as they walked to the smelting site.

Once they arrived, Isaabel watched for a moment, thinking of the humble fire pit that her husband had built to smelt tools in the land of Bountiful. Here in the Land of Nephi, low buildings had been constructed to house the furnaces, and large stones had been chiseled to act as work benches for the shaping.

Sam ran the site, overseeing everything from the gathering of tinder for the hungry furnace to the final decorative carvings on the hilts. A large rug had been placed on the ground, and rows of newly fashioned swords were lined upon it for inspection.

Isaabel's own nine-year-old son, Aaron, had the job of inspector. He ran a slim finger along the newly sharpened blades, hunting for any inconsistencies or nicks in the metal. When he saw his mother, he rose and crossed to her. Even at his age, Isaabel could detect concern in his expression. Her husband and son were very close, and Isaabel knew that Aaron missed his father greatly—even after just two days.

His gaze moved from Isaabel to Rebeka, then back again. Finally he asked, "Is there really going to be a battle?"

"I don't know, son," Isaabel said, her stomach churning at the thought of it.

"Sam says I may be needed to help fight." He puffed out his narrow chest.

Isaabel looked down at her long and lanky son and shook her head. "No, you will not fight."

"But Mother, what if the people of Laman outnumber us?"

Isaabel shuddered, knowing that her son would very well fight if Laman's people came upon them suddenly. In fact, she knew that even she would fight—but she did not fear for herself. She would do anything to protect her children from what would be a devastating battle—for it would not be nameless faces they'd be fighting. But surely it would not come to that. Agreements and negotiations could be made before any actual combat took place. She turned her attention back to her son.

Aaron started teasing young Lehi until the child tried to wriggle from her arms. But Isaabel couldn't let her youngest son play near the smelting area.

"Let's return and start the evening meal," she said to Rebeka. Isaabel knew that performing the normal daily tasks would calm her sister. Yet as the two women left the furnaces and walked to the cooking area, Isaabel couldn't help but wonder if the peace of the last two years was about to be shattered.

* * *

This is all like a dream, Eve thought. A dream where she could see herself below—crying, walking, and stumbling next to Jacob—flanked by their captors, Shem and Javan. It was hard to believe the ragged girl in the dream was her—and that it was really happening.

But it was all too real. Her wrists and ankles had been tied to Jacob's, making walking not only difficult, but painful. The humidity of the jungle was oppressive, weighing her down as perspiration ran along her neck and soaked her tunic. Insects took delight in her bloodstained skin and clothing. After many futile attempts of shaking them off, she gave up. Without looking at her reflection in a body of water, she knew that her face was dotted with swollen welts from insect bites. Her gag cut painfully at the edges of her mouth. Yet through the numbness and exhaustion, Eve knew that Jacob was worse off than she. The blood on his face had dried hours ago, but the swelling had increased and the bruising had blackened.

She marveled that he could see well enough to guide her along the darkened path. But it was Jacob who pulled her along, supporting her weak limbs and whispering words of encouragement. How could he even speak? She could barely comprehend that they were moving at all. All she wanted was to lie down in a soft meadow and close her eyes. She didn't care if death followed. She reasoned that it couldn't be any worse than what she experienced now.

Her entire body throbbed with pain. Instinctively she slowed, hoping that she could ease the blisters on her feet. But Jacob's whisper came ready and sure.

"Keep moving. It won't be much longer now." His words were slightly slurred due to his swollen lips, his breathing rapid.

If she turned her head far enough, she could catch a glimpse of Jacob. But each time she did so, she winced at seeing his injuries. If only she had escaped in the first place he wouldn't have been beaten. She might have had a chance when she was just with Shem, but she knew once both cousins accompanied her, it was nearly impossible.

She thought about her family from time to time, but it was only fleeting. At this moment, it was difficult to imagine a life carefree from worry, as hers had once been. It was hard to believe the things she normally fretted over, like having a shy nature or not understanding Nephi's speeches. None of that seemed to matter right now. What mattered was the simple act of surviving from one moment to the next.

Finally, just as Eve thought she would sink to the ground and topple Jacob with her, the two men came to a stop. She could hear irritation in their voices as they argued about whether or not to rest for a couple of hours.

Eve felt her knees start to give and she leaned against Jacob, hoping he had more strength to hold them up than she did. His skin was warm. He was feverish.

"Someone's following us." Jacob's voice was almost imperceptible above the howl of an unseen monkey.

Eve's questions caught in her throat. *Could it be someone looking for us?* Her father, perhaps? New hope sprung as she thought about the men of her family tracking them down. They would come in force and surprise Javan and Shem. She and Jacob would return home, where they would be safe and secure.

She wanted to cry out, to signal those who followed. But she could barely make a garbled sound through the gag. And she didn't want to induce more anger from Shem or Javan. She was relieved when her cousins decided on a short rest. Although she didn't expect to sleep, she was desperate just to stop moving.

Shem pulled the two off the path and led them several paces from the main trail. "Sit here," he said with a stern glare. "And don't make a sound." He turned to Javan. "You have first watch." Shem lay on the ground, promptly falling asleep.

Javan kept watch diligently, but Eve could see that his shoulders sagged with exhaustion. *Please Lord,* she silently prayed, *deliver us from these men.* The touch of Jacob's body next to hers and his closeness was her only comfort. She knew that under any other circumstance, she would feel extremely awkward and embarrassed. But here, now, concerns of propriety had fled.

Her stomach rumbled loudly, signaling what she already knew. She was hungry and thirsty. The last time she'd felt so fatigued with thirst had been those last few days on the ship. Eve felt Jacob's hot breath upon her neck as he turned to look at her. She didn't meet his gaze, afraid that the action would alert Javan. But she was aching to know how Jacob sensed someone followed them. *Father,* she ached to call out. *We're over here.*

She felt Jacob's body relax against hers and his hair tickle her shoulder. *He must be falling asleep,* she thought, glad that he could find a momentary lapse from their torturous journey. But she worried that his infected wounds would make him too ill to travel. Then what would Shem and Javan do?

A figure came out of the darkness without a sound. Eve saw the flash of shadow, the long dark hair, then Javan was knocked to the ground. She was sure that whoever it was, the person was too small to be her father or Nephi . . . or any of the men she knew for that matter. She struggled against the ropes, wanting to get away in the confusion. Jacob became alert again.

As the two watched Javan fight with the attacker, Jacob whispered, "Now is our chance."

Together they stood and began to back away. Just then, Shem awoke. It didn't take long before he figured out what was going on. He piled onto Javan and together they pinned the intruder. Without waiting for the two to notice their plan, Jacob and Eve made their way to the trail and, still tied together, they headed the opposite direction which Shem and Javan had been leading them.

As Eve forced her legs to move faster and faster, one sound kept repeating over and over in her head. The scream of a woman. The attacker had been a female—and she had risked her life to save them.

* * *

The moist breeze lifted the leaves of the surrounding branches, caressing the flaps on Nephi's turban. Zoram kept pace as they jogged along the animal trail. Exhaustion had finally consumed them the day before, and they had slept for a few hours, just enough to regain their strength. Then they continued on.

Nephi swiped at the bugs buzzing around his head and shoulders. Because of the increasing insects, he knew they neared a river. He and Zoram had covered a lot of land, three times faster than when they had traveled the opposite way with the rest of the family. With only themselves to worry about, they kept pushing forward at an almost inhuman speed.

The markings Jacob had made stopped in a thickly jungled area, but Nephi and Zoram weren't deterred. It hadn't taken Zoram long to figure out that Jacob, and likely Eve, had been tied together. He was able to track their footprints, noticing the unusual pattern they made. Nephi sensed that Zoram was at his breaking point, and for that reason, he kept the pace up. He knew once they slowed and let the magnitude of the events sink in, Zoram might not stay calm.

Nephi glanced at Zoram, recognizing the wild look of desperation that had crept into his eyes in the last hour. "Do you recognize this part of the trail?" Nephi asked as he analyzed the waist-high ferns.

Zoram followed his gaze, then looked toward the south. "Toward that ridge is the Kaminaljuyú village." His expression lightened. "We aren't too far now."

"No," Nephi conceded. "In fact, if we can keep our pace, we should be there in just a few hours."

Letting out a haggard breath, Zoram grimaced. "If they've harmed my little girl in any way—"

"Jacob will protect her."

But Zoram didn't look convinced. "I respect Jacob immensely, but he's not exactly a fierce warrior."

Nephi understood Zoram's point, but he still disagreed. "Jacob's childhood was anything but easy. He suffered all kinds of tribulation and abuse from Laman and Lemuel, though I protected him as much as was possible. He's nearly a man now."

"It does bring me a measure of comfort to know that Jacob is most likely with Eve," Zoram said. "And if those joined footprints are theirs, then they are obviously still alive and moving. But even if Jacob can hold off Eve's abductor, he'll be no match for the others once they reach Laman's settlement."

"You're right. The question is, will we be able to overtake them before they reach their destination? Or will *we* be fighting with more men than we can handle?" Nephi watched for Zoram's reaction, but was surprised to see him smile.

"I don't mind. The time has come to fight for what we believe in once and for all." Zoram took a labored breath, but didn't slow his pace. "I know the Lord told you that they will be a scourge unto our seed, but I also think that *we* will be a scourge unto *their* seed."

"Zoram," Nephi interrupted. "A battle can only take place with the Lord's help if we are defending our lives and our freedom."

Zoram threw him a glare. "You know that they will never stop until they get what they want."

"And what's that?" Nephi asked.

"Your death," Zoram said quietly. "They are all like Laban, who was deceitful until he died—even until his last drunken breath."

Nephi slowed his jog, then stopped and stared at Zoram.

"Don't you see why the Lord commanded you to slay him?" Zoram asked as he faced Nephi on the trail—his voice rough, questioning.

"Because it was 'better that one man should perish than that a nation should dwindle and perish in unbelief,'" Nephi said automatically. He opened the waterskin slung over his shoulder and took a long drink. When he finished, he wiped his mouth with the back of his hand.

Zoram's eyes darkened, his stance defiant. "What do you think Laman and Lemuel are teaching their children? Our nieces and nephews?" His voice turned to a low growl. "It is better that *we* should perish than our posterity be taught false teachings."

"I was *commanded* by—" Nephi tried to cut in.

But Zoram continued, "And if it has to be done by my hands, then so be it. I'd rather spend the eternities cut off from the Lord than let Laman and Lemuel pass down their wicked traditions, cutting off hundreds and thousands of others."

Nephi shook his head and grasped Zoram's arm. "Stop. You don't understand what you are saying. The Spirit has shown these things to me."

"Then why can't He show you where my daughter is?" Zoram cried. "Why can't He send an angel to rescue *her?*" His eyes filled with tears, and his body began to tremble.

"Is He not guiding us now? Showing us the way by preserving their tracks? It hasn't rained since we began our journey." Waving a hand, Nephi continued, "All of the Lord's promises will come to pass. If we are righteous, we will be blessed. If we are not, we won't. It's not for us to judge our brothers and to take their lives from them—to take away their right to make choices."

"How can you continue, knowing what the outcome of our posterity will be? How can you continue to teach and love . . ." Zoram's voice cracked, ". . . and hope? Why do you write our battles and grievances on your ore plates? So that our doomed posterity can see how many blessings our brethren threw away?" His shoulders sagged as he brought his hands to his face. "Eve has done nothing. She does not deserve to endure so much."

"You are right," Nephi cut in softly. "She does not. And for that reason, we must make haste."

Zoram licked his lips and nodded, but his gaze remained wild and ruthless. "Let's go." They started moving again, rushing and stumbling along the darkening path.

It wasn't long before the night was complete and the trail became a silvery strand beneath the moonlight. In and out of shadows they moved, battling against sheer exhaustion and physical pain from aching muscles. The one thing that hung heavy in Nephi's mind was that Jacob and Eve were worse off than they.

As midnight neared, Zoram slowed to a stop and rested his hands on his knees. Nephi waited for him to regain some stamina, although Nephi felt as if his own body would collapse.

After breathing hard for a few moments, Zoram straightened and turned to Nephi. "We have a guest."

"Where?" Nephi asked, looking toward the trees for any signs of human or beast following.

But Zoram shook his head and pointed at the ground. "There."

Nephi looked down, not seeing any signs of animal droppings, but then he saw a heel marking in the soft dirt. It didn't follow the footprints from Jacob's group, but was off to the side, as if someone were purposely trying to conceal their tracks.

Together, the men took a few steps forward, then spotted a second heel mark. Zoram knelt and inspected the print closely. "It's a woman."

Nephi looked at Zoram in surprise. "Do you think they have another woman with them?"

"I don't think this woman is *with* them. I think she's following them."

Silence ensued as Nephi thought about what that could mean. He did not doubt Zoram's discernment, for the man had been an expert tracker in the high sands of the desert. They followed the tracks slowly for a while, then increased their pace.

Zoram stooped again and gazed at the marks beneath the moonlight. "The deeper prints signify that the woman who follows is carrying a child in her womb."

Nephi let out a slow breath of air. The tracks could belong to any of his sisters-in-law, he thought, or even a woman from one of the mountain tribes such as the Kaminaljuyú. Their aching muscles forgotten, the two men moved quickly now, each flooded with a new sense of urgency.

Not much farther along the trail, Nephi and Zoram stopped simultaneously and stared at a body lying motionless on the ground.

✢—☙ CHAPTER 16 ❧—✢

Till I die I will not remove mine integrity from me.
(JOB 27:5)

The shouts seemed to bounce off the trees around them. Jacob guided Eve off the trail as soon as the screaming had stopped—female screams. The poor soul had tried to stop Javan and Shem, but in the process had no doubt sacrificed her own life. Dismay consumed him. He had to return and help her . . . even if it was just to bury her. A deeper shout now echoed through the trees. Javan and Shem were already in pursuit.

First, he would find someplace to hide Eve, then he'd return. He knew his older nephews had the advantage—it had been two years since Jacob had visited these forests, and now, in the dark, he didn't recognize any landscape marker or grove of trees. What made it even more difficult was the cloudy vision of his one good eye. One thing he knew for certain was that they'd never be able to outrun Shem and Javan while he and Eve were tied together. But both of them had been stripped of their daggers. Once out of close range, Jacob stopped and was able to untie their ankles. Although their wrists remained bound together, he was able to work off Eve's gag.

There has to be something, Jacob thought. *Something sharp.* He plunged on, nearly dragging Eve behind him, searching his mind for a solution. Then he heard it—the rushing of a river.

He deviated from their northern path. "We're going to the river," he whispered. He hoped to find a cave—something to conceal her while he returned to help the other woman.

Eve didn't say anything, and Jacob wasn't even positive she'd heard him. But her pace quickened with his, and soon he could hear the roar of water just beyond the next outcropping of foliage. As a waterfall came into view, Jacob stopped for an instant, taking in the familiar site. He remembered this place—it had been one of his favorite places of solitude. A sliver of memory flashed through his mind as he remembered coming here to ponder after his father's death.

Without a word, the two plunged into the pool at the base of the waterfall. Jacob inhaled sharply as the water startled his senses. It was refreshing and painful at the same time. The water drenched his torn clothing and brought relief to his aching limbs and ragged feet.

He turned to face Eve, who stood in the knee-deep water with her eyes closed.

"We must try to loosen the bindings," Jacob shouted above the tumbling falls.

Eve opened her eyes and nodded.

Jacob could see trepidation in her gaze, but also noted her absolute trust. "If we kneel together, then the water will soothe our wrists and ankles."

They knelt and Jacob began to twist and turn his wrist against Eve's. She gasped at the initial shot of pain.

"If we do it quickly, it will be over sooner," Jacob said, feeling ill as pain throbbed through his entire body.

After another moment of twisting and tugging, Eve cried out, "I can't do this. It's . . . too painful . . . isn't there another way?"

"Not unless we can find something sharp."

Eve looked away, hopelessness on her face. "I'd rather stay tied together then, even if it means—"

"Wait," Jacob said. "Remember I saw you here one day collecting water?"

Eve nodded.

"Even though it was a far walk from our settlement, you came here often, right?"

"Once in a while. I liked the taste of the clear water," she conceded.

"Is there a chance you ever broke one of the jugs, and shards of pottery remain?"

Eve's eyes were searching along the bank. "More than once." An earlier embarrassment could now prove to be life saving. Together they moved ashore and began to walk slowly, stooping every so often to peer at a rock or other object in the moonlight. They searched, but found nothing.

"Let's just see if we can find some shelter to sleep a short while." Eve's voice cut through Jacob's thoughts.

"Not yet," he said. "Shem and Javan will not give up easily." He looked at the river again. "But if there is a way to trick them into thinking we went a different direction . . ."

"How can we do that?"

"Let's walk in the shallow part downstream for a while to find a way to cut across."

"All right," Eve said.

They moved as quickly as possible, wading in the edges of the stream. The rocks were painful to walk on at first, gouging the cuts and bruises on their feet, but after a while, the water relieved them from further pain. Dark water swirled at their ankles, and sometimes to their knees. The sky's change from gray to murky green signaled to Jacob that dawn was fast approaching. With the new day, he knew Shem and Javan wouldn't be far behind. If Javan could locate the sword of Laban that easily, he was obviously a skilled tracker.

The landscape began to change, just as Jacob remembered. The river also grew more shallow, and he saw a part of the river that looked less threatening. "Can you swim?"

"Yes," Eve said in a hushed whisper.

Jacob noticed the tremble in her voice and looked at her. "Don't be afraid, Eve." He wished his words could erase the fear he saw in her eyes, but he didn't have time to convince her right now. "Remember, we're tied together, so what happens to you, happens to me." She visibly swallowed.

"Let's go," she said, keeping her gaze steady.

They picked their way across the rocks, balancing together as they moved perpendicular to the current. Once they reached waist-deep water, Jacob sensed Eve's fear. "When it gets to your shoulders, start to kick your feet. The river will probably carry us some distance before we reach the other side. We'll tread until we can touch ground again."

Eve took a shaky breath and nodded. A few more steps and the water had moved above her chest, then to the top of her shoulders.

"Bring your feet up," Jacob said. "Kick." As her body bobbed in the dark water, he began to kick, too. Together they swam with the current, muscling their way toward the opposite bank. The current was swift, but not so fast that they couldn't keep their heads above the water as they propelled themselves toward the looming trees.

"We're almost there," he said. Eve gritted her teeth, and her face was scrunched in determination.

Jacob kicked hard, pulling her with him until his feet, and hers, touched the silted river bottom. He stepped on something sharp. "Ow." He glanced at Eve, who looked thoroughly miserable as she sputtered water. "Hold on a minute." He looked down into the swirling water and felt along the bank with his foot, searching for the sharp object.

His foot hit it again. "We have to bend down and get it together."

Eve nodded and followed his lead. They both crouched in the water while Jacob fished for the object. He lifted it out of the water and held it up. The broken piece of metal glinted in the moonlight, and Jacob wondered where it had come from. But more importantly, he wondered if it would work.

"Come on," Jacob said through chattering teeth, gently guiding her to the bank of the river. The weight of his wet clothing made him feel even colder. They sat together, and he gripped the metal piece at an angle. But it kept slipping between his half-numb fingers.

Then Eve tried, but came up with the same results. "Maybe we can wedge it in a tree trunk, then use it as a saw."

"All right," Jacob said. His breath came short as they stood. The first signs of light had touched the sky. Time was ever so precious.

Shem and Javan could be paces away. Jacob spotted a rock, which he used to pound the piece of metal into a nearby tree, wincing as he did so. He hoped that the sounds of the river would mask the pounding of metal.

He looked at Eve, her dark hair wet and glistening against her face. A lump formed in his throat as he thought about how close they came—and could still come—to real harm. "Ready?" he asked. At Eve's nod, he brought his hands up—hers moving with his—and rubbed the rope against the metal.

It took several moments for the rope to begin fraying, but once the strength of the cord was compromised, the rest of the twisted strands broke easily. As the rope fell away from Jacob's wrists, a sense of relief coursed through him.

"We did it," Eve breathed, a rare smile lighting her face.

Jacob wanted to rejoice and wished they could build a fire to dry themselves. But as the forest around them brightened, his heart began hammering again. Eve's hand touched his arm, surprising him.

She began to examine his injuries, her touch lighter than a winged insect.

Jacob held back a groan, his rope burns beginning to throb all over again. He also felt a pulsing pain in his eye and cheek, but it didn't compare to the infected dagger wound. His neck and head also throbbed, and he was sure he looked a sight.

"We must find something to treat the swelling," Eve said.

"Later," Jacob said. They had been tied together for so long that it seemed strange to be separated from her. She stood so close to him that he could feel her warm breath against the dampness of his chest. Bumps rose along the back of his neck and arms. He stepped backward, pushing away any progress of thought.

Eve noticed his reserve and dropped her hands. She looked toward the river, trembling still evident in her body. Jacob wished he had a dry rug to throw over her shoulders.

Without another word, they turned and faced the line of trees. Jacob reached over and took Eve's hand. *So we don't become separated,* he told himself. Feeling the pressure of her slim fingers against his palm, Jacob led the way deeper into the forest.

* * *

"Is she still alive?"

Nephi crouched next to the woman's body and shooed away a group of rodents that had gathered to inspect her. She lay face down, her hair a twisted mass about her head. Zoram crouched on the other side of the body, his expression a mixture of horror and curiosity.

"Do you think we should touch her?"

But Nephi had already answered the question. He gingerly moved the thick, black hair from the woman's damp face. In the dim moonlight he could see the pooled blood on her forehead. Removing his turban, he tore it in half and pressed one end against the open wound. Dirt and debris covered her hair, face, and clothing—as if she'd been dragged to this place. *Perhaps the person who did this wanted her to be found. A glimmer of compassion?* he wondered.

Zoram moved closer and took the woman's wrist in his. "She's still warm—clammy, but warm."

"She's alive then," Nephi said, more to himself. When the blood was staunched, he started to wrap the piece of cloth around the woman's head. In doing so, he had to lift her head, causing the moonlight to illuminate her face in full.

"Elisheba," Zoram said with a gasp.

Even as Zoram spoke the words, Nephi could hardly believe the woman who was lying so helpless could truly be his sister. In addition to the injuries she'd sustained, her clothing was minimal and ragged, and her appearance savage. As he and Zoram examined Elisheba for any life-threatening injuries, Nephi was sickened with worry about what had happened to his sister. How did she get here, and who had done this to her? The last time he'd seen his sister, she had been so beautiful and well cared for. Now her face was lined with hard living.

A moan sounded, startling Nephi. Her eyes fluttered open, then closed immediately as a groan escaped her lips. Again, her eyes opened, this time focusing on the men.

Nephi tensed, her savage appearance causing him to suddenly wonder if she'd forsaken righteousness over the years and adopted his older brothers' way of living. The notion seemed almost unthinkable for his tender Elisheba, but Nephi could only imagine how difficult it would be to remain the lone believer amidst such wickedness. He wondered if she'd be angered to see him—if he should brace himself for a verbal onslaught. But none came.

"My prayers have been answered," Elisheba said, her voice raspy.

Nephi moved to her side and helped her sit up. "Elisheba."

"Oh, Nephi, is it really you?" Then her eyes moved to Zoram. "And Zoram, how did you come to be here?" She reached out a hand and stroked Nephi's face. "I am dreaming the most wonderful dream."

"It's no vision, Elisheba," Nephi said. He glanced at her bound forehead. "What happened to you? Where's your husband? Your children?"

A look of confusion crossed Elisheba's brow, and her hand moved to her stomach. "Is my baby all right?"

Nephi followed her gesture and remembered what Zoram had said about Elisheba's tracks. The woman they were following had been with child. "The only injury we found was on your head."

Elisheba nodded, drawing in a sharp breath as she did so. "I don't remember how I got here." She looked around, peering along the dark trail. Then her expression softened as she turned back to Nephi. "Have you come to take us with you?"

Nephi started to shake his head, then stopped himself. "You mean Raamah and your children? We would be overjoyed for you to return with us."

Her eyes clouded over. "They are lost to me," she said in a low voice, gripping Nephi's arm. "He does not even know about the new child." She looked at him, wildness in her eyes. "I must hide. If they find me, they will kill my boys."

"Who?" Nephi asked, but his sister scrambled to her feet, her body teetering with the action. He didn't know how she did it, but she effortlessly began to climb the hillside that rose from the trail.

"Wait," Nephi and Zoram said at once, following her.

Nephi reached her first, and he grabbed her arm. "Where are you going? Elisheba, you've been seriously hurt!"

Elisheba looked at him for a moment, but Nephi sensed she really didn't see him. "Why did you come back?" she asked.

Sensing that his sister was delirious, Nephi realized that whatever explanation he gave, she wouldn't remember. But he also knew that for her safety he needed to convince her to stay with them. There was so much he wanted to ask her. Had Ramah really abandoned her? Was her life truly in danger? Yet he sensed that these would need to be answered in time. But right now Elisheba's life—and the life of her unborn child—were in serious danger. "We must find some herbal remedy for your wound."

Elisheba absentmindedly touched the cloth on her head. Nephi saw her wince in pain and was glad when she finally nodded.

"How far are we from your home?" Zoram cut in.

"I don't have a home," Elisheba said, her eyes darkening again. "I sleep under a makeshift shelter beneath the trees and eat from the river."

A shiver trailed down Nephi's back. Had life grown so awful that homes had been destroyed or left to rot? Did the people of Laman roam the land with no place to rest at night?

He looked at the trail, torn with the knowledge that the longer they waited, the farther away Jacob and Eve would get. And once the pair was taken to Laman, Nephi feared what the outcome would be.

Nephi decided that the wisest place for them to go would be Laman's settlement. Not only would his sisters-in-law have what they needed to care for Elisheba, but that would also put Nephi and Zoram there when Jacob and Eve arrived. "Can you take us to Laman?" he asked his sister.

Her eyes widened as she shook her head. Then she felt along her clothing. "My dagger is missing." Her voice raised a notch. "Did you take it?"

"No," Nephi said. "The person who injured you must have taken it."

Confusion crossed Elisheba's features. "Why do you want to see Laman?"

"Because someone has captured Jacob and Eve. We were following their tracks when we came across yours."

Elisheba reached for a tree and steadied herself. "Jacob? Eve?" she whispered. Then she moaned. "I remember now."

"What?" Zoram asked. He strode to her side and gazed into her eyes. "Did you see them? Were they all right?"

"Yes. No . . ." Elisheba looked at Zoram. "I'm not sure." She touched her forehead, grimacing.

"Sit down, sister," Nephi said, moving to her side. He helped her to a boulder, where she sat in silence for a moment.

"I heard them walking along the trail. I hid myself and watched them pass." She paused, looking from one man to the other. "Shem and Javan had tied them together. They have grown into men, and they are just like their fathers."

Zoram let out a low breath of air. "Shem and Javan?" He rubbed his head, anguish in his eyes. "How could they? Why?" He looked at Elisheba. "How did Jacob and Eve look? Were they injured?"

Elisheba nodded slowly. "Jacob's face was . . . almost unrecognizable. I would have never guessed it was him. But now, I'm beginning to understand. Eve fared better, although she seemed to be struggling—"

"What happened after you saw them? Did Shem and Javan attack you?" Nephi cut in.

"I . . . attacked *them*," Elisheba said. "After I had followed them for some time, I became angry at the insults and laughter I heard coming from Shem and Javan. I couldn't just watch Eve and Jacob be mistreated, so I had to do something." Her voice broke, and it took her a moment to gain control of herself. "But all the while I thought of my two boys. They might behave in the same manner . . . after all they have been subjected to. Who am I to condemn anyone? I have failed as a mother to my children." A sob broke from her lips and she hung her head in shame.

Nephi put his arm around his sister's trembling shoulders. Guilt swelled within him as he remembered his earlier suspicions about his sister. Now he saw her for what she had been through and become—an outcast, a survivor. "Tell me what happened. Why are you alone?"

She took a trembling breath. "It was my skin." She raised her arms as if to explain. "It never grew dark like theirs. Whether it was from the sun's rays or from their darkened dispositions, I don't know. I tried to concoct remedies to lighten their skin, but they accused me of sorcery. They had suspected for some time that I continued to teach my children about the Lord's commandments. Raamah knew about it, but he never said anything—as long as I didn't speak about it in his presence. They accused me of being a traitor because of this, and said that I was somehow responsible for their darkened skins. I've been waiting for the past few months, hoping to be reunited with my sons . . . to bring them to your home."

Nephi stared at her, awed by her determination and courage. "You have done everything in your power, sister. You are nothing like Laman or Lemuel or their sons. Nor are you to blame for your husband's or sons' choices. As for Shem and Javan, they apparently came to our settlement to steal the sword of Laban. They must have come across Eve and Jacob, and decided to take them along, too."

Elisheba sniffled, then nodded. "I knew I had to do something for those poor children. And now that I know who they both are, I don't regret a single action. When they stopped to rest, I waited until Shem and Javan were asleep. I think Eve and Jacob were asleep, too. I tried to take away Shem and Javan's daggers, hoping to free Eve and Jacob and let them flee. I hoped that when Javan and Shem realized what happened, at least their weapons would be missing." She took a shuddering breath. "Shem woke up and the rest—well, you can see what happened."

"And Eve and Jacob?" Zoram asked.

"Are still with them," Elisheba finished.

"What do you think they'll do with them?" Zoram asked again. Nephi could hear the fear in his voice.

"I'm not sure I understand why they felt compelled to bring along Jacob and Eve in the first place," Elisheba said. "Unless . . ."

"Unless what?" Nephi prompted.

Elisheba looked furtively between the two men. "Unless they felt that by killing Jacob with the sword of Laban, they would have avenged their own fathers."

Nephi was silent. He couldn't even formulate a reply, let alone comprehend what would compel Javan and Shem to act in such a despicable manner. The awfulness of the situation rolled over Nephi's body like a cold wave.

"The killing would not be immediate though," Elisheba said suddenly, her voice full of confidence. "They would want to do a ceremony of some sort, make a spectacle of Jacob and Eve." She looked at Zoram, sorrow in her eyes.

"So there might still be time," Zoram said, straightening his shoulders. "You can lead us to the settlement where we can spy on them. Then at the right moment—"

"No," Elisheba said, staring at him with conviction. "I could *never* put your lives at risk. When I go back, it will be alone . . . to get my children at any cost."

* * *

Isaabel gripped Sariah's hand. The poor woman tossed and turned, perspiration soaking her clothing.

"Nephi," Sariah cried out again and again.

It broke Isaabel's heart to hear her mother-in-law so distressed. Sariah wasn't even coherent, yet she continued to call for her son. Isaabel knew she couldn't tell the woman that her son was gone, facing unknown danger. It would do no good to try and explain.

"Find Nephi," Sariah continued.

Her mother-in-law's words echoed the desire of Isaabel's heart. With each passing hour, her concern grew. There had been no sign, no word, and no indication of Nephi, Zoram, Jacob, or Eve. Sam and the others continued fashioning swords long after dark fell the night before. Isaabel had relieved Tamar of duty and placed her children in the next room to sleep so that she could keep vigil by Sariah all night.

Sariah had slept fitfully, but with the early signs of dawn, she had become distraught.

Does she sense something? Isaabel wondered. Did Sariah know something about her son that no one else did? Isaabel leaned over and stroked Sariah's forehead until the woman calmed and settled into a peaceful sleep again. Then Isaabel stood and left the room. She crossed through the cooking room and exited the small home. Standing on the threshold she took in the scent of the new day.

The beauty of the crystal blue sky and dew-laden trees was lost on her. Anxiety crushed against her chest as she realized another day had passed with no sign of her husband or the others. Where was Nephi, and what was he doing? What had happened to Eve and Jacob? She tugged her mantle against her shoulders and shivered in the morning air. The sound of an ax striking wood caught her attention. She walked around Sariah's home and saw a figure against the outer rim of trees.

Isaabel recognized the silhouette of Sam as he repeatedly hewed down one tree after another. She pulled her mantle tightly about her and started walking across the dew-touched grasses. As she neared Sam, she could see his clothing was soaked with perspiration. She wondered how long he'd been chopping.

She waited until Sam paused in his work to call out to him.

He turned, looking startled to see her. Using the turban flaps that draped over his shoulder, he wiped the sides of his face. "Did I wake you?"

"No," Isaabel said, noticing the dark shadows beneath his eyes. "I was keeping watch over your mother."

Sam nodded, gratitude flickering through his eyes. "How is she?" he asked through heaving breaths.

"She calls for Nephi."

Taking a step back, Sam rested his ax against a tree and let out a heavy sigh. "It is because of Nephi's absence that I cannot rest either."

Isaabel's eyes welled with tears, understanding that it was not just the women who suffered.

"How many people do you think live in Laman's settlement?" Sam suddenly asked.

Isaabel looked at him in surprise. "I'm not sure. Perhaps . . ." She thought through Laman, Lemuel, Raamah, and Heth, their wives, and quickly calculated the number of their children. "Around twenty?"

"Adding in another couple of children who could have been born over the past two years, and I'd say you are right." Sam rubbed his forehead and glanced at the lightening sky. "And our settlement? How many do we have?"

Isaabel was quiet for a few moments as she counted through the family members. "The same amount."

"Yes," Sam conceded. "Remember the vision that Nephi had of our posterity battling against Laman's posterity?"

Her stomach tightened at the thought, but she only nodded.

"And now . . . the Lord commands Nephi to prepare weapons of defense." Sam pulled off his turban and ran his fingers through his dark hair. "With only a couple dozen people on each side of the family, what would a battle look like?"

"I don't know," Isaabel said, wondering what Sam meant. "It would be over very quickly."

"Exactly," Sam agreed. "Our numbers are so few that neither side would have much of an army. Unless . . ."

"Unless what?" Isaabel prompted. "Laman recruited fighters from Kaminaljuyú?"

"Possibly. But then he would know that we could do the same." Sam turned and scanned the surrounding forest. Then he looked at Isaabel, and his voice dropped to a whisper. "I think it's already begun."

Isaabel felt cold fingers of dread touch her skin. "What do you mean?"

"I think Laman's tribe will capture our people, one by one, as they hide out in the surrounding hills." He took a step closer toward Isaabel. "I think they will watch and wait, until one of us is alone, then they will attack."

Isaabel covered her mouth with her hand. *Eve.* Eve had been alone. *And Jacob, too.* "What can we do?"

"Build a wall to surround our village. Arm everyone with a weapon, and never leave the settlement alone." Sam waved toward the ax. "When I realized that this must be our plan of action, I could not delay. When the others wake this morning, we'll devote the rest of the day to this wall."

Isaabel's mind reeled. What if Nephi and the others had been captured by Laman? She hated staying in the village and doing nothing, although a part of her knew that her duty was to protect her children and care for Sariah.

Sam met her gaze, his eyes reddened with exhaustion. "We may have already lost . . ." his voice cracked, "four of our own. We cannot lose another soul."

CHAPTER 17

*The Lord preserveth all them that love him: but all the
wicked will he destroy.*

(PSALM 145:20)

They ran, stumbled, and ran again. Eve could feel her breath
tearing against her chest as she fought to keep up with Jacob. His
hand gripped hers firmly, half pulling and half dragging her along.
Her wrists and ankles throbbed, and the heaviness of her wet clothing
weighed her down. She wanted to cry out for Jacob to stop. She
craved just a few precious moments of rest, but he urged her on, apol-
ogizing in the process.

Three days ago, Eve would never have imagined such a predica-
ment—literally running with Jacob for their lives. Suddenly he stopped
and pulled her into a crouch beside him.

"Shhh," he whispered in her ear.

Eve tried to still her breathing, but there was nothing she could
do about the pounding of her heart. It was also difficult to breathe
lightly in the fierce humidity. She strained to listen, but heard
nothing. Light drops of rain fell, warm and soft. Yet Eve was not
fooled; she knew the rain could become merciless in an instant. But
perhaps the rain would become a protector, washing their tracks and
scent. She was about to ask Jacob, when a short, low whistle sounded,
cutting like a knife through her chest. She knew, without a doubt,
that it belonged to one of her cousins.

Jacob's arm tightened around her, and Eve felt his body tense. His breathing warmed the top of her head, if only temporarily. She felt the thudding of his heart against her back.

The whistle came again, much closer this time. Eve sensed that Jacob wouldn't wait much longer in their hiding place.

Another whistle sounded, higher pitched, slightly farther away.

"Ready?" Jacob whispered in a barely audible voice.

Eve's answer caught in her throat, but she managed to nod once.

"Stay with me . . ."

The words were hardly spoken before Jacob pulled her to her feet and thrust her through some thick brambles behind them. Eve tried not to stumble against the slippery ground but commanded her aching legs to move forward. A shout sailed above them. Eve increased her pace, pushing her body beyond its limit. The branches caught at her skin and her clothing, tearing and ripping. But Eve didn't care. She knew that if they were caught again, receiving only a beating would truly be an act of mercy.

"Go!" Jacob hissed behind her.

Eve realized that if her cousins caught them, Jacob would sacrifice himself for her. She didn't want that on her conscience, nor did she want to imagine the devastation that his loss would cause her family—and herself. Pumping her legs harder, she ran through the drenched forest blindly. Then the rain suddenly stopped, and speckled spots of light descended through the trees, making it easier to see. But it also meant that Shem and Javan could see them better.

They plunged onward, and Eve felt as if time were slipping from her fingers. Were these leafy trees the last thing she'd see on earth? Were Jacob's torturous cries the last sounds she'd hear?

O Lord, her heart pled, *Spare us from this awful fate. Protect us with Thy power. You sent an angel of mercy . . . please don't let the woman's efforts be in vain.*

Another shout, and soon Eve realized that Jacob had moved in front of her. He grabbed her arm and pulled her to the right. But she tripped, and both of them tumbled to the ground. They both lay on the ground, panting, covered in leaves and dirt. Jacob's gaze met hers for a wild instant, and he reached for her hand. But instead of pulling her up, he said, "Hide yourself. I'll lead them away."

Eve shook her head frantically. "No, I want to stay with you."

"We'll both die," Jacob said, his eyes softening for a moment. "At least this way, you have a chance."

Eve latched onto his hand, squeezing hard. "I cannot let you be at their mercy alone. We must stay together . . . for better or worse."

Jacob stared at her for a long second, then finally he said, "All right, but if we are captured, let them take me . . . and you flee for help."

Nodding resolutely, Eve rose to her feet. She shook all over, but she knew they had already wasted precious moments. Footsteps could be heard crashing through the nearby trees, and she thought her heart would leap out of her chest. But no matter what happened, she wouldn't be alone.

Hand in hand, they started running again. The trees thinned, and the undergrowth increased. Soon, they neared the top of a hillside. With the foliage growing sparse, she felt more exposed than ever and imagined Shem or Javan pouncing on her at any moment.

She was too full of panic to take in her surroundings and see if anything looked familiar. As she gulped for air and forced her legs to keep moving, she wondered if death might be a better alternative to the physical pain she now experienced. Even still, she didn't want to give her cousins any sort of victory.

This thought propelled her forward through the moments when she felt she could no longer continue. *If Jacob can still run, then I can,* she finally decided. She clawed her way through the fortress of brambles before her, ignoring the searing pain coming from sharp thorns and branches that ripped her clothing and tore at her feet. She choked back her sobs as the pain nearly blinded her vision. Her fear of being caught outweighed the pain, but just barely.

As she made her way up the hillside where Jacob was leading her, the wet earth gave way beneath her feet. She reached out for something to grab, but her hands came away empty. Her body hit the ground, and she started to tumble downward. She tried to slow the momentum and grab onto any of the passing shrubs. But she was rolling too fast. She heard someone shout her name just before she stopped tumbling. Once the ground beneath her was finally still, the sky above seemed to pitch wildly. Dark clouds swirled against the blue sky.

"Jacob," she tried to call, but only a cracked whisper came from her lips. She had to get up and signal to him where she'd fallen. But the rain had started again, this time coming in torrents, and she couldn't move. As she tried to lift her arm, her throat strangled a scream. Pain seized her, driving through her entire body at once. Just before everything went dark, she prayed that Jacob would be the first to find her.

* * *

Nephi paced as Zoram stared at the trees above. They had just finished a simple meal of guava fruit and wild rabbit. Elisheba sat on the ground, huddled against a tree. Her bruises and lacerations had been attended to, but with the improvement of her condition, Nephi almost dreaded the questions he needed to ask his sister. He glanced at her, seeing a thin and broken woman—so pale and fragile, her clothing inadequate to protect her from the sun or the rain. She had curled up in Zoram's outer tunic, but her too-large eyes haunted her gaunt face.

How could Raamah let his wife live in such a manner? Nephi thought. The more he dwelled on his sister and her circumstances, the angrier he became. And she was with child! His heart ached just thinking about the worst that could have happened to her. So far, she claimed that her babe had not been hurt in the beating. But it might be too early to tell.

He stopped his pacing and turned toward her. Zoram noticed the action and brought his gaze around to follow Nephi's.

"How far to Laman's settlement?" Nephi asked.

Elisheba's eyes filled with tears. "We can be there by midday if we start now."

Nephi nodded, grimacing as he did so. "We have to at least try."

She stood, and Zoram offered a hand to keep her steady. "I—" she began, her voice thick with emotion. "I will take you as far as I am able."

Nephi knew she did not refer to her physical ability, but something that was far more difficult. He met his sister's courageous gaze, then he stepped forward and took her into his embrace.

She seemed to melt against him, her thin shoulders trembling. He could feel the protrusion of her stomach and thought of the niece or nephew who was about to be born into her world of sorrow and uncertainty.

Elisheba pulled away first, her chin trembling as she contained her sobs. "I miss my boys every moment of each day. The bones in my body cry out for them, grieve for them, and now . . . when I think I may see them again, I am unsure. What have they become? Will I recognize them? Will they recognize *me*?" Her voice faltered. "Do they despise their mother who abandoned them?"

Shaking his head, Nephi said, "You had no choice." He looked at his sister with all the sobriety he could muster. "You are not to blame."

"If I am discovered, this journey may cost me my life," Elisheba whispered. "But my life is worth nothing without my children."

"Elisheba," Nephi groaned with emotion, no longer able to hold back the questions. "What happened between you and Raamah? Why did he not keep his marriage oath?"

She brought a trembling hand to her brow and lightly touched the bruises on her face. "He tried to . . . he wanted to . . ." She paused for a moment, overcome with emotion. "Although the settlement had cast me out, Ramah hid me away in the forest and tried to preserve my life. But once they found out that he was hiding me and bringing me food they beat him. Then Anah came to warn me that they knew where I was hiding and that Raamah and I both were in danger. So in the end, I was the one who decided to leave. I knew that in order to preserve the life of my husband and children, I had to give them up." She took a shaky breath and looked at Nephi with luminous eyes.

Nephi's heart softened a little toward Raamah, but he still didn't understand one thing. "Why didn't you come to us?"

Elisheba clutched Zoram's outer robe that hung around her thin shoulders. "I just couldn't bear to leave them. Even though I couldn't see them, speak to them, I always hoped for a chance . . . a change of heart."

A grim smile crossed Nephi's face. "For many years, I have hoped for the same thing."

"And now?" Elisheba prompted.

"That hope is gone."

Zoram joined the pair, looking from brother to sister. "There is still hope for something."

Nephi arched a brow and waited for Zoram's explanation.

"My daughter," Zoram said in an anguished, yet determined voice.

"Of course," Nephi said, glancing at Elisheba. "We will do this for Eve and Jacob." He hesitated. "The others may be lost to us, but at least we can spare two people from Laman's influence."

Elisheba exhaled slowly. "All right." She turned toward the climbing jungle. "This way."

The three carved their way through the jungle mass, Elisheba leading the way. She kept one hand cradled around her belly, while using the other for balance as they walked through the thick undergrowth.

Nephi gazed past the heavy foliage, wondering about Eve and Jacob. Where were they? Had they already arrived at Laman's settlement? Would they still be alive when Nephi and Zoram came? And what manner of torture and humiliation would they suffer in the meantime? Finally, he thought about the sword of Laban and the means it had been of bringing the brass plates into the wilderness. All at the Lord's bequest.

In his heart, Nephi began to plead with the Lord as he had done so many times before. The Lord had always answered his prayers, although not necessarily in the manner that Nephi expected. He thought of his mother and her failing health, Eve and Jacob, and poor Elisheba. She had suffered so much—and still suffered. Yet even as Nephi realized the many precious lives that hung in the balance, he felt the strengthening hand of the Lord. It was as if the more difficult the situation became, the more the Lord extended His hand.

As he followed Elisheba, Nephi marveled at the inner strength his sister possessed. Not only had she risked her life earlier for Eve and Jacob, but she was now making another sacrifice by guiding them to Laman's settlement.

* * *

Isaabel moved through the motions of the day with a numb heart. As the sun expanded its warm grasp over the fields and livestock, her chest tightened with worry. It had been too long since Nephi and Zoram had left. She walked along the row of maize stalks, picking ripened ears as she went. Her basket was nearly full, but she was reluctant to return to the settlement. She felt closer to Nephi when she worked in the fields, as if she were in a better position to spot him the moment he emerged from the trees.

Young Lehi babbled contentedly on the ground in the next row, scooping the dirt and watching it sift through his stout fingers. Isaabel smiled as he continued to play in innocence. The little boy didn't know anything was amiss. For a moment, she wished she could exist in such a state of ignorance. Looking away from the baby, she saw her oldest, Aaron, keeping watch over the field. Sam had stationed him there and seven-year-old Joseph on the other side of the fields, and had positioned the younger boys at different lookouts around the settlement—all keeping watch as the women gathered and stockpiled food. Isaabel plucked another cob and tossed it into the full basket. "I guess we'd better return home," she said to Lehi.

She picked up her son and fastened him onto her back with her mantle. Then she hefted the basket, propping it against her hip. Isaabel cut across the rows, waving to Tamar when she passed by, then moved onto the open path. She could see the line of wood stakes that Sam was building. It would take many weeks to finish the project, she knew, but everyone was eager to keep busy.

By the time Nephi returned, he would be impressed to find the start of a well-fortified village.

If he returned.

Isaabel shook her head, trying to rid herself of the thought. When she reached her home, she quickly dumped the load of maize in the courtyard. She didn't want to enter the lonely house and feel the emptiness of Nephi's absence. She walked to Sariah's home where she knew she'd find Rebeka tending their mother-in-law.

She arrived at Sariah's courtyard and found her daughter, Sarah, bent over a piece of embroidery. Isaabel stooped to admire her daughter's handiwork. She was surprised to see Sarah stitching a complicated pattern of wildflowers.

"How did you learn that?" Isaabel asked. She removed her son from the makeshift sling and balanced him on her hip.

Sarah glanced at her mother, then focused again on the cloth. "Eve taught me. I can't wait to show her how much I've finished."

Tears stung Isaabel's eyes. "Is your Aunt Rebeka inside?"

Sarah nodded.

"Where are your cousins?"

"Deborah and Rachel grew tired of stitching, so their mother sent them for water."

"Alone?" Isaabel asked, feeling a jab of worry. She let little Lehi sit on the ground and crouched next to him, watching him pick up a rock and examine it.

"No, they went with Tiras," Sarah said.

Isaabel nodded. Dinah had a new babe, a son they named Meshech, and spent most of her time inside with him and two-year-old Seba. And with the absence of three men, Tiras had become everyone's protector. Just as she straightened, she heard someone call her name.

Turning, Isaabel saw Sam approaching. His looked exhausted, his face red with exertion. "Have you seen Tamar?" he asked.

"I just passed her in the fields," Isaabel said. "What's the matter?"

"We need to have a family council." Sam sounded hesitant. "These stockades will take too long to finish. We need another plan."

Isaabel nodded, knowing that Sam was right. If an attack came in the next few days, they would be far from ready. And each hour that passed, without the return of Nephi, just created more anxiety in her heart. She glanced at Sarah, who was still bent over her stitching and had surely heard every word.

"We'll gather here," Sam added. "Mother needs to be a part of this."

"Of course," Isaabel said. She watched Sam hurry away, then turned to see Sarah watching her.

"Why do we have to build the walls, Mother? Is Laman fighting with Father again?"

Isaabel knew these questions would come eventually. She sat next to her daughter, letting out a sigh. "We are just building the walls as a precaution. When your father returns, he'll tell us if we need to do anything else."

Sarah nodded, her face a mask of seriousness. "I wish we could all live together. Then my other cousins could see the temple."

"Me, too," Isaabel said, her thoughts churning. Not only was her husband in probable danger, but so were her children. She said another silent prayer—perhaps her hundredth that day—and pled with the Lord to spare her family.

"I'll go tell Rebeka about the council." Isaabel kissed her daughter on the top of the head, then she scooped her son into her arms and entered her mother-in-law's home. Rebeka and Dinah were both inside preparing food.

Isaabel slipped into Sariah's room and saw that she slept peacefully. After watching her for a few moments, she rejoined the women in the cooking room.

Dinah's young baby, Meshech, gurgled when he saw his aunt. "He grows bigger every day," Isaabel said as she smiled at her nephew.

Dinah beamed with pleasure. "He must take after his Uncle Nephi."

"Oh, I don't know," Isaabel said. "Tiras is quite tall, too."

Dinah smiled and lowered her eyes. Isaabel thought she detected a note of concern in her sister-in-law's expression.

Isaabel glanced at Rebeka, but her oldest sister just looked away. "What is it, Dinah?"

"Tiras grows tired of waiting for the men to return," Dinah began, her voice low. She glanced between Rebeka and Isaabel. "Each hour it becomes worse. Last night I had to talk him out of leaving to search for Eve and Jacob by himself. He fears . . . he fears that something awful has happened to Nephi and Zoram."

Isaabel looked at Rebeka, comprehending only a small amount of what her sister must feel having both her husband and daughter missing. But was the solution to send more of their family to find them?

"If Tiras left . . . we'd only have one man to protect us."

Dinah nodded, a sad smile on her face. "That's what I told him." She sighed loudly.

"I don't know what else we can do but continue to have faith," Isaabel said, knowing that her words carried truth. But once she'd spoken them, she felt they sounded trite. Rebeka's expression remained closed. "Sam has called a family council," Isaabel said, seeing Rebeka's eyes spark with interest. "I don't think it's necessarily good news, though."

Just then, a shout came from outside.

"That's Tiras," Dinah said, rising and picking up little Meshech. "The girls are back with the water."

Isaabel followed Dinah and Rebeka into the courtyard where some of the family had arrived.

Sam crossed to Isaabel. "Do you think Mother can make it outside?"

"She's sleeping." Isaabel glanced at the house. "It might be better to let her know our decision when she wakes. I don't think she is quite lucid, and reminding her that Nephi and Jacob are still gone will only upset her."

"All right," Sam said. Isaabel could see how their circumstances weighed heavily on her brother-in-law's shoulders. He'd always worked under the direction of Lehi or Nephi, but now Sam had to fulfill the leadership role.

"Let's begin," Sam called over the murmur of voices.

With Zoram, Nephi, and Jacob gone, the only men who remained were Sam and Tiras. The rest of the group consisted of women and children. Sam looked across the family members and asked Tiras to offer a prayer.

When Tiras finished, Sam waited a moment then said, "I do not need to tell you how much I worry, for I know all of you feel the same." His gaze met Isaabel's. She could see by his flushed features that this speech was not easy for her brother-in-law. His usual jovial nature had become grave.

"We must do more," Sam said, continuing over a few exclamations. "We must prepare supplies and food in the event that we are forced to flee our home."

Isabel gasped. Would it come to that? Would they become fugitives from their own family again?

Sam continued, looking directly at Isaabel. "Gather anything you think Mother might need for a journey." His gaze shifted. "The rest of you repair your tents and rugs. Fill baskets with dried meat and vegetables. Tiras has been repairing our bows, which we will add to the supplies."

Dinah stood. "What about the fortifications? Don't you think they will protect us?"

"They will help," Sam conceded. "But we only have two men among us, and the going is slow."

Nine-year-old Aaron rose to his feet, his face red. "I'm nearly a man. And I can fight like one." Joseph went quickly to his feet as well, standing next to his nephew Aaron with a look of equal determination.

Sam's expression softened. "Of course you both are. What I meant to say was that we have only two *full-grown* men."

Sam's acknowledgment seemed to satisfy them, and Isaabel noticed a slight smile on Aaron's face. But no matter what Sam said, Aaron was still a child and she would rather fight than let her son enter any battle. She was sure that if Sariah was lucid, she'd insist the same for her own boy.

"In addition, we'll build a well in the center of our village, so if we are cut off for some reason and have to depend on the walls to protect us, we'll at least have water."

Isabel nodded, grateful for Sam's foresight. But she also worried they would not have time to do all of these tasks.

A commotion in the home's entryway caused Isaabel to turn. Sariah stood there, balancing against the pole frame. Isaabel leapt to her feet and moved to aid her mother-in-law. Sariah's face was a sickly shade of gray, and her clothing hung loosely about her fragile frame.

"Mother, what are you doing out here?" Sam called, hurrying toward her, too.

Sariah leaned against Isaabel and stared at Sam. "What have you done with your brothers?" she asked, her eyes blazing. "Untie them at once."

Sam's face paled. He looked at Isaabel, desperation in his eyes.

"Mother," Isaabel said gently. "Sam has done nothing to Nephi and Jacob. They left to find Eve." She thought it better to be as frank as possible.

"Little Eve?" Sariah looked wildly at the surrounding family. "What's happened to her? Where is she?"

Rebeka stepped forward and took Sariah's other arm. "Eve will return soon. But you must rest so that you can listen to her grand stories."

Isaabel's chest swelled with emotion as she listened to Rebeka's brave and confident words. Rebeka's eyes were bright with unshed tears. Isaabel held back her own as she and Rebeka helped their mother-in-law back into the house.

"There now, let's get you comfortable," Isaabel said as they walked. Rebeka began to hum softly.

As the two women tucked the light rug about Sariah's body, Isaabel wondered if Sariah had seen something in a dream. A shiver passed through her body. Perhaps Sariah had seen Nephi tied up again by Laman, and perhaps it was really happening. *Right now.*

CHAPTER 18

Discern between the righteous and the wicked, between him that serveth God and him that serveth him not.
(MALACHI 3:18)

Jacob's body swung back and forth like a skinned carcass on a spit pole. Thoughts of cannibals entered his mind, but he could feel no heat beneath his body. He cracked open his good eye to see if he were really tied like a meal ready to be eaten.

Above, the sky was brilliant blue; wispy clouds meandered along as if nothing was amiss. Jacob saw that indeed, his hands and feet had been tied together, and he hung from a sturdy pole. The jarring movements and the weight of his body being supported by his tied hands and feet sent searing pain through his limbs. He strained to look toward his feet. Two men carried the pole. They jogged, maneuvering along a steep path quite easily.

Jacob closed his eyes again, grateful that at least he was alive, but he couldn't remember what had happened. *Eve.* His less damaged eye flew open. *Where was she?* He tried to move his head enough to see behind him. He saw only bare chests and necks adorned with jade jewelry—belonging to the two men who held the back of the pole. Their eyes met, and one of them shouted to the men on the opposite side.

Oh, no, Jacob thought, *now what?*

But the men kept moving and Jacob whispered a prayer of gratitude that it was no longer Shem and Javan who held him captive, although he wasn't exactly sure if what was happening to him was something to be thankful for. The jade jewelry about their necks indicated these men belonged to the Kaminaljuyú tribe. Before Laman and Nephi had separated, Jacob had become somewhat friendly with a few of its members—mostly through delivering his father's generous gifts. But that was more than two years ago now. He hoped that he'd have a chance to remind these tribal men of the earlier offerings.

As the strange procession continued, Jacob tried to coax what had happened from his throbbing head. He remembered Eve falling down the hillside. He had grabbed a root to prevent his own fall, but he'd watched helplessly as she tumbled out of his reach. With Shem and Javan closing in, he did the only thing he could think of. He lunged after her, half sliding, half rolling down the hill. Shouts had followed him . . . And then he remembered nothing, until now.

Were Shem and Javan with these tribal men? Or even worse, had these Kaminaljuyú people joined with Laman's tribe, and was Jacob was merely being led to his place of torture?

Suddenly the jarring movement ceased, and he felt himself lowered to the ground. All became still. With great effort, Jacob tried to see out of his eye. The light above kept changing, dark to light and light to dark, as if the sun kept disappearing behind a black cloud. When his eye began to focus more steadily, Jacob realized that he was in a small hut. There was no sunlight, only the glow of a dying fire. Then a strange scent reached his nostrils—smoke that carried a pungent, almost rotten-wood smell.

So that really is what's happening, Jacob realized. *They are preparing to sacrifice me.* He'd heard of the human sacrifices made by these people.

As the last fragment of light disappeared, Jacob was left in a stuffy grayness. He let out a low breath, feeling his pulse increase, which magnified the pain in his face and shoulder. But he pushed away thoughts of his own discomfort and tried to focus on what had happened to Eve. Did Shem and Javan follow him down the mountain and capture her, leaving him for dead?

A light flickered nearby, and instinctively his eyelid opened. An angelic face hovered just above his. Curiosity set in, and he tried to reach up and touch the beauty. If only to draw strength and power one last time before he closed his eye again.

"Eve," he whispered, the word sounding desperate on his lips.

But the voice was low and mellow. The dialect was familiar somehow, and Jacob recognized a few words. "Healer" was among them. The soothing speech continued, and he felt a cool pressure against his festering eye and swollen cheek.

"Where's Eve?" he tried to say through his thick throat. "Where is the woman who fell?" He couldn't remember the Kaminaljuyú word for *woman*, but as the healer continued her work, Jacob felt miraculous relief from the pain that spread through him. It was as if the dark night had left, leaving a new day in its place.

Unease filtered its way into his mind. Would these people heal him in preparation for sacrifice? His vision cleared for a moment, as if the pungent smoke that filled the shelter had healing properties of its own. He tried to speak again to the healer, to thank her, to question her. She continued to work in the dim light as a light melody escaped her lips. If Jacob had just entered paradise, he would expect nothing less from a chorus of angels.

He could see the outline of her face and shoulders now, and he was surprised at how young she seemed. She couldn't be much older than he, but her gaze held wisdom beyond both of their years. Her eyes seemed deeper than a well, black and warm. But it was her touch that mesmerized him. She continued to massage and flex his limbs. He didn't know how much time passed, whether the sun had set or risen. But with the moving hours, his body began to mend. And he was grateful to this healer who had most likely saved his life.

As Jacob slipped in and out of wakefulness, he tried, many times, to ask about Eve. But the healer continually hushed him, feeding him a strong hot liquid, or fanning the acrid smoke about the shelter.

If night blended into day, Jacob wasn't aware of it. But he did know that his body felt stronger and his mind clearer. He realized that the smoke the healer kept constant was helping him relax. On one hand, he knew this increased the pace of healing, but on the other,

Jacob feared the relaxation it brought on would prevent him from finding Eve. She could very well be in great danger . . . *if* she was still alive.

The thought sent desperation through Jacob, and the next time the healer left the enclosure, he turned to his side. Maneuvering toward the edge of the shelter, he tried to lift the propped wood. But the energy it took was too much, and he lay still for a moment. The only sound that filled the tent was his own breathing. Jacob decided he'd have to crawl to the entrance. A few gulps of fresh air would help him think clearly.

Footsteps sounded outside the shelter, and with tremendous effort, Jacob made a swift movement to regain his place. He closed his eyes just before he heard the person enter.

Fully expecting the healer to resume her routine, he was surprised when he heard, "Jacob."

He opened his eyes, recognizing Eve's voice immediately. A jolt of relief passed through him. But the woman before him had changed so much that he wondered if he imagined her presence.

Her hair was twisted in plaits and swept up, topped by a head-dress of green quetzal feathers. Her brow and cheeks had been painted with indigo-colored designs. Several jade and shell necklaces hung about her neck, and jade bracelets lined her upper arms. Her clothing consisted only of a long wraparound piece of cloth, brilliantly dyed in the hues of a rainbow.

She reached out and touched his cheek. "You are healing nicely."

Jacob was relieved to see her. He couldn't explain the warmth in his heart as he saw her alive and healthy, when he had feared the worst. He raised himself on his elbow and peered at her. "Eve?"

"Yes," she said, bringing her hands to her throat and fingering her jewelry. Above one of her wrists, a deep bruise spanned her arm.

"What happened? Are you hurt?"

"I'll be all right." But her face paled for an instant. "They dressed me like this . . . but—" Her voice faltered, and she lowered her head, avoiding his gaze.

"What's wrong?" Jacob asked.

She waited a moment before responding in a soft, tremulous voice. "I begged them to let me see you . . . one last time."

* * *

Black smoke rose from the high treetops, creating a stark contrast to the blushing sky. The sun had set, and the only light that remained came from its golden reflection against the billowed clouds. Nephi watched a flock of birds startle away as he and Zoram moved through the escarpment. Elisheba lagged behind, but refused to rest even when the men had encouraged her to.

"The first sign is always smoke," Elisheba said quietly, coming to crouch next to Nephi. They used the thick foliage to their advantage, and except for the scattering birds, there would be no sign of their approach.

"What are they burning? Old crops?" Zoram asked as he scanned the line of trees.

"They're not burning, they're smelting," Nephi explained, recognizing the color of smoke—it was the same that wafted from his own kilns when they were in use.

"Yes," Elisheba said. If she was surprised at Nephi's intuitiveness, she didn't show it.

Nephi continued to watch the smoke, wondering what advancements the people of Laman had made in the settlement. For an instant he thought longingly of his own village—the rows of fields, the neatly built homes, and the healthy flocks of sheep and gaggles of turkeys. His people had been industrious over the past two years. "What do they smelt?"

"All manner of metals," Elisheba said. "Gold, silver, copper, brass, iron. They make things mostly to trade . . . sometimes I can't even believe what they make trades for."

"Trade? Trade for what?" Zoram asked.

Nephi was curious to know the answer. The surrounding hills and seas provided everything that was needed for a prosperous life.

"Girls . . . sometimes women." Elisheba's voice cracked. "Or sometimes young boys who are used for work."

Nephi's stomach recoiled at the mention of women and young children used as slave laborers. "They don't harvest their own fields?"

"Fields?" Elisheba let out a short laugh. "My garden was the only one remaining when I was forced out. I don't think any of the men or women have plowed a field or planted a seed since your departure."

"What about all the seeds we brought from Jerusalem?" Nephi asked, feeling his face heat in anger.

"Gone. What wasn't planted before you left was left for critters and birds."

"What do they eat?" Zoram asked, his voice reflecting disgust.

"Beasts of prey. The slave children gather fruit when it's in season, but other than that, it's mostly meat." Elisheba turned her moist gaze to meet Nephi's. "That's why I kept a garden. I gladly shared the harvest with my sisters, but there came a time when they became too proud to take my offerings." She shook her head and tried to drop the conversation.

But Nephi wasn't finished. "At least the men keep busy by smelting and hunting?"

Elisheba corrected him. "Even the smelting is done by the slaves. But Laman and the others do hunt, although they are considered more victorious when they bring back more than just slain animals."

Wretched sorrow showed plain on Elisheba's face, and he decided not to press further. He looked over at Zoram.

"Counting the slaves, how many do you think live in Laman's settlement?" Zoram asked.

Elisheba looked surprised. "When the slaves turn twelve, they are given back to the Kaminaljuyú. Laman doesn't want any of them rising up in power or strength against him."

"They are returned to their tribe? Their families must be happy to welcome them back."

Elisheba dipped her head and stared at the ground. Then she looked toward the eastern mountains. "I come across these abandoned children quite often. Some of them have a difficult time integrating back into their culture. Their people see them as damaged." She pointed toward a rising hill and sighed. "They congregate and form colonies, scavenging off the land. I believe when there are enough of them, they'll band together and take revenge upon Laman."

With a solemn nod, Nephi caught Zoram's gaze. "So we only have to worry about four men, plus Shem and Javan?"

"Against us three," Elisheba breathed.

"We won't let you walk into danger," Zoram said. "Just Nephi and I will go down."

Elisheba's thin fingers gripped Nephi's arm. "You don't understand. You may have been the largest brother in stature, but now . . . with the savage way of life in Laman's village, any one of the men could overpower you—as if it were ten men to your one."

A grimace pulled at Nephi's mouth. He wondered if they had become like the fierce marauders they'd encountered on the journey from Jerusalem to Bountiful.

"Let's wait until night falls, when we can ensure better cover," Elisheba said.

Zoram's expression tightened. "The delay has already been too long. I can't wait any longer to rescue my daughter."

Elisheba shook her head. "You don't understand. It will be easier to rescue Jacob and Eve if we wait . . . the men become drunk after the evening meal and will not be able to fight back so readily."

Nodding at the wisdom of his sister's words, Nephi felt torn between Elisheba's and Zoram's wishes. "Perhaps we can creep closer and get a look at what is going on. If Jacob and Eve seem relatively secure, we can wait until darkness falls."

Zoram breathed out a sigh of relief and looked at Nephi with gratitude in his eyes.

"All right," Elisheba said.

The three moved silently through the thick undergrowth, keeping themselves concealed from any exposure. Nephi bent over, half crouching, half crawling. The hairs on the back of his neck bristled in anticipation each time he heard a bird or other sound in the jungle.

He thought he heard the sound of beating drums as they neared the village, but soon Nephi realized it was only the thudding of his heart. Elisheba became visibly distraught as they grew closer and closer. "Wait here," Nephi finally said. She hid herself among a group of fallen logs.

Zoram and Nephi covered the last hundred paces quickly, where they lay flat on their bellies and scooted toward the edge of the clearing. It took a moment for Nephi to gain his bearings. So much had changed that he hardly recognized the village as the one that his father had so carefully laid out.

Several of the huts had been razed and the main building extended. The gathering room in which Nephi, Lehi, and Jacob had studied the brass plates now looked like a haphazard collection of stones. With further scrutiny, Nephi realized it warehoused mined rock. Stacks of quarried stone sat in piles, surrounding the building. The workers moved in and out of the building, heads down, bent on the task at hand. With a sinking feeling, Nephi saw that Elisheba was right—the slave children were no more than twelve.

The young boys and girls scurried about the vast yard, carrying rock from the gathering room across the dirt courtyard to the smelting building. Sharp commands echoed in the early evening, and Nephi strained to see who the taskmaster was.

"Heth," Zoram breathed. "The one issuing the commands is Heth."

Nephi stared at the dark-skinned man with a bulging girth. The darkness covered his entire being, as if he'd been born that way. The Lord's words echoed through his mind. *They hardened their hearts against me like flint and I did cause a skin of darkness to come upon them.*

Incredulous, Nephi saw that Heth had done little to cover his body. He wore only a loin cloth, fastened with a girdle. Dark bands of dye covered his arms and legs. His hair had been shorn off, except for one extended lock that was twisted into a braid. If Zoram hadn't spoken the man's name, Nephi wouldn't have recognized Heth.

"I don't see them," Zoram said.

Staring into the gathering dusk, Nephi tried to pick out anyone else who looked familiar. "Perhaps they are being held in one of the huts."

Zoram shook his head. "It's too quiet here. The slaves are working like nothing has changed." He paused, then took a deep breath.

"Something must have happened to them before they reached the settlement, or perhaps . . . they're already . . ."

"Don't think that way," Nephi said. "They could be on the other side of the village." He pointed to a circle of rocks. "That is probably where they have their family meals. If we stay here, we might overhear something."

"No," Zoram said. "We can't just lie here and wait." He turned his pained expression to meet Nephi's gaze. "I have to know if she's . . . alive."

Nephi touched Zoram's shoulder. "What do you suggest?"

Zoram wiped the moisture from his eyes with a dirt-stained hand. "We should circle the village, see every angle for ourselves."

"We'd have to leave Elisheba alone," Nephi said. He glanced behind them as if checking on her. Even though he couldn't see into her hiding place, he could at least reach her quickly if he needed to. He looked at Zoram and saw sorrow and desperation in his eyes. Nephi knew that even if the trip around the village proved fruitless, at least they would be doing something instead of just waiting.

"All right," Nephi said. "I'll tell Elisheba of our plans. Wait here."

Zoram offered a smile of gratitude and scooted away from the clearing to await Nephi's return.

Nephi moved as fast as he could, considering he had to crawl most of the way. He found the pile of logs quite easily. A piece of cloth showed through one of the gaps between the logs. He'd have to tell her to conceal herself better before he left again. "Elisheba," he whispered. "It's me."

He waited a moment, then crept toward the opening. She may have fallen asleep, he thought, and he wouldn't be surprised—after all she'd been through in addition to carrying a child.

"I wondered how long you could stay away."

A jolt spread through Nephi at the sound of the words. He spun around, heart telling him who the speaker was before seeing with his own eyes. Every sinew in his body tensed and a wave of dread pounded through his chest. Taking a deep breath, Nephi addressed the brother he'd not seen in over two years.

"Laman."

CHAPTER 19

Justifying the righteous, to give him according to his
righteousness.

(1 KINGS 8:32)

Jacob stared at Eve, trying to comprehend her words in spite of the smoky haze filling the tent. He felt his throat tighten as he craved a single breath of fresh air. "Then am I the one to be sacrificed?"

Eve smiled, though it didn't reach her sorrowful eyes. "No, Jacob." Her voice was just above a whisper. "You will not be sacrificed."

"You then?" Jacob mustered himself onto his elbows, ignoring the fresh wave of pain it sent through his shoulder. "We can leave now. I'm well enough . . . I just need to get away from this intoxicating incense."

"There will be no human sacrifice of either of us," Eve said. She lifted her arms, clearly favoring her bruised arm, and removed a necklace from the many at her neckline. "Remember this?"

Jacob gazed at the stone she dangled in front of him. It looked strangely familiar, but his head throbbed, and he knew his mind would begin to drift soon.

"Remember the tribal girl I told you about who gave it to me?" Eve tied it back in place behind her neck. "It was just after your father's death, during our flight with Nephi. I never did find out more about the girl . . . until the Kaminaljuyú discovered us at the bottom of the ravine."

She lowered her head and continued in a halting voice. "When they . . . examined me . . . they discovered the stone. It belonged to the daughter of their king. She never returned on that day long ago." Eve raised her eyes to meet Jacob's. "They think I am her—changed and renewed—they think I am the king's lost daughter."

"Did you tell them your name and who your father is?" Jacob asked. He felt his mind cloud, and he fought desperately to maintain his focus, his consciousness.

"They think I became delusional in my absence. They said the necklace proves my identity." She hesitated as a single tear dripped down her cheek. "I am to be married tonight to the new chief. The Kaminaljuyú believe this is a miracle, that I have been protected by the goddess Ix Chel and returned to them."

Jacob felt his eyelids grow heavy, but still he fought. "Help me to fresh air, Eve." Her name sounded sorrowful upon his lips. "I must speak with the king. I must explain to him . . . even if it means trading my life for yours."

"No." Eve leaned over Jacob's relaxed form. "My fate will not be so bad." Her voice wavered as she gave a watery smile. "My power as a chief's wife can be used to release you when you are completely healed." Her face drew closer and she kissed his forehead, then turned away, hiding the tears that fell. "Good-bye, dear Jacob."

Jacob tried to lift his hand, grab her arm, and stop her. But she was out of reach. As she lifted the door flap, a dim glow temporarily filled the enclosure, then it faded again into dark. He was alone. And helpless.

He struggled to open his eyes, to move, to call out to Eve. He knew she was gone, but if he could attract some sort of attention, maybe he would be taken to someone he could explain things to. As Jacob tried to formulate a plan about how to do so, he slipped into a smoke-induced slumber.

Some time later Jacob's eyes fluttered open. He didn't know how much time had passed since Eve left, but he sensed darkness closing in around him. Night had fallen, and the forlorn call of the quetzal echoed through the trees.

He turned onto his side, wincing as he put weight on his injured shoulder. Focusing on nothing but the entrance, he scooted toward it. In the distance he heard ritual chanting. With dread clenching his stomach, Jacob realized that the wedding ceremony had begun. And Eve would be a part of it if he didn't do something quickly.

Jacob parted the door flap with considerable effort, but he was more determined than ever, as if the chanting pushed him forward. The fresh air struck his senses, startling him at first. After a moment, he began to breathe easier, his body adjusting to the clean air. His head started throbbing, but he ignored it. Standing with trepidation, he paused to let his weakened muscles become used to the new position. Slowly he walked, favoring his injured ankle. The chanting grew louder, and beyond the line of trees that edged the path, he saw the orange reflection of firelight.

The farther he walked, the brighter it became. Fighting exhaustion, he arrived at the edge of the dense foliage. In the clearing rose a great, stone structure—a graduated temple. He'd heard his father talk about them when they'd first arrived at the promised land, but this was the first time he'd seen one so closely. Its massive size seemed to touch the sky as steps led from the ground to a high platform. The stone stairs were dark with stains—blood, from human sacrifice. On the uppermost platform, the victims' hearts were cut out, then their bodies rolled down the steps.

Jacob looked away from the dark stains to the base of the great stone footings where a ceremony unfolded. Strange, surreal, colorful. Several fires blazed about the perimeter, which was carefully watched by young boys who threw in kindling every so often. A woman, who could only be Eve, sat perched on top of a platform carried by four men.

On the opposite side of the clearing, another platform was carried across the open space upon which a young man perched, most of his body covered in feathers. His elaborate headdress contained large blooms and bright green feathers to match Eve's. Nestled against the headdress was the stuffed head of a jaguar. The man's clothing was dyed different colors, setting off the gold jewelry on his arms.

The bridegroom, Jacob thought. This young chief, with his bright and eager eyes, was about to be joined with his bride. Jacob tried to recall the details that led up to this event—Eve had said something about her necklace. It was proof of the tribal girl's return to earthly life. Only an equally powerful emblem could counter such a convincing sign—no matter how false.

Jacob reached beneath his tattered tunic and felt for the gold ring that hung on a leather strap about his neck. The gold caught the glow of the fire and gleamed bright in his hands. Looking at the heirloom, Jacob thought about his father, Lehi, and the moment when his father had handed over the ring. The next day Lehi had passed from this life. Now, with all that had happened, this ring and the endless moments of education were the only things that remained of his father.

And those moments are more than enough, Jacob realized. He gripped the ring tightly in his hand, mouthed a silent prayer, then limped into the middle of the ceremony.

* * *

Nephi stared into the bloodshot eyes of his eldest brother. He had known he would see one, if not both, of his brothers on this journey, but he hadn't prepared himself for what he would say when that time came. And now, seeing this brother who had no mercy in his heart— dull hatred reflected in his gaze—Nephi knew that it didn't matter anyway. Nothing had changed.

It was difficult for Nephi to tear his gaze away from his brother's figure. His clothing and skin were altered, as if Laman had taken on the appearance of a fierce warrior. Whatever handsome features he'd once had were now twisted into the ugliness of many years of hatred and impetuous living. His hair was shaved off, save one long piece that was plaited with a blue-colored strip of cloth. The beard on his face was short, cropped. Laman's torso was bare, although he wore several necklaces with large gemstones dangling at the ends. About his waist he wore a thick leather belt, from which hung a loin cloth and a sword of fine workmanship.

"You've come to preach to me and my sinful people?" Laman practically growled. "I cannot believe that you came alone." He looked past Nephi, scanning the foliage.

Nephi was about to shake his head, then thought better of it. He might be able to get more information out of Laman if his brother thought he was unaccompanied. "Someone from your village has stolen something from us."

"Sheep? Fowl? Tapir? Surely you have more than enough tame beasts to feed your children." Laman chuckled. "Do not tell me you've come begging for food, little brother."

Contempt seized Nephi's chest, but he answered in an even tone. "The sword of Laban was stolen."

"Ahh." Laman fingered the hilt on his sword. "Your claim to greatness has vanished. Who took it?"

"I have my suspicions," Nephi said. "But before you deny that it was one of your people, I must tell you that I have come seeking something greater."

Laman brought his hand to his chin and stroked his stubbly beard. "What could be greater than the symbol of your pride? The sword you so easily killed another man with, all supposedly under the Lord's direction?"

Nephi inhaled sharply, wondering how he managed to take such abuse from his brothers for so many years. "I think you already know the answer. It's Jacob, and Zoram's daughter, Eve. I followed their trail here."

Lifting a shoulder, Laman said, "I remember Eve, and Jacob must be practically a man by now." A slow grin spread across his face. "I'd say yet another brother is tired of living under your rules."

"No," Nephi said, taking a step forward. "Their tracks show they were tied together and forced to march this way." He held Laman's gaze. "If you are claiming no knowledge of these events, I demand to speak with Shem and Javan."

Genuine surprise reached Laman's expression. "Shem? So that's where he went." He locked eyes with Nephi, showing no remorse, no regret, just increased curiosity. "And you think Jacob and Eve are with him? Interesting."

"Laman," Nephi said, his voice trembling with disgust. "The past is between *us*, not them. All I want is their safe return. Then I'll never bother you again."

"How much is their safety worth to you?" Laman asked, amusement dancing in his eyes.

"Name your price, and I will deliver it."

Stroking his beard again, Laman looked toward the sky. "Well, the price will be steep." He brought his gaze to meet Nephi's. "But one that I'm sure you'll be happy to meet."

"Of course," Nephi said. "You can send some of your 'slaves' with me, and I'll give them the goods to carry back."

"It all sounds so civil . . . and *righteous*."

Nephi held his breath, not liking the change in his brother's tone.

"Ah, well," Laman said, letting out a sigh. "No."

Nephi stared at his brother. "What?"

"First of all, Jacob and Eve aren't in my village. Second, I don't know where Shem and Javan are—or if they've done what you've accused them of. Do I need a third reason?"

Nephi shook his head slowly, feeling his neck heat with frustration. "I can wait until they return."

Laman folded his arms. "Always the noble one. Always the one who will sacrifice everything for the lesser cause." His voice seethed with anger. "This is *my* territory, dear brother. These people listen to me and follow my rules. You do not belong here, and I do not take orders from you. Neither will Javan, Shem, or anyone else living in this region."

Stepping back, Nephi tried to think of what he could do to tame his brother's temper. "I'm not giving orders. You are the one who suggested a price be determined."

"Don't speak to me unless I command it," Laman shouted, his face a dark red. He removed his sword from his girth and lunged toward Nephi.

Diving out of Laman's path, Nephi tumbled to the ground and rolled before he could pull himself up again. But Laman attacked again. Nephi spun out of the way, keeping clear of the metal blade.

In one swift motion, he gripped his own dagger and held it in front of him.

But the new weapon didn't deter Laman. Again he pounced, this time gripping Nephi's neck. Nephi reared backward and both men fell to the ground in a struggling heap. Laman used one hand to wrench his brother's dagger away, and Nephi watched helplessly as it scuttled across the dirt, out of reach.

Nephi looked up—Laman's face was a mere fraction from his, his hands around Nephi's neck. "Only in my bad dreams did I ever imagine that you'd return," he said, his breath rancid and hot.

Nephi fought for breath as he wriggled beneath his brother's weight, trying to gain some leverage with a knee or a foot. A satisfied look crossed Laman's face, and he released his grip. But then he grasped Nephi's hair and slammed his head against the ground.

"Hear me out." Laman's eyes blazed. "If you want your life to be spared, leave now."

"I will leave when I have Jacob and Eve with me," Nephi said through choked breaths as he strained against his brother's full weight.

Laman snarled and held his sword against Nephi's bruised throat. "Then you have made your choice." A shrill scream erupted in the air. Laman's sword wavered, but his hold on Nephi remained fast.

From the pile of logs, Elisheba emerged, frantically yelling. "Stop! Both of you! Can't you see that it's enough?" Tears coursed down her cheeks, becoming lost beneath her chin.

Laman turned to gape at his long-lost sister. He stared at the unkempt woman with tangled hair. Nephi knew it wouldn't take Laman long to realize that Elisheba had led him to the village.

"Who else came with you?" Laman asked, holding the sword precariously close to Nephi's neck.

He was just about to answer when someone else came crashing through the underbrush. It was Zoram. Nephi wanted to shout at the man to turn around and flee for his life. But it was too late now.

Eyeing the two people who now stood together, Laman shook his head. "If either of you move any closer, you'll never hear Nephi speak again."

Nephi swallowed thickly, realizing that Laman might only cut out his tongue—better than death.

"It's unbelievable that you would dare encroach upon my village." Laman nodded his head toward Elisheba. "She is like an animal, hardly recognizable." His gaze settled on Zoram. "And you are still a dog following at his master's heels."

Zoram didn't blink. "Where's my daughter?"

Laman smiled, obviously enjoying Zoram's distress.

"She isn't here yet," Nephi said. Sensing Laman felt wary about being outnumbered, Nephi decided to wait for the right moment when Laman's attention wasn't entirely focused . . . then he'd attack.

"And you believe him, Nephi?" Zoram asked, keeping his gaze steadied on Laman.

The clear surprise Nephi had seen on Laman's face had convinced Nephi that his brother hadn't been aware of Jacob and Eve's abduction. But Zoram's question planted a seed of doubt.

Nephi focused again on his brother—plainly reading pleasure on his face. There was no trepidation or fear in the man's eyes. Perhaps being outnumbered only brought more excitement to such a murderous heart.

Suddenly, Elisheba lunged for Laman. He immediately released Nephi and turned on his sister. She started to scream, but Laman quickly silenced her by covering her mouth with his meaty hand.

Elisheba struggled wildly beneath her brother's grasp, but his hold was too strong for her weakened condition.

Laman positioned his sword against Elisheba's protruding stomach.

"She's our *sister*, Laman," Nephi shouted as he leapt to his feet. "Let her go, she has done nothing to you."

"Look at my skin—the skin of my people. She cursed us. Her presence here will only mean more trouble." He gripped her hair and pulled her head back until she looked at Laman. "Only with her death will the curse be lifted."

"Your changed skin was not caused by Elisheba," Nephi said, his chest tightening in alarm. He'd never seen his brother so beyond reason. "Being cut off from the presence of the Lord is a result of your disobedience. Your change in countenance is merely a reflection of that."

But Laman shook his head and started to back away. "Take your preaching somewhere else, little brother." He spat on the ground. "From this day forth, I no longer call you my brother. You are dead to me. Go back to your land if you want your life to be spared." He took another backward step, dragging Elisheba along. "Our *sister* has already made her decision. And if you follow, my people will shower flaming arrows upon you, Zoram, and anyone else who dares to step foot on our land."

"Please don't follow," Elisheba said, her eyes wide with resolution. "This is my decision . . . I could never be truly happy without my family anyway."

Zoram moved to Nephi's side and the two men watched helplessly as Laman dragged Elisheba out of sight.

"Let's go," Nephi said in a haggard voice.

Without hesitation, Zoram nodded, and they moved toward the left, making a wide berth around Laman.

"What do you think he'll do?" Zoram whispered as they crept through the jungle mass.

"He'll make an example out of her—a terrible example." Nephi let a low sigh escape. "Laman can't believe we would just leave her behind, especially when we're seeking Jacob and Eve. He'll create a terrible spectacle, mostly for our benefit."

Zoram gripped Nephi's arm, stopping him mid-stride. "We could rush him right now, before he reaches the village. Two of us against him—it would be an easy match."

"I thought of that, but Laman's gaze harbored murder. And Elisheba would be sacrificed in the process." Nephi pulled from Zoram's grasp. "We need to get to our watch places before it grows too dark. If we can free Jacob, we'll have another man to fight with us."

Zoram nodded somberly, his jaw clenched tight. "I don't know if I will be able to restrain myself when I see Shem and Javan."

"Nor I," Nephi agreed.

CHAPTER 20

But when I speak with thee, I will open thy mouth.
(Ezekiel 3:27)

"The woman cannot marry your chief—she is already married to me."

The words that spilled from Jacob's lips surprised even him. The tribal people stopped their music and chanting and stared at him. Jacob had learned a few words of the tribe's dialect years before, but to be able to speak it so fluently now could only mean one thing. The spirit of the Lord was present.

The chief motioned for the men carrying him to lower his platform. He climbed off, brows pulled together in confusion. He strode toward Jacob. "You are the man we healed and now you say you are married to this woman?"

"Yes," Jacob said, holding up his father's ring. "This ring is proof of our union."

The chief turned to Eve, who stared at Jacob. "Is this true?"

Jacob watched her, his heart pleading that she would go along with the ruse. He translated the chief's question. After a brief hesitation, Eve nodded.

"Why did you not tell us?"

Again, Jacob translated when Eve answered, "I could not speak your language well enough to explain."

The chief's face drew into a frown, and his expression darkened.

"This is very ill indeed. Ix Chel will not be pleased. We will have to find something to satisfy her." His gaze moved over Jacob. "The only thing that pleases her more than a marriage is a sacrifice."

Out of the corner of his eye, Jacob saw Eve hesitatingly climb off of her platform. If he could just get close enough to tell her to flee. He didn't dare say it out loud since he didn't know how much Hebrew the chief knew.

The chief took a step closer to Jacob. "Let me see the ring."

Jacob gladly handed it over, feeling like the longer any mention of human sacrifice was delayed, the better chance they had. The chief turned over the gold jewelry, then looked at Eve again.

"I will leave the ring as a gift if you let us depart in peace," Jacob said, interrupting the chief's gaze.

When the chief brought his focus back to Jacob, his throat grew dry. The look was plain in the chief's eyes—he wanted Eve for himself. Perhaps the chief didn't mind that she'd supposedly been married to a man from a different culture.

Jacob inhaled and held his breath, waiting. He felt light-headed and wondered if he would collapse, making a spectacle of himself. Instead of the true hero trying to save the woman, his body would give out before he could even reach her. The thought permeated his mind, and he knew he'd gladly give his life to save hers.

His gaze met hers. She looked like an exotic queen with all the jewelry and colorful clothing that adorned her body. Even though her fair skin contrasted with the maple color of the tribal people surrounding her, she seemed to blend in with their beauty. Her paleness complemented their rich tones.

"I can bring more gifts from my homeland," Jacob said, hoping to persuade the chief. "We've made all manner of decorative pieces, swords, bows, and arrows. Crops and animals are plenty."

"You want to pay for what is rightfully yours?" the chief asked. He kept the ring in his palm.

"Yes. I want to do what it takes for our people to exist together in peace. I am sorry that you have been disappointed. But this woman, Eve, who is the daughter of Zoram from a land far across the high seas, is not your lost betrothed," Jacob said, trying to hang onto what seemed a thread of hope.

The chief closed his hand over the ring. His features twisted and turned in the dancing firelight. "All right." He opened his palm and extended his hand. "But I cannot take this ring that represents your union."

Relief washed over Jacob. As he reached for the precious memento, a voice cut through the air.

"If the chief doesn't want her, I'll take her."

Jacob spun around, ring in hand, and with revulsion saw Shem and Javan emerge out of the dark trees. The two men sauntered to the center of the clearing, standing close to Eve. "She belongs to us," Shem said in the local language, then pointed to Jacob. "This man is a liar. He abducted her."

The chief's face grew pale; he bowed toward Shem and Javan.

Jacob realized that the chief was afraid of the two men—possibly fearing to start a war between the two tribes. Helpless anger consumed him as he saw the terror on Eve's face.

"The god Yum Caax is angry," Javan said, his expression stern.

The chief visibly quivered.

Javan stretched out his arm and pointed at Jacob. "His sacrifice will appease Yum Caax's anger."

Jacob glared at Javan. "Your gods require no such thing; it is only your lust for blood that demands it."

The men laughed. Jacob took the opportunity to motion to Eve to try and escape. She shook her head emphatically, mouthing that she wouldn't leave without him.

At that moment, communicating with Eve amidst all the chaos, Jacob was flooded with an unexpected, yet absolutely peaceful sensation. He knew Eve was the woman he wanted to marry someday. After all this time of pushing his feelings away, it took a near-death situation to make him recognize them. Suddenly, what he should do next was clear.

"I'll be sacrificed for your god if you promise to let Eve return to her home."

The chief looked at Jacob with surprise, but nodded his consent.

A grin spread across Shem's face. "We will do our best to meet your dying wishes."

The two men stepped forward and grabbed his arms, and Jacob offered no resistance. He let them lead him toward the towering temple structure to the base of the first row of steps. As they passed by Eve, he mouthed the word *run.* He prayed that she would flee and not look back.

Jacob flexed his calloused hands as they walked, thinking about the months he'd spent hewing rock and laboring with them to build Nephi's temple. He hoped that the thick skin on his hands would serve a new purpose. As Shem and Javan led him past the last blazing fire circle, Jacob lunged forward, pulling the two men with him.

Straining against their resistance, he plunged them into the fire. The outer flames scorched his legs, and Javan let go with a cry of pain. Jacob used that free hand to grab a burning piece of timber. He shoved it against Shem's skin. Shem sprang back, batting at the licking flame.

Jacob didn't feel the pain, yet. He moved as if in a dream. Everything seemed slower, more methodical. He could clearly see what he needed to do to escape. He moved toward the fire again and grabbed another piece of burning wood. Before Javan could attack, he thrust the stick against Javan's torso.

A quick glance told him that Eve had eased away from the transfixed wedding throng and moved toward the outer edge of the clearing. *Please run,* he silently begged her.

Jacob grabbed one more burning timber, his eyes stinging and his chest practically suffocating with the smoke. He threw the timber at Shem, who dove out of the way and landed wailing on the ground. His clothing had caught fire. The tribesmen rushed forward and started to stamp it out.

The moment was now, and Jacob knew it. With Eve waiting beyond the clearing, he fled the scene. A few pursued him, but the others were caught up in putting out the flames. Sheer adrenaline pushed Jacob to the edge of his limits and on he ran. Several paces into the thicket, he slowed and crouched, searching.

Waiting until the sounds of his pursuers faded, he then whispered, "Eve?" He moved in a zigzag pattern, calling for her every so often. His heart thundered at the prospect of not being able to find her. What if the tribesmen had captured her again?

Then he felt something warm grip his ankle.

Here we go again.

* * *

Biting back her scream, Elisheba let her body go limp as Laman dragged her through the trees. She didn't expect to make it out of this situation alive, but perhaps . . . hope suggested . . . she'd be able to see her children one last time.

Tears stung her eyes as she thought about their reaction to seeing their mother treated this way. *No*, she thought. *Escape now so your children aren't witnesses to Laman's brutality. Surely he'll kill you if you fight back.*

She dug her heels into the ground, trying to create some resistance and slow Laman. But he didn't seem to notice. One part of her worried that the babe she carried would be injured by the exertion, the other part reminded her that she probably wouldn't live long enough to deliver the child anyhow.

Laman relaxed his grip beneath her arms, and she heard his labored breathing. Perhaps this meant he was weakening. She turned her head and clamped her teeth into his forearm. He just cursed and gripped her tighter.

"Don't start fighting now; you'll have all your energy spent before you see your husband." Laman chuckled, grunting and pulling her with some effort over a fallen tree. "Won't he be surprised to see you? Although I don't think he'll take you back or try to defend you as he did before."

The passing branches scraped her legs, and her shoulders ached—but not as much as her heart ached to hear about Raamah. For weeks after she left Laman's settlement, she hoped he'd come and rescue her . . . demand that Laman allow her back into the family. In her best dreams she wished he'd gather the children and lead them all to Nephi's land where they could be a righteous family again.

Laman continued, "Since you abandoned your husband and children, our settlement has granted Raamah a divorce."

"But you forced me to leave," she cried.

"We couldn't allow sorcery in our village." Laman's grin was mischievous. "Raamah has certainly had his pick of new wives from the local tribes, although he hasn't replaced you . . . yet."

That news alone gave Elisheba hope. Surely her husband still had feelings for her if he hadn't taken another wife. But Laman's next words stung her heart.

"But after tonight, he'll no longer have an excuse not to remarry . . ." Laman burst out with laughter. "Tonight is turning out better than I expected."

The foliage thinned, showing the many stars above in the black sky. The distinct smell of smoke reached her, and she assumed they were nearing the cooking fire.

"It will be enjoyable to debate what type of death you'll experience." He stopped in a common area several paces from a low-burning fire pit. He lowered her to the ground. Keeping one knee pressed against her chest, he called for a rope.

Elisheba felt any earlier resolve to flee leave her. She hoped to see Raamah or her children. A young child scurried forward, carrying the rope, and Laman deftly tied her hands and feet. He left her lying in the dirt alone.

After several moments, a few children crept near her. She looked at them closely, but it seemed they were all slave children. Did Laman learn nothing at Mudhail? Living in servitude for five years had not softened his heart against this evil practice.

"Do you know the boy Dedan?" Elisheba asked quietly. The children stared in silence as if they didn't understand her words.

Then one girl stepped forward, her hair a tangled nest. "Dedan?"

"Yes," Elisheba pressed. "And his brother, Noah. They are about your age."

The girl's eyes widened and she shook her head.

"Please," Elisheba said. "Tell me how they are."

Crouching, the girl made motions of a deer.

"Are they hunting?" Elisheba asked. The girl nodded. "With their father?" The girl didn't answer.

Elisheba felt satisfied, although she ached to see them—under different circumstances. If she'd understood the girl, there would be no spectacle in front of her children. She breathed out a sigh of relief. Her death would not be a terrible ordeal for them after all.

Then another thought made her skin grow cold. What if they had adopted the ways of Laman? What if they no longer missed her or loved her? Elisheba wondered what her sons had been taught by her sisters-in-law. What had Raamah told them? Had he continued to care for them as a father, or did he pass the responsibility to the other women?

Suddenly, the children scattered, and Elisheba looked up. Two figures strode toward her and for a moment, hope returned. Perhaps Zoram and Nephi had come back to rescue her.

But as the men neared, she saw their garish features reflected in the firelight. Laman and Lemuel.

Lemuel actually smiled at her, which changed to a sinister expression. As her two brothers dragged her along the ground toward the center of the settlement, she closed her eyes against the blinding pain and thought about her father. His heart would break to know what was happening, but if his teachings were accurate, she'd soon be in a better place—a place where she'd be protected by the loving arms of the Lord.

She only had to make it through the next terrifying moments.

When her brothers slowed their pace, Elisheba opened her eyes. They'd arrived at a huge courtyard lined with blazing torches. The unnatural light made the scene surreal. But the stake that loomed in the courtyard, thick and massive, was real enough. Slave children scurried about, bringing kindling to scatter at its base.

A shot of icy dread moved along Elisheba's back. *They intend to burn me at the stake.*

Two more men stood waiting near the stake. One of them was well-rounded with much drink and meat. *Heth.* The other man was tall, but his face was partially hidden by the shadows. As Elisheba was led toward the center of the courtyard, the man's features became clear. *Raamah.*

Reason fled Elisheba. She tried to cry out to him, but the only sound that came from her throat was a strangled gasp. If he'd noticed her effort, he didn't show it. His face remained a mask of stone as he watched silently. But she thought she could see dark emotion in his eyes. Fear, regret, pity, or hatred? She couldn't tell.

She noticed his clothing. A simple and threadbare tunic hung from his shoulders, whereas her brothers wore next to nothing—only their loin cloths. His hair also remained long and his beard full. Why hadn't he shaved his hair like the other men?

Heth stepped forward, no sympathy or endearment in his expression. He grabbed her wasted body from Laman and Lemuel. Relieved of his burden, Laman shouted into the night air, "She will go up in flames as do all those who betray us. When she is burnt, the curse that she bestowed on us will also become ash."

Elisheba shuddered at the spiteful words. Then Raamah came and took her other arm to help Heth position her against the stake. The touch of his hands was a betrayal—hands that had once cared for her, loved her. She closed her eyes against his swift work. How could her own husband . . . ?

She'd survived the past two months living as a savage because she'd held onto the sliver of hope that maybe Raamah had fought for her because he still loved her. But his actions tonight, his coldness, his blind obedience to Laman, showed her otherwise. It was as if her soul had died. Her husband had divorced her in heart and body. Now this final act would divorce them in God's eyes. She stared at him, knowing it would be her last memory on earth. Surely he could see past the filth, the malnourishment, the pain . . . to his once beloved wife.

Their gazes met, and the blackness of his eyes shifted in the torchlight. He had noticed her swollen belly. Her husband would now be the murderer of not one person, but two.

"I'll finish the rest," Raamah said, his breath brushing her cheek as he looked down at her.

Elisheba was about to respond when she realized he spoke to Heth. Her brother-in-law turned and moved to stand by Laman and Lemuel, his form illuminated by the torches. The courtyard was silent except for Laman's occasional ranting. "We've been betrayed by a sorceress. She'll never bother us again."

Where were their wives? she wondered. Anah, Puah, or Zillah? She suspected that Bashemath would never leave her home after nightfall. A few children had gathered, and Elisheba turned her head from them—not wanting to recognize their faces. If her own sons were among them, she'd die before the first flame reached her skin.

Swallowing hard, she felt the tug of the ropes about her arms as Raamah tightened the knots. His closeness sent a tremor through her, and she wished she could ask him what had happened. Why did he not come after her? Why did he insist on following Laman? Was his life here better than it could be anywhere else? But as he straightened, she saw that he thought nothing of her. His eyes were dead, his face haggard.

He leaned closer to fasten the ropes around her wrists. Until now, she hadn't noticed the unusual thinness about his neck and shoulders. *Perhaps he's been ill. Perhaps he's been poisoned and couldn't come for me.* Elisheba chided herself. *Stop.* She made excuses even as her own husband paved the way for her death.

Before he pulled away, Raamah leaned close to her for a final moment, and Elisheba thought he'd forgotten to tighten one of the ropes. Instead he whispered in her ear, so faintly that she wondered if she'd heard anything at all.

"The knots are loose. When the flames grow closer, make your escape, and don't look back—no matter what you see or hear."

Elisheba's heart pounded as Raamah stepped away from her and knelt, making a pretense of adjusting the knots at her ankles. She looked upon his dark hair. *No,* she wanted to shout, *they will kill you, too. Let it be over with. Let me die with you.* Yet through her convoluted thoughts, she knew she didn't want to die.

The wait seemed agonizingly long. As Raamah left her, she suddenly felt cold and alone—more alone than she'd ever felt. She closed her eyes and prayed, for she knew her life depended on the mercy of God. There was no other way. Her mind reeled at the words Raamah spoke. Perhaps he still did love her, or perhaps he just wanted to give her a final chance. He probably felt pity for her condition and couldn't bring himself to be responsible for the death of his unborn child.

The air surrounding her sparked with fear—or was it actual flames? Smoke wafted to her nostrils, and Elisheba opened her eyes. She realized she had blocked out all activity, all sound, and now . . . the tinder had been lit. Dark figures of people danced, their shapes eerily shadowed in the firelight.

Fire had seized the outer ring of tinder, and the smoke and heat increased. Elisheba felt her skin prickle, breaking into perspiration. She started to cough, violent spurts that left her stomach sore. The child within her moved rapidly, as if he or she sensed the imminent danger.

Elisheba struggled to remember exactly what Raamah had said. Gagging on the smoke that filled her senses, she tugged at the ropes holding her wrists behind the stake. The second row of tinder blazed, the heat becoming unbearable. The knot pulled loose on her wrists, but she kept her arms in position so that it wouldn't be noticeable to any of the frenzied dancers. Through the smoke, she thought she caught of glimpse of Raamah—dancing, but more slowly than the others, watching her.

Gritting her teeth against the exhaustion and heat, Elisheba leaned forward, pulling against the ropes. They loosened noticeably. She knew she couldn't last much longer without releasing screams of terror as the fire closed in. Perspiration poured down her face, and her tunic was soaked. But the rawness of the heat tortured her eyes and throat. Her nostrils stung, and she gasped for fresh air.

Tearing free of the ropes, Elisheba lunged away from the stake. Her feet struck the searing flames and she yelped in startled pain. Relying on Raamah's words and the commotion of dancing, she burst out of the ring of fire and plunged away from the celebrants. Shouts rose from behind, and she recognized Raamah's voice screaming at Laman—diverting attention. She kept running, unconscious of her burnt feet, her swollen belly, and her fatigued body. She hunched over and ran through the dusty passageways, past houses that she didn't recognize. Then she heard more shouting.

It was as if the turmoil was only a few paces from her, the yelling filling the settlement, reverberating off the surrounding hills. Elisheba forced herself to move forward, trying not to imagine what sacrifice Raamah was making for her—if not his own life. *I am not worth it, dear husband,* she thought. *I should have never returned, Nephi or not. It is my fault that you are forced to suffer.*

Tortured thoughts ran through her mind.

"Elisheba."

She strained in the darkness to see who had called her name. It was hard to distinguish the whisper. Perhaps Shem or Javan had finally caught up with her to finish the job. Elisheba moved behind a tree, ready to run.

"Elisheba."

She recognized Nephi's voice. She stepped from her hiding place and lifted a hand. Her brother moved toward her, and behind him was Zoram. Relief flooded through Elisheba at the sight. She rushed to Nephi and fell against him. As her brother held her, she let all her emotion escape.

"Are you all right? I'm so grateful you escaped!" Nephi hugged her to him tightly. "What was all that chanting and shouting?" When she didn't answer, he gripped her trembling shoulders. "Whatever has happened, we must leave the area. Zoram and I have searched all the buildings and discovered Jacob and Eve aren't here."

Elisheba's throat constricted. All of this had been for nothing? Was her husband still alive? What type of hunt was now underway for her? As she gained control of her crying, she looked down at her scorched feet. Nephi followed her gaze.

"They tried to burn you?"

Nodding mutely, she took a shaky breath. "Ra . . . Raamah saved . . . my life."

Nephi's expression softened. "Were your sons there?"

Elisheba shook her head, unable to speak.

"Raamah might have redeemed himself after all." Nephi took his sister's hands. "Can you walk?"

"The pain will never match the pain in my heart." Elisheba bit her lip to stop another round of sobs.

Nephi looked over her head at Zoram. "We've already lost precious time, let's move." He met Elisheba's gaze. "I'm going to carry you until we can bathe your feet in a river and wrap them with cloth."

Elisheba was about to protest, but before she knew it, her brother had picked her up and was moving at a surprisingly fast pace through the thick jungle. As Nephi and Zoram cut their way toward the closest river, Elisheba closed her eyes—against the memory of Raamah's last words, against the memory of her lost sons, and against the memory of her near death—and offered a bittersweet prayer of gratitude.

CHAPTER 21

A virtuous woman . . . her price is far above rubies.
(PROVERB 31:10)

"Jacob, it's me."

Slowly Jacob turned and saw Eve emerge from the bushes. He ran to her and pulled her into his arms. "You're all right?"

She nodded against his chest, and he drew away, feeling self-conscious about his impulsiveness. He was holding her so close that he felt the rapid beat of her heart against him.

"Now what?" she whispered. "Which way do we go?"

Refocusing on the present, Jacob stiffened as he heard shouts nearby. He grabbed her hand, then inhaled sharply.

"My hands," he said, turning them over. The pink flesh throbbed, and sections of burnt skin hung in patches.

"Oh, no," she said. "We must treat them right away."

"Once we are free from our pursuers," Jacob said, blinking away hot tears of pain. He looked at Eve's trusting face in the moonlight. "How is your arm?"

She turned it over. The black had faded to purple, rimmed with yellow. "The swelling has lessened."

"Hold onto my tunic with your other hand and don't let go," he said.

The two plunged ahead in the darkness, moving upward, above the tribe's temple where they caught a view of the ring of fire.

"Where is everyone?" Eve asked, her eyes wide as she looked down upon the scene.

"Looking for us," Jacob said. "Come on. We'll travel until we grow too tired. Then in the morning we'll try to figure out what direction we need to take."

They continued over the ridge, cutting through thick jungle mass, the rest and care that both of them had received at the hands of the Kaminaljuyú proving beneficial. Jacob's shoulder hardly bothered him, and the only pain came from his burns. He was grateful that Shem's and Javan's injuries would probably slow them down. *Or increase their desire for revenge,* Jacob realized.

Now the chase was personal.

The shouts faded, and Jacob saw that as a sign of success, unless some had given up while others continued the pursuit. Eve's hand tugged at his tunic. "Hold on. There's a curaiao plant." She crouched over the plant and broke off two fleshy green leaves with sharp spikes. "These contain a soothing gel that will seal your wounds and heal the burns."

"We shouldn't stop yet," Jacob said, straining to hear any unnatural sounds. But Eve ignored his hesitancy and took one of his hands. He tried not to cringe as she carefully applied the cool salve. As he watched her work, he marveled at her endurance. After all they'd been through, she looked even more strong and healthy than he'd ever remembered. Gone was the timid and delicate girl he'd once known. She'd been replaced by a woman who could fend for herself. *One who was almost married tonight.* If that had happened, she would have been lost to him forever.

Jacob felt a strange warmth in his chest as he watched the way Eve's hair covered part of her face as she concentrated. She had discarded the tribal headdress hours before. He looked down quickly before she noticed his gaze, watching her carefully nurse his wounds. The salve had begun its healing power already, and Jacob felt a remarkable relief.

"Thank you," he whispered.

She glanced at him and smiled, her gaze open and warm. "You're welcome."

He wanted to say something more to her, something about what he was feeling. He couldn't just tell her outright that he loved her. How would she react? They were still young, with plenty of time to think about serious things when they were older. But Jacob knew without a doubt that he never wanted anyone but her by his side.

Eve continued the application, then tore a strip from the hem of her turquoise garment and loosely wrapped his hands. "All finished." She stood.

"Eve?"

She looked down at him, her dark hair framing her pure features. "Yes?"

He hesitated, his heart pounding as he thought about revealing his thoughts to her. Yet on the other hand, he worried that they'd delayed too long already. "Thank you."

Her eyebrows drew together. "You already thanked me, but 'you're welcome' again." Then she laughed.

Jacob thought it was the most beautiful sound he'd ever heard. As he rose to his feet, he vowed to do whatever was in his power to hear it much more often. But the quiet moment was gone. He'd lost his chance. Dawn was still several hours away, but he didn't dare rest yet. "We should hurry."

Eve grasped the waistline of his tunic. It wasn't entirely necessary now, since the foliage had thinned considerably and the full moon lit the way well enough. But Jacob took comfort in her closeness.

They started down the ridge, careful about their footing. A low quetzal call sounded through the creeping vines. A shiver traveled along Jacob's back, and he stopped to listen. Eve covered her mouth, her eyes watering.

"Did you hear that?" he whispered.

Nodding, Eve moved her hand. "It was very close."

Another call of a bird—this one higher, louder. He held his breath, intent on hearing the minutest sound. "Too close," Jacob said. "And they aren't real quetzals."

"Shem and Javan?" Eve asked.

"Possibly." He paused as another round of bird calls began. "There are several of them and they are signaling each other. More than just Shem or Javan. I think your rejected bridegroom wants his bride back." He turned his gaze on Eve and saw her expression was as desperate as he felt. "Can you keep going?"

"I think so," she gasped.

He locked her hand in his, and they started to run.

* * *

Nephi watched Elisheba's steady breathing—shallow, but steady. "What do you think we should do?" he whispered.

Zoram shrugged. "I don't know. She doesn't look well at all." He adjusted the robe across her body.

The men had taken Elisheba about a half-day's journey from Laman's settlement, hoping it was far enough that he couldn't easily find them. But Nephi's heart still burned with desire to find Jacob and Eve. One look at Zoram told Nephi that he felt the same. As concerned as they were about her health, it was difficult to watch over Elisheba when they knew each passing hour brought more danger to others.

Where had Shem and Javan taken them? Why hadn't they gone to Laman's settlement to show off their captives—along with the sword of Laban? Nephi had tried asking these questions when Elisheba was relatively coherent, but she seemed just as confused about it as he was.

"I don't know how much longer I can just wait," Zoram said, his eyes filled with desperation. "Wait here with your sister, and I'll go."

"But I don't want you traveling alone." Nephi looked from his sister to Zoram. Both needed him. Both for different reasons. "There's no way we can track them now—too much time has passed."

Elisheba moaned and Nephi immediately turned to her, placing his hand on her forehead. Her skin was clammy. "The Kaminaljuyú," she whispered.

Nephi stared at his sister.

"The Kaminaljuyú," Elisheba said, her voice cracking with the effort. "They are east of here, in the high hills."

Nephi remembered the friendly tribe. His father had spent quite a bit of time in their village, teaching them about God. But when it became apparent that they were only interested in trade, not a new religion, the visits were restricted to business only. *Of course,* Nephi thought. *There might be a chance that a member from the tribe has seen or heard something.*

"I'll go find out," Zoram said, his expression filling with hope again.

"No," Nephi said. "Shem and Javan are still out there, not to mention their fathers."

"Both of you go," Elisheba said, opening her eyes to slits. "It will only take a few hours. I'm not going anywhere." She offered a feeble smile. "And I can't get any sleep with you hovering over me."

"But—"

"Go," Elisheba urged. She licked her dry lips. "You know the language, Nephi. And if you run into anyone, I'd rather you be together."

Nephi glanced at Zoram, who nodded, although there was concern in his eyes. Nephi looked at his sister. "Only a few hours?"

She nodded, a faint smile on her lips.

"All right. We'll leave some food and water within reach." He placed the sheepskin and a handful of moras berries by his sister.

"Nephi," Elisheba said.

He looked at her with anticipation. "Yes?"

"Can you give me a blessing before you leave?"

His throat suddenly become thick. Through all that had happened to his dear sister over the past two years, she had never lost her faith.

After the blessing, Nephi leaned over his sister and kissed her forehead. "We'll return before dark."

She simply closed her eyes. "I'll be praying for you."

Nephi smiled at the poignancy of his sister's words. "And we for you." He rose and stood by Zoram. "Ready?"

The two left Elisheba and headed east. The terrain was steep in some places and rocky in others, but the thought of Elisheba being alone spurred them to move quickly. They passed along the edge of a deep ravine until they reached the base of a hill.

"Straight up," Nephi said, the topography starting to become familiar to him. "Their village sits on a plateau, then a temple structure scales a hillside."

"Shhh!" Zoram suddenly said.

"What?" Nephi whispered.

Zoram pointed to a dense thicket. "Look."

Nephi crouched and saw the unmistakable color of clothing through the brambles. They crept closer to get a better view.

"It must be them," Zoram whispered. "Shem and Javan."

Nephi gazed at the two sleeping men. They were definitely younger versions of their fathers. Memories poured into Nephi's mind as he remembered his brothers from their youth. And now . . .

"It's the sword of Laban," Zoram said, pointing.

Then Nephi saw it. The sword that had given them the brass plates was secured at Shem's waist. Nephi felt anger rising in his chest. That sword was a family heirloom and because of Shem's greed, the seed of battle between brothers and their children had been planted.

Nephi determined that he would return the sword to its rightful resting place. But before he could take action, Zoram grabbed his arm. "Wait."

Surprised, Nephi looked at him.

"Why aren't they with Jacob and Eve?" Zoram asked.

Nephi understood. The fact that Jacob and Eve weren't with them was either a very good situation, or a very bad one. Recovering the sword of Laban was the least of their concerns.

"We need to capture them," Zoram suggested.

"What?"

"Threaten their lives until they tell us what happened." Zoram waved toward the sleeping men. "Look at them. They won't go down easily."

Zoram was right. Shem and Javan looked as if they'd never lived a day of peace, although Nephi remembered their youthful, carefree days of harmless pranks. Their expressions were hardened, their skin dark and bruised as if they'd spent most of their time outdoors in some sort of combative activity. Patches of bright red skin around their ankles and feet indicated that they'd suffered some burns.

With a quick nod, Zoram and Nephi sprang into action. Nephi crept toward the two and grabbed the sword, placing it to the side. Then he dove for Shem, and Zoram for Javan. Before the young men could react, Nephi and Zoram had them each restrained.

Shem cried out, reaching for his dagger, but Nephi pinned his arms behind his back.

"Hello," Nephi said.

Shem looked around wildly. It took an instant for recognition to dawn. Fear crossed his face, but only for a moment. It was soon replaced by arrogance. "What are you doing?"

Nephi's tone was somber. "You know what we want, nephew."

"Is this how you treat family?" Javan yelled, his arrogance not quite as strong as his cousin's.

"Shut your mouth, Javan, these men won't hurt us." Shem's eyes narrowed. "They are afraid of our fathers." He struggled vainly against Nephi's grip.

Nephi only hoped that Zoram could contain Javan . . . they hadn't eaten well for days, and the journey had been more than arduous. But one look into Zoram's eyes told Nephi that he had nothing to fear. The resolve of a man fighting for his family was unmatched.

"You want the sword back?" Shem asked, laughter in his voice. "Take it. We have much better weapons anyhow."

"We've already retrieved the sword," Nephi growled.

Shem looked down to find the sword was indeed gone. His face paled at the realization.

"So you intend to shed blood with the same sword you've murdered with before, and the same one that has spilt Jacob's own blood."

Nephi started, but tried to keep his composure. "Where are Jacob and Eve?"

"Ahh," Shem said.

"Where are they?" Zoram shouted. He tightened his hold on Javan, who looked about wildly.

Nephi noticed the anxiety and realized the answers they looked for would probably come from Javan, not Shem. "Get him out of here."

Zoram looked surprised, but Nephi saw that he understood. They would have to question the cousins separately. Together it would be hard to make them crack.

Nephi watched as Zoram hauled Javan off, who kept yelling for Shem to do something.

When they were alone, Nephi focused on Shem. All Nephi had to do was put a little fear into Shem so the pursuit would stop once and for all. And he knew it would not be so easy.

"Shem, you aren't going to like what you hear, but it's for your own good." Nephi inhaled, his muscles starting to tire from restraining Shem.

"Don't preach to me, Nephi! I know all about your false teachings," Shem spat. "You pray to a God that no one can even see. You brought my father out of Jerusalem to deprive him of his land of inheritance."

"Jerusalem has been destroyed," Nephi said, his voice full of authority. "Your grandfather, Lehi, saw this in a vision. You may not remember when he spoke to your father about it. If our family had stayed, we would have been killed or led into captivity. What Lehi did for our family was save us and lead us to a new land of inheritance."

"This land is nothing compared to Jerusalem," Shem growled. "My father's birthright was stolen, and he was wronged in the wilderness. He was wronged again while crossing the sea. And for that your people will pay with their lives."

Sorrow filled Nephi—Laman had not only passed on false teachings to his children, but hatred as well.

"Someday, Shem, someday our families will battle each other." He lowered his voice, remembering the awful scenes he had witnessed in his visions. "But the time is not at hand. The sword of Laban was perhaps a precursor to the boiling hatred that lies within your father's heart. This hatred does not need to be yours."

"No. My father is right," Shem said, wriggling beneath his uncle's grip.

But Nephi didn't budge. "It may be hard to doubt your parents. But if you take your questions to the Lord, the one true God, He will answer them. You will know for yourself. You won't have to rely on the *Lamans* or the *Nephis*—you will have your own assurance."

"You're lying," Shem said. "I don't need to ask anyone, let alone someone who doesn't even exist."

"He *does* exist," Nephi said quietly, his voice brimming with knowledge. "I have seen Him."

Shem remained still for a moment, staring. His expression twisted as a myriad of thoughts passed through his mind. "You've seen God?" he asked in a quiet voice, his face a picture of doubt mixed with hope.

"Yes."

Shem's face pulled into a scowl, and the defiance was back. "So what did He look like?"

"Brilliant, whiter than white, holy . . . sacred beyond any words I could use to describe," Nephi said, relaxing his hold.

"Was He . . . a man?"

"He was a man like you and me, but His countenance was unspeakable—like the brightest star." Before Shem could cast more doubt, Nephi continued, "In His presence I changed. I felt as if I had incredible powers—power to move a mountain, to command the waves of the sea, to heal death . . . to forgive my worst enemy." Nephi hesitated for an instant. "I have forgiven your father. And I forgive you for any wrongdoing you may have done against Jacob . . . or Eve.

"And now," Nephi took a deep breath. "You are free to go." He released Shem and took a step back.

Shem turned to face his uncle. He was covered in perspiration, and his body trembled slightly. Nephi didn't know if it was from fear or amazement, or if the Spirit had touched his nephew.

"You're letting me go?"

Nephi smiled sadly. He pointed to the sword of Laban. "If you really want the sword, take it. It's not worth losing lives, friendships, or family over."

Shem's gaze trailed to the fallen sword. It nestled against the soft green grass, gleaming in the sunlight. "You would *give* it to me?"

"Yes," Nephi said. "If that's what it takes to restore peace between our families."

Shem took a step backward, his eyes hardening. "This is trickery, and I won't fall for it."

"No," Nephi insisted, spreading his arms wide. "I am giving you the gift you seek." He paused, glancing at the sword, then he looked directly into the eyes of his nephew. "And there is so much more I would give if you would allow it. Shem, men are that they might have joy! All you have to do is come and receive it. Isaiah has said that every knee shall bow, and every tongue shall swear that there is no other god besides the Lord."

Nephi lowered his voice to a gentle whisper. "Regardless of whether you admit it now, you will someday. We all will. But if you want your life to contain joy now, you must pray to know the truth. If you pray for knowledge, you will receive it. The way is open. The way is clear. Your heart can be pure and clean again. You can enjoy real happiness."

Curiosity filled Shem's eyes, but left just as quickly. The old suspicions returned. "I will not let you deceive me as you and Grandfather deceived my father." His face grew red, and any earlier softening was replaced by anger. "You are the cause for my father's sorrow. You betrayed your own brothers and stole what was rightfully theirs."

"No," Nephi whispered. "The truth is right in front of you. All you have to do is accept it."

"There is only one truth. And it is not you or your God," Shem said. "This is only the beginning. My father will never rest until he has taken from you what you have taken from him. *I* will not rest. You and your family may have escaped danger today, but there is always tomorrow and the next day." He blew out a low breath. "You might think you are rid of us, but you never will be. We are no longer family. We are enemies."

Nephi hung his head. At that moment, Nephi grieved. He knew he'd lost his nephew. Shem's heart was so hard he couldn't recognize goodness, truth, or forgiveness when it was laid before his feet. Nephi stared at the steel sword on the ground, halfway between him and Shem.

Nephi heard a scuffle from Shem and when he looked up, his nephew was gone.

"No," Nephi cried. "Don't run away from the truth." He wanted to chase him down. He had seen a glimmer of hope in Shem's eyes— even if only for a moment.

Zoram crashed through the foliage, Javan still in his grip. "He's confessed."

"Let him go," Nephi said.

"Let him go?" Zoram asked.

"Now," Nephi said with resolution.

When Zoram saw his insistence, he released Javan. It only took him an instant to take off, leaving the two behind.

Sighing, Nephi bent over and retrieved the sword of Laban. He held it up to the light, then met Zoram's confused gaze. "I tried to explain to Shem that it wasn't too late to change . . ."

Zoram crossed to Nephi, a knowing look on his face. "The Lord commanded us to flee from Laman. The Lord knew that his heart had been hardened beyond measure. He's not your burden to carry, Nephi. Laman's tribe has brought upon themselves the sore cursing of the Lord and has been cut off from His influence." He placed a hand on Nephi's shoulder. "I don't even think a visit from an angel would change their minds. Think of all the witnesses that Laman and Lemuel received. They now live in this promised land with every luxury. But still they complain. Still they blame. Still they hate."

Nephi knew Zoram was right. But that didn't lessen the sorrow in his heart. He looked at Zoram, feeling his eyes sting with remorse. "What did Javan say?"

"Jacob and Eve escaped when Elisheba attacked. The Kaminaljuyú found them, and they believed that Eve was a lost daughter returned to them. Shem and Javan discovered them just as the chief was about to marry Eve. Jacob interfered with the marriage, and both escaped."

Nephi shook his head in disbelief, although his relief was evident. "Those two have been through quite an ordeal." He paused for a moment, then said, "So that means we can assume that Jacob and Eve are still together?" He turned the sword over in his hands. "We have no other alternative but to move toward home and hope they are going in the same direction." He put an arm around Zoram's shoulders. "Let's retrieve Elisheba—then we'll return."

Zoram nodded, the creases of worry on his brow fading. "It's a plan, my friend. Let's go home."

CHAPTER 22

Rest in the Lord, and wait patiently for him.
(Psalm 37:7)

Moist tendrils lay against little Sarah's neck. Isaabel smiled at her young daughter as she helped her harvest maize. The seven-year-old had worked hard, along with the rest of the children in the settlement, to prepare for any emergency departure. The men and boys continued fortifying the village, building lookout points and a well in the central courtyard.

The late-afternoon sun had finished its slow creep across the sky, and now every few moments the colors of the horizon deepened. Isaabel straightened from her bent-over position and gazed at the violet and orange streaks against the western hills. It signaled that another day had passed—another day without her husband.

Isaabel glanced at the baskets piled with maize. "It's time to carry these back."

Sarah let out a sigh. "Will Father know where to find us if we have to leave?"

Crouching to meet her young daughter's gaze, Isaabel thought quickly for a reply. "We'll watch for his return wherever we decide to camp."

Sarah nodded as if she understood perfectly.

"Do you think you can carry the baby while I carry the baskets?"

Sarah reached out for little Lehi, who protested the transfer to his sister's arms.

"I'm still here," Isaabel said with a chuckle. She balanced a basket against each hip and began the short walk to their house. Sarah continued to chatter as they walked, mostly about the things she wanted to tell her father when he returned.

Isaabel tried to hide her worry from the children. It was enough to have them in tears nearly every night. She well remembered the hatred of Laman and Lemuel, and the obstinacy of Heth and Raamah. And she knew what Nephi had seen in his visions. With Sam directing everyone as if preparing for war, the misgivings in Isaabel's heart multiplied.

Would she see her children battle against their uncles and cousins? It was devastating to consider. She often thought about Elisheba and her children—pearls among the rebellious. *Has she remained faithful?* Isaabel wondered. She shook these thoughts from her head. She didn't even want to consider the alternative.

To think about what had become of Jacob and Eve was heart wrenching. Eve was such a quiet and trusting girl. And Jacob held little interest for adventure—he'd rather mull over the brass plates and discuss building temples with Nephi. "O Lord," she whispered, "protect them all. Bring them safely home."

Baby Lehi squealed in Sarah's arms, and Isaabel turned to gaze at her youngest children. They had thrived in this beautiful land, and upon adulthood her sons would inherit large homesteads and farm-land on which to raise their own families. As they neared the first house, Rebeka came hurrying toward them.

"What is it?" Isaabel shouted when her sister neared.

"Sariah is asking for everyone to gather around her."

Isaabel's stomach twisted with dread as she remembered Lehi asking the same thing a short time before his death . . . and the precious blessings and farewell her father, Ishmael, had given before his death. On the other hand, she hated seeing her mother-in-law so ill and in great pain most of the time. There were days when Isaabel believed Sariah would be better off passing beyond this world of pain and uncertainty. Sariah spoke of Lehi often these days, as if she were going to be seeing him very soon.

Rebeka took the basket from Isaabel, and together they walked to her home. When they arrived, they dumped the supplies just inside the doorway. Isaabel gathered her baby from Sarah, and they followed Rebeka to Sariah's home.

Everyone had assembled and stood whispering in the front courtyard. When Tamar saw Isaabel, she ran to embrace her. But instead of tears on Tamar's face, Isaabel saw a radiant smile.

"What's going on?" Isaabel asked, releasing her sister from the embrace.

"Sariah has regained all of her strength."

Isaabel stared at her sister. "She's recovered?"

"It's unbelievable. Go see her. Dinah and Tiras are with her."

With Lehi clutched in one arm, and pulling Sarah by the hand, Isaabel entered the home. The room at the back belonged to Sariah, and Isaabel made her way quickly past the few children who ran about the cooking area.

Dinah and Tiras turned when she entered the room. They both stepped aside to reveal Sariah sitting up in bed, a rosy glow in her cheeks.

"Oh, Mother," Isaabel said. She moved to the bed and kissed Sariah's cheek.

Sariah grasped her hand and smiled at the children. "He's coming. I can feel it."

Isaabel felt her face drain of color. Did her mother-in-law dream of Lehi? "Who's coming?"

"Nephi. He'll be here soon."

Just Nephi? What about the others? Isaabel wondered. Sariah's dementia had periodically given her false hope, which was surely spurring this miraculous recovery. Isaabel worried that as the hours passed, Sariah would realize her mistake and sink again into despair.

Turning to look at Dinah, Isaabel raised a brow. How could the entire family allow Sariah to think this way? But Dinah just smiled and nodded. "Mother has felt his approaching presence."

Confused, Isaabel turned back to Sariah and squeezed her hand. "Have you eaten supper?"

"Oh, yes, and I'm still hungry."

"All right, I'll bring you something."

As Isaabel left the room, she motioned for Dinah to follow. Once they reached the cooking room, Isaabel hissed, "How can you encourage her false notions?"

Dinah stared at her for a moment. "What's happened to you, Isa? Don't you believe that Mother could know such a thing?"

"I . . . of course it's possible, but she's been delirious for so long."

"Not anymore," Dinah said, her eyes narrowing. "When she told me, I felt her words pierce my heart."

Isaabel opened her mouth, then closed it. Had she been so consumed with her own self-pity that she had ceased to hear the Spirit's whisperings? She glanced out the window. The family was quietly rejoicing. They all believed; why couldn't she?

Did she really think that the worst had happened? Had she lost faith? She looked at Dinah. "It's been so long," she said in a trembling voice. *Not now,* she told herself. *Not in front of the whole family.*

But it was too late. The tears came fast and hot, and Dinah embraced her.

"We have all been praying, pleading with the Lord to bring Nephi and the others back safely, but no one has been as earnest as Mother. Perhaps that is why she is the first to know, truly know. Plus she is the matriarch of the family, and a leader in her own right."

Isaabel pulled away from her sister-in-law. "Of course." She sniffed and wiped the tears from her face with her hand. Rebeka had entered the room, and she came forward. The two women embraced, both grieving their losses, but both hoping for the prayers of their hearts to be answered.

Hours later, when her children were asleep, Isaabel left her home and walked up the path a little way toward the woods. It had become her nightly routine. She'd stare at the early moon and the stars in the firmament and wonder if her husband watched the same sky. Where was he? Was he thinking about her? Did he wonder how the children were?

She stood alone, her mantle wrapped tightly about her, lost in her thoughts. Did Sariah truly have a premonition? Was Nephi on his way home? To her? Oh, how she'd missed him. Without him, nothing had been the same; nothing held the same value.

She gazed at the waving maize field, the dark stalks moving in the sweet evening breeze. In the morning, she'd make the final preparations and move into hiding. Tiras and Sam would alternate keeping watch over their settlement for any signs of Nephi or the others. Sam was convinced that they were still in real danger. Even after Sariah's announcement, he felt compelled to continue their plans.

Isaabel's gaze trailed again to the heavens. Exhaustion had crept in, so with a prayer in her heart and determination for renewed faith, she whispered, "Good night, dear husband, wherever you are. Sleep well."

* * *

"We're almost there," Nephi said, looking at Elisheba. His sister grew weaker each day—and now, each hour. He made her rest often, which she protested, but Nephi insisted. "By nightfall, we'll be standing on land blessed by the Lord."

Zoram quickened his gait, as if the prospect somehow infused new life in him. He flashed a grin at Elisheba. "Rebeka will be overjoyed to see you."

Nephi almost added, "And Mother," but he couldn't be sure that Sariah still lived. She had been so ill when he left, and he knew that she desired nothing more than a reunion with her dear husband.

With a brief smile, Elisheba trudged on. "It feels like ages since I've seen Dinah . . . and the others." She looked at Nephi. "Aaron must be a miniature you, and Sarah must be a grown girl now."

"She's seven, but she thinks she's seventeen," Nephi said with fondness. His heart ached at the thought of his dear daughter, her silky curls and merry eyes. He could almost picture her running toward him, flinging her browned arms around his waist. He glanced at Zoram, knowing how much he ached to see his own wife and children again—especially to have Eve returned safely with Jacob.

"Isaabel fared well with her baby's delivery?"

Nephi nodded, grateful that Elisheba was thinking of something else. "We named him Lehi," he said, a pang in his chest. A soft smile crossed his sister's face. The past couple of days had been filled with lamentations about Raamah and her children. She'd even said that her heart was so broken that her baby might be better off if raised by another woman. Nephi saw that she was so filled with melancholy that her thoughts were not logical. It was almost as if she'd given up. Nephi hoped that with time, Elisheba would start looking ahead—to the future. He knew that being around her sister and sisters-in-law again would eventually heal her spirit. They had all been praying for her, including Isaabel.

Isaabel, Nephi thought. He ached to see her, hold her, tell her everything was all right, at least for now. They had not been apart for this long since the first months they'd spent in Mudhail. But even then, they at least had caught a glimpse of each other once or twice a day. He wondered how she'd fared taking care of the children and watching over Sariah. If he knew her, she spent most of the day working in the fields, and every spare moment after that caring for others.

As he neared their settlement, Nephi felt like a parched camel approaching water. Every sinew trembled, his heart raced, and his feet wanted to sprint toward the village. He'd told Elisheba about the recently completed temple and about the home they'd built for Sariah.

Ahead of him, Elisheba's step faltered, and Nephi reached out to grab her arm. She mumbled a thank you, but Nephi kept hold of her elbow for support. They continued to walk as Nephi stayed by his sister. She was too stubborn to let him carry her any farther, and he'd finally let her have her way—although it meant the journey was slower.

A warm wind touched the bent treetops, making Nephi wish he could climb a tree and signal to his family that they were coming. He couldn't wait for the joyous reunion. His thoughts shifted to his nephews, Shem and Javan. He hoped that the encounter would have some sort of an effect on the young men. Even in their defiance he could see a glimmer of possibility in their eyes.

"Oh!" Elisheba cried out as she nearly stumbled.

Nephi tightened his hold. "I should carry you. It's not that much farther."

But Elisheba stopped walking and faced him, her eyes shining. "I don't think there's time."

"What do you mean?" Nephi said. "We can take the time you need."

Elisheba looked down at her protruding belly. "My pains have begun."

Nephi and Zoram both stared at her.

But her eyes had glossed over as she spoke again. "Leave me here. I will prepare for the birth." She smiled faintly. "I will be fine. I am not afraid."

Nephi glanced at Zoram, who said, "We can hurry to the village and return with a woman to help her."

Elisheba wandered from them and found a patch of grass to sit on. She crossed her hands over her belly and a look of peace came over her.

Although Nephi saw the wisdom in Zoram's words, unease crept through his chest. He'd seen a woman experience birth pains before, and never had he seen the woman look as relaxed as Elisheba did. It was almost unnatural. Something was wrong.

"No," Nephi said quietly.

Zoram looked at him in surprise. Elisheba didn't seem to be paying attention to them.

"It's too early," Nephi said. "Something must be done to stop the progress."

"Perhaps if we rest, the pains will stop on their own." Zoram glanced at Elisheba. "She seems to be handling it well."

"I sense something is wrong," Nephi said, keeping his voice low. "She looks too calm. She is ill, exhausted, injured . . . she has been so downtrodden these past months, years . . . I wouldn't be surprised if—"

"She gave up?" Zoram's gaze hardened as he looked from Elisheba to Nephi. "Why now when we are so close?"

Nephi nearly scoffed, but saw that Zoram's question was simple. "Because her life is gone. Her husband, her children, her future. Although our village offers a new start, her heart has been broken several times over. She is still full of sorrow and can't seem to find peace."

Zoram nodded his head slowly. "We'll have to carry her against her will."

"Think of it as saving her life," Nephi said.

Following Zoram, Nephi moved to his sister's side. She had a sheen of perspiration on her face. Without saying a word, Nephi leaned over and picked her up.

"Leave me here," she said, her eyes widening with alarm. "It is not fit for you to be around me during this time."

Zoram walked next to Nephi, ready to help when he tired.

"We'll just carry you a little farther; this area of the forest is unsafe. If the baby starts to come, we'll leave you," Nephi said.

Elisheba looked around for a moment, then eventually she relaxed against her brother's hold. Nephi walked as fast as possible, not only because it meant they'd arrive sooner, but because he didn't know how long Elisheba would let him carry her. Every few moments, her body tensed, and she inhaled sharply.

The warmth filtering through the trees began to fade as night crept on. Despite the warm air, Elisheba started to shiver. Nephi's shoulders and back ached, but he forced himself to increase his pace. If he ever thought of stopping to rest, all he had to do was look at his sister's agonized expression.

"I'll run ahead," Zoram said. "The women can begin preparations and be ready when she arrives."

Nephi just nodded, too out of breath to speak. Wanting to be there for the reunion himself, Nephi was torn as he watched Zoram disappear down the path ahead. He thought about the activity that would burst into action as soon as Zoram arrived. He could well imagine the happiness Rebeka would experience at seeing her husband. He thought about Isaabel and how she might be waiting in anticipation as he crossed through the fields.

The moon hung low in the sky—the violet-splashed horizon quickly fading to indigo. Nephi whispered to Elisheba, "We're nearly to the stretch of fields. We should soon be able to see the welcoming glow of torch lights. You'll have warm rugs and expert care from the women."

Elisheba moaned, but Nephi couldn't tell if it was from another pain or in acknowledgement of his words. Moments later, the cultivated fields spread before him. Pleasure swelled within his bosom as he remembered plotting the spaces and planning the food they would grow. He watched everything in this settlement grow from the ground up. By the third season, their crops provided more than enough for their needs, enabling them to store grain and seed for the year to come.

The moon hung low in the sky, seeming to touch the wispy tips of the maize stalks. Coming toward him, Nephi could see a figure hurrying across the expanse of land.

Isaabel? He nearly started running, but didn't want to jar his sister's poor body any further. His heart leapt as he thought about the sweet reunion with his wife and children.

The figure grew closer, and Nephi realized it was a man. "Sam?" he called out.

"No. It's just me."

"Zoram?"

He ran up to Nephi and stopped before him, breathless. "Everyone is gone."

"What do you mean?" Nephi asked, peering at Zoram's face in the moonlight.

"The homes are empty, every last one of them."

"Did you check the temple?" Nephi asked.

"Yes."

Incredulous at the news, Nephi shook his head. "Impossible." He trudged forward, Elisheba still in his arms. "Did you check for recent signs of any cooking fires?"

"Yes, I checked everywhere." Zoram looked at Elisheba, weariness on his face. "What do we do now?"

Nephi hesitated. "We need to try and find out where they went. But first, we'll take her to my home and make her as comfortable as possible." As he spoke the words, Nephi tried to sound confident, but the truth was, worry for his wife and children consumed him.

Reaching the edge of the fields, Nephi could see that indeed, there was no welcoming light, no waiting family. Perhaps they traveled to another village for a celebration. His stomach twisted at the next thought. Perhaps they went to seek a burial place for Sariah. But *all* of them?

By the time they reached his home, irrational thoughts churned in his head, each more wild than the first. *Shem and Javan beat us to them somehow, coming upon the women and children unawares. Elisheba may have slowed us just enough to allow Shem and Javan the advantage. Or maybe a terrible disease has taken hold and caused them to flee.*

Passing through the courtyard, Nephi followed Zoram and waited for him to throw open the door. Stepping across the dark threshold, Nephi immediately sensed the emptiness of the place. The floors had sticks and leaves strewn about—something his wife would never allow. And the smell of rotting vegetables pierced his senses. He knew that Isaabel and the children hadn't just been gone for a few hours or a day.

Zoram made his way through the dark and was able to light an oil lamp. The flickering glow reached the walls, landing on empty baskets. Where was the stockpiled grain?

It seemed that Isaabel had packed for a long journey. But *where*, and *why?*

"Let's get her into the bedchamber," Nephi said, his arms aching.

Zoram carried the lamp, lighting the way. Nephi carefully arranged Elisheba, who looked like she was half asleep, on the bed. Her pains had relaxed and her trembling subsided. That was a blessing, he decided. "Leave the lamp here, and I'll find another." Zoram arranged rugs about Elisheba's trembling body as Nephi moved through the small house, staring in surprise at its complete abandonment. He rummaged through the cooking room, looking for something he could feed Elisheba. At last he found a few over-ripe guavas.

With the fruit and his sheepskin he returned to Elisheba's side. He gently woke her and persuaded her to drink a little. Then he looked at Zoram. "We'll need more water before morning, especially if the baby comes."

Zoram nodded, his face drawn into a somber expression. "I'll go to the river and fetch it." As he reached for the sheepskin, Elisheba moaned pitifully.

Nephi put his hand on her forehead, then stroked her cheek, trying to soften her groans. He glanced at Zoram. "What should we do?"

"Women have experienced childbirth by themselves many times."

Nephi nodded. "But I can't leave her alone like this."

Zoram shifted on his feet, looking uncomfortable. "Of course not." After a moment he said, "Do you think Shem and Javan came back?"

Snapping his head up, Nephi stared at Zoram. He'd wondered the same thing. "Have you seen any signs?"

"Not yet, but our travel was slow. They could have easily beat us here if they didn't return to Laman's settlement first. Perhaps they came to steal the sword again, or to find Eve and Jacob. We weren't here, but they may have met up with Sam or Tiras . . ."

"You think our families were driven out?"

"Perhaps they fled when they saw them, or maybe they were threatened."

Nephi nodded, thinking. *Perhaps.* "It may not be safe to stay here too long."

"In the morning, we can look for tracks and follow." He sighed, then let out a yawn. "I'll go get that water."

Nephi settled next to his sister and watched over her during Zoram's absence, wishing he could do more for her. He held her hand and watched her eyelashes flutter against her cheeks in her sleep. Moments later, Zoram reentered the home.

"There's a well in the center of the village."

"A well?" Thoughts raced through Nephi's mind as he considered the reasons.

"And a wall has been started that runs along the north end." His eyes were wide with apprehension. "They were preparing for war."

CHAPTER 23

*Thus saith the Lord God of Israel, That which thou hast
prayed to me . . . I have heard.*

(2 KINGS 19:20)

That night seemed to be the longest of Nephi's life. He dozed
off a few times, only to be startled awake by Elisheba's moaning.
This caused him to kneel in supplication for the safety of his family
and the delay of Elisheba's birth. When those prayers exhausted
him, he fell into a state between wakefulness and sleeping. As soon
as dawn surfaced, he left the cloistered room where Elisheba
finally slept soundly, and discovered Zoram resting on the ground
outside.

He hesitated before waking Zoram, but he knew they had to find
answers as quickly as possible. Daylight would leave them exposed to
whatever caused his family to flee their home. But he was grateful
that Elisheba's pains had lessened during the night, and the danger of
early childbirth seemed to have subsided.

"Zoram," he said, nudging him.

Immediately, Zoram opened his eyes and sat, as if he were ready
for anything. "What happened?"

"Nothing. Elisheba is sleeping now—she seems much better."

"Good," Zoram said, rising to his feet. He arched his back into a
stretch and let a huge yawn escape.

"You could've had any bed to choose from, you know," Nephi

commented, a wry smile on his face. "You didn't have to sleep on the ground. Or you could've gone to your own home."

"Yes, well . . ." Zoram began. "It didn't seem right to get too comfortable, considering the pain Elisheba was in. And, I wanted to keep a lookout." He stifled another huge yawn. "Although I wasn't much good at that."

"I see." Nephi smiled and clapped a hand on Zoram's shoulder. "You're a good man."

Zoram looked away, his expression humble. "She'll be all right for a short while?"

"Yes, but let's hurry." Nephi felt a prickle of uncertainty spread through his body. He wanted to inspect the settlement before deciding what to do. Zoram followed him and they walked toward the center of the village. It felt strange to pass along the quiet roads that were devoid of any signs of life. Even the scraggly pet sheep had disappeared, likely following their masters.

The partially constructed well was noticeable even from a distance. The size of rocks weren't uniform—as if they had been chosen in a hurry. It had obviously been built at an expedited pace, although it seemed functional. Nephi paused by the well and peered inside to the murky darkness below. He frowned, wondering why they would build it, then leave so suddenly.

The two men did a cursory search of each home, finding much the same thing—food and bedrolls gone. When they arrived at the temple, Nephi gazed upon the holy structure, marveling at the beauty it emanated in the early morning sun. With a pang in his chest, he thought of Jerusalem, and all the beauty that had been destroyed because of the people's disobedience.

The structure looked so sturdy and strong that Nephi thought it would withstand any type of fierce battle. Beyond the temple site were the hilly pastures. He caught a glimpse of the flocks of sheep, but no shepherd in attendance. At least that signaled one thing to him. The move Isaabel had made wasn't intended to be permanent.

Nephi and Zoram walked around the temple and into the pastures. All seemed peaceful among the softly bleating sheep. Nephi rotated slowly through the open fields, assessing the surrounding terrain—the grazing land, the harvested fields, the line of the thick forest, and the rise of the hills beyond. Which direction did they go? There must be some sign of their departure other than abandoned homes.

"Father."

Nephi spun around and stared at Zoram. "Did you hear that?"

Zoram furrowed his brows and looked toward the hills.

"Father!"

A grin broke across Nephi's face, and his heart about leapt from his chest. He knew that voice. Faint as it was, it could be none other than his son Aaron.

Sure enough, moments later a figure burst out of the tree line, running toward him.

Nephi whooped with joy and ran toward Aaron. When they reached each other, they embraced fiercely. After catching his breath, Nephi inspected his nine-year-old son. "Where is your mother?"

"She's with the rest of the family, camping not far from here. Today it's my job to spy on the village."

Zoram reached the both of them and embraced Aaron. "Can you take us there?"

"Of course." Aaron grinned. "Everyone will be surprised to see you." He glanced about the pasture. "So where are they?"

"Who?" Zoram asked.

"Jacob and Eve."

Nephi stared at his son. "You mean they haven't returned yet?"

"No. Everyone's been saying that they're probably with you," Aaron said. He looked from his father to Zoram.

"They should be on their way soon, then," Zoram said.

In spite of his confident reply, Nephi felt every bit of fear coming from Zoram. The man's daughter was still not safe.

Nephi broke the silence. "We have your Aunt Elisheba with us. Let's go and tell her that we've found you." As they walked into the settlement, Nephi had mixed feelings. He was overjoyed to soon see his wife and other children, but returning without bringing Jacob and

Eve with them, the very reason they'd left in the first place—that was unthinkable.

Zoram fell into a heavy silence, his face drawn into a tight frown. Nephi knew better than to offer words of comfort to him. Besides, he couldn't think of any.

Aaron walked with them to fetch Elisheba. Nephi entered the home first, unsure of what to expect. But his sister was awake, her demeanor relaxed.

"Aaron's here," he said as he knelt by her side.

Her face lit up when she saw Aaron. She held out her arms to her young nephew and he shyly stepped into them. Nephi was grateful to see that some of her color had returned.

"How are you feeling?" he asked as soon as Elisheba released Aaron.

"The pains have diminished," she said. "I think the baby is safe now."

"Aaron is going to lead us to the others," Nephi said. "They are camping not too far from here. Can you travel with us to meet everyone?"

Elisheba shook her head. "I dare not right now. I'll be fine here; I know you'll be back soon."

With mixed feelings, Nephi left her side, leaving a jar of water and fresh fruit by her side. The three cut through the trees, climbing upward toward the makeshift camp. After several moments, Nephi smelled something cooking. His mouth watered in anticipation.

"At first we wondered if we should cook," Aaron said. "Finally, Aunt Rebeka insisted on it."

Nephi smiled and glanced at Zoram, but the man's face remained closed. The trees grew thicker, and soon they arrived at a clearing. The bustling scene was a welcome sight—children played, pet animals scurried about, and mothers called orders in the general chaos. *Home.* It was the only place Nephi ever wanted to be, whether that home was a humble tent or a fine edifice. Being apart from his family never felt right.

Isaabel crouched near the cooking fire, poking a long stick into a pot. As the voices around her quieted, she looked up. Her face mirrored relief, joy, and surprise all in one expression.

Nephi moved to her side before she could rise and take one step forward.

"Isa," he murmured into her hair, holding her tightly against him. Baby Lehi reached for Nephi from his sling on his mother's back. Nephi laughed and tickled the little boy's neck.

Isaabel didn't speak for a moment and just clung to him. "You're finally here. Alive and well."

"Father!" A screech sounded behind him. Without turning he knew it was his daughter, Sarah. Her small arms wrapped around his legs as she beamed a smile at him. "Wait until you see what I made you."

Nephi drew away from Isaabel and turned his attention to Sarah. Squeezing her tightly, he kissed her forehead and cheeks, then tickled her tummy.

After a moment, she bounded away to tell the other children that her father had returned.

Nephi straightened and looked at Isaabel. "We didn't accomplish what we set out to do."

She gazed at him with confusion for a moment before his words sank in. "Jacob? Eve? What happened?"

"I *think* they are on their way back home. We couldn't find them, but we know that they are together. We assumed they'd beat us here. They escaped Shem and Javan's abduction."

Isaabel's hand flew to her mouth. "Shem and Javan are to blame for all of this?"

"Jacob and Eve were literally saved by Elisheba."

"What do you mean?" Isabel voice raised a notch.

Nephi hesitated. *There's so much to tell.* "She was cast out of Laman's settlement when she was with child. We brought her with us."

"Cast out?" Isabel stared in shock. "Are Raamah and the children with her?"

Nephi shook his head slowly. "They were separated. Her pains started last night, but now they've subsided. She's in our home, resting. I told her we'd return as soon as possible." He took his wife's hands in his. "I hoped that you could help her through all . . . of this." The look that passed between them told Isaabel that the details would need to be revealed later.

"Of course," Isaabel whispered, her eyes brimming.

"Nephi!" a voice boomed behind him.

He turned as Sam pulled him into an embrace.

"We really missed you," Sam said in an emotional yet relieved tone.

For some reason, Nephi laughed. "I can see that. You've had a lot to deal with."

"Not only that," Sam said, "but your son over there thinks he's in charge of the whole operation."

Nephi smiled. "I sensed that." Several paces away, Aaron instructed some of the others to pack up their things, saying it was time to move back home.

"With the addition of you and Zoram, and hopefully with Jacob and Eve on their way, we'll have enough manpower to fortify our settlement quickly," Sam said.

"I saw the work you put into the village."

Sam nodded, but his eyes remained troubled. Nephi saw that there was much to discuss. "I must speak with Zoram," Sam said.

Nephi watched him walk toward Zoram where he stood with Rebeka. Her hands covered her face while Zoram held her, rocking slowly. In her hands, she clutched Eve's blue scarf.

Isaabel touched Nephi's arm, and he turned to look at her. "I'll start back right away to help Elisheba," she said. "I'll take the baby with me." She paused and lowered her voice. "Your mother is in the tent over there. She prophesied about your return and . . . I doubted her words." Tears glistened against her long lashes. She sniffled.

Nephi took Isaabel's hand and squeezed it. "There were times when *I* doubted my return." He embraced Isaabel again and kissed his baby son, saying, "I'll go to her now." Then he made his way to his mother's tent. For some reason, he felt more nervous to tell her about Jacob and Eve than he'd been to tell his wife. He'd seen his mother experience so much pain with her children over the years that he didn't want to be the bearer of more ill news.

The interior was mellow and dark when Nephi entered, but he saw his mother propped against several rolled rugs. Her sharp eyes met his in the dim light. A gentle smile increased the folds in her cheeks. "I've been waiting for you."

Nephi knelt at her side and kissed her, then put his arms around her.

"I saw you on your journey," Sariah said. "I knew you were safe, but I didn't want to leave this existence before I saw you again."

His eyes grew moist as he looked at his dear mother. She seemed to have aged years in the short time he'd been gone. The lines around her eyes were profound, but wise and kind. "How are you feeling?"

Her voice brightened. "Today is a good day, made even better by your arrival." She placed a hand on his cheek. "There is still worry in your eyes. Do not fear, son. I know that Jacob and Eve aren't with you. But they will be here soon."

Warmth spread through Nephi as he recalled Isaabel's words about his mother's prophecy. Could it be possible that the Lord had spoken through her to comfort the others? He gazed into his mother's eyes, seeing rich memories there, deep and abiding love, and a never-ending well of faith.

"We brought Elisheba with us," Nephi said quietly.

His mother's emotional resolve melted at last. "My Elisheba?" She clapped her hands together, a thousand thoughts flitting across her brow. "How is she?"

"She needs her mother. She's with child and has had some early pains." Nephi placed his hands over his mother's and squeezed. "We have to break camp, then I'll take you to see her." He leaned over and kissed her forehead. "I'll be back soon."

* * *

Elisheba turned over, supporting her stretched belly as she did so. The faint shadows in the room told her that the sun was high overhead. Any moment now, she thought, any moment Nephi and the others would return. She'd prayed for so long to be with Nephi and to live in this land . . . but she'd never expected to do it alone, without her husband and children.

Touching her stomach, she felt the babe within her kicking. She was so grateful that her pains had stopped, this miracle alone convincing her that there was hope after all. Elisheba closed her eyes, trying to push away the fear and sorrow that had consumed her during the past two years. It was now time to look toward the future. She needed to put her faith in the Lord and trust that He knew what was best for her—and that He could heal her broken heart. Only then could she properly give her child the love he or she deserved. Only through the Lord could she be the mother her child needed. Slowly she climbed out of bed and moved to her knees. It had been a long time since she had truly poured out her heart and accepted her dilemma.

She started to pray. "O Lord my God, blessed art Thou. Thou hast been generous and preserved my life. I thank thee for Thy tender mercies." She paused, feeling emotion swell within her breast. "I have desired only that my husband and children follow Nephi, when I should have strengthened my faith and listened to Thy will, not mine. If Thy will is that I continue on without them, I shall follow Thee."

The room seemed to hold its breath while Elisheba whispered her prayer. Tears filled her eyes as she ached for her former life, her former love, peace within the family. "Lord," she concluded, "I turn my burdens over to Thee and put my trust in Thee. I am Thy servant, here to do Thy will. I praise Thee, O Lord, according to Thy righteousness."

Opening her eyes, she felt as if the grief in her heart had lessened. Voices reached her ears, and Elisheba stood unsteadily, listening intently. They had returned. She then sank onto the bed, waiting . . .

Isaabel entered the room first, her eyes anxious as they met Elisheba's. She smiled through her tears then fell on her knees to the floor, and the two women embraced for several moments. Then Dinah and Tamar burst in the room, and Dinah practically knocked her sister over in jubilation.

"The men are bringing Mother," Dinah said, holding up two-year-old Seba for Elisheba to see. "He's grown since you saw him last."

Elisheba smiled at the dimpled toddler, then saw that the women carried babies in the slings across their backs. No doubt they had noticed or at least had been told about her condition.

"And this is Meshech," Dinah said with a smile. She removed her baby boy from her sling and presented the child to Elisheba.

Smiling, Elisheba looked at Isaabel expectantly.

"This is our Lehi," Isaabel said, lifting the robust child from his comfortable perch. He grinned.

"Lehi and Meshech." Elisheba's eyes filled with tears. "They are both beautiful children." Then everyone in the room was wiping their wet cheeks.

Elisheba asked question after question, keeping silent about her own experiences, but in time she knew she'd share the tale. She sensed they were curious, but were waiting respectfully until she was ready. One thing she knew for certain was that these women loved her, no matter what she'd done or what she'd been through. She felt the blessings of the Lord through their sisterhood. A warm peace crept through her soul, confirming that she'd made the right choice in coming to the Land of Nephi.

She was giving her unborn child a chance.

With the afternoon growing late, Elisheba felt her body tire, but she didn't want to be left alone. Tamar kept watch for the men to return with Sariah and at last Tamar made the happy announcement.

Entering the room, Tamar said, "She's coming." She laughed with delight. "Nephi's made a platform to carry her on—like a queen."

Tears pricked Elisheba's eyes as she thought about seeing her mother again. To her, Sariah *was* a queen.

Elisheba climbed off the bed, much to the women's protests, and walked haltingly out of the house to wait in the outer courtyard. The procession she saw jolted her heart. Sam, Nephi, Zoram, and Tiras—four strong and good-hearted men—carried Sariah as if she were royalty. And she was.

A huge grin broke out on Elisheba's face as tears streamed down her cheeks. As the men lowered Sariah to the ground and helped her from the makeshift bier, Elisheba crossed to her. She buried her face in her mother's neck, soaking her skin with the years of separation, the months of loneliness, and the hours of desperation.

In her mother's welcoming arms, Elisheba knew that the wounds of her heart could now finally mend. She closed her eyes, reveling in her sweet, familiar scent. After a moment, she pulled away and gazed at each person. The feeling of joy was so tangible that Elisheba felt as if she could gather it into her arms.

Sariah took her hand and squeezed. "I've prayed for two years that I would see you again."

"Me too, Mother," Elisheba whispered, squeezing back. "Me too." She wanted to pour her heart out to her mother, but now wasn't the time. Tiras moved to her side and they embraced. She wished she had better news to tell him about his father and his little brothers. She pulled away, smiling. There would be plenty of time later to tell him of the events over the past two years. For now, she relished the long awaited reunion.

Elisheba looked past the gathered crowd. Along the edge of the first field, she saw two people walking. She scanned the family quickly, everyone was here . . . unless . . .

Joseph was the first to yell. "Jacob! Eve! They're here!" The family tore out of the courtyard and ran toward them.

Elisheba grabbed her mother's hand and they hurried forward, too. Jacob was swept from one person to the next—Nephi, Isaabel, Dinah, Tiras. Eve was enveloped between her parents, laughing and crying at the same time. Sariah plunged forward, wetting Jacob and Eve with her tears.

Then Zoram stood back and removed the blue scarf he'd kept inside his tunic. With trembling hands, he gave it to Eve. She threw her arms around his neck and burst into tears.

But still Elisheba held back. She didn't know whether to laugh or cry. The last time she'd seen them, they were being treated horribly . . . by Shem and Javan. After several moments of wild rejoicing, a hush fell over the group. Jacob turned from Aaron, and spotted Elisheba. He ran to her, closing the short distance. Elisheba clung to him, so grateful that she had been there that fateful day to free him and Eve from certain death.

When he pulled back, Jacob said, "How did you get here?"

Elisheba smiled, but her lips trembled with sadness. "Nephi and Zoram brought me."

Zoram sidled up to the group and grabbed Jacob by the shoulders. Tears coursed along his cheeks. "Thank you," he whispered. "Thank you for bringing back my daughter."

Nodding, Jacob embraced the man.

After several more moments, Nephi called everybody's attention. "We all want to hear about Jacob and Eve's journey. But let's first get them something to eat and drink, and let them rest a little. But before you do," he looked at Jacob, "be sure to thank Elisheba for contributing to your rescue."

"What do you mean?" Jacob asked, his expression puzzled.

Nephi looked from Jacob to Eve. "Didn't you know?"

"No," Jacob replied.

Elisheba felt her heart drop as Jacob looked at her. Tears spilled onto her cheeks, uncontrollable now. But she nodded toward Nephi, giving him the permission to speak the words that were too difficult for her to utter.

Nephi explained the details quietly to the hushed family—how Elisheba's skin had remained fair when the others' skin went dark; how she was cast out of Laman's village, leaving her husband and children behind; and how she had defended Jacob and Eve, led Nephi and Zoram to Laman, and escaped after she was tied to the stake by Raamah . . .

She couldn't move. Jacob walked toward her and prodded her from the circle of women. She lifted her eyes to meet his, seeing the astonishment and gratitude there.

"I didn't know it was you," Jacob said.

Elisheba reached up and stroked his cheek. "What matters is that we're all home at last." She smiled through her tears.

"What about Raamah and the children?" he asked.

She lowered her head, blinking rapidly. "He sacrificed his life for me—so that I could escape and come here." She touched her belly. "I have a new life to bring into the world, a child who will be raised unto the Lord." She brushed the moisture from her cheeks, feeling a flood of warmth pass through every part of her being. And she realized that she *knew* where to find happiness. "This is where I always wanted to be, and this is where I'll be happy."

CHAPTER 24

*Come now, and let us reason, saith the Lord: though your
sins be as scarlet, they shall be as white as snow.*

(ISAIAH 1:18)

They had eaten, rested, and rejoiced. One by one the family began
to leave Sariah's courtyard for their own homes, until only Nephi and
Elisheba remained with Jacob and Eve.

Eve glanced over at Jacob, feeling relieved that it was finally all
over. They had narrowly escaped the tribal chief and his men. For
days they had traveled almost without pause, resting for two or three
hours at a time, always in fear of being discovered. Until now.

Elisheba rose, and Nephi followed. They each embraced Jacob
and Eve one more time. Then Jacob stood, too. "I'll take her to her
home." He looked at Eve. "Just like I promised I would."

After saying good-bye to the others, Eve followed Jacob out
through the gate. They walked slowly, so close that Eve felt her pulse
pounding throughout her entire body. The moon hung heavy and
full, casting its golden light across the crisscrossing trails. The fields
spread to the east, and the homes nestled together on the west. They
neared the first set of trees along the edge of the forest. Eve smiled as
she saw curling tendrils of smoke rising in the air from the various
courtyards. The familiar sight brought joy and intense pain in the
same breath. She had changed so much, and yet, she wanted nothing
more to do than the regular tasks day in and day out.

Walking in silence next to her, Jacob gazed across the same fields and forests, and Eve wondered what thoughts went through his mind. His shoulder had healed poorly, and she knew he still needed care for his burns. For herself, she just needed about three days of sleep. The bruises would fade, but she would never forget.

Once this night was over, Eve realized that everything would change between her and Jacob. They'd grown close, out of necessity and facing danger together, but here at home . . . would they resume their regular habit of saying little to each other?

She sensed that Jacob knew things were about to change between them, too. The past two days of their journey, he'd withdrawn more and more. Their conversations had been stilted, Jacob only speaking when necessary. He'd already begun the process of pulling away, and their relationship had become formal again.

"Eve?" Jacob said, stopping on the trail.

She turned and looked at him, surprised at the tenderness in his voice. Maybe he would admit that their friendship wouldn't be the same.

He withdrew the leather strap from around his neck, wincing in the process as he fumbled with his bandaged hands. "Here," he said, holding the gold ring toward her. "I want to you have it."

She took the ring from him, barely glancing at it. "Why?" she asked.

"My father gave it to me . . . as a token to remember him by."

"Well . . . uh . . ." Eve looked at the ring more closely. It was roughly made, but its brilliance reflected in the moonlight. "Oh, Jacob, I can't take this from you. It's from your father." She looked at him, surprised to see that his eyes glistened with emotion. She gently pressed it into his hands. "I'm the one who should give you something for all the trouble you went through to bring me back home."

He shook his head and dropped his hands, refusing to take back the ring. "That's not what I meant." He looked past her, as if struggling for words.

She saw the old Jacob, the reserved and too-intelligent-for-her Jacob, return.

"I want you to keep the ring for me, as a token . . . a token of . . ." He broke off and gazed at her. Eve felt her skin warm beneath his stare, and she realized she was holding her breath.

"I know we are young, at least in the eyes of others, too young to be betrothed . . . yet . . ." Jacob hesitated again, but his gaze was steady. "I already know what I want my future to be."

Eve's heart began hammering, and she tried asking him what he meant, but no words came.

"When we marry, you can return the ring," Jacob said with a self-conscious smile. He ducked his head, then looked at her again out of the corner of his eye. "The ring will represent our . . . promise. I hope this isn't too awful for you to consider."

Eve felt the breath leave her body. Of course it wasn't awful . . . in fact, it was wonderful and more than she ever dared hope or consider or even dream about. Well, maybe she'd dreamt about it. She stared at the ring, excitement pulsing through her. "Marrying you could never be awful . . . only . . . wonderful." She turned over the ring in her hand, trying to grasp the significance of what Jacob had said. He wanted to marry her . . . eventually. Her eyes met his, and she was sure her face had turned a brilliant red. Slowly, she tied the leather strap about her neck.

He watched her actions, a crooked smile on his face. "It looks nice on you."

Eve smiled back. Her hands hesitated near her neck, and she removed the necklace holding the jade stone. "And this will be my promise to you." She walked behind Jacob and reached up to knot the leather cord about his neck. Her fingers brushed against his browned skin, and she felt a quiver run down her arms. Stepping away, she took a deep breath.

"Now that we have *that* decided, I'll return you to your parents." He took her hand, and she knew he was trying hard not to show any pain. But the gesture was so sweet, that Eve continued holding onto him.

Together they had overcome danger. Together they had survived being beaten, chased, and nearly starved. And now they walked slowly along the trail leading to her home. Together—to their future.

* * *

Jacob felt his chest expand with joy unlike anything he'd experienced. It was as if the heavens had opened and spilled pure gold across the land. As he and Eve walked along the moonlit trail, he soaked in her features, every step, every sway of her hair, every flutter of her lashes . . . He knew that the Lord's hand had brought them together.

He couldn't take his eyes off of Eve. Her radiance shone through the exhaustion of their tumultuous journey. She met his gaze, making his breath stop for an instant. Although he'd known her since childhood, he felt he had just caught a glimpse of the real Eve. He couldn't believe he'd had the courage to ask her to marry him—and that she'd agreed. The necklace swung against her neck as if she'd worn it her whole life. Jacob grinned. If his body didn't ache so much, he'd spin her around, lifting her high into the air.

Just then a loud crack sounded to their left. Jacob stopped and peered through the forest that edged the trail. A dark shape seemed to grow, then melt against the trees. Eve hovered at his side. "What is it?"

"I'm not sure," he said. "I thought I saw something." He waited for a moment, then continued on, albeit more slowly. His heart thudded as he thought about Shem or Javan still in pursuit. Should he call for one of the other men?

The sound came again, and Jacob released Eve's hand. His fierce protective instinct took over before he could consider any consequences. "Wait here." He plunged into the forest, bent on defending Eve against anyone from Laman's tribe who might have followed them. It took only an instant for his eyes to adjust to the dim light caused by the canopy of trees overhead. He pushed through the forest in zigzag fashion, searching for any sign of broken branches, disturbed ground, or outright footprints. Then he saw a cloaked form crouched against a bush.

This man wasn't hiding, Jacob thought. He hadn't even attempted to conceal himself. To Jacob's surprise, the person was shaking. It definitely wasn't Shem or Javan, he decided—neither of them would be covered in a robe or hiding his face.

"Who are you?" Jacob said as he approached. Another fight would probably undo all the healing over the past days, but he was ready if need be. He walked slowly, trying to understand the sounds that came from the person. It seemed animal-like—yet almost like crying.

Then the head turned, and Jacob stared in shock at what used to be a face. A horrible change had taken place. The man's features were mutilated beyond recognition—two swollen eyes, a deep gash traveling from mouth to ear, nose broken. The dark skin was similar to Laman's group. But who was he?

"Who are you?" Jacob repeated. "What do you want?"

The man unfolded his long body and rose to his feet. The pain was obvious by his jerky movements, and Jacob wondered how much more of the man was injured in a similar fashion. He had charred skin hanging from his ankles, and his feet were bright red with what looked like fresh burns.

"Kill me," the man said, his voice guttural.

Jacob took a step back, troubled by the request. But the voice had startled him even more. "Raamah?"

"Jacob, I beg for your mercy." He lowered himself to his knees.

"No," Jacob said, moving to stop him. "Do not beg me. I cannot kill you." He reached for Raamah's arm, but recoiled at the sickening sight of burnt skin. Had this man been tied to a stake?

"I am unfit to even touch," Raamah said. He rose and took several steps forward, his full height towering over Jacob. "I cannot face my wife to ask for her forgiveness." His voice cracked. "I am as repulsive now on the outside as I have been on the inside."

A crashing sound came behind him through the underbrush. He turned to see Eve arrive. But it was too late to shield her from Raamah's appearance. She cried out, bringing her hand to her mouth.

"It's all right, Eve. It's Raamah; he's hurt." Jacob gazed at Raamah again, trying hard to ignore his clenched stomach.

Raamah reached up and pulled his robe over his head, covering most of his face. "I shouldn't have come." He took several staggered steps back, then turned away.

"Wait," Jacob called. "You need care for those burns." He continued as Raamah hesitated. "When my hands were burned, Eve found a remedy to heal them." He looked at Eve, hoping that she'd catch the meaning in his eyes.

"Yes," she joined in, lowering her hand. "The curaiao grows abundantly here. I can prepare a poultice for you to ease the pain."

"I earned the pain." Raamah kept his head lowered. "After all I've done, I don't deserve to live."

Jacob wasn't sure what Raamah meant, but he knew he had to help the poor man. "Come with us. There is plenty of room in our village. And I'm sure Elisheba will—"

"No!" Raamah said. "She cannot see me yet . . . I don't want her pity . . ."

"Don't worry," Eve said. "I can bring you the ointment as soon as I can prepare it. No one has to know." She looked at Jacob and received a grateful smile.

Raamah's shoulders sagged. "All right."

"We'll return soon." Jacob turned and motioned for Eve to follow him. He wasn't sure how they'd sneak back to Elisheba's without being noticed. As they exited the forest, the moonlight brought welcome illumination after the darkness of Raamah's encounter.

Jacob knew once he told Nephi about their brother-in-law, he would be welcomed with open arms into the community. He shuddered at the memory of the man's deformities. He'd once been so strong and self-assured—the broken man Jacob had seen in the forest was a mere shell of who Raamah once was.

"We must tell Elisheba right away," Eve said.

"But Raamah—"

"I know what he said, but did you notice how sad Elisheba looked when she spoke of her husband?"

Jacob nodded. He remembered it well.

They hurried back through the settlement and arrived at Sariah's home. Light flickered from within. Jacob called out softly and almost immediately Elisheba appeared at the doorway.

"What is it?" she said, pulling her mantle about her shoulders.

"Eve and I," Jacob began, glancing at Eve. When she nodded, he continued, "Raamah is here . . . hiding in the forest."

Elisheba's hand shot out, and she gripped Jacob's arm. "Where?" She looked toward the trees.

Eve stepped beside Jacob. "He doesn't want to be seen. His face . . . his body . . . have been badly burned."

Choking on a cry, Elisheba's eyes grew wide. "I must go to him. I must see him." She grabbed Eve's tunic. "What did he tell you?"

Eve glanced at Jacob. "He said . . . that he doesn't deserve to live. But Jacob talked him into letting us help him." Her gaze traveled back to Elisheba. "I promised to make him a poultice."

"Let me take it to him," Elisheba said.

* * *

The purple sky deepened to black as Elisheba set out on the trail that ran along the edge of the forest. Jacob had explained the location, and she was confident she could find Raamah easily enough. *My husband.* The thought of seeing him overwhelmed and scared her. She wasn't sure what to expect. Not only what he might look like, but what was inside his heart. But from what Jacob and Eve had said, they believed he was a changed man.

He did save my life, Elisheba reasoned. But he'd also allowed her to be cast out of the village. He could have grabbed their boys and taken the family to the Land of Nephi when it all first happened. Instead, she'd lived for months on her own, scraping for food and shelter.

Her emotions alternated between anger at losing her boys, pain because of her husband's cruelty, and complete sadness over the whole situation. She gripped the pouch filled with food and healing ointment. Over her shoulder she carried a waterskin. Knowing how stubborn he could be, he probably wouldn't let her touch him. But she'd at least try and help. Even if it was their last contact. She'd repay her debt to him—that of saving her life—then she could rest well, knowing she'd done everything she could.

But really, she wanted answers. She wanted to see if he'd really changed—if he *could* change. She wanted to know about her boys. And finally, she wanted to know why he hid from her now. Even as she trudged through the undergrowth, she couldn't believe she was actually going to confront him. After all this time and after so much had happened, she'd finally get the chance to examine his heart— *away* from Laman; *away* from Nephi.

Just the two of them—face to face, talking about Elisheba and Raamah.

She reached the area that Jacob pinpointed for her. Turning, she glanced down the trail and saw Nephi. He said he'd wait on the path in case she needed him. Her throat tightened as she thought about his faithfulness, his steady nature, and his constant love. She lifted her hand briefly to wave, then disappeared between the trees.

About thirty paces in, Jacob had said. *By a group of fallen trunks.* It was quite dark, but Elisheba walked with a sure foot. This was simple compared to her life before. She had adequate clothing, a full stomach from a good meal, and comfortable sandals. Living in the jungle had taught her a keen sense of smell and hearing. That was why she heard Raamah before she saw him.

The unmistakable snore of her husband.

She didn't know whether to laugh or cry. She crept forward and stood over him, watching his chest rise and fall. His face was concealed, partly by his robe, partly in shadow. For a mad moment she wanted to shake him awake and yell, *How did this happen to us? We had a beautiful family. We had so much love.* She hung her head, her tears long since spent. After several heaving breaths, her anger dissipated, replaced with familiar sorrow.

"I cannot change what's happened," Elisheba whispered.

Raamah jerked awake, and she covered her mouth. She hadn't meant to speak aloud. He rose to his elbows, and his robe fell from his head. His hair had been shorn like Laman's. But his face . . . even in the mottled moonlight, Elisheba gasped in horror.

His face was deformed—from burns, a battle—she couldn't tell. But her heart nearly stopped at the sight.

"Elisheba?" he said in a ragged voice. He lifted a hand and reached toward her. Elisheba's stomach recoiled as she saw his damaged skin. She closed her eyes as he touched her cheek. "Is it really you?"

After a long moment, she opened her eyes, looking past the broken skin into his gaze. "What happened?"

Raamah dropped his hand and pulled the robe back over his head. "Nothing that I didn't deserve—after the way I treated you."

"No," Elisheba said. "No one deserves this." Like a gentle river, she felt her anger start to shift. It didn't change their broken marriage, but she could never wish such torture on another person. "You saved my life."

"It was a small price to pay for what I've done." He struggled to a sitting position and inhaled deeply. With a guarded look, he met her eyes. "It was you who saved me."

Elisheba held her breath, not quite understanding. Had her husband changed?

"I've done unforgivable things, Elisheba." Raamah's voice came clear. She felt a prickle along the back of her neck as he said her name. "I should have followed Nephi when I had the chance, taking you and the boys, so that we could all be together with Tiras, too." He hung his head and whispered, "I could never expect you to accept me."

She remained silent. The last thing she'd expected was for her husband to ask her to come back. Her hands began to tremble, and she took several deep breaths. She couldn't just forget that he'd separated her from the children. "What about our boys?"

He visibly flinched and looked up.

"Where are they, Raamah? Where are my boys, my children?" Anger swelled against her chest.

"With my sisters," he said, his voice hoarse. "The boys haven't spoken to me in months. They told me I was dead to them."

Elisheba stared into his eyes, seeing the pain her husband felt. "They're so young."

Raamah held her gaze. "You don't understand. They have been taught to hate everything about Nephi, everything that is of the Lord." His voice softened. "Everything good that you taught them . . ."

Tears stung her eyes as her heart sank even lower. "How could you take my children from me? This would have never happened if you had let us go with Nephi in the beginning." Elisheba turned from her husband's deformities—not wanting pity to change her words. She stared at the branches on a nearby tree as tears dripped down her cheeks.

"I tried to bring them with me." His voice broke. "I begged Laman and the others. They taunted me . . . then they tied me to the stake."

Elisheba brought her hand to her mouth, holding back a sob. She turned and looked at him. "They set you on fire?"

"Only for a moment." He clutched his robe tightly. "Laman told me the gift of death was too generous. He wanted me to live in misery. When they doused the fire, Laman said if he ever saw me again, he'd burn Dedan and Noah." He brought his hands to his face and his shoulders started shaking.

Elisheba swallowed, her throat dry as she thought about her sons being a permanent part of Laman's tribe. She watched her husband grieve. His loss had been just as great as hers. *But I didn't betray him. I've suffered more,* she thought.

"Forgive me," he cried. "Forgive me."

The moment seemed endless as husband and wife stood close together, facing each other—but it was as if the divide was greater than a sea. Elisheba wrapped her arms about her torso, thinking about the child within her and the sons she'd already born. Her family had been fractured, and all that was left were two.

She lifted her head and gazed as Raamah. He was on his knees now, whispering *forgive me* over and over. He was a broken man— alone and destitute. Just as she had been. During that time, she'd prayed for her family to be made whole again. But what if that was no longer possible? What if Raamah and the baby were all she had left?

What if she turned away her husband and regretted it? Thoughts flashed through her mind of their marriage—how he'd never judged her for the five years of captivity in Mudhail, he'd never disrespected her father, he'd stood up to Laman when he tried to kill Lehi, he'd never tried to take another wife or concubine, and finally, he'd risked his own life to save hers . . .

Elisheba's heart swelled with love—surprising her. And she realized it had never faded. Her love for him seemed stronger than ever. *God's love.* She was feeling love toward Raamah as God felt toward all of His children. A flash of clarity passed through her mind, and she saw him as God saw him—repentant, contrite, heartbroken.

Tears slipping down her cheeks, she walked to her husband and knelt beside him. She gently drew his hands toward her and brought them to her cheeks. "I will try, Raamah—just as you forgave me so long ago. Even if it takes until my last breath for my heart to heal, I will find a way."

EPILOGUE

Hold thy peace at the presence of the Lord God: for the day of the Lord is at hand.

(ZEPHANIAH 1:7)

FIFTY-FIVE YEARS FROM THE TIME LEHI LEFT JERUSALEM

Nephi entered the temple, inhaling the familiar waft of copal incense. Jacob and Joseph were already waiting, and Nephi smiled at seeing them. Walking slowly, his sandaled feet echoed against the wood floor. He no longer had the stride of a young man, but rather the gait of one who had just passed his seventieth birthday. If only his father or mother had lived as long.

"Brother," Jacob said, standing with Joseph in respect as Nephi joined them.

Nephi motioned for him to sit down. In his hands, Nephi carried the stack of plates. The time had come to pass them on to Jacob. Looking upon his brothers, Nephi remembered the day he'd ordained them as priests. He knew that if anything should happen to him, Jacob or Joseph could ably take over and continue to teach the people.

Jacob had already taught sermons for many years among the ever-growing population. Nephi was convinced that there was not one word written by Isaiah that Jacob didn't know by heart. Isaiah loved the Savior. He had seen the Savior. That was the common bond that

Nephi and Jacob shared with the ancient prophet. Each of them had seen the Savior.

Nephi knelt next to his brother, smiling at Jacob's aged face. He nodded, his eyes narrowing somewhat. Jacob sensed something was going on. He'd surely noticed the plates Nephi carried.

"As you both know, the Lord asked me to record the history of our people on my other plates." Nephi placed the small plates on the floor and met his brother's gaze. "I have completed the Lord's assignment. And now, Jacob, these belong to you. Only write about the things that you consider the most precious. You may touch upon the history of our people, but save your writings for sacred preaching, revelation, or prophesying."

Jacob's eyes filled with wonder, and Nephi placed his hand on his brother's shoulder.

"The Lord has already called you to be a prophet of God," Nephi said. "These plates—your words—will be handed down from generation to generation. They will be a witness of our Savior and His teachings."

Lowering his head for a moment, Jacob was silent. Then he met Nephi's gaze. "The Lord does not give up on His people."

"No," Nephi said softly. "And that's what we want future generations to understand."

"*We* need to understand it as well." Jacob looked at Joseph. "'The Lord said, 'Have I put thee away, or have I cast thee off forever?'" Joseph nodded in agreement. "'Who is among you that feareth the Lord, that obeyeth the voice of his servants, that walketh in darkness and hath no light?'"

Jacob touched the plates that Nephi had set down. "Before you arrived, Joseph and I were discussing why some people have more faith than others. We feel it's time to review the Atonement and what it means to walk in His light."

Nephi noticed the acknowledgement in Joseph's face. "We'll hold a special meeting to review this doctrine. If I hadn't placed my trust in the Lord, we wouldn't be here today. It's only through Him that we can receive salvation."

Looking at the plates, Joseph said, "I've heard Isaiah's words quoted many times, but sometimes our people feel their sins are too great." His face twisted with emotion. "Look at you, look at Jacob. Both great men—men of God. You have not tasted sin as some in our family. We teach the Atonement will deliver us all, but . . ." He glanced away. "How can God forgive those who have knowingly sinned?"

Jacob touched his Joseph's arm. "He has already forgiven them."

"What?" Joseph said, looking from Jacob to Nephi as if he needed a second opinion.

Nephi nodded. "He's right. Our sins have already been forgiven if we but repent."

"All we need to do is kneel before God with pure intent and ask for His forgiveness," Joseph finished. "It sounds so simple when stated that way. I wish our children could fully grasp it."

"The truth *is* simple," Nephi said with a sigh. "The difficult part is to help our families open their hearts and let themselves contemplate the good things of God." He thought about Jacob's son, Enos, who had lately been questioning the words of God.

"Even before I witnessed miracles," Jacob said in a halting voice. "And even before I saw the Savior Himself, I *knew* . . . with every part of my soul. It has been difficult to see our people struggle so much."

"You were different from the other children," Nephi said. "You had a sober mind. Mother claimed it was because you were born under such harsh conditions. But Father sensed your uniqueness from an early age. There is something he told me that I didn't know if I would ever share with you."

Jacob arched a brow, waiting.

"Father had a vision, not long before he became ill." Nephi watched Jacob closely, hoping that the words might bring some comfort. "He knew you would be a prophet, and he also saw your son become a prophet."

"Enos?" Jacob whispered.

"I believe so," Nephi said.

Jacob let out a low breath. "My heart aches for my son to just find happiness, but if he is to be the mouthpiece of the Lord . . ." He buried his face in his hands. "I *know* that the Savior is real. I have seen Him. I know He will atone for all our sins. *I know it.* But to see a man such as my son change . . . to teach and prophesy . . ." He raised his wet eyes and held Nephi's gaze. ". . . is a miracle that can only come by the hand of God."

Nephi embraced his brother, feeling Jacob's thudding heart against his chest. "Your example, and your wife's, couldn't be better. Perhaps someday you'll be able to pass on these plates to Enos."

Jacob nodded, tears streaking his cheeks. "That would be a great blessing."

After several moments of sitting together, each man lost in his own thoughts, Nephi finally stood. "Isaabel will be expecting me."

Jacob and Joseph nodded in understanding and waved good-bye.

Retracing his steps, Nephi walked out of the temple. The day was still new, and the early mists clung to the surrounding foliage as he made his way back home. He knew right where Isaabel would be, and he looked forward to spending some quiet moments with her each morning . . . before the bustle of the day began. He'd often cautioned her to slow down, especially in her advancing years, but she continued to clean, cook, and garden as if she still had a houseful of children.

Now even their grandchildren were grown. There was rarely a moment in the day when Isaabel didn't have one of her grandchildren following her around, performing some task or chore in tandem. All the more reason to find his wife in her moments of solitude.

Ahead on the road, Nephi saw the familiar form of Raamah. The man walked with a heavy limp and still insisted on wearing a head wrap covering most of his face so that he wouldn't scare the young children. In one hand, he clutched a bouquet of white orchids.

He's taking flowers to Elisheba—just as he does every day. Since Raamah's arrival, Nephi couldn't remember a morning when his brother-in-law didn't wake early and pick flowers for his wife.

Approaching his brother-in-law, Nephi slowed. "How are you today?"

Raamah's concealed smile reached his eyes. "I'm doing fine, my brother."

Nephi bid farewell and continued on. Raamah had truly changed, becoming one of the most humble men in the settlement.

Rounding the final bend, Nephi saw the front courtyard of his home. Sure enough, Isaabel sat on her reed chair, working on a piece of embroidery. Even though her hair had turned white, and her face had finally given way to wrinkles, she was still beautiful. As he neared, Isaabel looked up and smiled. Patting the chair next to her, she waited as her husband approached.

Nephi leaned over and kissed her cheek, then he sat and took her hand.

For a few moments they remained silent, hand in hand, watching the azure sky lighten with another day.

"Did he tell you about their worries over Enos?" Isaabel asked.

"Yes." Nephi glanced at his wife. "I told Jacob that his and Eve's example is the most important thing right now."

A soft smile reached Isaabel's lips. "I'm sure you offered a little more advice than that."

Nephi grinned. "I couldn't resist."

"I wouldn't have you any other way." She squeezed his hand. "Enos has the best of everything between his father and his uncles."

Nephi looked at her. "He has a wonderful aunt and mother, too."

"Well, let's just wait and see if Enos finds his peace. Then we can all take the credit for ourselves."

Nephi laughed then pulled his wife's hands toward his lips. After a lingering kiss he said, "I think the only one who should get the credit is the Lord."

She smiled tenderly at him. "Of course." Then her gaze grew stern. "Now let go of my hand, or I'll never get anything done."

Nephi tightened his grip so that she had to tug her hand free. Then he chuckled as he watched her resume her work. After a moment, he turned his gaze toward the rising sun as its rays crested the tops of the dense tree line.

It would be another glorious day in the promised land, and he planned on spending the day doing what he'd done every day of his life—serving his family and the Lord.

╼═╍❖ CHAPTER NOTES ❖╍═╾

PROLOGUE

According to anthropologist John L. Sorenson, the main food staples for ancient Central Mexico included corn, beans, squash, chilies, and the amaranth grain (*Images of Ancient America: Visualizing Book of Mormon Life,* 36). In fact, historian Michael E. Smith tells us that maize was first domesticated between 5000 and 7000 B.C., and by 2000 B.C., agriculture was the main form of subsistence (*The Aztecs,* 29).

Other native foods that Lehi's family probably ate include manioc, jicama, sweet potatoes, guavas, and fish. First Nephi 18:24 states that Lehi's family planted "*all* our seeds into the earth, which we had brought from the land of Jerusalem" (emphasis added). Mosiah 9:9 mentions that Zeniff's people planted corn, wheat, barley, neas, sheum, and seeds for fruit (compare also Mosiah 7:22). Enos said the people of Nephi raised "all manner of grain, and of fruit, and flocks of herds, and flocks of all manner of cattle of every kind, and goats, and wild goats, and also many horses" (Enos 1:21) (*Images,* 36).

CHAPTER I

John L. Sorenson notes that a typical house in Mesoamerica would have consisted of "small, straight sticks (or even reeds or cornstalks) aligned vertically and tied to the house frame. The spaces between the sticks might be left open, allowing smoke from the cooking fire to disperse. . . . Most roofs were of thatch." Furniture was basically nonexistent, and meals were eaten on the floor. Tables served as workbenches, supporting a clay griddle and a flat stone for grinding maize. Consistent with how Lehi's family already slept, beds were floor mats, although a mat-covered pole platform or a hammock may have been used (*Images*, 60).

Book of Mormon text vaguely hints at the type of homes found among the Lamanites and Nephites. Third Nephi 8:8 explains that the city of Zarahemla "did take fire" from lightning—which would be easy enough with roofs made of thatch. Most families had a house large enough to meet the needs of their immediate family only. But in Alma 15:18, we learn that Amulek was taken into Alma's home and cared for. Upper-class families likely had larger homes to accommodate guests and kinsfolk *(Images,* 61).

Sorenson points out that "people in different cultural and ecological areas developed their own architectural styles, although there was wide sharing of concepts throughout Mesoamerica" (*Images*, 104). Maya scholar Michael D. Coe says that as early as the Middle Preclassic period, Maya emerged from a simple peasant life to a more complex society that included temple architecture with buildings and platforms as high as fifty-nine feet (*The Maya*, 56). Lehi's family arrived in Mesoamerica with temple-building skills, and they would have found the natural resources of hardwood timber and limestone readily available (*Images*, 105).

In Mesoamerica, medical healers used plants for treating various diseases and ailments. The women in Lehi's family likely knew how to treat many infections and wounds before arriving in the promised land. With new vegetation, they probably found new treatments and learned from local people what herbs and plants were effective. The active ingredient found in aspirin was extracted from willow bark, and was used effectively for pain control. The Mayan civilization was known for suturing wounds, performing obstetrics, doing dental work, and even making prostheses from jade and turquoise.

CHAPTER 2

Scriptures referenced: 1 Nephi 18:24–25; 1 Nephi 19:1, 3, 6, 10–13, 17–18, 20; 1 Nephi 20:1; 1 Nephi 21:11, 15; 1 Nephi 22:1–6, 8; 2 Nephi 21:22 (compare Isaiah 48); Jacob 4:1; Psalm 24:5, 7, 9.

The Mayan civilization has been present in Mesoamerica since approximately 8000 B.C. Historical author Lila Perl explains the stages of the Mayan civilization as follows: the Archaic period (8000 B.C. to 2000 B.C.), the Preclassic period (2000 B.C. to A.D. 200), the Classic period (A.D. 200 to A.D. 900), and the Postclassic period (A.D. 900 to A.D. 1500s). Lehi's family would have come to the promised land during the Mayan Preclassic period (*The Ancient Maya*, 6).

If Lehi landed on the Pacific coast in the area of Guatemala, he likely encountered the Mayan civilization of Conchas along the coast; and in the highlands, the Arévalo and Las Charcas (*The Maya*, 10).

Michael D. Coe notes that one of the most notable archaeological sites in the Americas is the ancient Mayan city of Kaminaljuyú. Kaminaljuyú is located on the west border of modern-day Guatemala City. Remains from the Las Charcas are scattered throughout the region, signifying major occupation of the Valley of Guatemala. Excavated remnants include cooking pits, carbonized avocado seeds, maize cobs, textiles, mats, rope, and basketry (*The Maya*, 52–55).

CHAPTER 3

Scriptures referenced: 2 Nephi 1:2–4, 7–8, 10, 13–15, 28–32; 2 Nephi 2:1, 11.

In Jerusalem, members of Lehi and Ishmael's families would have performed ordinances in the temple. All of the ordinances, including sacrifices, involved covenants of one sort or another. Pointers to temple ordinances like our own appear in Psalms 15 and 24; Isaiah 56:3–8 and 59:1–8. Examples of the Messianic language they used appear throughout the Book of Mormon: Holy One of Israel (2 Ne. 1:10;

3:2), Holy Messiah (2 Ne. 2:6, 8), Redeemer (1 Ne. 10:5–6, 14; 2 Ne. 1:10; 2:3), Lord (1 Ne. 10:8, 14; 2 Ne. 1:15, 19, 27), and especially Messiah (1 Ne. 1:19; 10:4–5, 7, 9–11, 14, 17; 2 Ne. 1:10; 2:26; 3:5).

The expression "fulness of the gospel" may have come from Lehi (see 1 Ne. 10:14), although Nephi is the one summarizing his father's words. But we find it again in Nephi's writing (1 Ne. 15:13). Both of these references tie to the last days, during the period of gathering. The act of people becoming holy is apparent in the words "Holiness to the Lord" (Ex. 28:36; 39:30) and in the language of officiating and worshipping in the temple (1 Chron. 31:18; Ps. 29:2; 93:5; 96:9). See also Ex. 19:6; Lev. 11:44–45; 19:2; 20:7.

CHAPTER 4

Scriptures referenced: 2 Nephi 1:15, 17–21, 25, 27; 2 Nephi 2:3–4; 2 Nephi 3:1, 23; 4:9, 11.

Incense burners were used throughout Mesoamerica for religious purposes. Archaeologist J. Eric S. Thompson explains that the Mayas believed that the jaguar god would appear in front of an incense burner. The Mayas used incense burners to summon gods and to have their prayers answered (*Maya History and Religion,* 292). John L. Sorenson notes that incense was used at sacrificial and religious rituals. He quotes A. V. Kidder, a well-known Mesoamerican archae-ologist: "The belief that pungent smoke is sweet in the nostrils of gods is one of the many extraordinary likenesses between Old and New World religions" (*Images,* 142).

The clothing worn by the Mesoamericans was quite different than what Lehi's family would have brought from the Near East. Suddenly they were plunged into a very humid and tropical climate. And yet similar to Hebrew custom, the Mayas and other surrounding cultures dressed according to their social status. The privileged Mesoamericans wore luxurious fabrics and valuable feathers from specific birds (*Images,* 88–90). The Book of Mormon is full of examples of clothing worn to categorize social standing. In Alma 1:29 we read about "silk and fine-twined linen," and later "very costly apparel" (Alma 4:6). Samuel the prophet condemned "costly apparel" (Hel. 13:27–28).

It is well known that jade was a valued commodity in ancient Mesoamerica. The Mayas harvested jade from deposits out of the Río Motagua, which runs through southern Guatemala (*The Maya*, 60). Other elite commodities included quetzal feathers and marine shells. The tail feathers of the quetzal were found in the bird's natural habitat throughout the forests of Guatemala and were used to decorate Mayan costumes. Maya scholar Michael D. Coe points out that "the most prized shell was the beautiful, red-and-white, thorny oyster, obtained by divers from deep waters off the Caribbean and Pacific coasts" (*The Maya*, 23).

Lehi undoubtedly met with a variety of different languages in Mesoamerica. Coming from Arabia, he likely developed knowledge of many Semitic dialects. Professor Brian Stubbs illustrates that even in the scriptures there are several strains: "(1) a Lehi dialect of Hebrew (with Arabic, Hebrew, and Egyptian names), (2) a Mulekite Hebrew dialect, (3) Egyptian, and (4) the unknown Jaredite language or languages" ("Was There Hebrew Language in Ancient America?" *JBMS* 9:2 [2000], 63). Coe notes that the linguistic category of the Mayan language also contains a number of dialects. For example, a Mayan from highland Chiapas would have a difficult time understanding someone from Yucatán (*The Maya*, 26). It is possible that the language Lehi brought to ancient America had some influence on the developing New World languages, or vice versa. Stubbs notes that there are many ties between Semitic languages and the language family of Uto-Aztecan (*JBMS* 9:2 [2000], 54, 56). In fact, "the Near Eastern element in the UA lexicon [Uto-Aztecan] may constitute 30 percent to 40 percent" (*ibid.*, 57).

CHAPTER 5

John L. Sorenson estimates that Lehi died at the age of fifty-seven. This takes into account that Lehi would have been born in 639 B.C. and married around 621 B.C., at the age of eighteen. Sorenson theorizes that Lehi was about forty-two at the opening of the Book of

Mormon record. Sorenson also estimates that Sariah was likely sixteen when she married Lehi. If Sariah was fifty-five when Lehi died, they would have been married thirty-nine years upon the event of Lehi's death ("The Composition of Lehi's Family," *By Study and Also by Faith*, vol. 2, 176–177).

Book of Mormon scholar Hugh Nibley points out that funerary customs are the most unchanged traditions throughout the ages. People take burial practices with them when they migrate. Thus, Lehi was likely buried in the same manner as he would have been in Jerusalem. Hebrew women traditionally mourned immediately upon death and continued for several days (*An Approach to the Book of Mormon*, 252). The Old Testament mentions that psalteries, or dulcimers—musical instruments with strings—were typical instruments played during this time (see Dan. 3:5). If Lehi's family didn't take these instruments on the ship, they could have created new ones in the promised land.

CHAPTER 6

Scriptures referenced: 2 Nephi 4:13–17, 20–23; 2 Nephi 5:3.

As in my previous volumes, I've followed the pattern of prayer found in Psalms 4 and 5. "O God of my righteousness," "Have mercy," "Hear my prayer," "Lead me, O Lord," and "Unto thee will I pray" were probably regular phrases used while praying.

CHAPTER 7

Scriptures referenced: 2 Nephi 4:24–28, 30–32, 34–35.

Throughout the fourth volume, I've made references to the moon as a way for Lehi's people to gauge the passing of time and season. Randall P. Spackman suggests that the principal Nephite calendar could not have been based on a solar year, but on a lunar calendar ("The Jewish/Nephite Lunar Calendar," *JBMS*, 7:1 [1998], 50).

"Because a twelve-moon year is about eleven days shorter than a solar year, after only three years a strict twelve-moon calendar would fall about one moon out of coordination with the solar year"(*ibid.,* 54). Spackman says that the ancient people in the Near East and in Mesoamerica knew centuries before Lehi's time that they had to add a thirteenth moon every three or four years. But there is no mention of a thirteenth moon in the scriptures, so Lehi most likely didn't use that system. This may be emphasized when Lehi took his family on the eight-year trek through the Arabian wilderness then across the ocean. Desert nomads and sea voyagers used the twelve-month lunar calendar. It would have been natural for Lehi to have adopted this system and continued following it in the promised land. The Book of Mormon text hints at the use of a lunar calendar in Omni 1:21: "And Coriantumr was discovered by the people of Zarahemla; and he dwelt with them for the space of nine moons" (*ibid.,* 54–55).

CHAPTER 8

Scriptures referenced: 2 Nephi 5:2–3, 5.

Following the death of Lehi, Laman and Lemuel murmur against Nephi. It becomes serious enough that the Lord commands Nephi to flee into the wilderness. In 2 Nephi 5:2–3 we learn that Laman and Lemuel do not want Nephi to rule over them—a commission that was given by both Lehi and the Lord. But there is more to consider. Not only were the brothers fighting for control over the family, but in Mosiah 10:12–17 we learn that Laman and Lemuel still believed they were forced out of Jerusalem, wronged in the wilderness, wronged while crossing the sea, and again wronged at the arrival in the promised land. To add to these insults, Laman and Lemuel most likely became angry when Nephi took the brass plates and the sword of Laban (2 Ne. 5:14), and probably the Liahona with him. Unfortunately the anger that Laman and Lemuel harvested for years never abated, and the Lamanites continued to teach their children to hate the Nephites for generations to come.

CHAPTER 9

Scripture referenced: 2 Nephi 1:23.

When Nephi was commanded by the Lord to leave Laman and take all those who would follow him, he traveled "in the wilderness for the space of many days" (2 Ne. 5:7). How many days they journeyed is unknown. With women, children, and possibly flocks, all on foot, John L. Sorenson estimates they traveled about eleven miles a day (*An Ancient American Setting,* 8–9). He reveals that it's highly plausible that the city of Nephi was located in the Valley of Guatemala. In the high-lands, the climate is mild and has been called the land of eternal spring; whereas along the coast, the climate is hot, humid, and tropical (*Images,* 194). Nephi and his people likely traveled by foot and had limited means of carrying their supplies. Sorenson states that they loaded their belongings on their backs. The Nephites are noted for their crop agriculture, rather than animal husbandry (*ibid.,* 46, 56).

Just as Lehi did in the wilderness, Nephi would have built an altar of thanksgiving with unhewn stone. This was in the tradition of keeping the Mosaic law (see Ex. 20:24–25).

CHAPTER 10

Scriptures referenced: 2 Nephi 5:8, 17–18, 20–25.

In 2 Nephi 5:14, Nephi tells us that he took the sword of Laban and copied it, making many swords for his people's protection. Scholar Matthew Roper points out that this doesn't necessarily mean that Nephi was able to make swords with blades "of the most precious steel" (1 Nephi 4:9). Roper explains that Nephi's swords may have been similar in pattern—"a straight double-edged slashing implement" that contrasted with other weaponry such as a cimeter. ("Swords & 'Cimeters' in the Book of Mormon," *JBMS,* 8:1 [1999], 39). We know that by 200 B.C., the people of Zeniff had all types of weapons: bows, arrows, swords, cimeters, clubs, slings, etc. (Mosiah 9:16).

As in the wilderness, Lehi continued to build sacrificial altars outside of Jerusalem. Professor David Rolph Seely explains that this was allowed by the Mosaic law because a sacrifice was "allowed only outside of the radius of a three days' journey from the temple in Jerusalem" (see "Lehi's Altar and Sacrifice in the Wilderness," *JBMS*, 10:1 [2001], 69).

CHAPTER 11

Scriptures referenced: 2 Nephi 5:14, 20–25.

As discussed in the preface, the Lord caused a skin of blackness to come upon the people of Laman (see 2 Ne. 5:21). First, the people of Laman were cut off from the Lord's presence. In other words, they lost the influence of the Spirit (see 2 Ne. 5:20). Because of their iniquity, the Lord also caused a mark to be placed upon them. Instead of being "white, and exceedingly fair and delightsome" (2 Ne. 5:21), the Lord caused a skin of blackness to come upon them. It is essential to note that the cursing was not the mark of blackness, but losing the Holy Ghost (*Studies in Scripture, Volume Seven, 1 Nephi to Alma 29*, 111). The darkened skin was a mark placed by the Lord, which was later lifted (see 3 Ne. 2:15). We do not know how the mark was given or how the mark was taken away, but for the purposes of a compelling plot, I have given the Lord's actions an immediate result.

CHAPTER 14

Scripture referenced: 1 Nephi 12:2.

CHAPTER 15

Scripture referenced: 1 Nephi 4:1.

In volume two, *A Light in the Wilderness*, one of the sons of Ishmael possessed the qualities of an expert tracker. Distinguished explorer

Wilfred Thesiger explains that the Bedu people had the necessary skills that it took to determine important information from a simple camel print. The tracker could decipher where the camel had been raised, whether or not someone was riding on it, and to which tribe the camel belonged (*Arabian Sands*, 52). This also translated into a tracker's ability to make such determinations when coming across human footprints.

CHAPTER 18

Scripture referenced: 2 Nephi 5:15.

Historian Michael E. Smith notes that the early Mesoamerican religions were centered on sun worship, agricultural fertility, and human sacrifice. For example, the Aztecs—who borrowed their religious theories from their predecessors—based their ceremonies on blood, sacrifice, and debt payment. They believed "that the gods sacrificed themselves in order to benefit humankind." One myth states that the gods jumped into a huge fire to create the sun; thus, they believed it took human blood to keep the sun functioning (*The Aztecs,* 192). This was done through auto-sacrifice (piercing of body parts as a substitute for the more powerful human sacrifice); or human/heart sacrifice. The person marked for heart sacrifice was believed to be destined to become a god. "When the day of the sacrifice arrived, he went with honor to meet his fate." Men and women were sacrificed according to the needs and requirements of a particular god (*ibid.,* 217).

Slavery was practiced in ancient Mesoamerica. J. Eric S. Thompson informs us that slaves were sent between Mayan regions in exchange for commodities like cacao (*Maya History and Religion,* 151).

CHAPTER 19

The goddess Ix Chel was also known as the moon goddess. The moon was considered a divine heavenly body by the ancient Mesoamericans. There are many versions of the moon goddess throughout the Mayan cultures, and she has also been associated with the Virgin Mary. The moon goddess also presided over fertility and child bearing (*Maya History and Religion,* 241–243).

J. Eric S. Thompson explains that the jaguar was seen as a protector. The Mayas believed in a jaguar god that represented war, sorcery, and the night and stars. Wearing a jaguar skin or head symbolized that a person was of high rank (*Maya History and Religion,* 292–293). Sorenson also points out that the jaguar acted as a guardian spirit, or nawal (*Images,* 141).

In this chapter, Nephi attempts to strike a bargain for Jacob and Eve's lives. In Alma 11, we learn of the measuring system that the Nephites used in commerce. John W. Welch explains that the Mayas and the Aztecs sold everything by volume. For their dry goods, the Aztecs used a wooden box that was "divided until the smallest unit was a twelfth part of the whole." For liquid, they used different sizes of jars. The Mayas used measuring terms such as "armload" and "the fistful." Bowls have been uncovered in Kaminaljuyú that meet a consistent mold of graduated sizes. Welch adds that there is no conclusive evidence that scales or weights were used in Mesoamerica ("Weighing and Measuring" *JBMS* 8:2 [1999], 47).

CHAPTER 20

J. Eric S. Thompson points out the similar characteristics of the major Mayan gods: they have a blend of human and animal features, they can be both benevolent and malevolent, they can be categorized in several ways, they have the ability to blend with other deities, a reigning godhead contained four deities, etc. (*Maya History and Religion,* 198–200). The god of Yum Caax is also known as "Lord of the Forests." This god is linked to agriculture and also determined whether or not someone was a successful hunter (*ibid.,* 289).

CHAPTER 21

Scriptures referenced: Isaiah 45:21–23; 2 Nephi 1:4; Mosiah 10:12–13.

Chapter 24

Throughout this volume, I made references to plants, herbs, and trees that are native to the region of Mesoamerica. The apazote seed (also called wormseed) comes from a tropical herb with a reddish stem and a pungent scent. The seeds, which are small and black, contain a toxic essential oil (ascaridol). An overdose may result in severe poisoning or death.

The curaiao plant that is used for a burn ointment is an aloe vera variety. The moras berries are simply blackberries. And the bark from a protium copal tree was a main source of incense used by the Mayan people of the Guatemala highlands. Jengibre is a ginger root. Lemongrass is an aromatic tropical plant with leaves used for making medicinal tea that is believed to alleviate stomach pain, fever, muscle cramps, etc.

Cassava is also called manioc or yucca. The bush grows up to eight feet and has greenish-yellow flowers. This bush's root and tapioca are often combined to create an intoxicating beverage. In powder form it's used to prepare farinha (cassava bread). Agave juice is a fermented drink (also called pulque), and it comes from the agave plant. John L. Sorenson points out that this might be the source of the wine referred to in Mosiah 11:15 (*Images,* 45). Jicama is a root vegetable similar to a potato with a flavor that is sweet and starchy. It is eaten raw or cooked in soup.

First Kings 6–8 describes the temple of Solomon. Nephi would have seen the temple before its destruction in 586 B.C. by the Babylonians. Solomon used quarried stone from nearby and cedar timbers from Lebanon, along with ornamentations of gold-overlay, lions, cherubim, and palms. From 2 Nephi 5:16, we learn that Nephi's temple was constructed after the same fashion, except for the many precious things that Solomon had. Regardless, Nephi says that the "workmanship thereof was exceedingly fine." Sorenson notes that Torquemada, "an early Spanish priest in the New World, compared the plan of Mexican temples with that of the temple of Solomon." He also discusses similarities found in the temples built on a hill or platform, different rooms for distinct ordinances, sacrifices made on altars, the graduated levels of the altars, and the orientation of the temple so that the solstice sun shines through the temple doors twice a year (*An Ancient American Setting*, 143).

EPILOGUE

Scriptures referenced: 2 Nephi 6:2; 2 Nephi 7:1,10; 2 Nephi 8:8, 16; 2 Nephi 11:2–3; Jacob 1:1–4.

Scholars S. Kent Brown and David Rolph Seely have made a case for Lehi's departure from Jerusalem taking place sometime during Zedekiah's first year of reign (see 3 Nephi, book heading). Brown and Seely state that Biblical scholars estimate that Zedekiah's reign as king of Judah began in 597 B.C. This places Lehi's departure shortly thereafter, and thus, the book of Jacob opens up around 542 B.C. when "fifty and five years had passed away from the time that Lehi left Jerusalem" (Jacob 1:1). The fact that Lehi saw the destruction of Jerusalem in a vision (see 2 Ne. 1:4) may indicate that Lehi didn't learn this on the trail through Arabia (an eight year journey), or while living in Bountiful (an estimated two or three years). Therefore, Jerusalem was destroyed many years after Lehi's departure, solidifying the notion of Lehi leaving during the commencement of Zedekiah's reign. When the destruction of Jerusalem is completed in 587 B.C., it has already been eleven years since Lehi's departure (see Brown and Seely article "Jeremiah's Imprisonment and the Date of Lehi's Departure," *The Religious Educator* 2/1 [2001]: 15–32). Thus, there was no Jerusalem for Lehi's family to return to. In *A History of Israel*, author John Bright details the fall of Jerusalem and the spread of destruction that started with settlements within fifty miles of the city (327–30).

Nephi wrote upon ore plates (see 1 Ne. 19:1), then passed them onto Jacob (see Jacob 1:1–2). A sharp chisel was likely used for engraving and could be worked by hand without a tool. Engraving was time-consuming and difficult (see Jacob 4:1). Nephi and Mormon refer to the plates they wrote upon as ore (see 1 Ne. 19:1; Morm. 8:5). Scholar John A. Tvedtnes explains that the plates Mormon used to abridge the Nephite records were most likely gold alloyed with another metal, possibly mixed with copper. Gold is a soft metal that is typically alloyed with silver, copper, or other metals for hardier use. Joseph Smith and the Eight Witnesses all concurred that the plates had an "appearance of gold" (*Insights: A Window on the Ancient World,* 23:5, [2005], 6).

In 2 Nephi 5:26 we learn that Nephi consecrated Jacob and Joseph as priests. In Old Testament law, an ordination would take place at the age of thirty. In 2 Nephi 5:28, we are told that thirty years had passed since the time Lehi left Jerusalem. This may indicate that Jacob and Joseph were close to the age of thirty upon their ordination. Since they were not descendants of Levi or Aaron (Lehi's family came from the tribe of Joseph), they had to operate under the Melchizedek Priesthood. Robert J. Matthews said, "It should be clear to us that the Nephites did not have an established order of priests and Levites such as that found in ancient Israel, because there were no Levites among them" ("Jacob: Prophet, Theologian, Historian," *The Book of Mormon: Jacob through Words of Mormon, To Learn with Joy,* 41). Matthews also points out that the Nephite leaders wouldn't have been able to perform the ordinances of the law of Moses unless they had the proper priesthood authority (*ibid.,* 41).